By permission of M. M. Pari... Paris...

Duchesse de Polignac
after the portrait painted
by M.ᵐᵉ Vigée-Lebrun in 1787

SEVEN SPLENDID SINNERS

BY

W. R. H. TROWBRIDGE

AUTHOR OF 'COURT BEAUTIES OF OLD WHITEHALL,' AND 'THE LETTERS OF HER MOTHER
TO ELIZABETH'

FOURTH IMPRESSION

BRENTANO'S

NEW YORK

1909

TO

ISABEL TROWBRIDGE AND CLAUDE NICOL

IN MEMORY OF

A VENETIAN SUMMER

PREFACE

IT may be postulated as an axiom of history that individuals are more important than events.

The importance, not to speak of the interest, of the latter decreases in proportion to their distance from posterity till they are finally submerged in the ocean of time. To this sweeping assertion there is, of course, as usual, an exception, and certain epoch-making events in the history of mankind—a Renaissance, a Reformation, a Revolution, for instance—rear their crests above the waste of time, like those volcanic islands in tropic seas whose summits tower as high above the waves from which they rise as their bases are sunk beneath them.

But with regard to individuals the opposite is the case. It has been said that the Muse of History has no politics ; on the contrary, she has belonged to every political party, from the Absolutists to the Republicans—save the Socialists. The faith of the latter, indeed, it is impossible for her to profess ; in history the Individual is all in all. The dagger of Brutus, the eloquence of Antony, the corpse of Cæsar, possess greater significance for us than all the influences that converted Rome from a republic into an empire. Apart from some examination paper or treatise by Herr Dryasdust of what account is the Agrarian Question, which once so deeply agitated the mistress of the world ? Yet the Gracchi are deathless. Or coming quite near our own times, can there be any doubt as to the relative importance and interest between the march of events in France's stupendous struggle for freedom and the careers and characters of the men and women who engaged in the front rank of that struggle ? The mere names of Marie Antoinette, Mirabeau, Marat, Robespierre, Napoleon, speak more than whole volumes on the Revolution. For the memory of a personality, let it be stated again, endures longer than the memory of an epoch ; a fact that all the greatest historians, both " scientific " and "unscientific," have always recognized.

But while history asserts the supremacy of personality, it also restores to events and epochs an importance in proportion to the interest of posterity in the individuals who influenced, or were influenced, by them. For it goes without saying that in history, as in life, every individual is not of equal importance. But it is not from the contemplation of the greatest and noblest alone that the most useful knowledge of mankind is to be obtained. Much may also be learnt from the small and the base. In the play of Human Nature as acted in the theatre of history the cast is large, and those who perform but a small part are as well worth watching as the great stars who, like those on the French stage, often appear in minor *rôles*, as in the case of Catherine the Great, in whom there were two distinct personalities.

To watch this great drama, in which the events of history are but individuals in action, to the best advantage, depends entirely upon one's seat, so to speak. There are scenes in which only stars of the first magnitude occupy the stage, when it is better not to go at all to the theatre unless one has a stall or a box. Fancy viewing Napoleon from the back-row of the gallery, or Gibbon's *Decline and Fall of the Roman Empire* condensed into a curtain-raiser! When such characters and episodes are on the boards, it is intolerable to be cramped for space and squeezed into some position in which one can neither see nor hear. For in history, perspective and proportion are absolutely essential. Likewise, there are times when the only place to observe certain actors is from the wings, the *coulisses d'histoire*, as in the case of the seven ladies whose interpretation of certain phases of human nature forms the subject of this book. It is true, from the *coulisses* persons and events will never appear as attractive as they look from the stalls. But they may at least be seen as they really are, which, after all, I take it, is the chief object of those who seek amusement in reading books of a biographical or historical nature.

*   *   *   *   *   *   *

To turn from the trivial to the serious.

It is very seldom that absolutely fresh information is to be obtained relative to historical personages which presents them in a completely different light from that in which they have hitherto been regarded. Only too frequently, especially as regards the lives and characters of persons of minor importance in history, the information is very meagre and the most careful search will reveal nothing new. This is practically the case in respect to the subjects of the seven *historiettes* which form this book. With the exception of the Empress Catherine and the Comtesse de Lamotte, it may be said that everything worth knowing is known. In regard, however, to the Duchesse de Châteauroux, the Duchess of Kendal, Elizabeth Chudleigh, the Duchesse de Polignac, and Lola Montez, though the material is apparently plentiful, its yield is comparatively small. Nor is it probable that anything fresh will ever be added to what is already known of them which will change the impression that history has formed of them.

It was, therefore, with considerable surprise that I received from Count Alexander Kielmansegg—a lineal descendant of the famous Lady Darlington, popularly known as the " Elephant," of whom mention is made in the memoir of the Duchess of Kendal—certain information which quite upsets all preconceived notions of her. As Count Alexander Kielmansegg's information, which is based on family documents, did not reach me till after the memoir in question had been written, I am only able to rectify my own and previous errors here.

" I am," he writes me, " in the best position to prove to you that all rumours about the scandals and financial difficulties of Lady Darlington in Hanover before her arrival in England are without the slightest foundation."

This proof is elaborated in some very copious notes[1] appended to the letters of George I's brother, the Prince-Bishop of Osnaburg, to General von Wendt, which have recently been edited by Count Erich Kielmansegg. These notes *establish beyond question that Lady Darlington was never the mistress of George I,* who recognized her as the daughter of his father, the Elector Ernest Augustus by the Countess von Platen ; that she was never separated from her husband, with whom she lived on the happiest terms till his death ; that she never left Hanover in disguise at the time of George's departure for England, but remained

[1] To quote these notes at length is impossible, they are to be found on pages 63, 64, 65, 66, 67 of *Briefe des Herzogs Ernst August zu Braunschweig-Lüneburg an Johann Franz Diedrich von Wendt,* Herausgegeben von Erich Graf Kielmansegg. Hanover and Leipzig.

behind for some months before following her husband, who had gone with the king; and that far from having squandered the fortune she had inherited from her mother the same property is still in the possession of her descendants. In face, too, of the fine portrait of her by Kneller (see page 76)—which justifies Lady Mary Wortley Montagu's statement that "Lady Darlington possessed fascination or no mean order in her youth"—I cannot believe, knowing Horace Walpole, that she ever became the "ogress" he depicts her—though it is undoubtedly true she was in later years enormously fat.

The stigma which has so long been unjustly attached to her name must be attributed to the slanders of the Jacobites and the old English prejudice against foreigners fostered by the unpopularity of King George I, whose position, it must be admitted, was one of extreme difficulty. Not the least of the reasons why he was so generally disliked was, as is well known, the belief in his cruelty to his wife, the hapless Sophia Dorothea. But here again it should be remembered that it was not her husband who was responsible for her imprisonment in the Castle of Ahlden, but *her own father*, the Duke of Zell. In this connection it is only fair to King George to add that the publication some years ago of his wife's letters to Königsmarck, by the permission of the Duke of Cumberland, to whom they belong, pretty well acquitted him of the charge of cruelty. These letters were, however, but a portion of Sophia Dorothea's correspondence, and Count Alexander Kielmansegg assures me that the remainder, which is unprintable, is of a nature to exonerate George completely.

As to the illustrations contained in this book, my thanks are also particularly due to Count Kielmansegg for the portraits of the Countess von Platen and Lady Darlington, as well as to Count Werner von der Schulenburg for the portrait of the Duchess of Kendal. This is the first time that portraits of these ladies have ever been published. My thanks are also due to MM. Plon-Nourrit et Cie., and to the Editor of the *Revue de l'Art Ancien et Moderne* for the use of certain other plates.

W. R. H. TROWBRIDGE.

London, 1908.

CONTENTS

LIST OF ILLUSTRATIONS

xii

THE
DUCHESSE DE CHÂTEAUROUX

1717—1744

MARIE ANNE DE MAILLY-NÈSLE, DUCHESSE DE CHÂTEAUROUX
[*After Nattier*]

To face page 3

I

"They were purple of raiment and golden,
   Filled full of thee, fiery with wine,
Thy lovers, in haunts unbeholden,
   In marvellous chambers of thine.
They are fled, and their footprints escape us,
   Who appraise thee, adore, and abstain,
O Daughter of Death and Priapus,
      Our Lady of Pain!"

               SWINBURNE'S *Dolores*.

THE DUCHESSE DE CHÂTEAUROUX

1717—1744

I

IT is impossible to mention the Duchesse de Châteauroux without calling to mind her sisters—Madame de Mailly, Madame de Vintimille, Madame de Lauraguais and Madame de Flavacourt. There is a subtle fascination in the mere sound of these stately and beautiful names so redolent of the *parfum de la vieille cour*, the fascination of luxury, licence and intrigue. At the very start one feels sure that the women who bore them had no vulgar ambitions, no commonplace loves or hatreds, no middle-class vices. Nor had they.

"From 1732," says the Maréchal de Richelieu, "when Madame de Mailly, the eldest, first appeared on the scene, till 1744 when Madame de Châteauroux, the youngest, left it, whether together, in succession, or as rivals, these five sisters found themselves bound to all the events of the times. In a word, the history of France during this period is nothing else but the romance of their lives."

As the Maréchal de Richelieu was the personification of the refined and cynical society of which he was one of the most typical members, it should be explained that by "romance" he really meant scandal. In this respect the origin of the sisters, descended as they were from the families of Mancini-Mazarin and Mailly-Nesle, was as romantic as their lives.

The Marquis de Nesle, their father—Madame de Châteauroux always boasted that hers was the Prince de Condé—was the head of one of the oldest and most famous families in France. In point of antiquity it ranked with the Rohans, the Tremouilles, the Montmorencys; in point of celebrity it was unrivalled. Associated with some of the most terrible crimes and noble chivalries of the Middle Ages, the name of Nesle was familiar to every Frenchman. As became a race so illustrious, their motto, like that of all the great noblesse of the sword, was superb. Beneath the knockers or *maillets*—whence the family name Mailly—on the doors of their palaces was inscribed in old French *Hogne qui vouldra*, or as we should write to-day *Frappe qui voudra*, "Knock who will." [1] And great was the number and low the repute of those who had literally interpreted this generous invitation. Nor were they ill-received by this last head of the house of Nesle, whose pedigree was the only respectable thing about him. For he was one of those men who drag a proud name in the mud in which great and worn-out families so often end. Having squandered, with noisy and reckless hospitality, his 250,000 livres a year on the lowest company, he was finally reduced to bankruptcy, and ended his days in an ignoble exile.

[1] *Hogner* signified "to growl" or "to grumble"; whence, applied to a *maillet*, "to pound" or "to knock."

The disgrace he had brought upon his name was enhanced by the scandalous reputation of his wife, from whom he had long been separated. The Marquise de Nesle, née Mazarin, had inherited all the characteristics which had rendered her race so conspicuous in the reign of Louis XIV. She had been one of the most notorious of the *femmes galantes* of the Regency. The most audacious of her gallantries and adventures, of which the least said the better, was the duel she fought in the Bois de Boulogne with a Madame de Polignac, over the lover of both, the Maréchal de Richelieu. It was from her that the Marquise de Flavacourt and the Duchesse de Châteauroux inherited the beauty for which their great-grandmother, Hortense Mancini, Duchesse de Mazarin, was so celebrated.

With such antecedents it is scarcely to be wondered that the Nesle sisters, possessing on their own account very vivid personalities, should have stamped them in a striking fashion on the history of their times. In this respect the Duchesse de Châteauroux was more successful than her sisters, who merely served to pave the road to power for her. Though less famous than her two successors, Mesdames de Pompadour and Du Barry, she is none the less significant as the first of the three Mistress-Ministers of Louis Quinze who, belonging to the noblesse, the bourgeoisie, and the people, from which classes they came in succession, typified in the most curious manner not only the three phases of the reign and the age, but the gradual passing of power from the highest order in the State to the lowest.

The Duchesse de Châteauroux, the representative of the noblesse, was much more typical of her stage in the process of national decay than either Madame de Pompadour or Madame Du Barry was of theirs. The incarnation of intrigue, she was, so to speak, the *mot d'ordre* of her class and period. Of the intrigues for which the Court of Versailles was famous none were more fell than those into which

Madame de Châteauroux and her sisters wove the "romance" of their lives. It is, therefore, necessary in depicting her to describe them. A knowledge of them is, indeed, absolutely essential to any knowledge of her—as essential as the loom to the tapestry, as the play to the actor, as atmosphere to personality.

These intrigues began in 1715 with Louis XV's succession to the throne, or two years, to be exact, before Madame de Châteauroux was born, and ended at her death in 1744. The object of the ambitions which inspired them was to snare power—an object that was pursued absolutely without scruple, with infinite cunning, and with the frenzy of a *sauve qui peut*. For in the press and rush to be first in the race the winner might be defrauded of the prize. "To have and to hold" was the motto of all.

In this lust of power one man was conspicuous above all others for the pertinacity of his ambition and the skill with which, having grasped power, he managed to keep it, in spite of persistent and cunning attempts to snatch it from him. This man was Fleury, the Bishop of Fréjus, Louis' tutor.

Fleury possessed two qualities of the greatest value in the realization of ambition—cunning and patience.

He was also, though perhaps he would have been the last to acknowledge it, very lucky. His father, whose influence was as small as his fortune, designed him for the priesthood, and to educate him for this career sent him at an early age to the Jesuit college in Paris. At six-and-twenty, when history next hears of him, it is to find him almoner to the Queen of Louis XIV. It would be interesting to know by what means he secured the influence that obtained him this post. Perhaps his advancement might be attributed to his good looks, which scandal declared, not without reason, made him particularly attractive to the fair sex, even when extreme old age rendered him incapable of inspiring any other than a platonic passion.

But by whatever means he arrived at Versailles, once there he was quick to acquire the art of pleasing. On the death of the Queen, the King appointed him almoner to himself. Fifteen years later, after patiently fishing for fortune, the handsome Abbé Fleury hooked the bishopric of Fréjus out of the slime of the Court.

The revenues of this benefice were paltry, and his diocese—"two hundred leagues distant from Paris, with a palace in the midst of a swamp, the silence of which was enlivened by the perpetual croaking of frogs"—was the dreariest in all France. He was, however, considered lucky to have got even this, for as yet his ambition had not been characterized by a display of the sort of ability that is capable of obtaining the great prizes of life. He himself, on the contrary, had a far different opinion of his deserts, and expressed his disgust in his letters, which he signed: "Bishop of Fréjus—by divine indignation."

It was another fifteen years before the Court saw him again, so slowly did the wheels of his fate and fortune revolve. He might, indeed, have remained at Fréjus for the rest of his life, but for the War of the Spanish Succession. Out of this event he had the luck to make capital, and returning to Versailles at the end of the reign he succeeded somehow—through the favour, perhaps, of Madame de Maintenon, with whom he was ever something of a favourite—in getting himself appointed tutor to the baby heir to the throne. This was the opportunity of his life, and Fleury, whose

> "Pride and perseverance
> Made a bishop of his reverence,"

as the old couplet says, was the man to make the most of it.

The Bishop of Fréjus was sixty-two when he acquired this important post, key to his future and complete supremacy. Had a young man been given his opportunity even the Regent might have had reason to dread him. But what prospect was there of Fleury at his age, were he thrice as ambitious and as able as he was deemed, of ever wearing the Regent's shoes? Philippe d'Orléans was in the prime of life; during his Regency no ambition would be so foolish as to attempt to undermine him, and afterwards it was inconceivable that he should not continue to remain the most powerful subject of the King. Besides, Louis was only five, and before he reached his majority Fleury would be either dead or too decrepit to cause the Regent anxiety. The man, however, whose whole life has been spent in climbing the mountain of Ambition, is not likely to stop while there is the remotest chance of reaching the summit; in the course of time climbing becomes second nature to him. So Fleury, asking for nothing, pretending he wanted nothing, seeing an Abbé Dubois made a cardinal while he remained only Bishop of Fréjus, continued in his sly, patient way to train his royal pupil to regard him as indispensable. So well did he succeed in attaching Louis to him, and so strong was the King's sense of habit, that frequently when his dismissal seemed imminent he managed to evade it by threatening of his own accord to leave the Court. Therefore, being cunning enough to suspect that the chances were greater than one would imagine of a tough and temperate old priest outliving a dissipated and drunken young prince, Fleury silently backed his life against the Regent's, and after waiting eight years had the luck to win!

When d'Orléans one day suddenly dropped dead the Bishop of Fréjus was the only person capable of taking advantage of the situation. Coveting the dead Regent's shoes the old fox deemed it safer to get some one else to steal them for him than to steal them himself, so he went to the boy-king and persuaded him to appoint the Duc de

Bourbon as Minister. This was a great triumph for Fleury, for Bourbon, who was a junior prince of the blood and weak, would, the crafty Bishop thought, be obliged to depend on *his* influence over Louis to maintain his position.

There was, however, a factor in this scheming that Fleury lost sight of, or utterly miscalculated. Bourbon had a mistress, one Madame de Prie, who governed him completely, and whose ambition and Fleury's were identical.

II

OF all the mistresses, whether of King or of Minister, who disposed of the destinies of France during the eighteenth century and hastened the end of the *ancien régime*, none was more bounteously endowed with mental and physical gifts than Madame la Marquise de Prie. Had she had the luck to have been a *maîtresse en titre*, she must have won for her fame a prominent place in history. As it was none wielded greater power, while it lasted, than she—not even the Pompadour.

Her beauty was enchanting; her friends and her foes were alike agreed on this point. One of the latter, Boisjourdain, said of her, " Madame de Prie was more than beautiful; she was seductive in everything."

A friend, d'Argenson, declared that he " did not think there ever existed a more celestial creature than Madame de Prie. She was the real flower of the sweet pea. A charming face, and even more graces than beauty; wit, genius, ambition, and supreme presence of mind, and with it all the most decent air in the world. Her fascination was great."

As to the character, however, of this enchantress, opinion was almost uniformly hostile. Historians influenced by her notorious profligacy, her unbridled arrogance, and her utter lack of principle in the conduct of public affairs, have generally painted her as a human tigress. Even Michelet, the Orpheus of history, who animated its very dust and treated it as it should be treated, as a fascinating romance and not as a corpse to be "scientifically" dissected, after pouring vitriol over her memory spilt a tear upon it. It is true she was a great libertine, but so were the majority of her contemporaries, though in this respect it was notorious that "when she had ceased to love any one she did not cease to retain much friendship for him and to do what she could for his advancement." The vices of her state-craft, however, are quite indefensible even on the plea of self-preservation. Dictated by an unbounded ambition, their corruption, as will be seen, was that of cold-blooded premeditation.

Such in the rough was the obstacle that suddenly rose up in Fleury's path, just as he was at last reaching the goal of his ambition.

It was inevitable that in the end the cunning old priest, with the influence he exercised over the mind of Louis, should triumph over this formidable adversary. Had Madame de Prie been content with the second place, or adopted towards Fleury tactics similar to those he had adopted towards the Regent, she might perhaps have long delayed her ruin, if not entirely escaped it. But she was too arrogant to affect subserviency, and her youth—she was but five-and-twenty—made her over-confident. She had, moreover, at the start a great advantage in possessing the loyal friendship of the great financier, Pâris-Duverney, who might be described as the Colbert of the eighteenth century. Knowing that the Treasury was all but empty, and that Fleury, who was personally poor and niggardly, had no other means of filling it than by counselling economy, which was repugnant to the luxurious Court, Madame de Prie trusted to maintain her position by pitting prodigality against parsimony. This policy, indeed, was not without

THE MARQUISE DE PRIE

To face page 10

its triumphs, and by her ability to cause a cascade of gold
to pour into the empty coffers of Versailles she succeeded
for two years in snapping her fingers at the Bishop of
Fréjus.

But while Madame de Prie, entrenched behind the credit
of Pâris-Duverney, felt secure from attack from Fleury she
was sensible enough to realize that her position was not
impregnable. A smile, an ankle, or a bosom, cleverly
displayed so as to capture the fancy of the boy-king, might
secretly, and in the twinkling of an eye, reduce her power
to zero. Conscious of this danger she prepared to protect
herself against it as far as it was possible. Being a woman
of courage and resource, the means she employed were at
once bold and crafty. To turn to her own advantage the
desires which she knew must sooner or later be aroused in
the King, who was now rapidly reaching manhood, she
resolved to take time by the forelock and provide him
herself with a mistress or a wife!

Madame de Prie had strong objections to the former,
which were, however, anything but scrupulous. Since precisely similar objections had influenced Fleury in his task
of forming the character of his pupil, with the view of
making it serve his own ambition, it is necessary to throw
some light on the character of this king of fifteen when
Madame de Prie took him in hand, in order to explain the
raison d'être of the intrigues that, so to speak, hatched
Madame de Châteauroux.

When a man has gained a reputation for viciousness, like
Louis Quinze, the memory of whatever virtue he may
originally have possessed is entirely lost—until his " white-
washers " appear. But even they, in spite of their zeal, are
never altogether successful, for in their efforts to obliterate
the stains from the monstrous reputation they desire to
cleanse, they make it grotesque, if not more hideous than
before. From this fate Louis Quinze has at least been

spared. Almost alone in the roll of infamy the "Most Christian Brute" lacks an apologist. Still, without the least intention of smudging his vices into virtues, it should not be forgotten that there was a time when even he was virtuous, though, alas! his virtue was only the negative sort after all—like chastity, of which Nietzsche so profoundly says that "the she-dog sensuality looketh with envy out of all she doth."

It was, indeed, only to his very frail health as a child, and the intrigues of those who had the care of him, that he owed the virtue he once possessed. He had the Regent to thank that he ever lived to grow up at all. It was certainly not from *fear* of the hatred his enemies would excite against him, if Louis died, that made Philippe d'Orléans so solicitous of the health of this child who kept him from the throne. If it had been true, as was so atrociously rumoured, that he had poisoned the little King's parents and elder brother, it is scarcely likely that he would have hesitated to sever the last thread by which the coveted crown hung. The truth was that the good-natured *roué* was not only incapable of murder, but really honestly attached to his little ward. So, knowing—none better than he—the danger to be apprehended from an early development in the sickly kinglet of the hereditary depravity of his race, he took such care of Louis that the boy passed out of childhood into adolescence, as the memoirs state, without being conscious of the change. And this at the Court of the Regent!

Similar motives of purity cannot, however, be credited to Fleury, who assisted d'Orléans in preserving Louis' innocence. For, realizing, as Madame de Prie did later, the danger to his influence of the awakening of love in the young King, the crafty tutor had endeavoured to nullify the danger by creating in the boy a prejudice against women. With this object he allowed the King to have only playmates of his own sex, whom he chose from the noble families who had everything to hope from his favour.

But this method of preserving Louis' innocence, or rather Fleury's influence, had brought fresh dangers to both in its train. It was remarked that the young Duc de la Tremouille, first gentleman of the bed-chamber and the King's favourite companion, began to give himself the airs of a Quélus or a Maugiron. If the power for which ambition intrigued at the Court of Versailles was only to be obtained by reviving the times and customs of the last of the Valois, neither Fleury nor Madame de Prie would have hesitated to turn Louis Quinze into a Henri Trois. But the menace to their influence was as great from a Ganymede as from a Hebe ; so, urged by a sense of their common peril, the rivals united to remove the too fascinating Tremouille from the Court.

Such being the nature of Madame de Prie's objections to providing Louis with a mistress, she chose the other alternative and gave him a wife. His marriage had already been arranged some years previously by the Regent, who had made it the excuse for a political alliance with Spain ; and princesses chosen as the future consorts of the kings of the two nations had been exchanged between the respective Courts. But Madame de Prie required a queen of her own making, so the little Infanta who was being brought up at Versailles was sent back to Madrid, an insult that was all but resented by Spain at the point of the sword. Diplomacy, however, succeeded in avoiding a war ; and Madame de Prie calmly ordered a list of the marriageable princesses of Europe to be made for her inspection.

"Of these," says de Goncourt, "there were exactly 100 ; but 44 were too old, 29 too young, and 10 impossible. Of the 17 that remained, Madame de Prie determined to choose the one most likely to be grateful to her for raising her to the throne of France."

But Madame de Prie was too crafty to be guided in her choice entirely by the gratitude of a woman who owed a crown to her. She had a striking instance of what such gratitude was worth in the "Termagant" Queen of Spain, who had been raised to that lofty elevation from the petty Court of Parma by the Princesse des Ursins, and whose very first act on arriving in Spain was to expel her benefactress. So Madame de Prie wanted in the queen of her making, "not so much gratitude as a great incapacity for public affairs, fecundity to provide heirs to the throne, and sufficient charm to arrest and hold her husband's fancy."

After some little difficulty a princess with these requirements was discovered in the person of Marie Leczinska, the daughter of Stanislas, ex-King of Poland. The possessor of this dubious dignity was one of those amiable but inefficient men whom fate pitch-forks now and then into the highest places, as if for the express purpose of proving their incapacity. It was, indeed, an unfortunate day for Stanislas when he attracted the notice of that most picturesque of kings, young Charles the Twelfth of Sweden, who tried to play—and succeeded too, for a sublime hour—the *rôle* of Alexander of Macedon in modern Europe. Raised by the victorious Charles to the throne of an anarchic kingdom, to which he had no claim, Stanislas lost his crown,

> ". . . after dread Pultawa's day,
> When fortune left the royal Swede."

Captured, forced to abdicate, and sold as a slave to the Turks, this ridiculous king had, when Charles's star once more began to rise, recovered his liberty and returned to his original obscurity, from which he ought never to have emerged. His ambition, however, had been fired by his romantic adventures, and in his retirement at Weissembourg in Alsace, where he subsisted on an irregularly-paid pension from the French Government, he had never ceased to sigh, like all ex-kings, for the vanished pomps of the throne he had lost.

When Madame de Prie turned her thoughts in his direction hope had sunk so low in Stanislas that he was on the point of marrying his daughter to a mere gentleman of the neighbourhood. The excitement, therefore, that was caused by the arrival of the couriers from Versailles to demand her hand for the King of France may be imagined. Poor Stanislas, on whom fortune seemed suddenly to have dropped literally from the clouds, exclaimed in a fervid transport, the honest soul—

"Let us fall on our knees and thank God!"

But before he could execute this pious wish, so great was his emotion, he first fell into a swoon.

His daughter, however, supported the news much more stoically. Indeed, some went so far as to say that in secret she had no mind at all for the match, having given her heart to the gentleman mentioned above. Nevertheless, her stoicism, whether natural or feigned, melted when Madame de Prie herself arrived a couple of days later with the *trousseau.* At the sight of the silk stockings and lace underclothing she exclaimed with naïve delight—

"Never in my life have I beheld such riches!"

Thus was it that Marie Leczinska became the wife of Louis Quinze, thanks to Madame de Prie, who "made her a queen," says d'Argenson, "as I might make my lacquey a *valet de chambre.*"

But this marriage, which Fleury had been unable to avert, while an undoubted triumph for Madame de Prie, damaged her prestige. With one hundred princesses to choose from, the Court of France could not forgive her for what it considered the humiliation of a *mésalliance.* Instead of the advantage she had counted on gaining from her victory, it contributed to her ruin. The very next year

Fleury succeeded in bringing about her disgrace, together with that of her lover, the Duc de Bourbon, and her financier, Pâris-Duverney.

Never was a fall from power more sudden, more complete, and more dramatic. Aware of the conspiracy against her, which caused her such anxiety that "she grew so thin that she was nothing more than a woman's head on a spider's body," she tried to crush it by inducing the King to dismiss Fleury. The promise of his dismissal she did, indeed, obtain, and flushed with victory she hastened to her queen with the joyful tidings. But in the very act of delivering them she received the news of her own banishment from the Court, and was carried fainting from Versailles! This was the first of those acts of treachery for which Louis Quinze was afterwards distinguished.

In the list of the women who have swayed, or sought to sway, the destinies of France, Madame de Prie is the only one who preferred death to disgrace. The manner in which she made her exit from the world was characteristic of a woman of the Regency. D'Argenson thus describes it—

"She gathered about her at Courbépine (the estate in Normandy to which she was banished) all pleasures. The Court people even came there; they danced, they made good cheer, they acted comedies. She herself played in one two days before her voluntary death, and recited three hundred verses by heart with as much feeling and spirit as if she were living in a lasting contentment. She had taken for her lover a nephew of the Abbé d'Amfreville— from whom I learned these circumstances. He was a sensible, intelligent, good-looking young fellow, and, above all, very civil. She informed him of the day and hour on which she intended to die, but he refused to believe her and exhorted her to give up the cowardly project. But Madame de Prie was ever a woman of great determination.

She gave her lover a diamond not worth 500 crowns and sent him to carry to a secret address in Rouen 50,000 crowns' worth of jewels. On his return he found her dead at the appointed hour. But what she had not foreseen were the terrible sufferings in which she died, they were so great that the toes of her feet turned back.

" Here," adds d'Argenson, " for those who give heed to it, is food for reflection on compacts with the devil, who comes at the agreed hour to twist our necks, though with Madame de Prie it was her legs." At the time of her death she was only twenty-seven.

Thus ended with her what, on account of the immense power she wielded, is often termed the " second Regency."

III

WITH the disappearance of Madame de Prie from his path, the Bishop of Fréjus became First Minister and a Cardinal. He was seventy-three when he became supreme and he was destined to remain so till the day of his death seventeen years later at the age of ninety! It is true his supremacy continued to be fiercely disputed ; but Madame de Prie was the only serious rival he ever had, for the Duchesse de Châteauroux did not arrive on the scene of this devilish struggle for power until it was time to screw the old rogue into his coffin. Few men in history have had their ambition survive so many checks and disappointments as he, or realized it so late and enjoyed its fruits so long.

The importance of this victory was enhanced by the spoils Fleury secured. His ambition and Madame de Prie's being identical, he was exposed to the same dangers as she had been, and obliged to defend himself after the same fashion. The preparations, therefore, which she had made for her protection were of the greatest value to him, and he reaped all the benefit from her queen that she had expected to reap, without its odium. Marie Leczinska, indeed, might be described as the first of the *maîtresses en titre*, and the least dangerous of them all to a minister.

Forced at fifteen into a marriage for which he had no inclination, Louis Quinze had at first resolved to follow the example of his late companion Tremouille, who had also been compelled to marry against his will, and treat his wife with cold disdain. This resolution, however, was speedily overcome, and for seven years there was no more faithful husband in France than its King.

"It is pleasant," wrote Barbier, "to see in a king so young, so handsome, and so charming, a heart so pure and a chastity so agreeable."

If ever a woman was praised in his presence—as was frequently done with an ulterior motive—Louis would reply modestly—

"But the Queen is better than that."

This devotion, so unusual in a King of France, is almost incomprehensible when one considers the character and appearance of Marie Leczinska. She possessed neither the charm of beauty nor the ugliness that is frequently even more fascinating than beauty. She looked what she was—commonplace and dull, " a *bourgeoise* who could never accustom herself to her unexpected and undesired rise in the world." For she was much more afraid of her husband than in love with him, and when in his company was always constrained and awkward. Nor were these disadvantages lessened by the fact that Louis was seven years her junior. There is, however, no accounting for tastes, and the King, who was too lazy to break a habit even when it bored him, might have remained faithful indefinitely but for the Queen herself and Fleury.

With all his craft, the Cardinal was sometimes weak enough to give the rein to his prejudices, but he only indulged in this dangerous gratification when the worms he trod upon were unable to turn. Disliking the Queen because she owed her position to his enemy, whom, out of gratitude, she would have saved if she could, and despising her insignificance, he took a mean satisfaction in perpetually humiliating her. Never, it must have seemed to Marie Leczinska, was fate more ironical than when it lifted her out of the poverty of her father's court at Weissembourg and placed her amidst the splendour of Versailles. Purposely kept short of cash by the Cardinal, the poor creature was often reduced to the necessity of borrowing from her ladies-in-waiting to defray the ordinary expenses of her household sooner than subject herself to the snubs of the all-powerful Minister. She could do nothing without first obtaining his permission, which it frequently gave him a pleasure to withhold. He once denied her even so small a distraction as that of entertaining her ladies and gentlemen at supper at Trianon, on the ground of an unnecessary expense. It was of no use to complain, as she once dared to her uxorious husband.

"You must obey the Cardinal," he told her, "in everything, as I do."

But the petty tyranny of Fleury was not the only trouble that made life a burden to Marie Leczinska. Considering it her "duty," a sense of which was very strong in her, to provide heirs to the throne, she was obliged to endure the frequent manifestations of constancy that Louis gave her long after they ceased to afford her satisfaction.

"Eh, quoi," she could not help exclaiming once in disgust, "toujours coucher, toujours grosse, et toujours accoucher!"

At last, her spirit having been previously broken by the Cardinal, her strength succumbed, and in losing the desire she lost the ability to continue to play the *rôle* of a *reine pondeuse*.

It was now that Louis Quinze, like the kings in the Old Testament, "did that which was evil in the sight of the Lord." There was no open rupture, no scandal, but it was noticed, says d'Argenson, that "if the King wished to pass his evenings, as was customary, with the Queen, to play cards or to talk, she was always too unwell to dress to receive him, or too fatigued to try to amuse him. So, in disgust, he took to passing his evenings first with his gentlemen, and then with his cousin, Mademoiselle de Charolais, or his aunt, Madame la Comtesse de Toulouse."

Or, to express it in the words of the cynical Maréchal de Richelieu, "It is impossible to say when, or where, or how the King ceased to be the best of husbands; but after he had been married seven years he realized one fine morning that he was only two-and-twenty, and seven years younger than his wife."

To the Court, whose spirits had long been depressed by the *bourgeois* domesticity of the sovereign, and the parsimonious *régime* of the Cardinal, who was so inconsiderate at eighty as to go on living when everybody wished him to die, the coolness between the royal couple gave the greatest relief. All factions—save the ruling one—united to widen the breach. Wit, ridicule, irony, and even example attacked in turns the virtuous precepts which Fleury had so craftily instilled into his pupil. To provide the King with a mistress from whose influence each hoped to profit was the ambition of all, from the Œil-de-Bœuf to the ante-chambers.

"Even the people," says de Goncourt, "urged him by their lampoons and songs to commit adultery, for they had been so accustomed by the Bourbons to the prestige of gallantry that they could not understand a young king, who was, moreover, the handsomest man in his kingdom, without his Gabrielle."

In a word, all France conspired to seduce Louis Quinze.

One day a courtier coming to inform him that the Queen had just given birth to a princess, which brought up the number of the "Mesdames," as the daughters of the sovereign were styled at the Court of France, to seven, said facetiously—

"Sire, c'est Madame Septième."

"Non," corrected Louis, "c'est Madame Dernière !"

At Versailles, where the twitch of an eyelid was regarded as of the deepest significance, such a retort, falling from the lips of the King, was not unnaturally interpreted as a sign that the Queen had been supplanted. It was no sooner repeated than the whole Court, the whole nation, became vibrant with curiosity.

"Who is she ? " whispered the Œil-de-Bœuf. "Who is she ?" echoed the ante-chambers. "Who is she ?" gossiped Paris and France.

Was it Mademoiselle de Charolais, who, since the age of fifteen, had provided the world with a fresh scandal regularly every year—a circumstance which she regarded as one of the prerogatives of her rank as a princess of the family of Bourbon-Condé, for whom the laws of morality made special exceptions ? Or was it the Comtesse de Toulouse, the widow of one of the royal bastards of the late reign, who, though twenty years the King's senior, was still fascinating ? Was it the lovely Duchesse This or the *spirituelle* Marquise That ? At Court the answer to this question was the chief, the only affair in the world, quite casting into the shade the fate of Stanislas, whom France was just then trying to replace on the throne of Poland, an adventure in which he was running the risk of his life, and France experiencing great humiliation. But echo merely answered Who ?

Baffled curiosity never thought of doubting if it might not be mistaken in the interpretation it had put upon the King's retort. Having ceased to visit the Queen there could be no doubt he had taken a mistress, *ça va sans dire*. He, moreover, confessed as much himself one night at supper with his gentlemen. For some young Duc d'Epernon or de Gesvres or another having cunningly insinuated the general conviction of the Court on the subject, Louis, slightly flushed with wine, suddenly rose, and in the midst of a breathless silence bade them drink to—La Belle Inconnue! And draining his glass he dashed it to the ground.

But why all this mystery? Was Louis Quinze ashamed of having left the path of virtue, or did it merely amuse him to have for once a secret from his Court?

IV

THERE was one person, however, to whom the identity of La Belle Inconnue was no mystery. That was Cardinal Fleury. No one understood the temperament and character of Louis better than his Eminence. The King was chiefly what the Cardinal had made him. Aware of the duplicity and insincerity natural to the race of Bourbon, he knew it was by fear and not affection that one could hope to rule the King. He knew too that at such a Court and with such a prince his vigilant cunning must ever be on the alert to detect and avoid any mole-hole of intrigue, the smallest one of which stumbled on unawares was capable of bringing a giant to the ground. So the crafty priest had forged out of Louis' tendency to hypochondria, which cankered his pleasures, a chain of fear, and riveted it to his victim with espionage. It was to Fleury that Bachelier, the King's favourite *valet de chambre*, owed his place, his

ANDRE HERCULES CARDINAL
DE FLEURY
Grand Aumonier de la Reine Ministre d'Etat

After Rigaud

[*From an old French print*]

To face page 22

title, and his fifty thousand livres a year. In return Bachelier betrayed the confidence of his royal master to his friend Barjac, Fleury's devoted and trusty servant, whereby it chanced that the Cardinal was always kept informed of everything the King did or said or thought.

With the machinery of such a system of espionage at his disposal, he had known before the Court, even before the King himself, when his Majesty's passion for the *reine pondeuse* began to cool. Nothing could have given him greater annoyance than the thought of the illicit connection which he was aware must inevitably follow sooner or later. No minister of an absolute monarch, even though he be as crafty as old Fleury, can contemplate with equanimity the advent upon the scene of some feminine influence—a Maintenon's, for all he knows—to rival his. So this venerable prince of the Church, who, when it had served his purpose, had done all he could to keep temptation out of the King's way, now resolved, like Madame de Prie, to take time by the forelock and himself provide Louis with a mistress as she had provided him with a wife—a mistress whom he could bully as he bullied the Queen !

" For this purpose," says the Maréchal de Richelieu, "the Cardinal wanted a woman sufficiently attractive to entice the King without enslaving him ; disinterested enough to love him for himself rather than for profit; poor and meek, to be thus the more easily kept in subjection ; and, above all, wholly lacking in a capacity for affairs. Being notoriously "—and with great reason, Richelieu might have added—" economical in his governance of the State, it was further necessary to him that the mistress of his choosing should have a husband who might be held responsible instead of the King for any vexatious consequences that might result from the *liaison*." And lastly, as a Jesuit, realizing that there still existed a certain traditionary superstition of morality, he wanted, to quote the mocking

Maréchal again, "a lady of quality, in order that there should be as little scandal as possible!"

As I said above, Fleury owed his success not only to his cunning, but to his luck. Such a woman as he required chanced to be at Court, and Bachelier had reported to Barjac, who in turn told the Cardinal, that the King already appeared taken with her, for "he blushed whenever her name was mentioned." The fair who had produced so significant an impression was the Comtesse de Mailly *dame du palais* to the Queen. Apart from the qualities that recommended her to Fleury, she possessed one that had recommended her to the King—a natural modesty. Married at sixteen to her cousin, a notorious *roué* by whom she had been shamefully neglected, she had sought consolation in a post-nuptial friendship with another man, of the sort which Madame du Deffand termed "quite a decent arrangement." Indeed, Madame de Mailly's lapse from virtue was so slight that she still retained a sufficient sense of shame to display diffidence, if not to feel reluctance, in beginning an amour with the King.

Such modesty, coupled with the gentleness of her nature, was just the quality to appeal to Louis. Secretly desiring a mistress, he was too timid to make the first advances. The boldness of a Charolais would have driven this novice in vice back into the shell of his chastity. As it was, he experienced considerable difficulty in conquering his shyness even with the aid of Madame de Mailly's modesty.

Once, however, he got the better of this sensual timidity, it will scarcely surprise one to learn that Louis "passed in a short time from an extreme reserve with women to the greatest licence." Indeed, so impartially did he divide his attentions that the Court came to the conclusion La Belle Inconnue was Woman in general. It was, however, to Madame de Mailly that he was the most devoted, and as it

pleased him to preserve the mystery of his amour long after
he had ceased to be shy, she was obliged to act in private
the *rôle* that it was her ambition to act in public.

The royal assignations followed the course of the royal
degeneration. At first they took place "at night in the
Bois de Boulogne chez Charolais"—who acted as *entremet-
teuse*—at her villa Madrid, to-day well known as a café-
restaurant. Then at Choisy, "that temple dedicated to
Love where there was only accommodation for ladies."
At last in the *petits appartements* of Versailles itself, into
which, after the respectable and solemn *coucher du roi*
demanded of him by etiquette, Louis would slip from his
royal bed in his grand state bedroom and join a select and
secret coterie at the famous *petits soupers*.

Petits soupers in the *petits appartements !* What scenes
of revelry and debauchery ! What an unmasking of that
"vice which lost half its evil by losing all its grossness" !
And what cabals and intrigues, in which the fate of a
minister, a mistress, and Europe were involved !

These *petits soupers* in the *petits appartements* are
anathema maranatha to the "scientific" historian, who
is much too dignified a personage to leave the Council
Chamber, where wars were declared, treaties broken, and
high policies of State elaborated, for the back stairs, whence
the motives that inspired these actions originated. But as
you and I make no pretence of being historians, there is
no reason why we should yawn, like Louis Quinze, while
ministers read tiresome dispatches from Berlin or London,
glanced over balance sheets, and argued whether France
should form an alliance with Prussia or Austria. I frankly
confess that I would rather get a glimpse of history *en
déshabillé*, so to speak, than behold her *en grande tenue* in
the Council Chamber of Versailles. Nor am I the least
ashamed to haunt the back stairs like a lacquey, since the
example has been set for me by no less a personage than

the successor of Richelieu and Mazarin—the Last of the Cardinals.

In fact, Fleury spent most of his life at Versailles eavesdropping at the doors of the *petits appartements*. With Bachelier and Barjac for his ears he heard the popping of every cork, the click of every glass. He heard the loud, ribald laugh of Charolais, who, said d'Argenson, "would have been a thief, a receiver of stolen goods, a flower-girl, had she been born among the people." He heard the indecent jokes, and perhaps laughed at them too, of old Maréchale d'Estrées, "who was invited for her fund of racy stories." And he heard every hiccough of the modest Mailly, who, according to d'Argenson, "had only one defect—she grew to love the wine of Champagne as her grandmother had loved it fifty years before her, and glass in hand would have drunk a Bassompierre under the table !"

His Eminence too saw everything, as he heard everything, that went on at Versailles. Perhaps not the least pleasing sight he saw was Madame de Mailly, sober and in all the *éclat* of her beauty. As, for instance, when dressed —and " no woman at Court knew how to dress better "— " in the Polish costumes she affected, lovely to behold, whether on horseback with a heron's plume *à l'aigrette* in her caftan of velvet, or driving in her carriage in yellow satin trimmed with sable."

Perhaps too the Cardinal had seen her when, according to Richelieu, " she would have made a picture for Giorgione or Titian, could they have beheld her like the merchants who came in the mornings to show her their wares, and whom she received in her bed of lace decked in all her diamonds, which she wore on every occasion, even when she slept."

It was this frail beauty's dream to be publicly acknowledged as the *maîtresse en titre*. Louis, doubtless, could have been induced to realize this dream for her much sooner than he eventually did, but for the Cardinal, whose opposition to her elevation was prompted by his passion for economy and his own interests. In regard to the former he had at the commencement of her amour, says d'Argenson "made the King give her 20,000 livres, paid once for all." Nor did Madame de Mailly, who was neither sordid nor avaricious, ever ask for more—save a mere forty francs or so on two occasions—and consequently was "frequently without a crown in her pocket."

But money was none the less necessary to her, and to cover the cost of what is ever an expensive *rôle* she was obliged to incur enormous debts. Fleury was aware of these debts, and as he dreaded that if she became the *maîtresse déclarée* she would avail herself of the usual prerogative of the position to pay them at the public expense, he had opposed her elevation on grounds of expediency. He had, however, a selfish motive as well. For as long as the King refused to recognize her the uncertainty as to her influence diverted into various channels the force of the current of intrigue against which, powerful as he was, he was ever obliged to swim.

It was so necessary to his safety to know everything that was transpiring that one can hardly blame him for attaching so much importance to the tittle-tattle of the back stairs. The eavesdropping and peeping through keyholes that was done for him by his valets saved him more than once from the fate of Madame de Prie. In this way he discovered that the bold princesses and ribald duchesses of the *petits soupers*, in order to bring about his fall, were flattering Madame de Mailly into the belief that if she could induce the King to dismiss him her dreams would be realized. With the ears of his Bachelièr and Barjac glued to the doors of the *petits appartements*, he heard this tool of a powerful cabal herself ask Louis—

"When are you going to get rid of your old tutor?"

All of a sudden the Court, which knew nothing of these secret revels beyond the fact that "they finished at five or six in the morning and the King remained in bed till four or five the next afternoon," perceived, says d'Argenson, that his Majesty "no longer spoke to Charolais." She left Versailles of her own accord, to avoid being asked to leave, and it was rumoured that "Madame de Mailly had been ordered to quarrel with her."

The Cardinal, had he desired, might, no doubt, have got rid of her too, but being necessary to him he punished her more cruelly. He now not only ceased to raise objections to her recognition as the King's declared mistress, but even persuaded Louis to gratify her. Diabolical Cardinal! For a *maîtresse en titre* to maintain her position required special and exceptional talent, which Fleury knew Madame de Mailly wholly lacked. On what, on whom could she depend to circumvent the machinations of the enemies with whom she would have to contend? Not on that beauty any more "which would have made Giorgione or Titian haunt her ante-chamber." The dissipation of the *petits soupers* had faded it; at eight-and-twenty she was *passée*. Least of all on Louis. Fleury had studied him too well not to know that, stripped of its mystery, his passion would die. No, to keep from falling on that slippery summit of her dreams the wretched woman would be obliged to look to *him* for support! With his aid only would habit, to which the King was a slave, continue to chain him to a mistress who had ceased to please him— perhaps for the brief span of life that an indispensable minister of eighty-five might still hope to enjoy!

Nor was the crafty Cardinal, to whom power was the breath of life, mistaken in his calculations.

The vanity of Madame de Mailly, who was "quite without hatred or malice," had no sooner been gratified than the King's passion, which had bloomed for five years in the shade, withered in the sunshine of publicity. "She ceased to be happy," says Richelieu, "the day she could no longer conceal her happiness."

To appreciate the full extent of Fleury's vengeance it should be added that the inoffensive Madame de Mailly had grown to love this king, who was "beau comme l'amour," as Vallière had loved his predecessor. It was his affection she coveted, not his money. "She had appeared content," says Richelieu, "with the 20,000 francs she had received at the outset, which, on the first morning of a royal *liaison*, was a price more than *bourgeois* for the favours of a Comtesse de Mailly." And now grown weary of her, but lacking the will to dismiss her, Louis treated her, to quote the Maréchal again, "like Peter the Great when in France, who made love like a porter and behaved in the same fashion." *Maîtresse en titre* of the King of France, Madame de Mailly did not cost him as much "as an opera girl costs a banker!"

Finding herself neglected by the King, ridiculed by the Court and bullied by the Cardinal, one would have thought a woman of Madame de Mailly's unselfish and docile nature would have followed the example of Vallière and retired to a convent. But this a wild hope of rekindling Louis' passion prevented her from doing, and in her despair she sought consolation at a source from which there seemed a reasonable chance of obtaining it, namely, the boasted devotion of her sister Félicité de Nesle—Madame de Vintimille to be.

V

THE unconventionality, to give it a mild name, of the lives of the Marquis and Marquise de Nesle had so disorganized their establishment that it became necessary in the interests of respectability for their relations to provide for their children. Madame de Mailly, who was at the time of this family conclave the only one of the five sisters married, had charged herself with the care of Félicité, the sister nearest her own age, and placed her as a *pensionnaire* at the convent of Port-Royal. Here Mademoiselle de Nesle, cut off from a world she had never known and temptations she had never experienced, had developed a malady that she neither tried nor desired to cure—a malady to which the Faculty would no doubt give a scientific name, but which will best be understood by calling it, like the cynical Richelieu, *nostalgie de roi*.

This complaint, though strange in a *pensionnaire of* Port-Royal, was particularly prevalent in the eighteenth century. But of all who have ever been afflicted with it, Félicité de Nesle had it in its worst form. To its victim the repose and security of the haven of Port-Royal seemed more dreadful than the tempests and shipwrecks of the ocean of the world. In the bosom of an eternal Lent she sighed for an eternal carnival. Consumed with the fever of baffled curiosity and ungratified desire, she spent her days glued to her window, like sister Anne in the fairy-tale, watching for the coming of the royal lover of whom she dreamt at night. Never did she hear the Angelus but she started as if it were the signal of her deliverance, the profane annunciation for which she pined. Moreover, not only was this dove weary of her mystical dove-cot, but she made no mystery of her desires. More than once she was heard to declare in the delirium of her *ennui*—

" My sister Mailly is good " (and foolish, she might have added); " she will call me to her. I shall make the King love me, and then I shall ruin Fleury and govern France ! "

In the hope that by some chance they might fall into the hands of the King, she wrote letter on letter to her sister imploring her to send her an invitation to visit

Versailles. At last, as she had hoped, one of these letters *did* fall into the King's hands. He read it and was amused. To amuse Louis! It was the thread to the labyrinth in which Madame de Mailly wandered, the thread she had dropped when Fleury had robbed her of her mystery and Time of youth and beauty. So Madame de Mailly, who had already thought of Félicité—whose name alone was a happy omen—as a reinforcement, no longer hesitated but sent her sister the golden key to Paradise—lost!

Born, as Richelieu expressed it with flippant irony, in the "hot month of August" 1712, Mademoiselle de Nesle was twenty-seven when she arrived at Versailles. It was rather late, one would have thought, to succeed in capturing the heart of Louis. A woman, however, is only as old as she appears to be. Ninon de l'Enclos and Diane de Poitiers made conquests at sixty, and kept them too! Nevertheless, they had retained some of their past charms, but Félicité de Nesle had never been beautiful. Her own sister, Madame de Flavacourt, in describing her years afterwards, to Soulavie, said that "she had the face of a grenadier, the neck of a stork, and the smell of an ape." While her husband, who hated her as much as she despised him, used to speak of her as "his little he-goat!" Indeed one *peut flairer* Madame de Vintimille—to call her by the name of the man she married—in all the memoirs of the time. Nevertheless, without charms, she charmed even her enemies.

"It needs," said Richelieu, "much art or much genius to be as ugly as that. If she had not the beauty which comes from God, she had that which comes from the devil and returns to him."

In her the repulsive became horribly attractive, even that *odeur de singe*, a feature that would have robbed even Venus of her loveliness. With this original ugliness, which she was clever enough to admit, and the first to make a jest of she was ever restless, capricious, inventive, malicious,

vicious, sparkling, a creature full of surprises, and of whom
nothing was certain but the unexpected.   On Louis "who
was the easiest man in the world to distract but the most
difficult to keep amused" such a woman was bound to
exert a powerful charm.   But Mademoiselle de Nesle had
not come to Versailles simply to amuse the King.   Behind
all her affected gaiety and folly she had a serious object,
and while her head appeared to be empty it was teeming
with ambition.   This object, which she never lost sight of
for a moment, was "to subjugate the King, to render his
yoke light but to accustom him to it, to tame him gently
but to tame him for ever."

She did not, however, take Louis captive by a sudden
assault; but insensibly insinuated herself into his esteem
and glided into his confidence, prying the while into all the
secrets of State with the air of a disgusted *ingénue* who,
having tasted forbidden fruit, finds it bitter.   At the same
time, the more artfully to conceal her designs, she continued
to display the greatest devotion to the sister she was supplanting.   But Madame de Mailly was under no illusions as to
her treachery.   She was, however, afraid to complain, lest
by doing so she should precipitate the catastrophe she
dreaded.   She had, moreover, herself succumbed to the
diabolical fascination of Félicité even while she resented it.
So, says Richelieu, "forcing despair to wear the mask of
hope and crowning with laurel a brow that called for the
willow, she consented to share the King with her sister,
preferring the martyrdom of secretly suffering near her
lover to the public affront of a dismissal without hope of
return."   And so well did she feign indifference that many
believing it impossible for a woman, even one so docile and
sweet-tempered as she, to endure such a humiliation,
declared she had found consolation in another lover.   But
even the prick of these thorns Madame de Mailly bore in
silence.

THE MARQUISE DE VINTIMILLE
[*After Nattier*]

To face page 32

Nor was the Cardinal less concerned at the designs of Félicité, in whom he at once recognized another Madame de Prie, but one infinitely more subtle, more hostile, more fell. That he should attempt to defeat her purpose goes without saying, and in the whole history of Court intrigues, which teems with so many strange incidents, there is none stranger than the struggle for power that now began between this old man close on ninety and this young woman fresh from a convent. It was the craft of instinct pitched against the craft of long experience, the fearless malice of youth against the feline malice of age. Such a struggle, which would at any time be remarkable, by reason of the contrast of the antagonists, is rendered the more conspicuous from the utter worthlessness of the object— the favour of Louis Quinze. For Louis, insincere and malicious by nature, unwilling to part either with his minister or his mistress, amused himself by playing them false in turns, and encouraging each in the very act of betrayal.

The marriage of Mademoiselle de Nesle afforded the King an excellent opportunity of displaying this characteristic duplicity. In her *rôle* of understudy to Madame de Mailly, etiquette and ambition alike demanded that she should marry. As she did not in the least *love* the King whom she had bewitched, she had none of her sister's modesty in regard to enriching herself at his expense. *Love* a king! It was an ideal worthy of a *femme de chambre* in the opinion of Félicité de Nesle. She knew that it was the importunate mistresses of kings who were the fortunate ones; in her opinion a Vallière or a Mailly deserved to be unhappy. She intended to get all she could out of her royal lover. So when it came to a question of her marriage she aspired high, and with her natural audacity demanded the hand of a Prince of the Blood!

3

It was not that her avarice or her pride desired this gratification, but her cunning and her malice. She knew that the Cardinal would bitterly oppose such an alliance, therefore from malice she wished it as a means of humiliating him. While her cunning told her that in case of some future reverse of fortune, a princely marriage would to a great extent break her fall.

But Louis, after consenting, to Fleury's vexation, married her instead to the Marquis de Vintimille, a quite unimportant and contemptible young nobleman of twenty. Her shame and Fleury's triumph were, however, mitigated by a further instance of kingly duplicity. For Louis settled 200,000 livres on the bride and made her a *dame du palais* to the Dauphiness, which gave her another 6,000 livres a year with quarters at Versailles. But this extravagance was, perhaps, less disturbing to the Cardinal than the fact that "the King came expressly from his hunting-box at La Muette to honour the ceremony, and that night took the husband's place, who was sent to sleep alone in the King's bed at La Muette!"

After this marriage, Madame de Vintimille's influence over the King rapidly increased. Nevertheless, try as she might, she could not bring about the fall of the Cardinal, "though she succeeded in preventing him from seeing the King for more than a quarter of an hour a week." Nor could the Cardinal dislodge her, though he employed the most brilliant wits at Court to sting her to death with ridicule, and all the craft of which he himself was a past master. But powerful as Madame de Vintimille had now become, she could not save Chauvelin, of whose ability Fleury had grown jealous, from disgrace. She had, too, in order to save her vagabond father from imprisonment, to suffer the further humiliation of beseeching the intercession of the Cardinal, who humbled her still more by granting her prayer.

Considering, however, Fleury's extreme age, Madame de Vintimille had merely to wait for the golden apple of power to fall into her lap. But cunning seldom fails to dig its own pitfalls. As the Cardinal, for all his craft, had made the mistake of driving Madame de Mailly to despair, whereby he had made Madame de Vintimille possible, so she in her turn over-reached herself. Merely to see her inveterate enemy sink into his grave within a month or a year gave her no satisfaction. In her vindictive hatred she wanted his disgrace as well as his death, and she never ceased to meditate how she might accomplish it, "feeling," says de Goncourt, "that she had within her the gage of victory."

In order to invest this "gage"—in other words, the child with which she was *enceinte*—with the importance her ambition attached to it, Madame de Vintimille desired that her *accouchement* should take place at Versailles. And thither the infatuated King himself brought her from Choisy, where she had for months kept him cut off from Fleury and all hostile influences. Naturally delicate, the strain of the intense excitement under which she had long laboured, caused not only by the high hopes she built on the legitimization of her child, but by the fear lest it should be stillborn, had reduced her to a state that occasioned the doctors the gravest anxiety.

Fleury, in the meantime, at eighty-nine, clinging to power like a miser to his money-bags, awaited this event on which his fate hung, with an apparent indifference, which afterwards gave rise to the foulest suspicions. For Madame de Vintimille perished with victory in her grasp!

Four days after her arrival at Versailles she was safely delivered of a fine boy, "which the King received into his own arms with much greater manifestations of delight than he had ever shown at the birth of his Queen's children."

With Louis exhibiting such inordinate joy over the child, and Madame de Vintimille reported to be convalescing, Fleury played his last card and left Versailles—an act that on previous occasions in the past had invariably brought the King to heel.   On this occasion, however, Louis manifested no sign of regret, and the old Cardinal might never have returned had not the health of Madame de Vintimille unexpectedly taken a sudden turn for the worse. Seized with violent convulsions, she shrieked out that she had been poisoned, and failing to obtain the least relief from the antidotes she took, the unhappy woman at last consented that a confessor should be sent for.   But the remedies of the Church were destined to give as little relief to her now terrified soul as those of the Faculty to her tortured body.   For the confessor himself dropped dead on the threshold of her room before he could reach her !   A few minutes later Madame de Vintimille likewise expired. Her romance of love and ambition had lasted but the length of a dream.

As if to set the seal to this horrible end, " horrors," says d'Argenson, " were perpetrated on her body before it was buried."   Following a ridiculous custom which prevented the palace of the King of France from offering hospitality to the dead, the corpse of Madame de Vintimille, loosely stitched up after a hasty autopsy, and wrapped in a sheet, was removed to the Hotel de Villeroy, where the servants— to continue in the words of d'Argenson—" left it in the stable to go and get drunk, whereupon the populace of Versailles who were rejoiced at her death, because they believed she wished to induce the King to reside permanently at Choisy, got into the stable and saying that she was a vile creature, who had stolen the King from her sister who was a good woman, they lit fire-crackers on her body, and subjected it to all sorts of insults ! "

What an end !   And what an opportunity for a moral

reflection! But to dig up a dead woman from the *oubliette* of history in which she is buried, to pelt her with the stones of morality, seems to me even more inhuman than "to light fire-crackers on her body." Besides, belated indignation is ridiculous, and I am sure that had Madame de Vintimille foreseen her end it would not have prevented her for one moment from going on with her *rôle*. Her soul, as Richelieu said of her looks, came from the devil and returned to him.

VI

LOUIS was overwhelmed by the shock of this death. When the news was broken to him he immediately took to his bed, and remained there for three days utterly prostrated with grief—and fear, people said. For he took no steps to investigate the truth of the rumour that the sudden end of the woman he mourned "was due to poison administered by the Abbé Brissard, a Fleuryiste, being warned, it was whispered, that a similar fate would overtake him if he dared to avenge her."

But Fleury, whether directly or indirectly responsible for this crime, was not the only person who benefited by it. On rising from his bed Louis departed for a secluded country house, taking Madame de Mailly with him, "to remind him of her sister." To poor Madame de Mailly, who in order to remain near the man she loved had endured the torture of witnessing his affection for her rival, there was nothing humiliating in being invited to weep with him over his loss. On the contrary, after her bitter winter of neglect, it seemed to her as if the summer had returned— the short summer of St. Martin. So she encouraged the hypochondriacal King to pour his grief into her ears, and realizing that on its continuance the length of her lease of happiness depended, she mingled her tears with his while he read over the "two thousand odd letters he had exchanged with her sister," and sighed with him when he would pause to exclaim—

"Ah, Madame de Vintimille was not so wicked as they say!"

But while the minister and the mistress were only too willing to encourage him to indulge a grief which gave the kingdom to the one and the King to the other, the Court was impatient to put an end to a state of affairs that threatened to revive the melancholy bigotry of Louis XIII. So the Duc de Richelieu, the gayest, the greediest, the cleverest, and the most unscrupulous of the courtiers, having consulted with a few of his friends, formed a conspiracy to remove both the minister and the mistress, and to replace them with others. As it was agreed that he should take the place of the Cardinal, it was only a question of finding a substitute for Madame de Mailly.

"After running over in my mind," he says in his monstrously wicked and witty Memoirs—"after running over in my mind the beauties of the Court, I thought I could do no better than give the preference to one that at first sight of her some months before the King, turning pale, had thrice in succession exclaimed, 'Mon dieu, qu'elle est belle!' She was indeed beautiful. Moreover, being the sister of Mesdames de Mailly and de Vintimille, she appeared to me a most suitable candidate, for such a mistress would make the King the least faithless possible to poor Madame de Mailly, since she would be replaced by her sister, a thing she had already tolerated, and the least blamable in the sight of Heaven and the world, since the scandal would be confined to a single family."

It was thus that Marie Anne de Mailly-Nesle, Duchesse de Châteauroux, acquired the leading *rôle* in this drama of intrigue, which may very aptly be termed "The Fatal Amours of Louis Quinze."

"She was not one of your ordinary beauties," wrote Richelieu ; "with her nymph-like form and her regal carriage, with her blue eyes full of genius and her enchantress's voice, with her mouth made for kisses and commands, and with her superb blond hair waving on a brow of ivory like the hair of the Antiope of Correggio or the Venus of Titian, she was a morsel for a king. But she was far more beautiful than these masterpieces of art, for she was a masterpiece of Nature. She had speech, movement, life ; her eyes called for homage, her lips for pleasure, her heart for love. Such a woman was born to reign."

And this, like Madame de Vintimille before her, was her ambition. Descended, so to speak, from a long line of intrigues, all the traits of which she inherited, the Duchesse de Châteauroux possessed a remarkable aptitude for the difficult *rôle* she undertook to play.

Nothing is more erroneous than to fancy that the mistress of a king is necessarily an *amoureuse*, least of all the mistress of a French king. Never were women colder, less sensual than the Maintenon or the Pompadour. The *maîtresse en titre* was, with few exceptions, essentially a woman of vast ambition, wholly absorbed in obtaining and maintaining her power. It is, perhaps, no exaggeration to say that she regarded the bodily "duty," as Marie Leczinska expressed it, of her office as its sole drawback—the thorn, so to speak, to the rose of power for which she hankered. Such women were utterly devoid of passion, utterly incapable of love ; and, paradoxical as it seems, when they frankly polluted themselves, like a Vallière or a Mailly, they were far less depraved than when they deliberately and coldly made a sin for which they had no inclination the means of achieving their object.

Madame de Châteauroux had an energetic, almost male

character, at once sharpened and softened by precocious experience. Her wit could be amiable as well as malicious, and her coquetry, which was either piquant or modest as she desired, seemed natural because it was refined. There never reigned at Versailles a mistress surer of herself; her every action was premeditated, and she studied her *rôle* with as much care as an actress at the Conservatoire. If she made mistakes, she was determined they should not be at her own expense, and if she fell, to fall from such a height that her fall should still be a triumph and her disgrace a homage. She belonged to the class of women-sphinxes, one of those creatures who regard themselves as the axis of the world, and to attain their ends will see with a light heart and without the least remorse everything tumble to pieces around them. Such a woman was not one to surrender at the first assault, but after a siege.

"If the heart," said Richelieu, "that glittered in her eyes burnt, like all new worlds, to be discovered, it did not suffer common exploration or hasty possession."

When she came to Versailles she was known as the Marquise de la Tournelle. Her husband, it was said, had died of unrequited love of her, leaving his widow with a fortune quite inadequate to support her in the manner she desired. So beautiful a woman could not lack opportunities of acquiring a grand position, and the Prince de Soubise, of the semi-royal family of Rohan, had offered her marriage. Such an alliance would have satisfied the ambition of an ordinary woman, but not that of Madame de la Tournelle, who openly boasted that Condé and not the Marquis de Nesle was her father. Félicité de Nesle had had the audacity to aspire to a Prince of the Blood; Marie Anne, become a widow, refused to accept the hand of any man short of the King of France, and it was only since he could not offer her his right, that she condescended to accept his left.

Warned, however, by her sister's mistakes, she determined beforehand to secure the guarantees which Madame
de Vintimille had failed to demand. To obtain them she
played the prude—a part that never fails to subjugate an
amorous king—and teased Louis to distraction by feigning
fidelity to the " beau Agenois," a nephew of Richelieu, with
whom it was rumoured she was as madly in love as he was
known to be with her. But the Duchesse de Châteauroux
never loved any one or anything but power. When it
suited her purpose to appear to surrender to the King she
did not scruple to be false to Agenois, but in a manner
which threw all the odium of her treachery on him. To
effect this she employed Richelieu, whose aims depended
on the success of hers, to concoct a plot by which his
nephew was sent to a distant part of the country, and
while absent made to believe that his mistress was faithless. This ruse succeeded precisely as Madame de
Châteauroux, knowing Agenois, expected it to. For in a
fit of pique he married another, whereupon the artful prude
consented to receive Louis, " disguised as a doctor," for the
first time alone.

In return for this ineffable favour she demanded " that
when she wanted money she was to send her notes and
obtain it at the Royal Treasury ; that she should be created
a duchess, and her letters patent verified by the Parlement ;
and that her children, if she had any, should be legiti-
matized. Finally, as a pledge of the fulfilment of these
conditions, she demanded the immediate dismissal of her
sister Madame de Mailly."

Such demands were more in keeping with the coarse
manners of the Court of Whitehall than with the polished
Court of Versailles. Here, though the Treasury was
regarded by a *maîtresse en titre* as a bank whose funds
were her personal property, she had formerly made her
drafts upon it with as little publicity as possible. She had,

too, while wielding the greatest power, carefully avoided anything that might savour of ostentation. Madame Scarron was perfectly satisfied to be known as the Marquise de Maintenon. To be created Duchesse de la Vallière was Mademoiselle Louise La Beaume Le Blanc's crowning humiliation. As for the legitimization of the royal bastards, this had never been done *before* they were born. That a *grande dame* of the Court of Versailles should have been capable of setting the above price on her favours, and that the successor of Louis XIV should have paid it without a qualm, was significant of the degeneration of society, which now became perceptible to all close observers.

The dismissal of Madame de Mailly was the sole condition in this cold-blooded, soulless affair that did not outrage etiquette. It was, however, the only one to which Louis raised any objections. This was not because he had any sense of honour in the matter, or pitied Madame de Mailly, or regretted to part with her. He merely dreaded the scene that he knew she would make. With all the wish in the world, he had not the will to send her from him. But the haughty mistress was inexorable. Shylock was not more determined to have his pound of flesh than she was to have everything she demanded.

She very nearly overreached herself in this matter, for between her stubborn pride and Madame de Mailly's prayers and reproaches the King was so distracted that had there been any one capable of taking advantage of the situation, the Duchesse de Châteauroux might have remained Madame de la Tournelle for the rest of her life. Richelieu, however, as usual, came to the rescue by duping Madame de Mailly into believing that her voluntary departure from the Court would prove her love to Louis in a manner so convincing as to rekindle his for her.

Having brought herself to the point of acknowledging

THE COMTESSE DE MAILLY

[*After Nattier*]

To face page 42

the wisdom of Richelieu's advice, the wretched woman lost no time in acting upon it. Louis' behaviour on this occasion was typical of his natural duplicity. Finding that she was going, he pretended to deprecate her departure.

" At any rate," he said, as she staggered half fainting from his presence, " I shall expect you at Choisy on Monday, Madame la Comtesse. Remember, Monday," he repeated, adding playfully, " and don't keep me waiting."

Poor Madame de Mailly! She had no sooner left Versailles than the order was given to dismantle her apartments and nail up the doors. Monday she was ill with brain fever, and it was Madame de Châteauroux who went to Choisy with the King as *maîtresse en titre*.

Madame de Mailly's subsequent career was not without a certain pathetic interest. On leaving Versailles she took refuge with the Comtesse de Toulouse in Paris, having no home of her own and no money, for " never shade crossed the Styx poorer than she on leaving Versailles." A Noailles by birth, the Comtesse de Toulouse, like all her family, had the virtue of fidelity to her friends in misfortune. Through her intercession the fallen favourite finally obtained a pension from the King sufficient to enable her to pay her debts and the grant of apartments in the Luxembourg. At first grief and despair threatened her reason and her life ; but eventually a sermon of the revivalist priest Renault, whom she heard preach, led her to accept her fate with resignation. Her repentance expressed itself in a more practical fashion than Vallière's, for she renounced the world without entering a convent, and devoted the rest of her life to the poor, without neglecting her prayers.

The natural submissiveness of spirit, which, quite apart from her lack of ability, would have rendered her incapable of playing with success the difficult *rôle* of King's mistress, is illustrated by the following anecdote :—

Happening once accidentally to inconvenience some persons as she was taking her seat in church, a brute who recognized her, hissed out—

" What a fuss for a harlot ! "

" Since you recognize her," was the gentle retort, " pray to God for her."

Her death, which occurred several years after that of the sister who had so cruelly supplanted her, recalled her for a fleeting moment to the memory of the Court which had quite forgotten her. But Madame de Pompadour, it is said, was the only person at Versailles who manifested the least concern.

VII

WITH Madame de Vintimille's death the struggle for power, which had hitherto been a private, became a national, and even an international affair. Persons became synonyms for politics, politics acquired a purely personal character. The watchwords of the Cardinal's policy had been " Economy and Peace." It is to the persistency with which he endeavoured to adhere to these principles during his long supremacy that he owes the rather favourable esteem with which history is inclined to regard him— history being altogether too dignified to consider his conduct when absent from the Council Chamber. He had not, however, always been able to maintain this policy. When the War of the Austrian Succession broke out, it was impossible that France should remain neutral. He was for supporting Maria Theresa, because the nature of her resources seemed to guarantee a certain and speedy triumph. But in this he suddenly found himself opposed by what passed for public opinion, of which the spokesman was the Maréchal de Belle-Isle. To him the situation of Maria Theresa offered an excellent opportunity of breaking the power of Austria, which for centuries had been regarded as the hereditary enemy of France. Belle-Isle's policy was to sow discord in the Empire, by securing the election of an emperor hostile to the House of Hapsburg and at the same time too weak to maintain himself without the aid of France. Fleury had been forced to adopt this policy, to which he was opposed, at the cost of much of his prestige, for Belle-Isle had been actively supported by Madame de Vintimille.

Another such blow and the Cardinal's power must have been completely broken; and it was such a one that Madame de Vintimille was preparing to deal him when she died—at a time most unfortunate for France. This event deprived Belle-Isle, whose plans had so far prospered and who was absent with the army in Bohemia, of support at Versailles when he most needed it, a circumstance of which the Cardinal hastened to take advantage. By Madame de Vintimille's death he had recovered his power, but it was not safe so long as Belle-Isle, in whom he had a personal enemy and a dangerous rival, remained undiscredited. Belle-Isle, however, who lacked only loyal support to have proved himself the ablest general and minister France had had since the great days of Louis XIV, was not to be ruined easily. Nor was Fleury, to whom power was life, the man to hesitate to go to any extreme to be rid of such a rival. The only way of effecting this appeared to be by refusing to send Belle-Isle the reinforcements he demanded, whereby the French army was shut up in Prague without supplies and completely cut off in the depth of winter. Of the humiliation to France that would be occasioned by the fall of Prague, Fleury cared nothing. Ministers, before and since, have procured peace with dishonour, but seldom has the honour of a State been sacrificed to such base ends as in the present instance.

In Belle-Isle, however, the Cardinal met the first *man* he had ever had to deal with. Tired of waiting for reinforcements that never came, and conscious of treachery which had devoted him to ruin, the high-souled Marshal determined to save the honour of his country and bring home his army besieged in Prague, cut off in the midst of a hostile and foreign country, starved, frozen, and with the alternatives before it of an impossible victory or inevitable captivity. This too seemed as impossible as victory. But one night in the middle of December Europe beheld a handful of heroes all rags, skin and bones, and covered with wounds, pressing over the trackless snow towards France. It was the garrison of Prague escaping from its prison, followed by a horde of Uhlans, Hussars, and Pandours, against which it protected itself with thirty cannon that vomited fire as they flew from flank to flank—the first appearance of horse artillery in modern warfare, and invented by Belle-Isle, who, sick, wounded, and worn out, rode in the midst of his men encouraging them with hope.

For ten days and nights, starved and dying, they struggled on over the frozen mountains. But they reached France. This retreat from Prague electrified the world and deserves to be remembered, for it was one of the most glorious, and almost the last, of the great deeds of the *ancien régime*. But this is not the place to dilate on the genius of Belle-Isle. I merely mention him in passing, because at the very time he was saving the honour of his country, its king was too busy bargaining for the favours of Madame de Châteauroux to think of it.

To oppose the rise of this woman in whom he scented another Madame de Vintimille, the Cardinal, enfeebled by the weight of his ninety years and dispirited by the success of Belle-Isle, scarcely attempted. His day was virtually over, and within a month of Madame de Châteauroux's recognition as *maîtresse en titre* " he stole into his grave," as Richelieu says, " in order to escape the funeral of his power."

The news of his death was greeted with every manifestation of joy by the nation.

" Gentlemen," said the King, on being informed of it, to those who surrounded him, " henceforth, I am my own prime minister."

" Say rather," whispered Madame de Châteauroux to Richelieu, " no more priests ! ".

Having obtained power, the favourite, who herself said that her ambition was "haute comme les monts," was determined to use it in guiding the ship of State. Hitherto she had been too busy thinking of herself to find the time to think of France, but now she gave her attention wholly to the State.

In face of the invasion with which the kingdom was threatened after Belle-Isle's heroic retreat from Prague, no one was so pusillanimous as to advise the King to sue for peace. For once the voice of faction was silent and the whole nation was united in the desire to continue the war till the previous disasters had been atoned for by victories. Prompt and energetic action was needed at once, and Madame de Châteauroux was lacking in neither ability nor daring. She filled the most important offices of the ministry with her confederates and warmly supported Belle-Isle— though she afterwards abandoned him, when the disasters of the war dimmed his star, and threatened to cloud her own.

Furthur, to spur the patriotism of the nation, of the value of which in such a crisis she was fully aware, as well as to flatter the vanity of the man on whose favour her own existence depended, she unceasingly urged Louis to take the command of his army in person.

"You will kill me with all this energy," the lethargic king complained, loath to leave the luxury of the Court for the hardships of the camp.

"So much the better," she retorted ; "it is necessary for the salvation of your kingdom that you should be re-born!"

He finally consented to gratify her. The news that the King of France would in person lead his troops to victory, awoke an enthusiasm throughout the nation that was in itself a gage of victory. She had placed her hand on the pulse of public opinion, as well as on the heart of the King. The people compared her to Agnes Sorel. Nattier painted her as Dawn—the dawn of a new era!

Having found the energy to take the field, Louis, or rather his generals, rewarded the popular expectation by a series of rapid and brilliant successes. The pride of Austria was humbled in the dust in her Flemish provinces. But Madame de Châteauroux, knowing the nature of Louis Quinze, was afraid to run the risk of even a temporary separation from him. Before he started for the front, it had been agreed that she should follow him. To minimize the scandal of such an action, the King invited several ladies, among whom were three Princesses of the Blood, to accompany her. But this precaution produced the very opposite effect to what was intended. The announcement that the royal mistress had left the Court for the camp caused the greatest offence to the nation.

The King had been very popular with the army, "tasting the soup of the invalids and eating the bread of the soldiers." But with the arrival of the women his popularity vanished. The soldiers of the bodyguard even went to the length of singing at night, within hearing of the royal tent, a vulgar song very much in vogue at the time in Paris, of which the refrain was :—

> "Ah, Madame Enroux,
> Je deviendrai fou
> Si je ne vous baise,"

substituting for " Madame Enroux " " Belle Châteauroux."

Indeed, so hostile was the behaviour of the good people of Lille, that it was thought advisable for the favourite and her companions to go to Dunkirk and await the King.

Here, presentiment of coming evil, the first person Madame de Châteauroux met was her mortal enemy, the Comte de Maurepas.

VIII

THIS hatred, which was mutual and very vigorous, originated in the expectations that each had built on the fortune of the Dowager Duchesse de Mazarin, who was the aunt of Madame de Maurepas, as well as of Madame de Châteauroux, and by whom the latter had been brought up and educated. On the strength of this tie, Madame de Châteauroux had not unnaturally counted on inheriting the whole of her aunt's property. The Duchesse de Mazarin, however, after encouraging her niece in this belief, had, with contemptible mockery, left all she possessed to Maurepas and his wife, who proceeded to " rub in " their victory by immediately obliging Madame de Châteauroux to leave her aunt's house, where she was living, in order that they might enter into possession.

To " get even " with Maurepas had ever since been one of the prime objects of Madame de Châteauroux's life. The knowledge that he had tried to prevent her from becoming *maîtresse en titre* had been one of the chief motives of her demand to be created a duchess. To

4

mortify Madame de Maurepas, whom she would thus out-
rank, she had obliged the King to command Maurepas
himself to prepare the patent of her title for verification by
the Parlement. This, however, gave him the opportunity
of retaliating in a similar petty manner. For a pen in the
hands of Maurepas was as dangerous as a rapier in the
hands of the immortal d'Artagnan. He had a special
talent for composing lampoons and epigrams. Of all
those that flooded France in the reign of Louis Quinze and
were said to "temper despotism," none were more malicious,
more stinging than the ones that emanated from him. In
preparing the royal diploma which created her a duchess,
Maurepas defamed her in the most discreet manner
possible.

"Considering," it ran, "that our very dear and beloved
cousin, Marie Anne de Mailly-Nesle, widow of the Marquis
de la Tournelle, is issue of one of the oldest families in the
kingdom allied to ours ; that her ancestors have for many
generations rendered great and important services to our
crown ; that she is attached as *dame du palais* to our very
dear companion the Queen ; and that she joins to all the
virtues the most excellent qualities of heart and mind
which have won her just and universal esteem, we, Louis,
by the grace of God, King of France, deem it suitable to
bestow on her the duchy of Châteauroux with all its
appurtenances and dignities, etc., etc."

But Madame de Châteauroux was not born to perish
from the stab of ridicule. Maurepas might sneer as much
as he pleased, she had the supreme, if foolish, satisfaction
of sitting on her *tabouret* at Versailles while his wife was
compelled to stand.

It was in the sphere of politics, however, that this hatred
sought and obtained the most effective revenge. Maurepas
had belonged to the party of the Cardinal, who observing
the favour he enjoyed with the King, one of whose com-

panions he had been as a boy, had made him Minister of
Marine at twenty-one in the hope of securing his fidelity.
But Maurepas, treacherous by instinct, was only faithful to
Fleury because he hoped to inherit the reversion of his
power. Indeed, so cleverly did he play his cards, and so
broken had the Cardinal been during the last year of his
life, that Maurepas had virtually been chief minister.
When reconstructing the ministry on Fleury's death, the
Duchesse de Châteauroux would, had it been possible, have
excluded him from the cabinet. But Louis was too manifestly opposed to the dismissal of a minister whom he
liked personally, and who, more than any one with
whom he came in contact throughout his reign, had the
knack of making the most tedious details of state business
appear amusing. Under such circumstances, the *maîtresse
en titre* was too sensible to force the King to part with the
minister against his will. Moreover, she realized that
Maurepas would be less dangerous to her in the ministry
than out of it. She could not, however, forbear "putting
out one of his eyes," as she expressed it, by effecting the
fall of his only adherent and intimate friend Amelot, whom
she made the King dismiss "because he stammered."

But Maurepas, though humiliated by his haughty and
vindictive cousin, was not crushed. He quietly bided his
time, and let no opportunity slip of "getting even" in his
turn. The indignation excited by her arrival at the theatre
of war owed its force to his vilifying lampoons. He had,
indeed, even attempted to prevent her departure altogether
by warning Louis of the popular disaffection to which
such an act would expose him personally. But Madame
de Châteauroux had cleverly removed him before Louis
was convinced, by getting him sent on a tour of inspection
of the seaports of the kingdom, beginning with those in
the South, as the farthest away. Her annoyance, therefore, may be imagined when on arriving at Dunkirk, she

found her enemy there in his official capacity, having finished his tour of inspection, and ready to take all possible advantage of the unpopularity now attaching to her.

While she was waiting for the King at Dunkirk a cabal, the seeds of which had been previously planted by Maurepas, sprang up in a night like a mushroom. To bring about the fall of the favourite this cabal, which included generals, bishops, ministers, and princes of the blood, gave the utmost publicity to the scandal caused by her presence in the camp, being quite indifferent as to its effect on the popularity of the King or the stability of the throne. Thus it was reported that the monarch shared his favours equally between the duchess and her sister, Madame de Lauraguais, who was one of the ladies who had left the Court.

This infamous rumour, which was only too true, is an instance of the depths of infamy to which Madame de Châteauroux was capable of descending to gratify her lust for power. For, discovering that Louis appeared to be amused by her sister—of whom, by the way, she was as fond as Madame de Mailly had been of Madame de Vintimille—she had with consummate cynicism done her best to further the royal inclination, whereby she made of " fat, ugly, jolly Lauraguais, who had neither ambition nor ability," a trusty and useful friend.

The Duchesse de Châteauroux recognized the gravity of the situation. Of the faction by whose aid she had climbed to power there was but one person on whom she could rely—the Maréchal de Richelieu. But with such an ally, possessing a powerful artillery of craft and the advantage of being first gentleman of the bedchamber to the King, whose confidence he thus obtained and kept, the *maîtresse en titre* felt able to cope with her enemies. Conscious of the mistake she had made in leaving Versailles,

she dared not rectify it by returning ; that would be to
expose the King to the influence of Maurepas, which was
equivalent to her fall.   So she resolved to remain with
him, come what may.

Louis had scarcely arrived at Dunkirk, when his attention was called to the critical state of affairs on the
Rhenish frontier.   Inflated with martial ardour by his
conquests in Flanders, he desired to repeat them in Alsace,
which the Austrians were invading.   So he set out for
Metz with his mistresses.   In the army, no doubt, if not in
the nation, indifference would have followed the indignation
caused by their presence at the seat of war, but for the
cynical indifference of Louis himself to scandal, which
stripped his journey across France of the last shred of
decency.

It was a royal debauch rather than a royal progress.
Wherever the King lodged there lodged Mesdames de
Châteauroux and Lauraguais.   To keep him in good
humour they invented every kind of amusement for him.
Banquets, dances, and dramatic performances were the
order of the day.   It was as if the *petits soupers* in the
petits appartements had followed the King to the wars !

At Rheims the sudden illness of Madame de Châteauroux
caused the whole army to come to a halt.   She declared
that she had deen poisoned by Maurepas, but she did not
derive the advantage she hoped from this shameless accus-
ation.   Louis, to whom sickness was ever repulsive, telling
her that he would bury her magnificently if she died,
pushed on to Metz, bidding her follow him if she recovered !
His callous indifference effected a speedy cure, and she
lost no time in joining him again.

It was at Metz that the scandal was destined to reach
its *dénouement.*   The good people of Metz were inclined to
be of the same temper as the good people of Lille.   So
the King made a concession to virtue and lodged the

Châteauroux and the Lauraguais in the Abbey of St. Arnould, but had a long wooden gallery built to connect the Abbey with his own lodgings, four streets away, and which, to conciliate the scandalized inhabitants, the Prior declared was " to enable His Majesty to go to mass the more easily."

Louis was, however, prevented from using this gallery for one purpose or the other by an indigestion that ensued after one of his *petits soupers.* Immediately, on the advice of Richelieu, the two duchesses—Madame de Lauraguais also was a duchess, an old and widowed duke of that name having been pleased to gratify the *maîtresse en titre* by marrying her at the King's request—left the Abbey and established themselves in the royal chamber. And now began the fiercest and most shameless intrigue of the *ancien régime.*

The three confederates, whose fates hung on the life of the King, refused to allow any one to approach him but the doctors in their pay, who bled, purged, and vomited Louis till they reduced him to the brink of the grave. Even then the door was closed to the very Princes of the Blood. At last Louis himself became alarmed, and demanded to see his confessor. Forced to admit him, and fearing that he would refuse the King absolution unless she was dismissed, Madame de Châteauroux endeavoured to cajole the Jesuit into consenting not to exact this condition. He, torn between anxiety to please the cabal without and the favourite within the sick chamber, finally withdrew without confessing the King—" to reflect."

But scarcely had he gone, when Louis groaned loud enough to be heard in the antechamber, where the indignant cabal was waiting, ravenous for the blood of the haughty mistress—

"Bouillon ! My Bouillon ! And Father Pérusseau ! Quickly !"

Louis Quinze

[*From an old French print*]

According to Richelieu, who was capable of seeing the humour of the most serious situation, they " did not know whether it was bouillon or the Duc de Bouillon, or both, that he wanted." But their perplexity was put at an end by that peer of France himself rushing into the room. To keep out the others was now impossible and in they came —Maurepas and Fitz-James Bishop of Soissons at their head, the princes, generals, ministers and Pérusseau closely pressing behind.

Seeing the excitement of the crowd of courtiers who gathered round him, Louis, thinking his last hour had come, whimpered to be confessed. Hereupon the Bishop of Soissons—a son, by the way, of James II's famous Duke of Berwick—sternly ordered the duchesses to leave the King. On the advice of Richelieu they retired to an adjoining room.

Suddenly Monsignor Fitz-James opened the door, and standing on the threshold, his face red with anger, fulminated as if he were pronouncing an excommunication—

" The King commands you, mesdames, to withdraw from here at once ! "

Madame de Châteauroux, says Richelieu, gave the Bishop a look full of contempt, while Madame de Lauraguais, "who was always laughing," made up a face at the prelate. Compelled to obey, they contested every inch of ground in their retreat. From the room adjoining the sick room to which they had withdrawn, they now returned to their quarters in the Abbey. But Fitz-James held the winning trumps in this scandalous game of power. The news *Louis se meurt !* cried through the streets of Metz, had rekindled, as if by magic, the popularity of the King. In the terror and uncertainty as to what would happen if the King should die, his vices were forgotten and forgiven in the recollection that he had left the delights of Paris and Versailles to chase the Austrians out of France.

Immense crowds at once rushed to the churches to offer up prayers for his life. But the haughty Bishop of Soissons declared that the doors of every church in Metz should be closed while the duchesses remained in the town.

This was equivalent to letting loose the mob on the mistresses. Now thoroughly alarmed for their lives, the sisters took refuge with the governor of Metz—Belle-Isle. Madame de Châteauroux and he had differed over the conduct of the war ; the Duchess, in fact, had even gone to the length of using her influence against him. But the hero of the Retreat from Prague was a man too far above the titled rabble of the Court to descend to their contemptible level for his revenge. He rendered the wretched women every assistance in his power. He lent them one of his own carriages, in which, with the armorial bearings painted out and the blinds lowered, they fled to a distant château, the owner of which he had previously persuaded to receive them.

Affairs having come to such a pass Richelieu found his position of first gentleman of the bed-chamber untenable, and exiled himself to Switzerland.

As for Maurepas, cynically satisfied with his triumph, he left Fitz-James, Bishop of Soissons, whose ambition was to be another Fleury to the new king, to empty the remaining vials of his wrath on Louis. Nor did this pompous and arrogant priest spare the dying sinner. For Louis' repentance he cared nothing. It was as a victim, rather than as a penitent, that he regarded him, and lest the King should escape the torments of the next world, Fitz-James gave him a foretaste of them in this. Never was the *amende honorable* to God, so often made by Louis Quinze, more pitilessly exacted from him than now. For Fitz-James was not content with a private confession, but literally blackmailed his conscience-smitten victim into a public one as well by the threat of refusing him Extreme Unction.

" Messieurs, Princes of the Blood, and you great nobles," he thundered in his grandest and most pontifical manner to the crowd of courtiers assembled round the royal bed, "his Majesty charges us Bishop of Soissons to inform you of his sincere repentance of the scandal he has caused in living with the Duchesse de Châteauroux, and asks pardon for the same of God and man. He has learnt that she is waiting not far off in the hope of recall and he has sent to order her not to approach within fifty leagues of the Court."

" And Madame de Lauraguais too," murmured the King, on whom the fear of death and eternal damnation lay heavy.

" He would give his kingdom to M. de Fitz-James, if he asked for it," whispered Bachelier to Barjac.

At the conclusion of this scene in which God was profaned by prostituting the consolation of religion to the basest ends, Soissons, followed by his acolytes, stalked out of the room as if he had pronounced an excommunication rather than an absolution.

The King thought to be dying was left to the care of the nurses, while the generals and high officials prepared to hail a new sovereign in the Dauphin who, with the Queen and the Princesses, was now hastening to Metz. But an Alsacian surgeon having obtained permission of the physicians to administer a powerful emetic to the sick man, with the most fortunate results, Louis rapidly began to regain his health. This event, at once unexpected and undesirable, occasioned Maurepas, Fitz-James and Company the gravest anxiety. What if the King should revenge himself for the humiliation to which they had subjected him? Their fears, however, were somewhat alleviated by his apparently sincere desire to be reconciled to his wife, whom he greeted with every mark of affection and the most profuse apologies for the manner in which he had neglected her.

But this chastened mood did not last long. Louis was no sooner restored to health than he became more bored than ever with the Queen, "with whom it was always Holy Week." To get rid of her he resumed the command of his troops as soon as possible and had the satisfaction of capturing Fribourg, which put an end to all further danger from Austria.

The news of this last feat of arms, coupled with that of his recovery and repentance, restored his popularity. His return to Paris after the fall of Fribourg was made the occasion of an unparalleled outburst of loyalty. It was now that the title of Louis le Bien-aimé, Louis the Well-Beloved, was bestowed on him. But the extreme irony of such an epithet applied to such a king was utterly lost on the multitudes who crowded round the carriage of the returning conqueror and were so fascinated with their own loyalty and his remarkable personal beauty—then at thirty-four, in full bloom—that, according to Richelieu, "they disdained to pick up the louis d'ors that the equerries threw into their midst!"

Even the thick hide of Louis' cynicism was pierced by this reception.

"What have I done," he exclaimed, in unfeigned astonishment, "that I should be so loved?"

On his restoration to health he had begun to repent his repentance. After the capture of Fribourg he recalled Richelieu. On the night of his triumphal return to Paris he went in disguise to Madame de Châteauroux.

By an ironical coincidence the day of her rehabilitation was the day of her deepest shame. Drawn by an irresistible desire to see once more the sovereign whose sceptre she had wielded for a few sublime moments, Madame de

Châteauroux had ventured heavily veiled and on foot into a thoroughfare along which Louis was to pass. Carried away by the general excitement she had unconsciously raised her veil as he approached to see him the better. This act of imprudence had betrayed her to the crowd. Reviled and spat upon she had barely escaped with her life.

Louis, who took her completely by surprise, found her prostrated with the terror and shame of this experience. At such a moment he seemed to her agitated mind the personification of all the humiliation she had suffered through him. She taunted him with the insults to which his abandonment had subjected her, and haughtily bade him return to his palace and the sycophants who had effected her fall. It seemed to him that he had never desired her so much as now. He implored her pardon on his knees, and reinstated her then and there in her former position, with all its honours and emoluments. But she would accept nothing, grant nothing, she told him, till he had given her "the heads of her enemies."

Louis Quinze was not revengeful by nature, but the recollection of the humiliating manner in which his fears had been exploited at Metz rankled. He could forgive the penance which had deprived him of his mistress, but he could not forgive the wounds his dignity had received from the arrogant Bishop of Soissons, who not only exacted the *amende honorable* in public, but " had ordered the demolition of the scandalous wooden gallery that blocked four streets, which he purified with holy water before restoring the traffic." Conscious that the cabal into whose hands he had fallen were capable of silencing him by poison if he showed a disposition to be vindictive, Louis had concealed his resentment. Subtle and treacherous, as he had need to be in the atmosphere of subtlety and treachery in which his life was passed, he bided his time. This the splendid, popular ovation he had received that day assured him had come, and even before Madame de Châteauroux had asked for the "head" of Fitz-James the order exiling that prelate to his diocese, where he compelled him to remain for the rest of his life, had been signed.

Maurepas, however, had escaped the royal anger. He alone had thought of the possibility of the King's recovery and had refrained from associating himself in any way with Fitz-James's profane farce. His "head," then, Louis had no desire to sacrifice.

"I will grant you everything you wish," he told the restored favourite, "but you must not ask me to part with Maurepas. He amuses me, and besides he makes the work of the Navy so easy. Choose some other way of humiliating him."

The beautiful duchess was too crafty to insist. Her enemy could wait, she would not forget him.

"Well, then," she said, "I demand that the Comte de Maurepas write me in your behalf inviting me to return to Court and bring me the letter in person."

To this petty and malicious revenge Louis consented. But Maurepas was not the man to heed its sting. He could swallow pride without its choking him, and he not only wrote the letter recalling his enemy to Court and brought it to her in person, as she desired, but submitted to the "Allez vous en!" with which, snatching it from his hand, she drove him out of her presence like a dog.

Fate, however, gave him a grim revenge. The intense excitement of all the incidents connected with her fall and restoration proved too great a strain on Madame de Châteauroux's health, which had ever been delicate. Soon after Maurepas had left her, and while she was preparing to depart for Versailles, she was seized with violent pains and a high fever. To proceed in such a state was out of the question, so instead of going to Louis she went to bed, declaring, as she invariably did when taken ill, "that Maurepas had poisoned her."

In vain did they purge and vomit and bleed her; in vain did the King pray her to recover, and send "money to all the churches in Versailles"; in vain did her indomitable will struggle against pain and fever, and vexation of spirit. At length, convinced that she was dying, she in her turn made the *amende honorable* to God, and having been confessed and absolved, "expired in the arms of Madame de Mailly, whom she had sent for to beseech her forgiveness."

"She died," says de Goncourt, "according to a wish she had expressed as a child, on the day of the Conception of the Virgin."

Destiny granted this singular wish in a most ironical manner, for during her death agony Madame de Lauraguais gave birth to a daughter in the room above! Two days later Madame de Châteauroux was buried in St. Sulpice, "an hour before that usually appointed for burial, and with the watch under arms to protect her coffin from the fury of the populace."

This death plunged the King once more into the deepest grief. To his dead favourite he granted the "head of her enemy," which he had refused her when living, by banishing Maurepas from Versailles, to which he was not permitted to return till the next reign, thirty years later. For some months after his loss Louis was a prey to morbid melancholy, till one day in the Forest of Sénart he happened to meet Madame d'Etiolles—Marquise de Pompadour to be.

After that there was no longer any question of remembering the Duchesse de Châteauroux.

Of these five sisters, whose careers are so closely bound up in that of Louis Quinze, Mesdames de Lauraguais and de Flavacourt failed to succumb to a tragic and premature fate, as they failed to acquire the importance of the other three. They may, indeed, only be said to have come on the scene between the acts. On the death of Madame de Châteauroux the Duchesse de Lauraguais lost all interest for the King. She continued, however, for the rest of her life, which was tolerably long, to enjoy a great place at Court, owing chiefly to the friendship she formed with Madame de Pompadour, over whom she acquired considerable influence.

As for the beautiful Marquise de Flavacourt, whom Nattier painted as Silence (his masterpiece) and Voltaire extolled in verse, scandal having coupled her name with the King's, her husband, a fiery and jealous man, threatened to shoot her if she dared to imitate the example of her sisters. This threat produced so wholesome an effect on Madame de Flavacourt that when Richelieu offered to help her in her turn to become *maîtresse en titre* she declined on the ground that "she preferred the esteem of her contemporaries"!

She outlived most of them, and died in 1800 at the age of eighty-five, owing her escape from the guillotine to a *bon mot* which she uttered during her interrogation at the bar of the Revolutionary Tribunal.

EHRENGARD MELUSINA VON DER SCHULENBURG

DUCHESS OF KENDAL
"THE MAYPOLE"

1667 ?—1743

**EHRENGARD MELUSINA VON DER SCHULENBURG,
DUCHESS OF KENDAL**

*[Reproduced for the first time by the courtesy of Count Werner von der Schulenburg,
from the portrait in his possession]*

To face page 65

II

"In a twilight where virtues are vices,
   In thy chapels, unknown of the sun,
To a tune that enthralls and entices,
   They were wed, and the twain were as one."
                              SWINBURNE'S *Dolores*.

EHRENGARD MELUSINA VON DER SCHULENBURG, DUCHESS OF KENDAL

"*THE MAYPOLE*"

1667 ?—1743

I

A COURT more unlike Versailles than Herrenhausen, a King more unlike Louis Quinze than George the First, or a *maîtresse en titre* more unlike the Châteauroux than her Grace of Kendal, it is impossible to conceive.

There is something Maeterlinckian about that Court of Hanover of George's—a sense of vagueness, remoteness, unreality, and mystery. The period seems vague and the locality remote, as times and places always do in regions where barbarism attempts to mimic the civilization which it desires to assimilate. And the people, how strange they seem—grotesque, Maeterlinckian people. They are like corporeal passions rather than human beings. Conceive them, if you can : the old Elector Ernest Augustus, proud, choleric, cruel, grasping, adulterous ; the old Electress

Sophia, haughty and condescending, clever, dissimulating, unbelieving, philosophizing, and for ever dreaming of ascending the throne of England, if and if and if——! the Medea-like Countess von Platen, most ferocious and infamous of *maîtresses en titre ;* the ignorant, selfish, sullen, unprepossessing, licentious young prince, George ; his beautiful, high-spirited, ill-treated, disillusioned, desperate young wife, Sophia Dorothea ; and her fascinating and fatal lover, Königsmarck. Did you wish a subject for a drama you have one here to hand in this Gothic Court, whose fiercely-clashing passions make the shedding of blood inevitable and foreshadow the tragedy to which they are drifting.

You know the story—who does not ?—of the " mysterious disappearance " of Königsmarck—how at midnight, on leaving the apartment of the Princess, who has consented to flee with him the next day, he is suddenly attacked and hacked to pieces outside her door by the assassins of the terrible Platen, whose love he had spurned ; how, as he falls, being a chivalrous villain, he cried, " The Princess is innocent ! " though her kisses were still warm upon his lips ; how the Platen, coming out from some corner where she had been concealed with the old Elector, taunted her victim as he lay gasping out his life ; how he cursed her with his dying breath ; how, stung to fury, she stamped his mouth to silence with her heel ; and how to save the Electoral honour the corpse of the murdered man was walled up in a fire-place !

There is more than one version of this " mystery," but they all agree in the main, and this being the most dramatic and most probable is the most popular. Nor was the fate of the Princess less tragic. You remember she was torn from her children and, vainly protesting and pleading, sealed up in the flower of her youth and beauty in a lonely castle for the rest of her life—thirty-two long years.

THE COUNTESS VON PLATEN

[*Reproduced for the first time by the courtesy of Count Alexander Kielmansegg, from the portrait in his possession*]

To face page 66

And the curtain having fallen on this nightmare tragedy, how grotesque is the scene when it rises again. The proud and cruel old Elector and his monstrous mistress are dead now, but the dissimulating and dreaming old Electress still lives, kept alive by her dream. Was there ever a dream less likely to be realized than hers? And yet she all but realizes it! Though *fifty-six* times removed from the succession to that throne of which she has dreamed so long, she at last finds herself by one of the romantic miracles of destiny on its very steps. Then, as if to help her tottering feet to mount them, fate sweeps away one by one the encumbering and numerous progeny of the dying queen whose place she covets, only to strike her dead just as her dream comes true!

And while she dreams and schemes the young, ignorant, coarse, sullen, selfish, licentious Prince turns into a middle-aged, grotesque Elector with an abnormal lust for hideous women, with two of whom and two Turkish slaves, trophies of some forgotten battle, he passes his time contentedly, undisturbed by any thought of his guilty wife, who is storming out her life in her living tomb. Till behold! Caprice with magic wand alights on this strange scene and changes Herrenhausen into St. James's, with romantic Jacobite risings thundering in the air, mingled with the thud of proud and handsome heads falling from young and shapely necks, while in some mad moment virtue with the aid of vice blows the shimmering South Sea Bubble!

Is it not all like some weird dream? Surely those times never *really* existed? Was there ever really a fourteenth-century Florentine tragedy at Hanover; or a King of England who could not speak English, whom the English *would* have instead of a fascinating Stuart prince who could; or a splendid South Sea Bubble; or Turkish slaves selling offices at St. James's; or hideous old hags from

Germany getting themselves made countesses and duchesses in England?

But if it *should* all be true, what in the name of wonder is George the First doing in such a *galère* of romance? Perhaps, if Vandyke had never painted those exquisite portraits of King Charles, the "Martyr King" might not seem so romantic to us as he does. But George had no Vandyke to idealize him, or no Cromwell to immortalize him by cutting off his head; nor if he had would it have made much difference. Nevertheless, though the least picturesque of kings, his claim to impress the imagination is scarcely less inferior to that of the most romantic of sovereigns. He is like one of those pictures of the Impressionist school, at which the longer you gaze the more you discover in it—an Impressionist picture superbly framed.

II

THE origin of the family of Schulenburg was literally lost in the mists of German history. When it first emerges from that hyperborean darkness it appears to have possessed the enormous number of quarterings that were considered the *sine qua non* of nobility. In a short time it became so prolific that the trunk of its genealogical tree cleft itself into two gigantic and umbrageous branches, known as the "Black" and the "White" von der Schulenburgs. It was to the latter and younger line that Ehrengard Melusina belonged.

Time had made this family very illustrious, and it was the proud boast of the Schulenburgs that they had provided the Holy Roman Empire with "four marshals, twenty-five generals, six ministers, and four bishops." The name was, however, scarcely known outside Germany till the laurels won by Johann Mathias, Ehrengard Melusina's brother, gave it a European reputation.

I am afraid that Herr Dryasdust is the only person who still remembers him, but in his own day Count Johann Mathias von der Schulenburg was a very conspicuous figure. Like most soldiers of fortune, his life was a romance. What he didn't know about war and the world wasn't worth knowing. He began his military career as a boy in the service of the Emperor, but after he had fought in seven campaigns against the Turks the spirit of adventure induced him to quit the imperial service for that of the Duke of Savoy, which in turn, after a time, he abandoned for that of the King of Poland, who was also Elector of Saxony—the famous Augustus the Strong, the "Saxon man of sin," as Carlyle called him.

It was now that Johann Mathias first began to distinguish himself as a strategist. The reputation he acquired in the wars of the Poles against Charles the Twelfth of Sweden was further enhanced in the War of the Spanish Succession, when he once more returned to the imperial service. The manner in which he handled the forty German battalions he commanded at Malplaquet excited the admiration of Marlborough, who expressed the highest opinion of his talents. After the Peace of Utrecht the Emperor covered him with dignities, but a sinecure at the Court of Vienna had no charm for a man of his restless spirit. Chafing for action, he offered his sword to the Republic of Venice, whose eternal enmity with the Turks kept her constantly at war. His heroic and brilliant defence of Corfu won him the undying gratitude of the Venetians, who, contrary to their custom with mercenaries, entreated him to become commander-in-chief of their armies. He readily accepted an invitation at once so flattering to his pride and so tempting to his temperament, and having been naturalized as a citizen of the Republic, he died in its service thirty-two years later in 1747 at the age of eighty-six.

But though the Schulenburgs were so distinguished they were very poor. Their marshals, generals, ministers, and bishops had a happy faculty of spending as they went the fortunes they made, and never had any money to give or bequeath to their numerous relations. They could, however, always find employment suited to their rank to relieve their needs at one or other of the German Courts. Thus Ehrengard Melusina, when sixteen or seventeen, like her famous brother before her, had bidden farewell to the dilapidated ancestral castle at Emden in Saxony, where she was born, and departed for the Court of Herrenhausen, at which the Schulenburg influence had obtained for her the post of maid-of-honour to the Electress Sophia.

George, who had just made his ill-starred marriage with Sophia Dorothea of Zell, no sooner beheld her than he straightway fell head over ears in love with her. The openness with which he proceeded to indulge his passion did not in the least shock the Electoral Court, where morals, if they ever existed, had become brazened by the example of the intrigues of Ernest Augustus with the infamous Platen. Even the indignation that might have been expected of the Electress Sophia, who was far superior to her surroundings, merely expressed itself in out-spoken contempt of her son's utter lack of taste in his choice.

" Look at that mawkin," she exclaimed scornfully to the Countess of Suffolk, when that lady was once visiting Herrenhausen, indicating her maid-of-honour, who was standing behind her chair, "and think of her being my son's mistress ! "

And Lady Suffolk, covered with confusion, which, however, quickly vanished when she remembered that the " mawkin " did not understand English, glanced up and looked at the singularly tall, gaunt, and particularly ugly

Graff von der Schulenburg
Comm: General der Venetian. Trouppen.

COUNT JOHANN MATHIAS VON DER SCHULENBURG
[*From an old German print*]

creature, who, as Horace Walpole more politely declared at a later period, was " by no means an inviting object."

Every eye, however, they say, forms its own idea of beauty, and George's no doubt discovered charms in the gaunt giantess that others were unable to perceive. His devotion continued, and the only concession that was ever made to appearances either by him or " Mademoiselle de Schulenburg," as Ehrengard Melusina was always called at French-speaking Herrenhausen, was their decision that the two daughters she gave birth to should be known as her " nieces "—a ridiculous fiction that deceived nobody.

As it was not, however, in George's nature to be constant, Ehrengard Melusina was obliged to share her lover with others, which she did with an apparently placid indifference. Her most formidable rival was the Baroness von Kielman-segg, the wife of the master of the horse at the Electoral Court. This lady was commonly reported and believed to be the daughter of Ernest Augustus and the Countess von Platen, and consequently a sister *de la main gauche* of George. The relationship by no means prevented her mother, as to whom at least there was never any doubt, from bringing her to Herrenhausen when she grew up for the express purpose of captivating her brother. Such nightmare morals were entirely in keeping with the characters of all concerned, and quite common in the semi-civilized Courts of the Holy Roman Empire. George had succumbed, as the terrible Countess von Platen meant him to, and the result of this monstrous intrigue was a daughter who in later years became the mother, in lawful wedlock, of the celebrated Admiral Howe.

As a concession to appearances, to which she never after-wards gave the slightest thought, Madame de Kielmansegg had married the man by whose name she was known in order to provide her child with a legitimate father. Shortly after this event she had inherited a large fortune from her

mother—whom the good people that have regretful doubts
as to the existence of hell may be relieved to learn suffered
the tortures of the damned in this world before departing
for the next by dying blind and haunted by the ghost of
Königsmarck. But Madame de Kielmansegg soon dissipated her inheritance in reckless extravagance, which,
coupled with numerous indiscretions, had so offended George
that he relegated her to the second place in his esteem
and returned to his former allegiance to Mademoiselle de
Schulenburg, who was generally regarded as the Sultana
Validé of the Electoral seraglio.

Ehrengard Melusina had passed nearly thirty years in
this way when an event destined to change the whole course
of her life occurred in England. This was the death on the
1st of August, 1714, of Queen Anne, who had scarcely
breathed her last when the Privy Council, in accordance
with the terms of the Statute of 1705, met immediately and
commanded the persons named in the Statute as Lords
Justices to issue a proclamation declaring that "the high
and mighty prince, George, Elector of Hanover, had become
our rightful and liege lord, King of Great Britain, France,
and Ireland."

The swiftness with which the Privy Council had acted
utterly confounded the Jacobite leaders, Bolingbroke and
Atterbury, who, instead of boldly supporting the claims of
the Pretender, wasted precious time in futile intrigues.
Multitudes crowded round the heralds as they proclaimed
the foreign king. Not a voice of protest was raised. Parliament assembled at once, and the Peers and Commons sent
congratulations to the new sovereign upon his happy and
peaceable accession to the throne, beseeching him to confer
upon his kingdom the blessing of his royal presence as soon
as possible. The funds, too, expressed their sympathy by
rising seven points.

A week later, on the 6th of August, the envoys from

England arrived at Herrenhausen. Their news, which would have transported any other prince with delight, was received by the phlegmatic George with indifference, if not regret. Indeed, it seemed doubtful at first if he would accept the throne that was offered him at all.

Lockier, the Dean of Peterborough, who knew him well, says that "had there been strong opposition in England to him, he would not have stirred a foot. For the family did not expect the crown; at least nobody in it but the old Electress Sophia."

The fact was that he was perfectly content with being the Elector of Hanover, and he could not imagine a place where he could possibly be happier than in his beloved Herrenhausen. It took the English envoys, with the aid of the rapacity suddenly awakened in the Electoral Court, three weeks to prevail upon him to set out for his kingdom.

Ehrengard Melusina was even more strongly averse than George to the idea of leaving Hanover. His objections were based on a combination of sluggishness and selfishness, hers on selfishness and fear. At forty-eight—the age to which she owned, though perhaps fifty-six, as some declare, would be nearer the truth, but it really doesn't matter—she not unnaturally preferred the ills she knew to those of which she had had no experience. She knew exactly what to expect of life at Herrenhausen, where she was quite content with her position and—strange as it may seem considering the rapacity she afterwards developed—her pension, which, though extremely small, was quite sufficient for her needs in so frugal a Court. Moreover, she disliked the English in spite of, or perhaps on account of, the extravagant encomiums that she had heard everlastingly lavished upon them all her life by the Electress Sophia.

According to Lady Mary Wortley Montagu, however, her objections were chiefly inspired by her fears of the people of England, " who," she thought, " were accustomed to use their kings barbarously, and might chop off George's head in the first fortnight," which made her dread being involved in his ruin.   In this respect her fears were not altogether unjustified, for in no country in Europe, unless it were Turkey, was head-chopping so common as in England.   Woe betide the man who fell into the power of his political opponents in those days !   Unless he could escape from the country he was generally obliged to face the axe ; while the hangman's rope was ever ready to relieve the tax-payer of the burden of contributing to support the existence of meaner offenders against the law.

George himself, on a visit he paid to England in his youth, had had evidence of his subjects' fondness for decapitation.

" They cut off the head of Lord Stafford yesterday," he wrote home to his mother in his phlegmatic way, " and made no more fuss about it than if they had chopped off the head of a pullet."

When her Electoral lover, in spite of all her remonstrances, finally made up his mind to depart, Ehrengard Melusina tried to restrain him by inspiring him with fear of a similar fate.   But when George once made up his mind, he was not the man to change it.   Fear, which, like all his race, he completely lacked, was the last thing to appeal to.

" Oh," he replied sardonically, " I have nothing to fear, for the king-killers are all my friends."

So, on the 31st of August, after a delay of three weeks, bidding a tearful farewell to his loyal Hanoverians, who ran after his coach imploring him not to forsake them, he set out for England, accompanied by his ministers, servants, and two Turkish slaves, trophies of some forgotten battle of his youth when he helped Sobieski to save Vienna from the infidels.

Ehrengard Melusina, piqued to find her powers of per-suasion ineffectual, remained behind, and, for a spinster of forty-eight, behaved in the most preposterous way, running about the gardens of Herrenhausen embracing the linden-trees, clinging to the marble statues, and declaring that she, at all events, would never desert so cherished a spot.

Madame de Kielmansegg, on the contrary, had no objec-tions whatever to quitting Hanover, where her debts, which George utterly refused to pay, had long made her life insupportable. Mortified by the loss of her supremacy, she had ever since been seeking vainly to recover it, and believing that Ehrengard Melusina's refusal to go to England gave her the opportunity she desired, " she dis-guised herself "—a difficult thing to do, one would think, considering she was as corpulent as the other was lean—in order to escape her creditors, who would have prevented her departure had they suspected her intention, and posted after George.

Madame de Kielmansegg at this time owned to forty, and all trace of the beauty and " fascination of no mean order," which Lady Mary Wortley Montagu says she possessed in her youth, had long since vanished. Time and dissipation had made her even more hideous than the rival she hoped to supplant. According to Horace Walpole, who as a child was terrified at the mere sight of her, she had " two fierce black eyes, large and rolling, beneath two lofty arched eyebrows, two acres of cheeks spread with crimson ; an ocean of neck that overflowed, and was not distinguished from the lower part of her body, and no part of it restrained by stays. No wonder that a child dreaded such an ogress ! "

George, however, overtaken by this monster as he was slowly journeying towards England and despondently wondering " how he was going to pass the lonely winter evenings at St. James's " without the society of his abnormal favourites, received the proof of her devotion with every mark of gratitude, and a seat was at once provided for her in his coach.

But the news of her rival's departure and reception was no sooner broken to Ehrengard Melusina than her jealousy overcame all other considerations. Instantly packing her trunks, and accompanied by her "nieces," she too posted after George. As he travelled as slowly as it had taken him to make up his mind to travel at all, she managed to overtake him just as he was about to embark for England. Her reception was no less cordial than Madame de Kielmansegg's had been, and on the 20th of September, three weeks after leaving Herrenhausen, and nearly two months after the death of Queen Anne, George arrived at Greenwich with the most grotesque crew of adventurers in his train that ever landed on these shores.

Accustomed by the Stuarts to expect a certain air of dash and dignity in their kings—of which the tradition had been maintained by William of Orange—the multitudes who watched the state entry of the Hanoverian into London were disgusted to behold a little old man of fifty-five, of so insignificant and unprepossessing an appearance as to rob him at once of popularity. Had he come with alacrity on the death of the late Queen and shown any disposition to win the regard of his subjects, it is possible that they might have found excuses for the defects of his personal appearance. But when to an utter lack of kingliness was added his delay in coming to receive so splendid a crown, which seemed almost tantamount to contempt, even the most indifferent were offended.

The popular disgust was still further accentuated by the report that he neither spoke nor desired to learn the language of his subjects. Nor did the people in his train tend to soften this bitter impression. At the sight of his hideous mistresses—whose ludicrous contrast at once in-

THE BARONESS VON KIELMANSEGG, COUNTESS OF DARLINGTON

[*Reproduced for the first time by the courtesy of Count Alexander von Kielmansegg, from the portrait by Sir Godfrey Kneller in his possession*]

See Preface

To face page 76

spired the coarse and ready wit of the mob to bestow on
the lean Schulenburg the name of the " Maypole," and on
the fat Kielmansegg that of the " Elephant "—at the sight
of his strange, horrific-looking Turks, and uncouth horde
of German officials and menials, it is not surprising that
the public should have believed they had only come to the
country to plunder it.

What George said, or thought, when he saw the anger
on the faces of his new subjects, and heard the mockery
with which his Turks and his mistresses were greeted is not
related. But Ehrengard Melusina, emboldened by the
sight of the protecting bayonets of the soldiers who lined
the streets through which she passed, leant out of the
window of her coach and exclaimed in the broken English
she had picked up in waiting upon the Electress Sophia—

" Goot peoples, vy you abuse us ; ve only gom for all
your goots."

" And for all our chattels, too, damn you ! " retorted a
fellow in the crowd.

Whereupon so significant a laugh translated his words,
the sense of which might otherwise have been lost to her,
that the " Maypole " quickly withdrew her gigantic skeleton
form and Jezebel face from view, and was never afterwards
known to address the British Public.

III

THE unpopularity of the foreign king, fanned by the
followers of the Pretender, soon burst into a Jacobite
rebellion in which for the moment all the fears of Ehrengard
Melusina seemed likely to be realized. In 1715, when the
" Chevalier de St. George "—(how picturesque these Stuarts
were even in the choice of an incognito !)—landed in

Scotland, there was every likelihood that the horde of Hanoverian invaders would return to Herrenhausen, if they got out of the country alive, much quicker than they came. Jacobites were to be found everywhere—in camp, court, and parliament ; on the bench and in the pulpit ; in every county, parish, street, and coffee-house. But though their sympathy with the fascinating and treacherous race of Stuart was unmistakable and their numbers probably far in excess of the Whigs, the latter had at their command, as the French Ambassador wrote his master, " the longest purses, the best swords, the ablest brains, and the handsomest women." In a word, in an age of corruption such as has never been known in England, the very enthusiasm of the Jacobites was purchasable. It was not because their convictions lacked courage that their cause failed, but because their courage lacked convictions. They merely contented themselves with noisily expressing their sentimental loyalty to " King James," whereby the English people were enabled to gratify their passion for head-chopping at the expense of a few reckless and chivalrous survivals from the days of knighthood. O Derwentwater, beautiful and brave !

Talking of the " Fifteen," nothing is more ludicrous than the self-satisfied, sanctimonious air that all historians—I have never yet come across an exception—assume when they declare that we owe the political and religious liberty we enjoy to-day to George the First and the Whigs *because* they saved England from absolutism and priest-craft. It would be interesting to trace the origin of this assertion, which is so manifestly superficial as scarcely to need refutation. I fancy it must have first been uttered by sycophancy, whose voice is particularly persuasive to cant, by which it has ever since been persistently echoed, until, like an oft-repeated lie, it has come to be believed Supposing, however, that the Old Pretender *had* succeeded in 1715 in inflicting absolutism and the Popery on England. Do you think, judging from what you know of the English character, the evil would have been any heavier to bear than the "liberal" despotism of the haughty Whig oligarchy which so long ruled England as if it were a sort of Venice with a German prince as Doge? Or can you imagine that the dreaded Roman priestcraft would have been any more bigoted than that of the Protestant and Agnostic cant under which so many characters have been dwarfed, so many hearts broken, and so much intellect insulted in "free" England? Or again, granting all the worst evils of a Stuart restoration, can you doubt that the example of the great French Revolution would not have freed us in England as well as the rest of Europe? As a matter of fact George the First and the Whigs, in my humble opinion, *retarded* our liberties. Had a Stuart been on the English throne in 1789 we should, like the French, have got what we enjoy to-day one hundred years sooner.

Mais, revenons. George, having faced and survived the dangers of 1715 with a contemptuous coolness that seemed to turn his very courage, of which there never was a question, into an insult, continued to be unpopular. Conspiracies to dethrone him were constantly in the air. After the "Fifteen" came the Atterbury Plot. For all his stubbornness and courage he never knew but that some day he might be compelled to abdicate. Consequently, in such an atmosphere of insecurity, and with Whigs buying and Jacobites selling honour, principles, convictions, what wonder that the Germans in his train, whom interest alone had brought to England, should make hay while the sun shone? George himself set the example, and gave every encouragement to rapacity.

Gifted with a fine sardonic cunning, he let it be seen from the very start that he intended to do as he pleased, at the expense of the kingdom in general and the Whigs in particular. On arriving in England he confessed frankly that he knew very little of the Constitution of the country, but he added significantly, "I intend to put myself entirely in the hands of my ministers, for they will be completely answerable for everything I do."

Equally significant was his reply to some great Whig lord who asked him shortly after his coronation what he thought of England.

"It is a very odd country," he said in his German-French. "The first morning after my arrival at St. James's I looked out of the window and saw a park with walls and a canal which they told me were *mine*. The next day Lord Chetwynd, the ranger of *my* park, sent me a brace of fine carp out of *my* canal, and I was told I must give five guineas to his servant for bringing me *my own* carp out of *my own* canal in *my own* park!"

Accustomed to be absolute master in his Electorate, it was difficult to explain to him that in England the proprietary rights of the sovereign were nominal. He enlarged Kensington Gardens at the expense of Hyde Park ; talked of turning St. James's Park into a kitchen-garden ; and as if this were not enough to exasperate the people, he showed his utter contempt for their representatives by demanding an increase in his Civil List of £500,000. To refuse was impossible without giving the Stuarts another chance. Moreover, George was himself something of a Jacobite, and though it was his intention to remain King of England if he could, he was none the less ready to go with a good grace if he was turned out, as he expected to be. With such a man there was nothing to be done, then, save to let him have his way.

"Never mind," he said to an honest German cook who complained of the extravagance in the royal kitchen, so very different from the economy practised in the Electoral one, "England will bear the expense, so steal like the rest ; and," he added with a laugh, "be sure you take enough."

And take enough and more than enough you may be sure they did. The Hanoverian ministers Bothmar, Bernsdorf, and Robethon not only made fortunes by acting as political go-betweens, but the two former aspired to seats in the House of Lords ; Robethon more humbly seeking a baronetcy. Mustapha and Mahomet, the Turkish slaves, were made pages of the back-stairs, posts in which they served George at St. James's as Bachelier and Barjac served Fleury at Versailles, and did as well a thriving trade on their own account by the sale of petty offices. While as for the mistresses, not even the women of the Restoration had more ravenous appetites. They devoured anything and everything indiscriminately—titles, pensions, bribes, monopolies—treating England as "a land of promise to be made the most of while it lasted." It was utterly useless for Sir Robert Walpole, himself corrupt, to protest to the King against this demoralizing rapacity.

" I suppose *you* too are paid," was all the answer George deigned him.

But the rapacious corruption of the Hanoverians dwindled to insignificance beside that of Ehrengard Melusina's. The inordinate greed she now evinced was a striking contrast to the placid contentment in which she had passed her life at the frugal Court of Hanover, where, according to Tolland, George, like a *bon bourgeois*, " had been wont to keep a strict account of the Electoral expenses, which he defrayed in person on Saturday nights." Nothing was more fantastic in the complete transformation which was now effected in the character of this hitherto unassuming and colourless spinster than the pomp she gave to her avarice. George having become a British king she determined to become a British peeress. As the first step in this direction it was necessary that she should be naturalized,

6

and her impatience being unable to support the tedium and delay of the legal requirement usual in such cases she purchased an Act of Parliament to this end.

Since, however, *one* patent of nobility seemed to her incompatible with the dignity of a family which had furnished so many marshals, generals, ministers and bishops as the Schulenburgs, the pride of Ehrengard Melusina demanded as many patents of nobility as there were degrees of rank in the peerage. It was an old tradition at the Court of St. James that Ireland should always be plundered before England, so to conform as far as possible to this custom of which he saw the advantages, and at the same time to gratify the favourite companion of his long winter evenings, George determined to foist her upon the peerage of Ireland. Ehrengard Melusina von der Schulenburg thus became Baroness of Dundalk, Countess and Marchioness of Dungannon, and Duchess of Munster.

The vanity of the newly-created Irish peeress, however, was only whetted by these high-sounding dignities. Title-hunting developed into a passion with her, and she set about collecting coronets as one would collect pictures, or books, or gems. Soon to her four Irish patents of nobility, George, with his customary indifference to public opinion, was persuaded to add three English ones, and Ehrengard Melusina was created Baroness of Glastonbury, Countess of Feversham, and Duchess of Kendal in the peerage of England. But even with this dazzling string of titles which rivalled those of a Spanish Don, she was not content. Her collection still lacked a princely diadem, and as this was not to be procured in the British peerage, she sought it in the Holy Roman Empire. So to please the Elector of Hanover, who as King of Great Britain had become a person of the first consequence, the Emperor created her Princess of Eberstein.

It was, however, by the ducal title of Kendal, which had

hitherto never been conferred on any one save royalty, that she elected to be known. In this connection there is a certain satirical humour in the arms with which she was furnished by the College of Heralds. In Doyle's *Official Baronage* they are described as containing a "lamb passant," a "lion rampant, imperially crowned," and "two wild men all proper and each wreathed about the middle."

Of course, the modest stipend on which Mademoiselle de Schulenburg had subsisted without complaint would not suffice for the state that the Duchess of Kendal and Munster, Princess of Eberstein desired to maintain. Since her titles were quite devoid of the territorial *cachet* which gives to rank its particular dignity and splendour, her Grace was obliged to compensate herself for the acres she lacked by seeking her ducal revenue elsewhere. Consequently George was appealed to for the requisite income, and he came to the assistance of his favourite with a generosity typical of his conduct to his compatriots in the altered circumstances of his life. By royal command a pension of £7,500 per annum was settled on the Duchess, "the same to be payed out of the English Treasury." And, if this sum should prove inadequate, the King gave her to understand that she was at perfect liberty to procure whatever she required by the exploitation of the private sources in which it was sure to be found.

With such encouragement it may be taken for granted that her Grace lost no time in obtaining an income suitable to her rank. Since opportunities of enriching herself were constantly offered her, none of which she let slip, she soon made an enormous fortune. One of these opportunities occurred when the Duke of Somerset resigned the post of the Master of the Horse, whereupon she prevailed upon the King, instead of filling it, to leave it vacant and confer the salary upon her. But to enumerate the number and extent of her resources would be impossible. The chief and most lucrative was her influence over the King. Quickly discovering that there was a market for the favour she enjoyed, she established a business, so to speak, for the sale of it, even, says Etough, "employing brokers to hawk state appointments." She sold everything that was saleable; and, according to Walpole, "would have sold even the King's honour at a shilling advance to the best bidder."

As an instance of her enterprise, she invested a bribe paid her by Lord Sunderland in the famous monopoly to supply Ireland with copper coin, which she resold at a profit to Woods. Being shrewd enough to realize the advantage of giving full value for what she sold, the volume of the trade she did was constantly on the increase. Throughout the whole of George's reign she never had a bad year. Among her most profitable customers was the family of Bolingbroke, who had been obliged to flee the country in the Jacobite rebellion of 1715. From his father, who desired to be created a viscount, she received £5,000 to this end; and he also paid her £4,000 for a two lives' tenure of a post in the Customs worth £1,200 a year. While the Marquise de la Vilette, the rich French widow whom Bolingbroke married in exile, paid her the monster bribe of £11,000 to obtain his pardon of the King, by which he was enabled to return and settle in England!

But though scrupulous in fulfilling her engagements, she had not the least scruple as to how she made money. Finding that the supply of the commodity in which she trafficked was not exhausted by home consumption, the enterprising spirit of avarice with which she was possessed caused her to seek foreign markets, where, as there is always a demand for what she had to sell, she quickly found purchasers.

The French Ambassador in a dispatch to Louis Quinze wrote:—"The Duchess of Kendal has sent me word that she desired my friendship, and that I should place confidence in her. Being convinced that it is highly essential to the advantage of your Majesty's service to be on good terms with her, I assured her that I would do everything in my power to merit her esteem and friendship. I am convinced that she may be advantageously employed, and that it will be necessary to employ her, though," he added with true diplomatic cunning, "I will not trust her more than is absolutely necessary."

The business proposals of her Grace, as the Ambassador's letter may virtually be considered to be, were at once accepted by the French King, who wrote, "that since there is no room to doubt the Duchess of Kendal's ascendency over the King of Great Britain, you will neglect nothing to acquire a share of her confidence."

It would be interesting to know just what her Grace received from this contraband trade in state secrets. Perhaps the vouchers exist in some forgotten pigeon-hole of the French Archives and investigation may some day bring them to light. The Duchess herself was too wise to keep any record of such transactions, and so secretly were they carried on it is doubtful if their existence at the time was even suspected. This was probably due to the fact that the friendly relations between France and England, whose interests during the whole of George's reign were for the most part identical, rendered the services of the Duchess superfluous, the money she received from the French Court being rather in the nature of a retaining fee, so to speak.

It was not only with France, however, that she did business abroad. The instinct of race—for one can scarcely dignify it by the name of patriotism—caused her to consider German interests after her own. Flattered by the desire of no less a personage than the Empress to correspond with her, the Duchess openly supported the interests of the House of Austria at the Court of St. James. It was, no doubt, to reward her zeal as much as to please George the First, that she was created Princess of Eberstein.

That the accumulation of wealth by means so scandalous as those employed by her Grace should entail ruin and misery on others goes without saying. A letter in Mist's *Journal* by an anonymous writer observed : " We are ruined by trulls, nay, what is more vexatious, by old ugly trulls such as could not find entertainment in the most hospitable districts of Old Drury." The attention of this insult was brought to the notice of Parliament, and Mist was sentenced with a fine and imprisonment.

The most notorious of her victims, whom she was accused of "pursuing to prison and even beyond the grave," was John Ker of Kersland. He had formerly been a government spy, among other things, and from having been sent on frequent missions to the Court of Hanover during the reign of Queen Anne, where at her death he chanced to be, his excessive vanity, encouraged by the confidences with which he was entrusted, led him to consider himself as chiefly instrumental in bringing about the Hanoverian Succession. On the accession of George his services being no longer required were dispensed with, and as their remuneration only consisted of " one hundred thalers and two medals," Ker's wounded vanity provided him with a grievance, when on soliciting the post of Governor of the Bermudas he found that the appointment was sold to another by " one of the foreign concubines " after he had refused to purchase it. Exasperated by neglect and harassed by debt he vented his spleen in a public denunciation of the Germans, "whose notorious rapacity even extended to the Colonies in America, where they appointed and continued governors at pleasure, not only exacting vast sums but receiving the revenues ordered by the public to support them."

As a result of this plain-speaking, a negotiation which

JOHN KER OF KERSLAND
[*From an old print*]

To face page 86

the Duchess of Kendal, whom he particularly denounced, had opened with him, ended in a prosecution; whereby Ker found himself " deprived not only of the King's favour but of his justice." For, as he complains in his memoirs, " the torrent of corruption that inundated the Court when the Hanoverians alighted here, having infested every department of state, from the Lord Chancellor downwards, never has the law been more distorted in any case to suit political views than it was in that in which this infamous woman was plaintiff."

Ker's ruin, however, which he attributed to her " inexorable hatred " was not altogether due to her Grace. Vanity and folly had already launched him on the road to the debtor's prison in which he died when he rashly undertook to thwart and expose her avarice. Attacked, she defended herself with the only weapon she possessed or knew how to use—corruption. As a matter of fact, she was too phlegmatic to be maliciously vindictive, and the placid indifference which passed for the amiability with which she was generally credited was seldom ruffled.

There were times, indeed, when the weapon with which she had destroyed Ker was used as a shield to protect her friends as well as herself. The most notorious instance of the " protection " her corruption displayed occurred in the South Sea Bubble time. To give the history of this gigantic swindle, which may be termed the apotheosis of corruption, would require an article to itself. But since the credit of the Duchess was involved in the general panic the means she employed to save it make some account of this picturesque speculation necessary.

IV

THE desire to get rich quickly that exists in every one was pricked to madness by the extraordinary success of the Mississippi Company in France. The immediate and enormous, but fictitious, profits of this huge monopoly had let loose the spirit of gambling all over Europe. Excited by the example of the French Company the South Sea Company in England, which had been established for ten years and was doing a legitimate business quietly, honestly and profitably, suddenly made a proposal to the Government to pay off the National Debt. Instead of rejecting so Quixotic a proposal the Government foolishly allowed itself to be tempted by the suggestion to get rid of its obligations by unloading them on the public. But before accepting the proposals of the South Sea Company, being smitten with the fever of speculation that was rife, the Government was still more foolishly tempted to tender for others in the hope of obtaining more favourable conditions. Hereupon the Bank of England entered into the competition and became the most formidable rival of the South Sea Company. Or, as Aislabie, the Chancellor of the Exchequer, who was at first opposed to the whole scheme, expressed it at his trial, "the spirit of bubbling had become so universal that the very Bank became a bubble."

In such a contest it was natural that parties should be formed, and as inevitable that corruption should direct their conduct. It was also natural and inevitable that the trading instinct of her Grace of Kendal should take advantage of a state of affairs so well suited to the display of her genius for making money. She offered her influence for sale as usual and the Company bought it after the Bank

had purchased Sir Robert Walpole's, who was persuaded
to sell his when he found that his protests against the folly
of the Government proved unavailing.

A fierce struggle now took place between Walpole and
the Bank on the one side and the Duchess and the
Company on the other. By dint of enormous bribes and
the purchase of the persuasive eloquence of Aislabie, the
bill in favour of the Company rapidly passed the Commons
and was sent to the Lords. Here, where the only remnant
of common-sense left in the country appeared to exist,
there was a serious danger that the bill would be lost. But
the Lords, too, in the end, after some delay, were bribed,
like the Commons, into passing it.

The impetus that the Government had given to speculation by the passage of the bill now caused all sorts of "wild
cat" schemes to be jobbed upon the public, and Parliament
was deluged with petitions to legalize all manner of
companies. It seemed as if every crank in the country
desired to turn his fad into a company. The most
ridiculous petitions for patents were submitted and
granted; such as for "the breeding and providing for
bastard children"—the first idea, by the way, of the
Foundling Hospital; for "planting mulberry trees in
Chelsea Park to breed silk-worms"; and "for carrying on
an undertaking of great advantage, but nobody to know
what it is"! A clergyman proposed a company "to
discover the land of Ophir and to monopolize the gold and
silver which that country was still believed to produce." In
brief, like Sydney Smith's French lady whose whole nature
cried out for seduction, the whole nation seemed to cry out
for its financial seduction.

Change Alley became like the Rue Quincampoix, where
the crush of all conditions of people delirious with the fever
of gambling became so great that "a hunch-back made a
little fortune by the letting of his hump as a desk on which

impatient speculators might scribble their applications for shares." In the course of a few days multitudes were raised from poverty to riches beyond the dreams of avarice. Then came the crash. The first blow to credit was given by the South Sea Company itself. In spite of the more favourable advantages it enjoyed several of the new companies came into competition with it, and to crush them the South Sea Company decided to take legal proceedings. This, however, had the undesirable effect of directing the attention of the public to its own methods of doing business. Confidence began to shake and stocks began to fall; "and when," as Mr. Justin McCarthy says in his admirable *History of the Four Georges*, "people ask whether a speculation is a bubble, the bubble, if it is one, is already burst."

Thousands of families were reduced at once to absolute beggary, "some of whom," to quote a writer of the time, "after so long living in splendour were not able to stand the shock of poverty and contempt, and died of broken hearts, while others withdrew to remote parts of the world and never returned." In the crash Cabinet Ministers were disgraced. Aislabie was found guilty of "most notorious, dangerous and infamous corruption," by the very Commons he had persuaded to pass the bill in favour of the South Sea Company, and imprisoned in the Tower. Craggs, the Secretary of the Treasury, died suddenly on the very day he was to be indicted in the House, and his father, the Postmaster General, poisoned himself a few days later.

The Duchess of Kendal was one of the few who were implicated in the swindle to escape unscathed. With lives and reputations being broken all around her she was in an extremely critical position. The enormous profits she was known to have made by speculation, the fraudulent companies she was suspected to have helped to float, and the notorious part she had played in the passage of the bill,

coupled with the universal hatred and contempt her
rapacity had long excited, marked her out for the vengeance of her enemies. But she proved to be more than a
match for them, and dexterously extricated herself from
their clutches by an act of corruption more audacious than
any she had yet practised.

Realizing that her safety from impeachment, which
would have resulted in her imprisonment and banishment,
depended on that of Knight, the Treasurer of the South
Sea Company, she urged him to leave the country before
he was arrested. He promptly took her advice and fled
to Antwerp, where, however, on the request of the British
Government, he was seized. But the crafty Duchess had,
in the meantime, been making a practical use of the credit
she enjoyed with her letter-writing friend the Empress, and
the States of Brabant, acting on orders from the Court of
Vienna, refused to give up the absconding Treasurer and
contented themselves with confining him in one of their
own prisons!

Defrauded in this way of the proofs of her guilt her
enemies were obliged to abandon their intentions respect-
ing her Grace, since to denounce her without the possibility
of establishing her guilt would have been futile and merely
have served to expose them in their turn to her vengeance.
Knight's flight and confinement in Brabant, however, were
generally attributed to her collusion in order to *screen*
her share in the great swindle. The popular indignation
expressed itself in caricatures, which were common at this
period, and attempted to temper corruption in England just
as the epigrams "tempered despotism" in France. The
one that had the greatest vogue was known as the "Brabant
Screen." It depicted Knight in travelling costume receiving his safe conduct, which was given him by the Duchess
of Kendal from behind a screen.

Being a woman of few words, and those uttered in a

language quite unfamiliar to English ears, it was never known what her Grace thought of the caricature or the hatred of herself that it implied. But it is highly probable that with her fortune, and her person immune from attack, and her influence over George supreme, she cared absolutely nothing.

V

THE vast credit the Duchess of Kendal enjoyed, though always used to advance her own interests, was not, however, entirely confined to the unscrupulous amassing of a great fortune. She devoted not a little of her time and attention to politics, less perhaps from any real inclination for intrigue than from a shrewd sense that in a country where political corruption was rampant a knowledge of the business of the State was essential to the security of the throne on which her own depended. Since her trade in royal patronage was largely of a political nature she gained considerable experience of the science as it was practised in England. She was thus able to give George sound advice even when it conflicted with her own personal prejudices. Her readiness to co-operate with Sir Robert Walpole, whom she thoroughly disliked, in getting rid of Carteret and the Hanoverian Bernsdorf at a critical juncture probably saved George from a compulsory abdication. She was, too, responsible for the King's timely reconciliation with the Prince of Wales, which was purely a matter of policy, for next to his wife, George hated his son more than any one on earth.

Walpole, who was a shrewd but prejudiced judge, declared that "her intellects were mean and contemptible." Nevertheless, since George would never consult him save in her presence, which showed how much importance he attached to her opinion though he did not always follow it, Walpole was obliged to come to some sort of an understanding with her, whereby both were able to gratify their dominant passion—his being to govern and hers to plunder the country.

It was, however, no doubt true that her ability, which in the mistresses of kings is often but another term for ambition, was mediocre. But had her love of power been equal to her love of money it is not improbable that she would have established a reputation for statecraft equal to that of a Maintenon, a Châteauroux, or a Pompadour. Frederick the Great's celebrated sister, the Margravine of Baireuth, referring to her in her memoirs declared that " the Duchess of Kendal had neither vices nor virtues, she was, in fact, one of those persons who are so good that they are good for nothing ; her sole object was to keep her influence and to prevent any one from disputing it." Taking it for granted that such was her object—and there is no reason to suppose the contrary—it was paltry enough to prove a paltry mind. But if the success of a *maîtresse en titre* is the chief test of her ability, it must be admitted that the Duchess of Kendal ranks among the most conspicuous of her class. According to Lady Cowper " she was as much a queen as ever there was in England."

To account for George's ludicrous attachment to this old and forbidding skeleton of a giantess, it was rumoured that he had married her morganatically. Etough, writing to Dr. Birch on the subject, asserts that the ceremony had actually been performed by the Archbishop of York. It is quite possible that the report was true, and the fact that such marriages, though common enough in Germany, were regarded in England, where hitherto they were unknown, as bigamous would be sufficient for reasons of expediency to account for the mystery in which the present case was shrouded.

The Duchess, however, by the assumption of an extraordinary semblance of piety, endeavoured to convey the impression that her relation to George was purely platonic. It was her custom to attend as many as seven Lutheran chapels on Sunday. But these assiduous efforts to appear respectable only excited ridicule, and on one occasion the minister of the Lutheran chapel in the Savoy publicly mortified her by refusing to administer the sacrament to her on the ground that she was living in a state of adultery. She was at the time considerably past fifty! How she revenged herself on the zealous Lutheran is not known ; but being determined to partake of the communion she found another and less scrupulous minister of the same faith in the city to gratify her.

The real secret, however, of her influence was tact. She thoroughly understood George, she knew all his tastes, prejudices, and moods, and was ever ready to humour them, even to the extent of suffering him to woo young and attractive women without wearying him with reproaches. Such complaisance naturally obtained for her the reward she desired, and she had the satisfaction of displaying the influence in which she traded to the very best advantage For she was not only lodged near the King in St. James's Palace, but since " he was in the habit of consulting the ministers in her apartments every day from five till eight," she had the supreme pleasure of acting as hostess on his behalf.

But though the bond that united him to her was so strong, the Duchess, like all her tribe, was ever anxious about its strength. To keep George from being bored was as essential to her as to keep Louis Quinze from being bored was to Madame de Châteauroux. The day a *maîtresse en titre* fails to amuse her king the days of

Le Roy d'Angleterre

Georges-Louis I.e du nom, cy devant Electeur d'Hanover, fils d'Ernest
Auguste Duc d'Hanover et de Sophie princesse Palatine, est né le 28.e Mar 1660
a esté proclamé Roy de la grande Bretagne a Londres le 12. Aoust 1714.

KING GEORGE THE FIRST
[*From an old French print*]

To face page 94

her supremacy are numbered. Considering that "one of George's recreations was cutting paper into different shapes," the Duchess should have found it easy, one would think, to provide him with entertainment in his idle hours. Nevertheless, she was known to complain of the great difficulties she had in this respect, which, no doubt, accounts for her readiness to support his infidelities—especially since Madame de Kielmansegg was no longer an object of jealousy.

On arriving in England the Duchess had quickly and completely eclipsed her once formidable rival; and the "Elephant," too fat and too lazy to contend with her, had contented herself with the title of Countess of Darlington and the free rein to rapacity that George gave her.[1] The numerous other rivals the Duchess had since been compelled to tolerate are too insignificant to mention, save one who appeared in the last year of George's life, and threatened for a while to bring her Grace's influence to a humiliating end.

This was Anne Brett, an Englishwoman, whom the King, according to Walpole, "took as a mistress out of compliment to his English subjects to atone for the contempt with which he had so long treated them." A coronet was promised her as the price of her favours, but after a brief and troublous reign her insolence caused her fall, and when George set out on his last journey to Hanover it was the Duchess of Kendal and not Miss Brett who accompanied him.

These journeys "home" were the great events of George's life. One, if not the chief, objection he had made to leaving Hanover was the clause in the Act of Settlement which compelled him, if he accepted the crown, to remain in England. It had, however, been intimated to him that this clause might be repealed, and taking advantage of the whip hand the events of 1715 gave him over the Whigs, he

[1] See Preface.

brusquely informed Parliament that he would no longer put up with the obnoxious restrictions to his movements. The liberty he desired was consequently granted him, and his visits to his Electorate—where the people always received him with bonfires and every sign of joy when he arrived, and always wept when he left—became so frequent and lasted so long that, as Lord Peterborough expressed it, "he seemed to have forgotten the accident which had happened to him on the 1st of August, 1714."

The great pleasure which he always anticipated from these visits was, however, on the occasion of the last he was ever destined to make, dashed by a presentiment that his days were numbered. On bidding farewell to the Prince and Princess of Wales he told them with tears in his eyes that he should never see them again. This uncanny presentiment had haunted his mind, prone to superstition, ever since he had received the news of the death of Sophia Dorothea, which had recalled to his memory a prediction made to him in his youth by a French fortune-teller, to the effect that "he should take care of his wife, as he would not survive her a year."

This prediction was destined to be fulfilled, but it was indigestion rather than superstition which really shortened his life. For after gorging himself on melons at the house of a Dutch nobleman with whom he stayed for a night *en route* to Hanover he was suddenly taken ill. The following morning his condition was so serious that his suite advised him to remain at his Dutch host's a few days longer. George, however, obstinate to the last, was resolved to continue his journey as far as Osnaburg, where his brother the Prince-Bishop lived.

"When he arrived at Ippenburen," says Coxe, "he was quite lethargic; his hand fell down as if lifeless, and his tongue hung out of his mouth. He gave, however, signs enough of life by continually crying out as well as he could articulate, 'Osnaburg! Osnaburg!'"

The horses were put at the gallop, and George reached there that night, to die in his brother's arms.

As for the Duchess of Kendal, believing his attack to be merely a trifling indisposition, she had remained behind for some unknown reason, and was unconcernedly proceeding to follow her lover when a courier arrived to inform her of the gravity of the King's condition. Alarmed, she hurried forward with all speed, but she had only gone a few miles when she was stopped by another courier who was bringing her the news of George's death.

Distracted by news so utterly unexpected and terrible, which deprived her at one blow of a devoted companion of nearly fifty years' standing and a position equal to that of "a queen, if ever there was one," the Duchess of Kendal exhibited every sign of grief and despair. "She even beat her breasts and tore her hair, and immediately separating herself from the English ladies in her train, took the road to Brunswick, where she remained in close seclusion about three months."

Her Grace survived the abrupt and dramatic termination of her career as *maîtresse en titre* for nearly seventeen years. It is rather curious to note that her retirement into obscurity synchronizes almost exactly with Cardinal Fleury's emergence from it, and that its duration continued till 1743, the year in which both she and the Cardinal died at very nearly similar ages, greatly in excess of those usually allotted to the human species.

But though the obscurity in which these last seventeen years of the Duchess were passed was as profound as the corresponding period of old Fleury's career was effulgent rumour from time to time illuminated the darkness with a grotesque ray of light. Drawn back to England after George's death by the immense fortune she had so un-

7

scrupulously amassed in that country, she passed her time between Kendal House, Twickenham, and a villa at Isleworth. It was at this latter residence that there occurred the ridiculous incident which revived, by reason of the laugh it created, a fleeting memory of her Grace in the world which had long forgotten her. You may take it with Jesse as an evidence that her long connection with George was really founded on a sincere mutual attachment, or with Lady Mary Wortley Montagu solely on interest, as you please; or again, as an evidence that the Duchess's remarkably cunning faculties were impaired in her declining years.

"In a tender mood," says Walpole, on whose well-known account of this grotesque incident the memory of the once notorious "Maypole" has perhaps been saved from almost complete forgetfulness—"in a tender mood George the First promised the Duchess of Kendal that if she survived him, and it were possible for the departed to return to this world, he would make her a visit. The Duchess, on his death, so much expected the accomplishment of that engagement, that a large raven, or some black fowl, flying into one of the windows of her villa at Isleworth, she was persuaded it was the soul of her departed monarch so accoutred, and received and treated it with all the respect and tenderness of duty, till the royal bird or she took their last flight."

After this event her Grace relapsed once more into obscurity till her death, chronicled in the gazettes one morning, revived the memory of her rapacity and corruption for a fleeting moment. Unlike most of her tribe, she had managed to preserve the greater part of the enormous wealth she had accumulated in her days of power. She left it to be divided equally between her two "nieces," one of whom, created by the indulgent George, Countess of Walsingham, it is interesting to note had married the Earl of Chesterfield, of letter-writing fame.

For some years after the Duchess's death Kendal House, where she died, having been converted into a tea-garden, continued perhaps among inquisitive customers to keep alive a certain interest in her and the corrupt age in which she had played so prominent a part, till it, too, in the course of time disappeared. History, in which she is buried, preserves no trace of her grave. But it seems to me that no more suitable epitaph could have been inscribed on her tomb than two striking lines of Oscar Wilde's, which will serve also as an epitaph for George the First—

> "And the damned grotesques made arabesques
> Like the wind upon the sand."

CATHERINE II
EMPRESS OF RUSSIA

1729—1796

CATHERINE II., EMPRESS OF RUSSIA
[*After Schebanoff*]

To face page 103

"O garment not golden but gilded,
  O garden where all men may dwell,
 O tower not of ivory, but builded
  By hands that reach heaven from hell;
 O mystical rose of the mire,
  O house not of gold but of gain,
 O house of unquenchable fire,
    Our Lady of Pain!"
                            SWINBURNE'S *Dolores*.

CATHERINE II
EMPRESS OF RUSSIA

1729–1796

I

It is universally admitted that the Empress Catherine II was one of the most remarkable women in history. To find her counterpart it would be necessary to search the records of antiquity; but perhaps even among the female prodigies of the pagan world she is without a rival. In the modern Christian era, at all events, she is a unique figure.

Like Augustus who found Rome brick and left it marble, she found Russia a wilderness and left it the most formidable power in Europe. It is entirely to her that Russia owes its spirit of nationality. She welded its loosely-bound tribes and races into one solid, homogeneous mass, thus realizing what Peter the Great had only been able to dream. To accomplish such a task unaided would have been impossible even for her, but to her belongs the credit of having discovered and selected those capable of helping her. The ministers and generals whose names are associated with hers in the creation of the Russian Empire merely carried out her instructions; even Potemkin, who alone of her servants possessed the creative faculty, was inspired in all he did by her personality. Nor was she great only as an Empire-builder; she excelled equally as an administrator, giving light to what she created. In a word, she did for Russia what her famous contemporary Frederick the Great did for Prussia—she civilized it.

To draw a faithful portrait of this "She-Louis Quatorze," as Carlyle called her—an epithet, by the way, much more apt than Eulogy's "Pole Star" and "Semiramis of the North," or Detraction's "Messalina" and "Circe"—requires space, as the first essential. When Madame Vigée Lebrun contemplated painting the Empress, some one advised her "to take the map of Russia for canvas." There were, however, two distinct women in Catherine—Catherine the Empire-builder and patron of art and literature, and Catherine the adventuress and light-o'-love, the splendid sinner in fact whose career may very readily be confined to the limits of a *coulisse d'histoire*, which is its proper place.

It is the latter only that is attempted here.

Sophie Augusta Frederica of Anhalt-Zerbst was born in 1729 at Stettin in Russia. The name of Catherine by which she afterwards became so famous was not given her until she was received into the Greek Church at the time of her marriage to the Grand Duke of Russia.

The family of Anhalt was Lutheran. Its lineage was neither particularly ancient nor illustrious; it possessed, however, the privilege of intermarrying on terms of equality with reigning houses, and though the vassal of the Kings of Prussia, was supreme on its own estates. In a word, it was only one of those three or four hundred princely houses which on the reconstruction of the Holy Roman Empire were " mediatized "—that is, very generously compensated in cash for their previous semi-independence. This particular house, however, was more fortunate than most of its kind and managed to escape absorption. The Dukes of Anhalt are to-day sovereign princes of the Germanic Confederation.

In 1729 this family consisted of four branches, of which that of Anhalt-Zerbst was the youngest and least important. Prince Christian August, its head, was, indeed, nothing more than a " highly connected " major-general in the Prussian service, who held the post of Commandant of Stettin. He was a serious, painstaking man with considerable military experience and the usual pipe-clayed sense of duty that was characteristic of the Prussian general of his time. In the opinion of the astute French Ambassador at St. Petersburg, the Marquis de la Chétardie, he was " a good fellow in his way, but of quite unusual stupidity." His wife was Jeanne Elizabeth of Holstein-Gottorp, whose family connections were destined to have an important influence on her daughter Catherine's career. She was a flighty and intriguing woman, very anxious that her daughter should make a brilliant match. She was shrewd enough to realize the value of mental accomplishments as a means to this end, and Catherine was given a much better education than was customary for girls of her rank to receive.

But beyond the fact that she gave promise of developing into a good-looking woman the young Princess of Zerbst showed no sign of those intellectual qualities which the admiring Diderot compared many years later to a "candlestick bearing the light of the world." Indeed, one of her teachers afterwards declared that she "expected her to turn into quite an ordinary woman." For recreation she was allowed "to play in the streets or on the ramparts of Stettin with the children of the townspeople." Occasionally she went with her mother on visits to her relations in Holstein. On the whole her childhood was extremely uneventful. She herself wrote to Grimm at a later period that she could "recall nothing interesting in it."

Events, however, were occurring in Russia which were to bring it to an abrupt end. The Empress Elizabeth, whom a palace revolution suddenly pitchforked on to the throne, being childless had adopted her nephew, who was also Catherine's first cousin, Peter of Holstein-Gottorp, for whom she was anxious to find a wife. The Empress would have preferred a princess of France or Austria, countries with which Russia was then allied, could one have been found to accept what was considered in Western Europe a very dangerous honour. But while the French and Austrian Courts invented courteous pretexts for declining the Empress's offer, being desirous of keeping on good terms with her, they as courteously offered to find a suitable wife for the Grand Duke. In their choice, of course, they intended to be guided entirely by their own interest. This was to add insult to injury, and the offended Elizabeth, whom diplomacy tried in vain to pacify, at her wits' ends for a wife for her nephew, turned in desperation to the man she mistrusted above all others—Frederick the Great. He was only too willing to be of service to her on such an occasion, and he at once recommended to the Empress the daughter of the Commandant of Stettin. Her humble place in the list of German princesses would, he thought, be more likely to make her grateful to him for her elevation than any other candidate he could select. Moreover, her obscurity would scarcely disqualify her in the eyes of the Empress, who would herself but for his death have married Jeanne Elizabeth's brother, to whom she had been passionately attached.

In the latter supposition at least Frederick was not deceived. Thus it chanced that one day when Catherine was fifteen Christian August received a letter from the Empress of Russia requesting him to allow his wife and daughter to pay her a visit. Money to defray the expense of the journey was sent with the invitation, the object of which, though not openly stated, even the heavy-witted Christian August could not fail to guess. Jeanne Elizabeth, whose ambitious projects for her daughter had never in her wildest dreams aimed so high, insisted on starting for Russia without a moment's delay. To this Christian August made no objection beyond expressing the hope that " by some arrangement his daughter might marry the Grand Duke without changing her religion;" and to strengthen her in the Lutheran creed in which she had been brought up the honest man gave her as a parting present, "a work of Heineccius on the fallacies of the Greek faith with a commentary in manuscript that he had made on the same."

The journey, made in the depth of winter, took nearly a month, and the discomforts were so great that at Mittau, where the mother and daughter were lodged at a posting-house "like a pigsty," Jeanne Elizabeth began to doubt the wisdom of having accepted an invitation to so barbarous a country. At Riga, however, the splendour of their reception revived her hopes. Here, lodged in the Castle in magnificent rooms "with sentries at all the doors," the recollections of the posting-house faded from her memory.

"When I sit down to table," she wrote to Christian August, "the trumpets in the house, the drums, flutes, and hautboys of the guard outside sound a salute. It seems to me as if I must be in the suite of Her Imperial

Majesty, or of some great princess. It never enters into my head that all this can be for poor me, accustomed as I am at Stettin to have only one drum beaten for me, and sometimes not even that."

Catherine, on the other hand, appeared utterly indifferent to the splendour which had turned her mother's head. Already she had begun to display that crafty calm which was characteristic of her manner till she usurped the throne eighteen years later. The splendour, however, was not lost on her, she loved it as much as her shallow mother ; but it meant a great deal more to her. She always felt born for majesty, and this conviction had been emphasized by a fortune-teller who had " seen three crowns in her hand." Nothing was lost on her that she saw or heard. On reaching Moscow the first thing that was pointed out to her was " the barracks of the Preobajenski regiment which had placed the Empress Elizabeth on the throne." Here, at the end of the journey, their reception was so splendid that Jeanne Elizabeth was obliged to take to her bed. On Catherine it produced an exhilarating effect.

" It is the grandeur that sustains her," said her exhausted mother. And her own ambition, she might have added.

II

THE Grand Duke of Russia—in those days there was but one—whom the young Princess of Anhalt-Zerbst had come to Russia to marry, was an imperial degenerate. He was at this time sixteen, having been born a year before Catherine, and, like her, in Germany—at Kiel. His mother, who was a daughter of Peter the Great, had married the Prince of Holstein-Gottorp, and till his aunt, the Empress Elizabeth, suddenly mounted the throne of Russia he had lived at Holstein. From the age of seventeen he had been trained for the profession of arms, beginning in the barracks like a private soldier and passing through every grade. But this training, which produces such admirable results in normal natures, had the most disastrous influence on the degenerate Peter. He learnt to prefer the barracks to the Guards' mess, his inferiors to his equals, and became imbued with the spirit and ideas of a drill-sergeant instead of those of a field-marshal. He also developed a taste for drink. Catherine remembered "seeing him drunk at the age of ten," when she first met him on visiting Holstein with her mother, long before either she or he had dreamt of going to Russia or marrying one another.

His tutor, who had been given absolute authority over him, was, according to a French observer, "good for training horses, but not princes." The man was, in fact, a savage and ignorant brute. He not only encouraged his pupil in drinking and depravity, but terrorized him as well by preposterous punishments; such as knocking him down with a blow of the fist, depriving him of food, or compelling him to kneel for a long time on dried peas spread on the ground. Born to a great destiny, no base-born child could have been more neglected or brutalized. The love, gentleness, and care that a boy of his delicate health and abnormal temperament required, and by which alone the development of his latent tendency to degeneracy might have been prevented, were entirely absent. No wonder, then, that he had become both a liar and a coward; vicious and violent; pale, sickly, and uncomely—"a crooked soul in a prematurely-ravaged body." Poor Peter!

That Catherine should be disgusted when she met her future husband goes without saying. But she was careful to conceal her impressions; already at fifteen she had learnt the value of dissimulation, in which she afterwards became a past-mistress, and without which at such a

Court as the Russian she must have been irretrievably lost. Disgust of Peter, moreover, was tempered by ambition. She saw in him not a husband, but a crown.

A chill which developed into pleuro-pneumonia, and the conduct of her foolish mother, who became inveigled in political intrigues, very nearly cut short Catherine's chance of becoming Grand Duchess. She saved the situation, however, by her modesty and sense. Having come to Russia on approval, so to speak, she realized that to be acceptable it was essential to become Russian. To lose no time she set herself from the start to study Russian, and so great was her zeal to acquire the language that she was in the habit of getting up in the night and repeating the lessons she had learned during the day as she walked bare-foot up and down the room. The immediate result of this midnight exercise in scanty attire was an illness from which it was thought she would not recover. Believing her to be dying, her mother, with the consent of the Empress, wished to send for a Lutheran pastor.

"No," murmured the sick girl, "send for Simon Todorski."

Such a request at such a moment in a girl of fifteen was remarkable. Todorski was a priest of the Greek Church. If she recovered, would not the fact that she had desired to die in the Russian faith prove that she was at heart a Russian? The success of this ruse was her first triumph in diplomacy; and Catherine on her recovery followed it up by requesting the Empress, of her own accord, that she might be received into the Greek Communion. The request was granted, Jeanne Elizabeth, whose behaviour had estranged the Empress from her daughter, was politely desired to return to Stettin, and Catherine was married to Peter.

Marriage, however, clipped the wings of her ambition. At a Court like that of Russia, where palace revolutions were of frequent occurrence, everybody was under espionage. The Empress kept the Grand Duke and the Grand Duchess under the closest surveillance. Elizabeth Romanof was a typical Russian: she was sensual, deeply pious, and superstitious, cruel, cunning, and neurotic. As became a daughter of Peter the Great, she was tall, beautiful, and majestic. The following character-sketch of her by the Chevalier d'Eon, that man-woman or woman-man so famous in the secret service of Louis XV, paints her to the life—

"If one is not buttoned and cuirassed beforehand against inspection her eye glides under your clothing, lays you bare, pierces open your Ibreast, and when you discover it, it is too late; you are naked, the woman has read you to the root of your soul. Her frankness and good nature are only a mask, in France and in all Europe she has the reputation of being *clément*. On her accession, indeed, she swore on the image of St. Nicholas that no one should be put to death during her reign. She has kept her word, and though, it is true, not a head has been cut off, *two thousand tongues, two thousand pairs of ears have been!* The same contradictions are to be found in her private life. Now impious, now fervent, sceptical to the point of atheism, bigoted to the point of superstition, she passes whole hours on her knees before an image of the Virgin, talking with her, questioning her, and demanding of her from what regiment of the Guards she shall choose her next lover."

Indecision was the chief note of her character. She was utterly unreliable. In the world in which she lived it was her strength. The Baron de Breteuil relates in one of his dispatches that in 1760, "as she was in the act of signing the renewal of the treaty concluded in 1746 with the Court of Vienna, and had already written 'Eli . . . ' a wasp settled on the end of her pen; whereupon she stopped, and it was six months before she made up her mind to finish the signature."

To complete the portrait of this singular woman it should be stated that she was also a sensualist and a drunkard. She had many lovers, though, unlike her more celebrated successor, she did not make a parade of them. It was to one of her lovers, the French physician L'Estocq, that she owed the success of the conspiracy which brought her to the throne. The precarious state of her health, on which many political intrigues were based, was due to her passion for drink, to which in the end she succumbed, "dying with a saucer of cherry-brandy at her lips."

With the terrible eye of the Empress upon them, marriage at first produced scarcely any change in the lives of the young couple. The reports of their conduct at this time which were made out for Elizabeth have been preserved. "The Grand Duke," she was informed, "passes his time in childish pursuits unworthy of his age." "The Grand Duke passes his time entirely in the company of valets." "The Grand Duchess is very silent and industrious, her chief occupation is learning the Russian language." "The Grand Duchess is negligent in the observances of the Orthodox religion, and *excessively familiar with the young lords of the Court, and even the pages and valets.*"

The spies of the Empress soon discovered that the Grand Duke not only tolerated the light conduct of his wife, but actually encouraged it. To keep them in order a Madame Tchoglokof was appointed as a sort of nurse to the young couple, whom she scarcely ever let out of her sight, even coming into their bedroom during the night. The cunning that Catherine displayed in outwitting this argus caused Peter to call her "his Madame la Ressource." In time she even succeeded in corrupting the terrible Tchoglokof herself.

Peter now "got drunk almost daily," and though twenty

THE EMPRESS ELIZABETH
[*From an old print*]

To face page 112

still played with soldiers, even taking his toys to bed with him at night! Indeed, his behaviour in general was such as to give rise to the most sinister apprehension. Once Catherine found him " in full uniform, booted and spurred, standing with a drawn sword before a rat suspended in the middle of the room, which had been tried by a council of war composed of valets and condemned to death for having eaten a paste sentinel placed before a cardboard fortress."

The removal of the Grand Ducal Court to Oranienbaum, a château that Elizabeth gave the couple as a country residence, afforded Catherine all the opportunities she desired for doing as she liked. For with such a husband it is scarcely to be wondered that the Grand Duchess should resume the flirtations that Madame Tchoglokof had been appointed by the Empress to prevent.

Chief among her admirers was her chamberlain, Sergius Soltykof, "beau comme le jour." All through her life Catherine was very susceptible to masculine beauty. Beginning to flirt with Soltykof merely for the sake of amusement, she fell passionately in love with him. The relation between them was soon the talk of the Court Peter as usual encouraged it; and this time even the Empress shut her eyes "for reasons of State." Catherine was now twenty-six, and she had been married ten years without a child. The succession was at stake, and the daughter of Peter the Great, herself childless, was resolved that it should be ensured. So Catherine was afforded every facility in meeting Soltykof; but after the birth of the Grand Duke Paul the Empress, to prevent further scandal, advised Soltykof "to travel for his health," which in Russia was equivalent to a mild form of banishment.

The question of Paul's paternity has given rise to many speculations. Paul, who closely resembled his reputed father Peter in many traits, was wont to declare that the House of Romanof ought to be called the House of

8

Soltykof. Peter himself was certain that Paul was not his son, and his attempt to repudiate him was one of the causes of his death. At the time some even went so far as to state that Catherine was not Paul's mother.

"The child," wrote the French Ambassador, "is, they say, the Empress's own."

And since Elizabeth took it away from Catherine as soon as it was born this report was believed by many.

This period, however, of Catherine's life had also its admirable characteristics. A great deal of her time was spent in reading. "After a year of French novels," as she says, she came upon Voltaire. From that moment commenced that remarkable intellectual development which was the chief factor in the Europeanizing of Russia.

III

WITH the departure of Soltykof, Catherine's passion for him quickly cooled. It was ever thus in all her affairs of the heart. The absence of a lover invariably had the effect of extinguishing the fire of the hottest passion into which she flung herself. It was not that she forgot—she never forgot, and her treatment of those she had once loved was always generous—she simply ceased to care. In her later years, when her passions for men degenerated into the prostitution that has left such an indelible stain on her fame, a fresh face had always the power of creating a fresh fancy. But in her youth and prime it was only separation that could snap the spell of a sexual enchantment.

No sooner had Soltykof gone into exile than there arrived at St. Petersburg a personage who was destined to indemnify her for his loss. This was Stanislas Poniatowski, one of the most romantic adventurers of the eighteenth century. His origin, on his father's side at least, was very obscure. For the latter was not a Poniatowski at all, but the illegitimate son of a Count Sapieha and a Polish Jewess whom the Poniatowskis had adopted, for what reason is unknown. But base-born though he was, he had brains and luck, which enabled him to marry a Czartoriski, which family was the most illustrious and most powerful in Poland.

Fortune, however, though it blessed this union with several children, failed to provide their parents with the means necessary to maintain a position worthy of their rank. Consequently when Stanislas was sixteen his parents, taking advantage of the fact that the Elector of Saxony was also the King of Poland, sent him to Dresden on the chance of his procuring there [the employment that they had been unable to obtain for him at Warsaw. For capital he had nothing more substantial than extraordinary good looks and great ambition. Failing to invest either profitably at Dresden, the boy had wandered on to other cities in Germany, whence he passed into France and England, always with the same object. In Paris he made friends in high places, but debt brought him to prison, from which the generosity of the celebrated Madame Geoffrin, in whose *salon* he had shone for a moment, effected his release. Disgusted with this experience, Stanislas next went to London, where after five years of vagabondage his luck suddenly changed.

Wretched though his condition was, his name was still a passport to society. At some social function, very likely at the Polish Embassy, he met Hanbury Williams, one of the craftiest diplomatists and most brilliant libertines of the age. Stanislas, with his youth, his beauty, and a temperament almost feminine in its refinement, could not fail to attract the notice of such a man, whose type is familiar enough to the readers of that class of fiction which is said " to leave a nasty taste in the mouth." To Williams, who had just been appointed Ambassador to Russia, young Poniatowski was a veritable *trouvaille*. In his diplomatic career he had acquired a great deal of useful information in regard to the chief personalities at the Russian Court. He knew that the health of the Empress was extremely precarious, and that her successor was as incompetent as his wife was clever ; it was the latter, then, whose favour his cunning told him he should attempt to win.

"Who knows," thought Williams, "in a country like Russia all things are possible, and some fine morning a palace revolution may turn this Grand Duchess, like Elizabeth before her, into an Empress in her own right."

As the means to his end Poniatowski seemed specially suited. Williams had heard enough of Catherine to infer that she was not averse to an intrigue, and great though her devotion might be to the banished Soltykof—was it not the gossip of the ante-chambers that she had once waited for him till three in the morning at a rendezvous to which he never came ?—the wily diplomatist was too much of a cynic to believe in the deathlessness of any passion. Broken hearts could always be mended, and who was more likely to patch together deftly the shattered fragments of the Grand Duchess's than his charming young Pole ? So Williams, who had already won his affection by numerous little attentions, bound the ties of gratitude, on which he based the success of his political mission to Russia, the tighter by taking Poniatowski with him to St. Petersburg as his secretary.

The project worked like a charm. To Catherine William's *protégé* was a revelation. If not quite as handsome as Soltykof, he had what Soltykof had lacked, and what Catherine till then had never suspected the existence of—an artistic soul. Poniatowski had mixed in the best society in Paris and London ; he possessed a most cultivated mind, and he could talk enthusiastically and sensibly of literature, art and philosophy, subjects that deeply interested her. And with all the charm of his person and the glitter of his mind he had *sensibility*, a peculiar Byronic air and temperament that had not yet been acquired or developed in Russian society. In a word, Stanislas Poniatowski had a *heart*, which Catherine determined to win.

The danger of such an intrigue was from the first apparent to the young Pole, but the society of Williams had tinged his natural courage with cynicism and prosperity had revived his ambition. In Catherine, moreover, there was something of the basilisk, and she seldom failed even in old age to strike a responsive chord in the breast of the man on whom she had fixed her eyes. Poniatowski was the last in the world to resist the appeal she made to his senses.

"She was," he says in the memoirs which he wrote at the end of the delirious career to which her spell now lured him, "at that perfect moment which is generally for women who have beauty the most beautiful. With her black hair she had a dazzling whiteness of skin ; eyelashes, black and very long ; a Grecian nose, a mouth that seemed made for kisses ; perfect hands and arms, a slim figure, rather tall than short ; an extremely vivacious manner, but full of nobility ; while the sound of her voice was agreeable, and her laugh as cheerful as her nature, which caused her to pass with facility from the most sportive, the most childish amusements to the driest mathematical calculations. So," he adds ingenuously, "in gazing at the Grand Duchess, I forgot that there was a Siberia."

The lovers, conscious of the perils of detection, behaved with the greatest prudence and caution. But not even the cunning of Madame la Ressource was able to avert suspicion. An accident which very nearly proved fatal to Poniatowski brought the *liaison* to the knowledge of Peter. The Pole, who was in the habit of disguising himself as a "ladies' tailor or one of the Grand Duke's musicians" in order to get access to Catherine, was caught slipping out of the Château of Oranienbaum in the early hours of the morning, and dragged roughly by the soldiers who seized him into the presence of the Grand Duke.

"Confide in me," said Peter, who had conceived almost as great a liking for Poniatowski as Catherine herself, " and it can all be arranged."

He was absolutely indifferent to his wife's conduct. She could live as she pleased for all he cared, so long as she did not come between him and his mistress Elizabeth Vorontzof. Of this woman the French Ambassador declared, " It is impossible to imagine anything uglier than her face ; she is in every way like a servant at a low inn." In this, how-ever, lay her charm for Peter ; boon companion as well as mistress, she was ever ready to get drunk with him. But though Peter's complaisancy in regard to Catherine's in-fidelities was well known, it was not to be relied on. So, fearing more for his mistress than for himself, Poniatowski chivalrously refused to explain how he came to be at Oranienbaum at such an hour and in disguise.

His silence only served to exasperate Peter, who in a fit of passion would have run him through on the spot with his sword but for the friendly intervention of a compatriot who chanced to be present. Peter, hereupon, had recourse to dissimulation. Feigning to believe that the Pole's nocturnal visit threatened his life rather than his honour, he had him placed under arrest.

Catherine, however, succeeded in procuring his release after two days by resigning herself to the degradation of supplicating Elizabeth Vorontzof to intercede for him. Flattered by the sight of the Grand Duchess, who had ever treated her with contempt, at her feet the Vorontzof deigned

STANISLAS AUGUSTE
PONIATOWSKY,
Roi de Pologne.

To face page 118

to be magnanimous; and at his mistress's request Peter at last consented to release Poniatowski. But perhaps the manner in which he forgave his wife's lover was even more degrading to Catherine than the necessity which had obliged her to humble herself to Elizabeth Vorontzof.

"What a fool you have been!" he exclaimed when the Vorontzof brought the Pole into his presence. "It could all have been arranged before if you had only taken me into your confidence."

In such circumstances it was easy for Poniatowski to regain the favour he had lost, and Peter's good-humour being increased by apology and flattery he suddenly declared with a laugh that since they were all reconciled there was but one person wanting to complete their happiness.

"And with that," relates Poniatowski, "he went into his wife's bedroom, pulled her out of bed without leaving her time to put on her stockings or shoes, or so much as a petticoat, and said as he brought her back with him, 'Well, here he is, and now I hope you are satisfied.' Whereupon we all sat down to supper merrily, and did not separate till four in the morning!"

It was not, however, from the jealousy of the Grand Duke, but from that of the Foreign Ambassadors, who had divided the Russian Court into two factions, that the chief danger was to be apprehended, and to which this *liaison* was at length destined to succumb. It is only in a formal biography of Catherine that it would be desirable or possible to explain in detail the various stages of the diplomatic war which the Powers waged at St. Petersburg. It is merely sufficient to state that Poniatowski's favour with the Grand Duke and Grand Duchess, and his connection with Hanbury Williams, whose mission was to persuade Russia to ally herself to England and Prussia, caused the presence of the Pole to be regarded by France and Austria as fatal to their interests. His removal, there-fore, became a matter of the first consequence to these Powers.

But Madame la Ressource, as may be expected, was not the woman to be deprived of her lover without a struggle. She made his enemies and friends hers, and proved herself a crafty and dangerous adversary. One of those intrigues of private ambition which exist at all Courts unexpectedly provided her with the weapons she needed. The Grand Duke's devotion to Elizabeth Vorontzof had created in her father a hunger for power, which nothing short of the Chancellorship of the Empire would satisfy. To realize this ambition he had formed a party of all who hoped to profit by the Vorontzof influence over the feeble Grand Duke, whose accession to the throne, owing to the delicate health of the Empress, might occur at any moment.

The intrigues of this cabal, and the factors on which they relied for success, had greatly alarmed the reigning Chan-cellor, Bestujef, whose power had been shaken by the defeats which Frederick the Great had inflicted on the Russian arms. Recognizing the ability of Catherine, who, he foresaw, would undoubtedly, on her husband's accession, become a person to be reckoned with, Bestujef endeavoured in his turn to save himself by winning her friendship. Through Poniatowski, to whom he had, from the Pole's arrival in St. Petersburg, been well disposed, he suggested to Catherine that as the triumph of the Vorontzofs would, on Peter's accession, be as injurious to her prestige as fatal to himself they should unite to defeat them. To do this he proposed to secure for her on the death of the Empress an equal share in the government with Peter— on the understanding, of course, that he retained the Chancellorship.

With such a husband as Peter, Catherine had, no doubt, many times dreamt of this possibility, but now for the first time it became a definite purpose. To persuade her to accept Bestujef's proposal was easy. Apart from her own ambition, which was fired by the sense of her vast superiority to her husband, the thought of crushing the hopes of the Vorontzofs would alone have sufficed to ally her to the Chancellor. She was not the woman to endure the humiliation of seeing herself overshadowed on the throne by her husband's mistress.

But in preparing for the future Madame la Ressource by no means forgot the present. Shortly after she had come to terms with Bestujef, France and Austria induced the King of Poland to order Poniatowski to return instantly to his native country. He departed for Warsaw, but not for long. Catherine's pride as well as her love were now at stake. She insisted that Bestujef should obtain his recall.

"And," she added furiously, "as Ambassador of Poland, or Russia must make peace with Prussia!"

Bestujef, who had no wish to humiliate France and Austria, urged the difficulty of such an undertaking in vain. But Catherine, knowing the power which the Chancellor's treasonable proposal to her gave her over him, was firm.

"Oh," she replied dryly, "the Prime Minister of Poland would go without his bread to please you."

And Poniatowski had returned in triumph.

The Franco-Austrian faction, however, had not forgotten this humiliation. Two years later they got their revenge. For having got scent of Bestujef's project to associate Catherine on equal terms with Peter in the government on the Empress's death, they insinuated to Elizabeth that proofs of this conspiracy would be found among his papers. Elizabeth, thoroughly alarmed for the safety of her own crown, instantly ordered his arrest. His rival Vorontzof was appointed Chancellor in his stead, and in the storm Poniatowski too was driven from Russia.

His experiences at St. Petersburg were merely the prelude to a career of splendour, danger and intrigue generally. Having become Autocrat of Russia, Catherine, who never forgot her lovers, made him King of Poland. But in Poniatowski's case this display of grandiose generosity in which Catherine always delighted, was inspired less by tender recollections of the past than by her consummate strategy, which required that Poland should be sacrificed to enable Russia to advance.

To have saved Poland from extinction was perhaps impossible, and Poniatowski, in spite of the noble virtues he displayed when king, was certainly not the man to do it. For his elevation, as Catherine intended, by stimulating the jealousy of the Polish nobles to a pitch of turbulence that required foreign intervention to restore order, led directly to the dismemberment of the country. All appeals to Catherine were useless. One which Poniatowski made to her in person during her famous journey to the Crimea only subjected him to a bitter public humiliation. On this occasion they discovered that not only had love died since they had parted thirty years before, but that its very ashes had been dissipated.

Finally, on the Second Partition of Poland, Catherine, with a cruelty that was unusual in her, compelled the unhappy king to abdicate on the anniversary of the day on which she had given him his crown. After this last humiliation Poniatowski retired to Russia and tried to accept the inevitable stoically ; but the fate of Poland had broken his heart, and her last king did not long survive the freedom of his country.

IV

CATHERINE did not escape unscathed from the storm that had driven Poniatowski from Russia. The fall of Bestujef had rendered her own position extremely precarious. It is true no proofs of a conspiracy could be found among the Chancellor's papers, and though under sentence of death—which Elizabeth, however, changed to banishment—he had generously refused to incriminate his accomplice, for which she as generously rewarded him later on. Nevertheless, Catherine was regarded with suspicion. The Empress refused to see her or receive any communication from her ; Peter threatened her; the Vorontzofs insulted her; and the whole Court neglected her. Under such circumstances, and in such a country as Russia, she might naturally feel the gravest anxiety as to her fate. Anything might happen to her—imprisonment, torture, Siberia, death.

But powerful minds rebound from the errors they have committed, or the misfortunes that have befallen them, with a force proportionate to that which has impelled them to disaster, and possess a self-sustaining energy that causes them to recuperate when lesser minds would sink.

Madame la Ressource, now as always, was equal to the occasion. She knew that if she could but obtain an audience of the Empress she could retrieve her position. Elizabeth, ill, weak, and easily imposed on, could be bullied into pardoning her. To procure this audience she feigned an illness and remained for days in bed. It was rumoured that she was dying. In such a condition the Empress was obliged to see her, and in the audience that was finally granted her Catherine succeeded in completely regaining the Imperial favour. She did more. She managed to discredit her husband, who from that moment till his accession three years later, was forced to rely altogether on his crafty wife for such consideration as he received from his exasperated aunt.

Having escaped being crushed in the fall of Bestujef, Catherine at once set to work with characteristic coolness and energy to rebuild the shattered conspiracy. In the case of Poniatowski, as in that of Soltykof, absence had quickly cooled her passion. The perils that beset her were scarcely conducive, one would think, to the formation of another. Nevertheless, not long after Poniatowski's departure she began an intrigue with Gregory Orlof that was to be fraught with immense consequences for her.

When first heard of at the Russian Court he was five-and-twenty—five years younger than Catherine, whose lovers, by the way, were always her juniors—and exceedingly handsome. All the Orlofs were noted for their great personal beauty and herculean strength. There were five of them, five brothers singularly devoted to one another, but Gregory was the strongest and most beautiful of all— "a giant with the face of an angel."

There was, however, nothing else angelic about him. He was at once a debauchee and a *spadassin*, spending his time in gambling, flirting, and drinking, "ever ready to pick a quarrel and knock down any one who opposed him." He had plenty of courage—the reckless, fatal courage of the Russian. It was traditional in the family. The first Orlof, a common soldier in the time of Peter the Great, known by his comrades as the Eagle, having been condemned to death for some act of insubordination, had, on mounting the scaffold, displayed such supreme coolness that the Czar, carried away with admiration, pardoned him. Gregory's contempt of death was by no means inferior to that of his ancestor. At the battle of Zorndorf he had received three wounds without leaving his post. No danger was too great for him to face, no risk too hazardous to deter him. He was ever ready to run blindfold into any adventure, and to stake his fortune on the cast of the die, the more so as he had nothing to lose. His whole life, in a word, was a sort of madness.

After the refinement and sensibility of the accomplished Poniatowski, the violence and brutality of this unveneered Tartar, who had neither intellectuality nor education, appealed to Catherine with all the fascination of novelty. To call such a woman fickle, who with all her lovers never knew what love was, would be to misunderstand her temperament altogether. As extravagant in passion as she was grandiose in statecraft, it pleased her to go from one extreme to the other. Attracted by Gregory Orlof's beauty, she loved him because he was all that the Pole was not, and also "because of the four regiments that he and his brothers seemed to hold in the hollow of their hands."

The perils through which Catherine had passed could not fail to produce a profound impression on her mind. Conscious of her own vast superiority to those on whom her fate depended, she was not the woman to put up with the anomaly of such a situation. Intrigue alone she knew could give her the prestige worthy of her ability, and passion having drawn her into politics, ambition now followed her and kept her there. In Gregory Orlof she found not only a lover, but a confederate. Having once condescended to notice him he was not the man to need any further encouragement, nor to make a mystery of the favour bestowed on him. The recklessness with which he openly expressed his admiration of the Grand Duchess pleased Catherine and fell in with her plans. She liked to have her name associated in the barracks with that of Orlof, " whom the officers adored and for whom the soldiers would have gone through fire." Moreover, there was nothing to fear. The Empress was now utterly indifferent to scandal; and Peter was too occupied with his own mistress, Elizabeth Vorontzof, to resent it even had he been able to do so.

Besides Gregory Orlof and his brothers, Catherine found active and loyal supporters in the Princess Dashkof and Count Panine. The latter, who was destined to be one of the chief ministers of her reign, had been a *protégé* of Bestujef, who had thought of him as a possible lover of the Empress herself. Elizabeth, indeed, had for a time regarded him with anything but indifference. An intrigue, however, had removed him, and for some years he had been attached to various Russian embassies abroad. But Elizabeth did not forget him, and when she required a tutor for the Grand Duke Paul she had appointed Panine to the post. His sympathy with Bestujef, whose fall he had foreseen in time to avoid being involved in it, had naturally brought him into connection with Catherine, to whom he was a most valuable ally by reason of his influence over the Empress.

In the Princess Dashkof she had a friend of quite another sort. This woman, who was born the year that Catherine came to Russia, was in the habit of boasting that she alone had brought about the revolution that gave Peter's crown to his wife. Having stated this many times and being a woman whose cleverness nobody disputed, she persuaded some of the ablest men in Europe, Voltaire among others, to believe her. But Catherine, who quarrelled with her afterwards, was unkind enough to deny her any share whatever in the great event. Frederick the Great was scarcely more flattering. He declared that "she was nothing more than the silly fly buzzing on the wheel." Perhaps the exact truth as to her usefulness would be to describe her as the oil that lubricated the machinery by which the wheel was set in motion.

PRINCESS DASHKOF

To face page 126

For she was a Vorontzof by birth, being the youngest
sister of Peter's mistress, a fact that caused Catherine's
friendship for her to serve as a screen to a conspiracy that
by its very nature threatened the Vorontzofs no less than
Peter. She had been brought up apart from her family,
which to a certain extent accounted for her readiness to
conspire against rather than with them. Her appearance
at Court had attracted considerable attention, for she could
not speak a word of Russian, her education having been
conducted entirely in French. In this language she had
read all the books that Catherine herself had read. This
served at once as a bond between them, for since Poniatowski had gone there was nobody at the Russian Court who
understood scientific or social problems, or could discuss
philosophy, history, or literature—subjects in which the
future Empress took the greatest interest. So Catherine
and little Vorontzof—whom they speedily married to a
colourless Prince Dashkof—became fast friends, and the
friendship of the younger woman coupled with jealousy
of her sister Elizabeth, whom she knew hoped on the
Grand Duke's accession to persuade him to repudiate his
wife for her, made the Princess Dashkof ready to join any
scheme that Catherine might suggest. She had too the
love of intrigue natural to a clever and ambitious woman
at a Court where successful intrigue was capable of
realizing any dream.

But Catherine had another and far more important ally
than any Orlof, Dashkof, or Panine—her husband's utter
folly and weakness. At the beginning of the intrigues
which she set in motion after the fall of Bestujef, she had
in mind nothing beyond securing the prestige and respect
due to her as the wife of the future Emperor. This she
appeared to have secured when the Empress Elizabeth
finally succeeded in drinking herself to death. Peter,
however, whom she believed she had completely subjected

by the manner in which she had exploited his fears for the last three years, suddenly undeceived her.

He no sooner came to the throne than he flung all restraint to the winds. He was now thirty-four, and for twenty years he had been kept in galling bondage by his aunt, who, believing him to be a fool, had treated him like one. But for this, judging from the way he behaved when he gained his freedom, the Empress is scarcely to be blamed.

His first act was to make peace with his hero Frederick the Great, who had beaten Russia to her knees. This might be chivalrous, but it was highly impolitic, and cost him at the start the popularity of the army. But he did more than merely make peace. He also introduced the Prussian uniform into the Russian army. Further, all that Frederick had lost he restored to him, and declared his "readiness at Frederick's bidding to make war on hell with all the Russian Empire." At a banquet at which he celebrated this alliance he proposed the toast of "The King our Master." Thus at one stroke he antagonized both the army and the powerful faction which under the late Empress had ruled the country, and whose sympathies were with Austria.

Having offended the army, he next made himself accursed to the Church. Declaring his intention of abolishing the Greek religion and compelling his subjects to become Lutheran, like his beloved Prussians—though he personally, like Frederick, had no religion at all—he confiscated the estates of the clergy. But even Peter, mad as he was, did not suppose that these immense changes could be effected without a protest, consequently, with a shrewdness that one would not have expected in him, he attempted to win the sympathy of the masses by proclaiming himself a reformer. As an earnest of his intentions in this respect he began by abolishing the Secret Chancery, a court worse even than the Inquisition, and all exiles were recalled and State prisoners pardoned. But his reforms were so sudden and sweeping that even those they were meant to benefit objected to them. Revolutions in Russia had hitherto been confined to the Court, but now the whole nation was disturbed. And the people, steeped in barbarism, resented, like the army and the clergy, changes for which they were utterly unprepared.

Playing with explosives, like a child with fire, it was but natural that he should blow himself up. Since to prevent him from doing so was impossible—for even Frederick warned him of his danger in vain—domestic and foreign intrigue alike prepared to reap all the advantages that were to be derived from this fatality. It was not long in occurring. For Peter, as if resolved on self-destruction, having laid the mine which was to destroy him, applied the match to it himself.

The change which had taken place in him on his accession was in no respect more fraught with danger to him than in his treatment of his wife. He had immediately flung off the mask of docile subserviency he had worn for three years, and proceeded to subject Catherine to all the humiliations and terrors that she had made him suffer. To prove his contempt, he subjected her to the paltriest annoyances and the grossest insults he could devise. Knowing that she was fond of fruit, he ordered that none should be served at her table. On every state occasion he paid such marked attention to Elizabeth Vorontzof, that a stranger would have believed her rather than Catherine to be the Empress. Nor did he neglect to take advantage of the infidelities of the latter, to which he had ever manifested unfeigned indifference, to increase her mortification and alarm.

Shortly before the birth of her son by Orlof, of whose paternity there was not the least doubt, Peter publicly called attention to her condition.

9

" God knows," he shouted across the table at a certain banquet, "where she gets her children from, but at least I know that they are not mine!"

At another banquet, in the presence of the entire Court, he addressed her in a loud voice by a low epithet, and even gave orders for her arrest, which, however, at the instigation of his uncle, the Prince of Holstein, he was induced to revoke. To these insults and threats he added others that were well calculated to drive her to desperation. When drunk, a condition from which he was seldom free, he talked of divorcing her in order that he might marry his mistress.

" I should not be surprised," the French Ambassador reported to Versailles, " knowing the Empress's courage and violence, if she were driven to some extremity. Her friends would risk anything for her, if she required it."

The idea of removing Peter by a revolution had been suggested to her before the death of the Empress Elizabeth. But feeling sure that she would be the real mistress, Catherine had very shrewdly refused to take any measures to usurp the throne on Peter's accession.

" I prefer to abandon myself to the course of events," she had declared to the Princess Dashkof.

She had no desire to have recourse to violence, which would create for her many enemies. Besides, the frequency of revolutions in Russia by no means argued that they could be organized easily. She hoped to come to the throne quite quietly and naturally, when Peter had drunk himself to death after a reign not likely to be long and during which she would from the first be the real sovereign.

Peter's unlooked-for independence, however, had speedily disillusioned her. Even then she did not at first desire to use violence. She still preferred that he should himself weave the rope that would serve as his halter. She had, therefore, attempted to put up with his ill-treatment by behaving in a manner that was calculated to make her as popular as he was unpopular. Thus, while Peter expressed his contempt of Russia and Russian institutions, Catherine was careful to conform scrupulously with all the customs of the country of her adoption, particularly in regard to the strict observation of the religious ceremonies of the Greek religion, which her husband threatened to suppress. In the art with which she never failed to turn every blunder he made to her own advantage she displayed talents that no political actress has ever excelled.

Peter's increasing violence finally warned her of the folly of waiting for the popular discontent to culminate before taking measures to assert her independence. She had, therefore, from the date of the banquet in which she had been publicly insulted and threatened with arrest, been engaged in hatching the conspiracy which was to put the supreme power in her hands. To achieve this it was essential in any event to make sure of the support of the army. So Princess Dashkof and Panine undertook to recruit the officers of the regiments stationed in St. Petersburg, while the Orlofs proceeded to win over the soldiers. But just when or how Catherine and her confederates expected to effect their *coup d'état* neither she nor they had the least idea. They relied entirely for success on the only god in whom Catherine believed, whom she called " His Sacred Majesty Chance," and who up till now had never forsaken her.

V

THE story of the crisis, as related by Catherine herself in a letter to Poniatowski, is intensely dramatic.

The corruption of the army could not be effected without

exciting suspicion, nevertheless though there were "thirty or forty officers and 10,000 men in the plot there were no traitors for three weeks." Peter at last, however, got wind of the conspiracy on the eve of a mad and extremely unpopular expedition against Denmark in defence of his native Holstein. He immediately signed a manifesto in which he declared his intention of divorcing Catherine, disowning the Grand Duke Paul as his son, and marrying Elizabeth Vorontzof. He was at the time at Oranienbaum with his bodyguard of 1,500 Holstein troops commanded by the celebrated Marshal Munich, his mistress and several women of the Court who were to accompany him on his expedition. Catherine was at Peterhof, whither he had ordered her to stay during his absence, and alone.

His Sacred Majesty Chance, however, disclosed the existence of his fatal manifesto before it could be published ; and the knowledge of the danger to be apprehended by all engaged in the conspiracy caused the Orlofs, though their plans were still but half formed, to act at once.

Catherine, at Peterhof in complete ignorance of what was happening, was suddenly awakened at six in the morning by Alexis Orlof.

" It is time to get up," he said calmly, as he entered her room, " all is ready for your proclamation."

She asked for details, he merely told her that the plot was discovered. At such a moment she understood that there was no time for further explanation. She dressed quickly and got into the carriage that was waiting. The horses, which had already done twenty miles at furious speed, broke down on the return journey to St. Petersburg. At this critical juncture, when time was life, His Sacred Majesty Chance again came to the rescue. A peasant's cart was discovered coming along the road, the horses which drew it were seized and the furious race against time was continued faster than ever.

On reaching St. Petersburg Catherine and Alexis Orlof, accompanied by the former's hairdresser whom they picked up on the way, proceeded to the barracks of the Ismailofski regiment which Princess Dashkof had prepared. They found twelve men and a drummer who at once beat the alarm.

"Then the soldiers," says Catherine, "began to appear. They kissed me, embracing my hands, my feet, my dress, and called me their saviour. One was sent for a priest who, like the soldiers, did what he was told ; and all swore allegiance to me, shouting ' Long live the Empress ! ' "

They next hastened to the Simeonofski regiment, where the same scenes were enacted. The officers of the Preobajenski regiment, one of whom was a Vorontzof, alone attempted to restrain their men, who, however, instantly seized them, and rushing to the Church of Our Lady of Kazan, where Catherine was being proclaimed Empress of All the Russias, begged her pardon for being the last to swear fealty. She then went to the Winter Palace, where the civic authorities came to pay her homage.

Peter, in the meantime, utterly unaware of what had happened, left Oranienbaum and came to Peterhof to arrest his wife in person. At the sight of him the servants, shaking with terror, told him the Empress had fled. Filled with misgiving, he instantly entered the palace and rushed like a madman through the empty rooms and gardens, followed by all his attendants, and calling Catherine again and again. Suddenly a peasant appeared who gave him a letter from his French valet informing him that his wife had been proclaimed in his stead. To confirm the information he had received, he sent three of his staunchest and most trusted adherents to St. Petersburg. None of them returned. A soldier, however, returning from a twenty-four hours' leave of absence, confirmed the news.

Having fifteen hundred Holstein troops with him and all the great Court officials, Peter did not believe that Catherine's plot could possibly succeed. He therefore determined to strike the first blow—on paper. He ordered one of his ministers to draw up several manifestoes, and at the same time prepared to fortify himself at Peterhof. But Marshal Munich, in whose advice and fidelity alone any trust was to be placed, declared that Peterhof could never stand a siege. He urged his master to go to Kronstadt, but by the time that Peter could be persuaded to follow this advice it was night. It was hereupon agreed that the journey should be made by water as being the quickest and safest route. On arriving at the sea-shore, however, only a couple of pleasure barges were to be found. But the night was fine, the Gulf of Finland was as still as a lake, and urged by Munich, Peter, accompanied by his mistress, several women and servants, embarked in the barges. His Holstein troops returned to Oranienbaum to await further orders.

The Imperial party, which in its composition was now as ridiculous as Catherine's when she entered St. Petersburg, arrived at Kronstadt at one in the morning only to discover that the fortress had declared for Catherine. Marshal Munich was for landing in spite of the threats of the governor, who threatened to fire on the barges. The Emperor, he declared, had but to show himself and the place would submit, for the soldiers would never dare to fire on him. But Peter was prostrate with terror. Heretofore his forts and soldiers had been merely toys. The women, no less terrified, implored him to return to Peterhof.

But Munich urged him to go on to Reval, where he would be sure to find a man-of-war, in which he could proceed to Pomerania, where the army he was to lead against Denmark was waiting for him.

"Do this, sire," said the old soldier, who had had many strange experiences in his life, but never one equal to this, "and six weeks afterwards St. Petersburg and Russia will again be at your feet. I answer for it with my head."

But Peter's courage and energy were exhausted. He could only think of getting back to Oranienbaum and his Holsteiners, and the barges were turned about.

Catherine, in the meantime, was anything but idle. On arriving at Oranienbaum, after spending the night rowing about the Gulf of Finland, Peter was greeted with the unpleasant information that his wife at the head of 20,000 men was marching on him. She led her troops on horseback—riding astride, as was ever her custom—and wearing the uniform of the Preobajenski Grenadiers. Beside her rode Princess Dashkof, similarly clad. The soldiers had stripped off the hated Prussian uniforms that Peter had given them, and returned to their former ones, which, too, by the way, had come from Germany, but so long ago that the fact was forgotten. They were burning with enthusiasm for the Empress and a desire to fight the Holsteiners.

This news completely finished Peter. He instantly wrote to Catherine and offered to divide his power with her. But he received no reply. The time when such a proposal, once the height of her ambition, would have been acceptable, was past. An hour later Peter humbly abdicated without any conditions.

Catherine received the news of her husband's submission at Peterhof, in the very palace in which he had intended to arrest her. She at once sent Panine to bring him to her. He cried like a whipped child when he saw her; and crawling on his knees like a Russian serf, endeavoured to kiss her hand, beseeching her to allow him to keep "his mistress, his dog, his negro, and his violin." But "fearing scandal," she says with sardonic cynicism, " I only granted him the last three, and sent him under the command of Alexis Orlof to a very pleasant and retired place called Ropscha until decent and comfortable apartments could be got ready for him at Schlusselburg."

Thus did Peter, as his fatal friend Frederick the Great said sneeringly, " let himself be dethroned just as a naughty child lets himself be sent to bed."

VI

IT pleased Catherine to boast that in the revolution which gave her the throne of Russia not a drop of blood was shed. Peter's death, three weeks later, she always maintained was due to apoplexy. It is true that she behaved with extreme magnanimity to all who had assisted her husband. They had, as she said to old Marshal Munich, only done their duty. But Peter, who, feeble and contemptible though he was, could not fail to render her tenure of the throne insecure while he lived, did not die naturally.

The true story of his death has never been told, very probably it never will be. At the time it was universally believed and stated that his end was violent. The French Ambassador wrote to Versailles that "he had by him everything that could justify the generally received opinion." As may be expected, there were numerous versions of this event. They all agree that Peter was poisoned by a glass of Burgundy. At the lying-in-state, which Catherine ordered, those whose duty it was "to kiss the corpse on the mouth, according to the custom of the country, were blistered on the lips." The account which enjoyed the greatest vogue is thus related by Castéra, few,

PETRUS III IMPERATOR
OMNIUM ROSSIARUM

CZAR PETER III.

To face page 136

if any, of whose statements in his admirable *Life of the Empress Catherine* have ever been refuted.

"They did not carry him to the imperial castle of Ropscha, as had been announced to him; he was secretly conducted to Mopsa, a small country house belonging to the hetman Razoumofski. He had been six days in this place, without its being suspected by any one, except the ringleaders of the conspiracy and the soldiers who guarded him, when Alexis Orlof and Teplof appeared and told him they came to intimate his approaching deliverance and to ask a dinner of him. Glasses and brandy, according to the custom of the country, were immediately ordered. While Teplof was endeavouring to amuse the Czar, Orlof filled the glasses, and mingled that which was to carry death to the prince with an infusion which one of the Court physicians had the villainy to compound on purpose.

"The Czar, suspecting no harm, took the poison and swallowed it. He was soon seized with agonizing pains, and on Orlof's presenting him with a second glass, rejected it and upbraided him with the horrid crime he had committed. He screamed aloud for milk, but the two monsters again presented poison to him and forced him to take it. A French valet, who was greatly attached to his master, ran in. The Czar flung himself into his arms saying—

"'It was not enough to tear from my head the crown of Russia, but they must have my life besides!'

"The valet had the boldness to intercede for his unhappy master, but the villains forced this dangerous witness out of the apartment, and continued to abuse the Czar. In the midst of this tumult there entered the youngest of the Princes, Baratinski, who commanded the guard. Orlof, who had already thrown down the Czar, pressed upon his chest with his own knees, holding him fast at the same time by the throat with all his force, while the other hand grasped his skull. Baratinski and Teplof then passed a table-napkin with a sliding knot round his neck, and the murderers accomplished the work of death by strangling him."

The manner in which Catherine received the news of this event, which there is not a shadow of doubt she connived at, if she did not instigate it, testifies, as Waliszewski says, "to her resources as an actress." It is also a striking example of her power of dissimulation, in which no woman or man has ever surpassed her.

The news was brought to her by Alexis Orlof in person, "covered with sweat and dust, and his clothes all in disorder," just as she was about to hold a court. It was agreed that the news should be kept secret for twenty-four hours, and the Empress appeared before her court without betraying the slightest trace of emotion. The following day, still feigning ignorance, she contrived to have the fatal news broken to her while at a banquet. Whereupon she immediately retired with streaming eyes and was not seen for several days.

That "His Sacred Majesty Chance" in placing Catherine on the throne received great assistance from her personality may be gathered from the following impression she produced on the Chevalier d'Eon three years before these events.

"The Grand Duchess," says d'Eon, "is romantic, ardent, passionate; her eyes are brilliant, their look fascinating, glassy, like those of a wild beast. Her brow is high, and if I mistake not an awful future is written on that brow. She is kind and affable, but when she comes near me I draw back with a movement which I cannot control. She frightens me."

VII

IF the Courts of Europe had any scruples, which is extremely doubtful, about acknowledging the accession of Catherine, they were very careful not to express them. To have done so would have been of no avail, and only served to exasperate a sovereign whom no power could afford to offend. But though the Foreign Ambassadors vied with one·another in hastening to congratulate her, she herself was far from assured as to the stability of the throne she had mounted under such questionable circumstances.

Among the masses, whose opinions, however, counted for nothing, she was regarded with horror as the murderess of her husband, whose reforms had rendered him immensely popular in the underworld of Russia. The great nobles objected to her on the score of her German origin. The clergy were lukewarm, and the army, accustomed by many palace revolutions to treachery, was ready to transfer its allegiance at the command of any officer sufficiently powerful to seduce it. Disaffection did not lack objects round which to rally. It was not forgotten that there still languished in the fortress of Schlusselburg a scion of the blood of Peter the Great, the Emperor Ivan, whose crown had been snatched from him in the cradle. In lieu of him, who many believed to be sane in spite of reports to the contrary, there was Catherine's own son, the Grand Duke Paul. It required little to make a conspiracy in his favour successful.

Quick to realize these dangers, Catherine set herself at once to remove them. The undertaking in which she displayed her unparalleled power of dissimulation in a fashion which alone would have rendered her remarkable, took her ten years. They were her apprenticeship in the statecraft which was to make her known as Catherine the Great and Russia the most formidable state in Europe.

To propitiate the masses she maintained the reforms that Peter had instituted. To appease the nobles she showed herself magnanimous to the great officials who had been opposed to her elevation, sacrificing to their interests those of several who had shown themselves friendly to her but whose ability or influence she knew to be worthless. In this way she did not hesitate to throw over Princess Dashkof; Bestujef was at once recalled from exile. She flattered the clergy by restoring to them their estates which Peter had confiscated, and proving herself the champion of the Greek Church whenever it was menaced. She excited the patriotism of the army and the nation generally by her repeated attacks on the Turkish Empire and the policy by which she finally absorbed Poland. Ivan was foully murdered in his dungeon at Schlusselburg, probably without her connivance though she has been accused of this crime, but certainly by the orders she gave that he should immediately be put to death at the first attempt to release him, an attempt which she knew would likely be made, as it was. While her son, the Grand Duke Paul, for whom she never had the least affection, she kept in a state of complete subjection, which, though it turned him into her bitterest enemy, rendered him throughout her reign a nullity.

To have accomplished all this by herself would have been impossible, so she naturally relied for support on the power of the Orlofs to whom she owed her throne. Her gratitude and sense of dependence fed the fire of her passion for Gregory Orlof. Free for the first time in her life to gratify her passion, she gave it the rein. Nor was Orlof slow to take advantage of the vast favour he enjoyed.

The familiarity with which he treated her was declared by all to be "unparalleled in any country since the foundation of monarchy." In the ten years of his ascendency he and his brothers received from her 17,000,000 roubles, exclusive of presents of palaces and jewels. On their estates they were the absolute lords of 45,000 serfs.

For Gregory Orlof's benefit she created the institution of First Favourite, a position that corresponded to that of the *maîtresse en titre* in France, and to which official recognition had hitherto never been given in any country. He wore her miniature studded with diamonds as a special mark of her favour. The distinction and power he enjoyed created for him many enemies and added to her dangers which she relied on his courage and her skill to overcome. But fortune and ambition turned his head. Having helped her to secure her throne, Gregory Orlof dreamt of mounting it with her as her consort. At the first proposal of such a thing the infatuated Catherine was willing to grant her lover even this distinction. Panine, however, convinced her that such a step would cost her all she had won.

"The Empress can do what she likes," he told her, "but Madame Orlof will never be Empress of Russia."

Orlof received her refusal haughtily, and discovering that his devotion was based on his own ambition she began to weary of the ascendency that he and his brothers had acquired over her.

The idea of dismissing so powerful a subject had no terror for her. She knew that he would be incapable of resenting it; in the very fact of his power lay his weakness. Once she decreed his fall the jealousy and envy he inspired would promote it. But to get rid of him she had recourse to dissimulation. Turkey, humbled by repeated Russian victories, was seeking for peace, and the idea occurred to Catherine to entrust the negotiation of the treaty to her favourite. Never for a moment suspecting her real design Orlof set out for Foksani with a regal retinue. On bidding him farewell she called him "her angel of peace."

It was on this journey that the first signs of his approaching insanity, which boundless ambition and power had developed in his primitive nature, were noticeable. The "angel of peace" no sooner arrived at Foksani than instead of making peace he broke off all negotiations with the Turks, quarrelled with the Russian Commander-in-Chief whose victories he proposed to outshine by attacking Constantinople itself. At Jassy, whither he went to make preparations for continuing the war, he displayed a splendour that startled even the Asiatics in his train who were habituated to the luxury of Eastern princes. At a certain *fête* he wore a costume decked with diamonds which was valued at a million roubles.

Suddenly, in the midst of this insane exhibition of splendour and arrogance, he was informed that one Vassiltshikof, "a very dark, rather good-looking young lieutenant," was installed two weeks after his departure from St. Petersburg not only in his place but in his special apartments. The shock of this news restored him to his senses. In a moment he was the old, energetic, courageous, passionate Orlof whose indomitable audacity ten years before had made his mistress Empress of all the Russias. Jumping into a carriage he started instantly at full gallop for St. Petersburg, a thousand leagues away, stopping only to change horses!

But this colossal, Orlof-like attempt to conquer destiny was in vain. Not far from St. Petersburg he was stopped and told that he must go into quarantine since he had come from the plague-stricken South. Permission, however, was given him to proceed to the Imperial palace at Gatshina which had been prepared for him. Orlof fell into the trap

GREGORY ORLOF
[After Rokotoff]

and discovered that in this ignominious end to his meteoric exploit his star had set.

He was stripped of all his honours, and a special ukase was issued which "permitted him to travel for the benefit of his health." The millions, however, which he had received in money, lands, palaces and jewels he was allowed to retain, with the single exception of the Empress's diamond-studded miniature. As if dazed by his fall Orlof made no attempt at resistance. He realized the futility of contending, devoid, as he knew himself to be, of genius or education, with the consummate craft of Catherine. The quiet, almost pathetic submission of this magnificent subject softened her. After a time she permitted him to return to Court, and treated him as was her custom with all her discarded lovers and offended nobles, in the most generous manner. She obtained for him the title of Prince of the Holy Roman Empire, and showered gold on him afresh. But Gregory Orlof's day was over.

"I owe greatly to the Orlof family," wrote Catherine at this time to an intimate friend; "I have covered them with benefits and I shall always continue to protect them, for they can still be very useful to me. But I have taken my stand. I intend to live according to my own pleasure and in entire independence. As for Prince Gregory, he can do whatever he pleases; he is free to go or stay, to hunt, to drink, to gamble, to keep mistresses."

He did neither the one nor the other. Debauched, disillusioned, *blasé*, he fell in love, deeply and sincerely in love, with his nineteen-year-old cousin, a very beautiful and charming girl who loved him as devotedly in return. In Russia such marriages were illegal, but Catherine came to the rescue of this passion in distress. Over-riding the civil and religious law she permitted them to marry by special ukase. Princess Orlof was appointed lady-in-waiting; the Prince received a palace at St. Petersburg. Here the happy couple lived the quietest, most retired of lives; "becoming, if such a thing be possible, more devoted to one another each day than the day before."

After three years of this beatific existence, Princess Orlof developed consumption, and Gregory began once more to struggle against destiny. He took his wife all over Europe in quest of health only to bury her at last at Lausanne. "Half in the land of the living," he returned to St. Petersburg—to die six months later—broken-hearted and mad. His mental disease, in which "his terrified vision beheld the avenging shade of the murdered Peter everywhere," had details which the French Ambassador wrote to his master at Versailles "he dared not mention even in cypher."

VIII

THE real difficulty of drawing the portrait of Catherine on a canvas, which from lack of space is reduced to the dimensions of so brief a memoir as the present, is not fully apparent till one comes to sketch in the colossal figure of Prince Potemkin of the Taurida, or Patiomkin as he is called in Russia. Under the circumstances, therefore, the rudest *ébauche* of this extraordinary man, who was a genius or a madman, or both, must suffice. To the Russian autocracy what Richlieu was to the French monarchy, the part he played in the career of Catherine the Great may be compared in its importance to that played by the Prince of Denmark in *Hamlet*.

Potemkin was born in Smolensk, a considerable provincial town on the Dnieper, ten years after the woman with whom his name is so closely associated first saw the light at Stettin. Very little is known of his early days. He came of an old but impoverished family, and since his parents had not the funds necessary to provide him with a more lucrative career they destined him for the Church. After commencing his education for this calling, to which no one could have been more unsuited, but for which he professed so great a liking that several times in later life he seemed seriously to contemplate returning to it, his inordinate ambition got the better of him, and having borrowed five hundred roubles, which he never repaid when a million was to him as nothing, he set out for St. Petersburg.

Here he discovered some female relation whom he interested in himself and through whose influence he obtained a lieutenancy in the regiment commanded by Gregory Orlof. Realizing that his promotion was only to be obtained by his own efforts, he endeavoured to attract the favourable notice of his commander, in which he was speedily rewarded. Orlof, who was at the time engaged in fomenting the conspiracy which was to place Catherine on her husband's throne, and was anxious to win the support of his subordinates, marked him out for his zeal as an officer whose confidence was worth winning. Flattered by the attentions and promises of the Orlofs, with all of whom, especially Alexis, he soon became a great favourite, young Potemkin readily threw in his lot with theirs. All the officers who took part in the revolution which deprived Peter of his throne and life were promoted. But Potemkin, who, it is said, had personally attracted Catherine's notice on the day when she proceeded to march against Peter at the head of her troops by offering her the plume from his own cap on perceiving that this ornament was alone lacking to complete the uniform she had hastily donned, was rewarded with the post of chamberlain to the Empress. From that moment he began to dream of supplanting Gregory Orlof.

To put him in his place, Alexis Orlof, who had noticed his growing favour with Catherine, picked a quarrel with him at a game of billiards, and unintentionally knocked out one of his eyes with a cue. Overwhelmed by this misfortune, which, though it left him half blind, did not seriously disfigure him, Potemkin left the Court and returned home to Smolensk. In his case, however, absence appears to have achieved for him the very opposite to what it did for others. Catherine missed him, and even wrote to tell him so. Potemkin needed no further encouragement, and, as soon as his wound had healed, he returned to Court, and proceeded to pursue his ambition with more cunning and more fervour than ever.

Orlof having finally fallen from favour and power, Potemkin, who had cleverly made use of Vassiltshikof to hasten this event, which he saw to be inevitable, had no difficulty in removing this good-looking nullity likewise from his path. The passion, however, with which he had succeeded in inspiring Catherine was not destined to last. But to be supplanted in her affections by another did not greatly trouble Potemkin. It was power not love that he had sought, and having tasted the former he was not the man to be deprived of it. No one understood better than he the curious, complex nature of Catherine, who was at once the slave of passion and ambition, which in her were two separate, distinct, and equally powerful forces. To retain his ascendency it was, therefore, necessary for him to control both these forces—to govern her mind through her ambition and her heart through her passions.

To Potemkin, confronted with the waning of Catherine's love, the difficulty of the latter did not appear insuperable. It was in the former that his real difficulty lay. He knew that if he could continue to rule Catherine's mind he would possess the key to the problem of continuing to rule her heart. It was through his success that Catherine became known as the Great.

From the moment she had mounted the throne she began

PRINCE POTEMKIN OF THE TAURIDA

To face page 146

to conceive the grandiose projects with which her reputation for statecraft is associated. Aware that her schemes for the development and aggrandizement of Russia could not be carried out without suitable assistance, like all great rulers, she was anxious to discover and reward talent wherever she could find it. In the colossal courage, energy and force of the unintellectual Orlof she had found the best specimen of the best type of Russian till Potemkin crossed her path. She had recognized his superiority from the first. In his ability and ambition she saw her own reflected. He was just the man she had need of, and in the exultation of her discovery she had given him, in her sumptuous generosity, both herself and her Empire to rule.

When her passion for him cooled—as it did in two or three years—he would have fallen, like Orlof, had there been any one to fill his place. But in Russia, backward and benighted till she lit it up with the torch of her intellect, there was a dearth of the sort of ability of which she had need. In Europe, even in Russia, she knew she might find men beside whom Potemkin would appear insignificant, but none who understood her and Russia as he did. Experience had proved his worth, and though she ceased to love him, Catherine had no intention of deserting him. She would have lost a lover sooner than such a minister. A lover could always be replaced, but where would she find another Potemkin? He was indispensable to her ambition.

With such a control of her mind, it was therefore not difficult for the crafty minister to recover the control of her heart, or the degraded desires that with her passed for a heart. On the means he employed he counted to render its loss a second time extremely doubtful. In a word, possessing all the avenues of approach to the Empress, Potemkin had merely to close them to whomsoever he chose. Moreover, being cynically indifferent as to whether she had one or a hundred favourites, at the same time or in succession, he was quite ready to further her pleasures in this respect.

Had Catherine's *liaisons* ceased with Gregory Orlof, or even had she attempted to conceal the degrading prostitution into which she flung herself at a time of life when the worst of her sex are wont to abandon it, history, perhaps, in consideration of her genius, to which at the same time she gave the world signal proofs, might have glossed over her monstrous licentiousness. For her admirers were quite as numerous as her enemies and far more capable of influencing posterity in her favour.

"I know," said Voltaire, whom her great qualities had fascinated, but who perhaps wisely refused to accept her patronage after his experience of Frederick the Great's, "I know that she is reproached with some trifles about her husband, but these are family affairs with which I do not meddle."

But Catherine, who like most colossal personalities lacked the moral sense, chose to show her contempt of the world's praises and execration, not only by parading her licentiousness, but by declaring that the number of her lovers was their excuse.

"By associating with me," she once said with a laugh, "they become trained for the service of Russia." Of one whose "promise" was cut short by death, she wrote, "He did his best, he was learning."

These "minor favourites" as they are called, to distinguish them from Poniatowski, Orlof and Potemkin, fill too prominent a place in Catherine's career to be altogether ignored. They were all noted for their good looks, they were also equally conspicuous for their utter lack of brains; and with one exception they were all young—very young. The moment one was dismissed his place was at once filled by another. Dismissal was always due to one of two reasons—weariness on Catherine's part, or the folly of the favourite in attempting to use his favour to cause the fall of Potemkin. The post, which from the day Catherine usurped the throne till the day of her death was an official one that enriched all who held it, was the dream of every handsome youth in the Russian Empire. The humblest might obtain it. Beauty of face and form was the sole qualification to the favour of the Empress.

Zoritch, a Servian in the Russian army, was the only foreigner among the favourites. He was entirely without education and admitted that he was a barbarian. He was, however, strikingly handsome, and even in the reign of Alexander I " old ladies still talked of the Adonis of thirty years ago." Catherine tried to educate him, but after eleven months, finding it impossible, she tired of him.

At first she had some difficulty in getting him to leave the palace. He threatened to "cut off Potemkin's ears." A *douceur*, however, of a million and a half roubles and an estate with two hundred thousand a year to keep it up overcame his disinclination to be separated from "his lady," as he always spoke of the Empress. He turned his fortune to a better account than any of them, for he founded on his estate, at his own expense, a military school for two hundred young officers without means which became a very useful institution.

Korsak, his successor, who changed his name to Rimski Korsakof as being more aristocratic, was quite of a different stamp. He too was quite uneducated. His ignorance was the laughing-stock of the Court. He tried, however, to rectify this deficiency by ordering a library.

" The books," he said, " must be like the Empress's, large

ones for the bottom shelves, and smaller and smaller as the shelves go up."

Potemkin, "who always received a present from a new favourite as well as one from the Empress," netted 750,000 roubles a year by the advent of Korsakof!

Like Zoritch, the amazing ignorance of this favourite brought about his dismissal, but in another way. He had the folly to make love to one of Catherine's maids-of-honour, a fool like himself with whom he plotted to ruin Potemkin.

Perhaps the most amiable of all was Lanskoi.

He was the only one for whom she felt anything that might be said to approach real affection, or whom she inspired with a passion that was not wholly sordid. Lanskoi was but two-and-twenty when he became favourite. Catherine's age at the time was fifty-one. He was of good family but poor, so poor indeed that his fortune at the time of his elevation was said to "consist only of five shirts."

Like the others, Lanskoi's education had been neglected ; he tried, however, very hard to improve his mind. Catherine wrote to Grimm "that he had read all the poets one winter and all the historians the next." He also tried to acquire Catherine's taste for beautiful things, and spent immense sums in collecting antique gems, coins, and pictures. His "sweetness and grace" made him extremely popular, and as he had no ambition and detested politics, his death was almost as much regretted by Potemkin as Catherine herself.

Lanskoi was the only one of the favourites who died in favour. His death, due to the premature exhaustion of his constitution, utterly prostrated Catherine. She refused to see any one for a fortnight ; all State business was suspended. Potemkin at last induced her to see him. He mingled his tears with hers and gave her "Zimmerman's book 'On

RIMSKI KORSAKOF

To face page 150

Solitude'" to read. She erected a mausoleum to the dead
youth in the grounds at Tsarskoe Selo within sight of her
windows—and three months later Lanskoi's place was filled
by another !

He had cost her during the four years of his reign over
seven millions of roubles.

The generosity with which Catherine treated these
creatures is without a parallel in history. Compared with
it that of Charles the Second of England or the French
kings is insignificant. During the thirty-four years of her
reign her favourites cost Russia, in cash alone, nearly one
hundred million roubles, or about twenty millions sterling.
Of this enormous sum Potemkin received fifty millions,
which he wasted on his own luxury and display. But he
was cheap at the price, for in return he gave Russia the
Crimea and the Caucasus; broke the power of the Turks;
converted the Black Sea into a Russian lake; and re-
organized the army which was destined a generation later
to save Russia from Napoleon.

Nor was he of less value to the glory of the Empress
than to the grandeur of the Empire. For by providing
this great actress with a stage specially adapted to display
her peculiar genius to the best advantage, he enabled her
to perform the *rôle* of "Semiramis of the North" in a
manner to excite the admiration of one of the most
brilliant audiences in history—an audience which included,
among others, such men as Diderot and d'Alembert,
Voltaire, and Frederick the Great, Joseph the Second and
Grimm.

It is true that the performances of this "Catherinized
Princess of Zerbst," as the Emperor Joseph described her,
frequently failed to please the over-bearing minister who
stage-managed her, so to speak. If the familiarity with
which she had been treated by Gregory Orlof had shocked
the Foreign Ambassadors, that of Prince Potemkin of the

Taurida rendered them speechless. Drunk with power and splendour he did not hesitate to "appear before her half-dressed to hold a Council of State or to receive Ambassadors." Such marks of the fantastic eccentricity for which he was noted, amused Catherine and she would on such occasions jest with him on his appearance. But if she criticized or rejected his advice he would fall into an ungovernable rage in which he would insult, threaten and command her. To those who beheld these extraordinary outbursts it seemed as if he was irretrievably ruining himself. For Catherine was not always as good-natured and easy-going as she appeared. She was wont to call "the volcano her cousin." Nevertheless in the most violent explosion it was impossible to induce her to sign an order before she had cooled. Whenever she was lashed to fury by the arrogance of her minister, she was always in the end dazzled into subjection. For Potemkin's rage having exhausted itself, he could always save himself from the consequences by flattery at which he was an adept. His cunning in this respect was never more remarkable than in the manner in which he advertised Catherine's tour of the Crimea, which as a display of magnificence has not had its parallel in modern times.

To assign such a man his proper place in the category of Statesmen or Empire-builders is very difficult. Some would dismiss him with contempt from serious considera-tion. Others, like the Prince de Ligne, would ascribe to him "genius, nothing but genius." But all must admit with the Comte de Ségur, who detested him, that "he was colossal like Russia." He said of himself that he was the "spoilt child of God." Considering that his supremacy ceased only with his death he was, perhaps, right.

This event was an ironical commentary on the splen-dour of his life. He died suddenly "on the high road under a tree in horrible agony, literally biting the earth."

Catherine was greatly distressed by his loss. "On learning the news," wrote the French *chargé d'affaires*, "she lost consciousness, the blood ran to her head, and she was obliged to be bled."

To Grimm she expressed her sorrow as follows—

"A rude and terrible blow was struck me yesterday. My pupil, my friend, almost my idol, Prince Potemkin of the Taurida is dead! Alas, now more than ever have I need to be *Madame la Ressource!*"

Fortunately, the tremendous structure that Peter the Great had designed, and of which only the façade existed when she mounted the throne, was now finished. With the passing of Potemkin, the "Pole Star" too began to set. She died suddenly five years later from a stroke of apoplexy on the 7th of November, 1796, having lived sixty-seven and reigned thirty-four years.

The career of Catherine after Potemkin's death was un-redeemed by a single ray of the old splendour. She and her reign were visibly on the decline. Prompted by a senile infatuation for Plato Zubof, the last of the favourites, she gave him the position that Potemkin had held. She declared that he was "the greatest genius that Russia had ever seen," and so great was the spell under which she had fallen that "she advanced a page who had chanced to pick up a handkerchief her favourite dropped." She was sixty-two at this time and Zubof was exactly forty years her junior!

She was alone in her faith in his genius. Set free by the death of Potemkin from the gilded cage in which, like all the other favourites, he would otherwise have shone for a moment without a morrow, Zubof displayed a grasping ambition coupled with utter incapacity. He not only took advantage of his position to enrich himself and his relations at the expense of Russia, but in a ridiculous attempt to ape Potemkin, whose ostentation alone he was capable of copying, he set himself to ruin the credit of all whom he thought stood in his way.   Insolent with everybody he had the folly to make no exception even in favour of the Grand Duke Paul, whom Catherine had treated as a nullity all his life.

On Paul's accession Zubof was lucky to escape with banishment.   He succeeded, however, in procuring a pardon.   But it was an evil genius that prompted Paul to this act of clemency.   Four years later when the mad Emperor was done to death at midnight in his palace by one of those conspiracies of profit through murder which they call revolutions in Russia, it was Plato Zubof who struck the son of Catherine " the first blow on the temple with a gold snuff-box, and then helped to strangle him with a sword-sash as he lay stunned on the floor."

At the same moment, Paul's eldest son was waiting in an adjoining room for the news of this brutal murder, which he had instigated, to be brought to him.   Thus Alexander I, the greatest of all the Czars with the ex-ception of Peter the Great, mounted the throne over the dead body of his father just as Catherine had done over the corpse of her husband.   It is interesting to note that he was Catherine's favourite grandchild and had been brought up by her.

It is also interesting to note that Catherine alone of the chief actors in these two atrocious crimes, was never tor-tured with remorse.   Orlof and Alexander after careers of remarkable splendour both died mad and haunted by the ghosts of the men they had helped to assassinate. Zubof, who had joined the conspiracy against the Emperor Paul in the hope of playing the *rôle* of Potemkin to Alexander as he had attempted to play it to Catherine,

PRINCE PLATO ZUBOF
[*After Lampi*]

To face page 154

gained nothing from the crime in which he had participated. Retiring to a lonely castle he passed the remainder of his life haunted by a mad terror of death and poverty. At the mere mention of death he would shut himself up for days in solitude. The poverty he dreaded turned him into a miser. When he died twenty millions of roubles were found buried in his cellars.

ELIZABETH CHUDLEIGH
DUCHESS OF KINGSTON

1720—1788

ELIZABETH CHUDLEIGH
[*Duchess of Kingston*]

To face page 159

IV

"I have passed from the outermost portal
   To the shrine where a sin is a prayer;
What care though the sinner be mortal?
   O our Lady of Torture, what care?"
                    SWINBURNE'S *Dolores.*

ELIZABETH CHUDLEIGH
DUCHESS OF KINGSTON

1720—1788

I

A MORE remarkable specimen of the aristocratic adventuress than Elizabeth Chudleigh is not to be found in English history, in which the type has been very common during the last two or three hundred years. To the novelist in search of original and sensational material her character and life will prove a veritable mine. Taking her career as a whole, she might serve as the heroine of a romance in the grand style of the old school of fiction. Or you may take her in sections, so to speak, like Thackeray, who used her in this way both as the model for the fascinating Beatrice in *Henry Esmond,* and the repellent old Baroness Bernstein in *The Virginians.* Her numerous and startling adventures would furnish the plots for as many works of fiction.

As in the case of the Duchess of Kendal, her biographers

do not agree as to the exact year of her birth. The majority, however, are of the opinion that this event occurred in 1720—a date which I am quite ready to accept without further argument, as it is really a question of no importance. Little is known of her parents beyond the fact that they were first cousins descended from an old Devonshire family, her mother's branch of which was settled in Dorset. When Elizabeth was said to have reached her sixth year, her father, who was lieutenant-governor of Chelsea Hospital, died, leaving his widow and only child quite unprovided for. Mrs. Chudleigh, however, like a sensible woman, faced her difficulties courageously. Conquering her pride, she rented a house in Conduit Street, procured a " paying guest "—a lady according to some ; a young man according to others, who in the course of time gave Elizabeth her first lesson in love—and made the most of her aristocratic connections.

In this manner Mrs. Chudleigh supported herself and her daughter modestly and uncomplainingly till the latter was sixteen, when chance threw a valuable patron in their way. This was William Pulteney, a man well known in the great world as a distinguished politician, a brilliant wit, and a leader of taste and fashion. Like all public men with such claims to distinction, he had many secret enemies jealous of his success who were only waiting for the chance to detract him openly. With this his acceptance of the earldom of Bath and his marked interest in Elizabeth Chudleigh furnished them. They declared that he had sold his political convictions for his title, and that his interest in the beautiful girl in whose company he was frequently seen was anything but platonic. From the former stigma history has been unable to clear him, but the latter in that day of loose morals was soon forgotten.

It is uncertain whether there was any truth in the scandal which went to the length of asserting that he had picked up his acquaintance with Elizabeth in the streets. At any rate, if the circumstances under which their acquaintance was formed would have lowered her in the esteem of most men, they had no effect on Pulteney, who was many years her senior. Recognizing that she was not only beautiful, but gifted with a quick and intelligent mind, which appealed to his own mental accomplishments, he endeavoured to give her the education in person that her mother's slender means had denied her.

His efforts to cultivate her were, however, doomed to failure. She was too restless and impatient to apply herself to the study of books. Her maxim on every subject, as she herself confessed, was to be " short, clear, and surprising," and in this respect at least she certainly succeeded. Pulteney also attempted to curb an inclination to extravagance which he detected in her. But though, as his enemies declared sarcastically, he had studied the value of a penny to such a nicety that he deemed it improvident for a thirsty man with only the price of a pot of porter in his pocket to indulge in another, he utterly failed, as her future career will testify, to initiate his *protégée* into the science of economy. Never having possessed any money, Elizabeth, not unnaturally, did not know its value; nor, burning with a desire for a life of luxury and possessing the friendship of a man who was able to give it to her, had she the least intention of learning.

It was not till Pulteney's complete failure to form her to his liking caused his interest in her to slacken that she could induce him to give her the key to the great world she longed to enter. From pity of her poverty, and the vanity of having the credit of discovering a beauty whose appearance in society was sure to create a sensation, he yielded at last to her importunities to "do something" for her. Pulteney, who at this time "blazed like a meteor in the hemisphere of opposition," was one of the chief favourites

11

of Frederick, Prince of Wales, who never succeeded in anything, not even to the throne. Employing the influence
which such a connection gave him, the "meteor" obtained
for his *protégée* the post of maid of honour to the Princess.
Thus, as if by the waving of a magician's wand, Elizabeth
passed in the twinkling of an eye from a mean obscurity to
a life of splendour more dazzling than even she had dreamed
of. It is only in real life and trashy novels that such tran-
sitions are possible. So the novelist who would care to weave
Miss Chudleigh's relations with Pulteney into a romance, if
he has any desire to stand well with the critics, had better
leave so "unconvincing" an episode out.

II

ELIZABETH had no sooner appeared in the Court of the
Prince and Princess of Wales at Leicester House than her
beauty and wit created as great a *furore* as that which the
lovely Gunnings evoked when they came to London some
years later. She was toasted by bucks and statesmen;
besieged with admirers who were ready to lay their
fortunes, coronets, and hearts at her feet; and flattered by
the friendly approval of her own sex. Best of all, she
instantly won the friendship of her mistress, the Princess
of Wales, whose favour was to prove of inestimable value
to her for twenty years.

Sensational as was such a change in her life, it was but
the herald to a career in which the sensational wa .ver to
be the dominant feature. Dazzled but not intoxicated
by the astonishing success which unleashed her ambition,
the penniless maid of honour shrewdly took stock of her
resources, and resolved not to throw herself away on any
one less than a duke. Specimens of this delectable species

WILLIAM PULTENEY, EARL OF BATH

[After the painting by Reynolds in the National Portrait Gallery]

To face page 162

of the human race are not to be snapped up easily even by beauties in a more exalted station of life than Miss Chudleigh. But fortune, which had thrown a William Pulteney in her way, remained faithful, and in time rewarded her patience by placing a Duke of Hamilton at her feet.

This nobleman, whose title and family were among the most distinguished in Europe, no sooner beheld her than he fell passionately in love. Being but nineteen he was still in tutelage, and his guardians unfortunately were not prepared to view the fascinating maid of honour in the same light as their ward. Consequently, fearing lest his passion and her ambition should forestall their intentions for his future, they compelled him to set out on the *grand tour* which he was contemplating, and for which all the preparations had been made. As this tour of the principal capitals and countries of Europe was *de rigueur* in those days to all men of rank and fashion, and could scarcely be accomplished under two years, his Grace's guardians trusted to time and absence to cure his infatuation. But Miss Chudleigh had no intention of letting so eligible a *parti* slip from her hands. Before the Duke departed he proposed and was accepted, each swearing undying love, and vowing to keep it alive by the interchange of letters.

Some months later the delicate state of the Princess's health compelling her to abstain for a time from the round of excitement and gaiety in which she delighted, her maids of honour were relieved of their duties. Miss Chudleigh took advantage of her leisure to visit her aunt, a certain Mrs. Hanmer, who lived at Lainston in Hampshire, a small village near Winchester, where another relation, a Mr. Merrill, was lord of the manor. Of the maid of honour's surprising experiences at Lainston there are several versions, all of which, however, agree that Miss Chudleigh returned to London the lawful wife of the

Hon. Augustus John Hervey, a lieutenant in the Navy, and a younger son of the Earl of Bristol.

The most probable story of this episode, which was destined to wreck the character and life of Elizabeth Chudleigh, is to the following effect. It seems that she arrived at Lainston greatly disappointed at not having heard from her nineteen-year-old Duke since his departure. In the hope of dispelling her melancholy, Mrs. Hanmer one day proposed that they should go to the races at Winchester, where they chanced to meet Hervey, who was spending a few days' furlough in the neighbourhood. To see the beautiful Elizabeth, with Hervey, as with all other young men, was to fall head over ears in love with her Possessing all the dash and recklessness in affairs of the heart with which men of his calling are so generally credited, he determined to win her, and, as time was pressing, to win her with dispatch. He disclosed his intention to Mrs. Hanmer, who, being doubtful of her niece's ducal prospects, and realizing that there was only one life between Hervey and an earldom, was readily disposed to assist him. Hervey consequently returned with the race party to Lainston, and flung himself with energy into the task of winning Elizabeth. Piqued by the Duke's silence, on which she could not help putting the most unfavourable construction, and carried away by the suddenness of an offer whose passion struck a sympathetic chord in her own nature, the cunning Elizabeth completely lost her head and allowed herself to be rushed into a marriage which she immediately and bitterly repented.

They were married secretly within a week of their meeting, at eleven o'clock at night in a little chapel adjoining Mr. Merrill's house. The witnesses were Mrs. Hanmer, her maid Ann Cradock, Merrill, and a friend of his, a Mr. Mountenay, who was visiting him and who held in his hat the candle by the light of which old Mr.

Amis, the rector, was enabled to perform the service. The secrecy of the ceremony was insisted upon by both Hervey and his bride ; the former from fear of the anger of his father, on whose generosity he supplemented the slender pay he received from the Admiralty ; the latter from necessity. For were it known she was married, she would have been obliged to forfeit her post of maid of honour, on which she was entirely dependent for support.

The idyl lasted a few days longer, and then Hervey returned to the *Cornwall*, and a two years' cruise in the West Indies. He had no sooner left her than Elizabeth realized the folly into which she had been led, and a violent hatred of her husband completely extinguished what attraction he had possessed for her. The idea that she should have committed such a blunder rendered her desperate, and she returned to her duties at Leicester House, firmly resolved to enjoy to the full the illicit pleasures of life, since the lawful ones were denied her.

III

THE Court of George II was, if possible, even more licentious than that of the Restoration. Public opinion was inclined to treat vice with indulgence, and provided frailty were fair and aristocratic, no distinction was made between it and chastity. At Leicester House, which was the centre of the smartest society in London, the Prince and Princess of Wales themselves set the example of charity to sin, which they encouraged by the looseness of their own actions and opinions. To have kept her virtue in such a world, if she had not already lost it, as was hinted, before arriving there, would have been impossible to Miss Chudleigh. To have pretended to keep it would have been still more out of the question. Before her departure for Lainston, ambition, if not timidity, had restrained her from plunging with the rest into the dissipations of the Court. But on her return, no longer having that incentive to abstain from indulging her inclinations, she dived, so to speak, fearlessly into the sea of vicious frivolity, and swam on the crest of the wave. Never was her success greater, never were her admirers more numerous. Her audacity knew no limit, and the ambition that had once urged her to seek a grand and honourable marriage, now goaded her to obtain notoriety at all costs.

" Notwithstanding," declared a fashionable journal of the day, " all her foibles and the impudent sallies of her youth, which may be looked on as shades in a beautiful picture, Miss Chudleigh is the *coryphée du bon ton*, the pattern of taste, elegance, wit, and polite conversation at Court; the soul of all public diversion, and her judgment the standard of delicacy in the most sumptuous entertainments."

The public, however, were not always so indulgent to her caprices, and her conduct one night in her box at the *Beggar's Opera* was so annoying to the pit that she was literally hissed and groaned out of the theatre.

A few months later, on the return of the Duke of Hamilton from his *grand tour*, she experienced another and more bitter mortification. " He came back," said Walpole, " shattered in health, wealth, and person by the excesses to which he had been addicted on his travels." But as soon as he arrived in London he sought out Miss Chudleigh and besought her to redeem her promise. Her surprise at such an unexpected request naturally led to explanations, and her vexation may be imagined on discovering that all his letters to her had been intercepted. She was, of course, obliged to refuse him, and as she dared not give him her reason, he departed in a sulk of which he was cured some time later by the beautiful Miss Gunning who, coming as poor and as ambitious into the great world as Miss Chudleigh, had the luck to obtain all that the latter had strived for and lost.

About the same time Hervey returned from his cruise in the West Indies. Being still inflamed with passion, which time and absence had failed to cool, for the beautiful girl he had married under such romantic conditions, he made haste to claim her—secretly, of course, be it understood. But she, to whom the very thought of him had become horrible, haughtily refused to see him. His amazement at such behaviour was quickly changed to exasperation. He wrote her that unless she gave him an interview, he would divulge the secret of their marriage to the Princess of Wales. This threat had the desired effect, and she consented to visit him at his lodging in Chelsea. The interview, as may be expected, was of the stormiest character. Miss Chudleigh, or rather Mrs. Hervey, described it afterwards as an "assignation with a vengeance."

Indeed, this meeting so seriously affected the health of the maid of honour, as to oblige her to seek a change of air. The consent of the ever-indulgent Princess was readily obtained, and the maid of honour chose Chelsea, then a secluded riverside village, as the place in which to recruit, as she said. To the profligate world in which she moved, however, the most innocent indisposition of a maid of honour was sufficient to arouse suspicion, and Miss Chudleigh's, which was of a nature that the secrecy of her marriage rendered anything but innocent, was the subject of much indecent mockery.

Ever peculiarly sensitive to ridicule when the laugh was *against* her, though she could bear it well enough when it was *with* her, she attempted to silence the jests at her expense by taking the bull by the horns, so to speak.

" I hear," she said to Lord Chesterfield one day, with an

air of indifference, that people are absurd enough to say that I have had twins."

"Indeed?" he replied. "I always make a point of believing only half what the world says."

At such moments, and there are many in her career on record, the power of repartee, for which she was noted, completely deserted her.

The scandal, however, soon subsided. The Princess of Wales had no intention of losing the companionship of so congenial a maid of honour for the sake of setting an example in respectability for which she cared nothing; Society willingly took its cue from her Royal Highness, and considered Miss Chudleigh's compulsory retirement from Court, under such trying circumstances, sufficient punishment for her fault. She was, if anything, more beautiful, more captivating, and more popular than ever after this escapade, and the Duke of Ancaster, among others, carried his admiration to the length of an offer of marriage. The painful necessity of refusing so desirable a *parti*, for which she was unable to give any explanation, even to her mother, made her situation so embarrassing that she decided to go abroad for a time.

On her return she met with a cordial reception, and between an innate love of pleasure and a desire for notoriety, which had now become a passion with her, she made herself very conspicuous. But scandal was powerless to lessen the consequence Miss Chudleigh enjoyed in Society, or to damage her in the esteem of the Princess of Wales, into whose favour she ingratiated herself more and more.

Her audacity, perhaps, reached its limit at the famous masquerade given by the Venetian Ambassador, to which she went as Iphigeneia at Aulis. The accounts of her appearance in this *rôle* are familiar to all who have read the memoirs of the period.

" Miss Chudleigh's dress, or rather undress," wrote Mrs. Montagu, after describing in detail the costumes worn by some of the most notable persons present, " was remarkable. She was Iphigeneia awaiting sacrifice, but so naked that the high priest might easily have inspected the entrails of his victim. The maids of honour were so offended that they would not speak to her."

Horace Walpole was equally explicit as to the scantiness of her attire, and wrote to a friend that Iphigeneia was " so naked that she might have been taken for Andromeda ! "

On this occasion even the Princess of Wales pretended to be shocked, and laughingly threw a veil of gauze she was wearing over the nudity of her brazen maid of honour.

This freak succeeded in establishing Miss Chudleigh's reputation as a *femme galante*. George II, who was present at the masquerade, saw fit to fancy himself in love with her, and a couple of nights later went to another masquerade in the hope of meeting her. But an attack of gout—she was barely thirty—prevented her from attending ; and the old King, on learning that she would not grace the festivity, returned to St. James's in disgust. Opportunities of meeting her, however, were not lacking. At a bazaar at which she was assisting, he gave her " a watch which cost him five-and-thirty guineas—actually disbursed out of the privy purse and not charged on the civil list ! " He also shortly after gave her further proofs of his regard by kissing her in public, and bestowing on her mother the post of housekeeper at Windsor Castle, which was worth £800 a year.

After this, no wonder, as Walpole remarks, that the fame of the " virgin Chudleigh " should become " historic." Moreover, as the income of £400 a year which she received as maid of honour was totally inadequate to defray the jewels, the toilettes, and equipages with which she now sought to dazzle the town, the world agreed to charge their cost between the King and Admiral Howe, whose attentions to the beauty were no less marked than his Majesty's. So protected, there was nothing, short of publishing her marriage to Hervey, that she was not capable of doing. And to show her utter indifference to the scandal caused by her conduct, " she took charge of a child, which was said to have been found on the stairs leading to her apartment at Windsor, and strengthened the report that it was hers by giving it her own name and keeping it with her till it died."

IV

BUT if a conscience hardened by vice failed to mar the pleasures of the Bacchanalian revel in which her life was spent, the thought and the sight of her husband continually disturbed her peace of mind.

"Captain Hervey," says her principal and anonymous biographer, " like a perturbed spirit was continually crossing the path trodden by his wife. Was she in the rooms at Bath, he was sure to be there. At a rout, a ridotto, or a ball, there was this fell disturber of her peace, embittering every pleasure and blighting the fruit of happiness by the pestilential malignity of his presence."

Disillusionment had long since turned his love into resentment. Having obtained promotion in the Navy, which rendered him independent, he had no longer any reason for keeping his marriage a secret, especially as he believed that its publication would cause his wife great annoyance. Consequently he had given her a proof of his disposition to trouble her, by again threatening her with an intimation that he would inform the Princess of Wales of their marriage. But this time the shot failed to hit the target at which it was aimed. Miss Chudleigh at once told

CAPTAIN HERVEY
[*After Gainsborough*]

To face page 170

the Princess herself, counting on her mistress's friendship, which was the base of her prestige, to survive the shock. Nor was she mistaken. Though it was contrary to all the regulations of the Court for a princess to have a married woman as a maid of honour, her Royal Highness, to gratify a whim, was as capable of outraging Court etiquette as Miss Chudleigh of outraging public decency. She would not have cared if her maid of honour had confessed to bigamy.

Hervey, finding that his threat was unavailing, was left to discover other modes of annoying his wife. For him, however, to hold his peace on the subject of the marriage was impossible, and rumours that Miss Chudleigh had been secretly married to him many years now first began to circulate. But the public, so long accustomed to be regaled with sensational stories of her doings, paid little heed to this particular one, on the ground that *everything* which is reported of a person cannot be true, even though that person was Miss Chudleigh.

That, with the memory of this terrible blunder constantly before her, she should have committed another equally disastrous, is not perhaps surprising; but that the second should have been a repetition of the first is almost incredible. Nevertheless, such was the case, and as in the former, so in the latter instance it was ambition which contributed to her undoing.

In 1759, on learning that the Earl of Bristol, to whom Hervey was heir, was likely to die, Miss Chudleigh's objections to proclaiming her marriage were easily overcome. It flattered her to think that in the event of her husband's elevation to the peerage she would become Countess of Bristol, and she promised herself all the benefits and none of the disadvantages of being recognized as Hervey's wife. But on confiding her intentions to her aunt, Mrs. Hanmer, or her cousin Merrill, at whose house the marriage register of the church at Lainston was kept, she was informed that in the haste of the nocturnal marriage which Mr. Amis the rector had performed fifteen years previously, no record of the ceremony had been made in the register. As she felt certain that if Hervey was informed of this fact he would not hesitate to take advantage of it to repudiate her claim to be his wife, Miss Chudleigh immediately rushed down to Lainston and compelled the rector, who was then on his death-bed, to insert the record of her marriage in the register. But having thus, as she thought, rendered the certainty of becoming Countess of Bristol doubly certain, she discovered a while later that her cunning, like her ambition, had but overreached itself. For she had no sooner established the proof of her marriage, than the Earl of Bristol unexpectedly and completely recovered from his illness.

At the same time, to increase her mortification, she received another ducal offer of marriage. But Miss Chudleigh's seemingly eccentric aversion to matrimony failed to produce the same effect on the Duke of Kingston as it had on the Dukes of Hamilton and Ancaster. Instead of rushing off in a fit of pique to offer his strawberry leaves to another beauty by whom the honour would be duly appreciated, his infatuated Grace suggested to Miss Chudleigh that, since her objections to so humdrum a condition as wedlock were insurmountable, she should unite her career to his in a manner more in keeping with her reputation. Flattered by so significant a tribute to her charms at a period of life when age had begun to rob them of the power of fascination—she was now thirty-nine—Miss Chudleigh accepted the second proposal of his Grace with as much pleasure as she had experienced mortification in rejecting his first.

The Duke of Kingston, with whose destiny that of the elderly but still attractive maid of honour was now linked, was, says Walpole, who expressed the general opinion, "a very weak man of the greatest beauty and finest person in England." In justice, however, to his character, it must be added it was also the general opinion that his Grace was a man whom nobody could help liking. While in the opinion of Miss Chudleigh, whose senior he was by nine years, the Duke's attractions were still further augmented by the immense and unentailed fortune he possessed.

The pursuit of pleasure had ever been the chief, indeed the only, occupation of this fortunate individual. But, though naturally prone to profligacy, the Duke of Kingston had had the good luck, paradoxical as it sounds, to escape the snares of vice by forming one of those *liaisons* in which health, wealth, and reputation are so frequently lost. The unexpected virtue, so to speak, of this questionable amour was all the more remarkable from the fact of the scandal in which the latter had commenced. Believing that he could not carry back to England from Paris a more suitable souvenir of the hospitality he had received, he had persuaded the Marquise de la Touche to accompany him. Their elopement had made a great noise at the French Court, for the lady had not only left behind a husband who adored her, but three children as well. The Duke was accused of having outraged honour and decency, not to speak of having carried off one of the most beautiful ornaments of Versailles, and indignation had expressed itself in such a manner that his Grace had never since ventured to return to France.

Time, however, had caused the memory of this scandal to be all but forgotten in England. Madame de la Touche, after her lapse from virtue, had conducted herself in such an exemplary manner at Thoresby, the Duke's seat in Nottinghamshire, where they principally resided, as "to win the love of all the neighbourhood." While her influence over her lover at whose table she had "done the

honours, like a duchess, for many years," had been so
beneficial that, instead of developing into a debauchee and
rake, he had remained a mere innocuous duke.

Fate, however, determined to rescue his name from a
respectable oblivion by throwing Miss Chudleigh in his
way. From the day of their first meeting, the favour
which the Marquise de la Touche had so long enjoyed
began to decline. As soon as she realized that her reign
was drawing to a close, the Marquise refused to struggle
against the inevitable, and decided to take her departure
before she should be subjected to the shame of being
asked to go. But her fall was not without its compensa-
tions. On returning to France, she had the good fortune
to be reconciled to her husband and children, while
Society, too, agreed to forget her past. This rather
difficult feat it had successfully accomplished, and the
very name of Madame de la Touche might have been
forgotten had not the desire to be revenged on the rival by
whom she had been supplanted, tempted her some years
later to write *Les Avantures trop galantes de la Duchesse de
Kingston*, in which she sought to gloss over her own relation
to the Duke, by depicting that of her enemy in the blackest
of colours.

It was not long, of course, before Miss Chudleigh with
her passion for notoriety, and her complete indifference to
public opinion, gave the world to understand by her conduct the position in which the Duke of Kingston stood to
her. Had she been his wife she could not have enjoyed
greater consideration, or lived in greater splendour. But
warned by the fate that had overtaken Madame de la
Touche, she made haste to provide against the day when a
wrinkle or a grey hair should furnish a grave for his Grace's
love.

One of her means of enriching herself was to persuade
the Duke to make her presents of villas and lodges, and as

she had but to express a wish for it to be gratified, she
soon became the possessor of considerable landed property.
To her passion for acquiring houses, a rage for building
succeeded as a natural sequence. Having obtained from
her indulgent lover a piece of ground in Knightsbridge, as
the site of her town residence, she had the effrontery to
call the mansion erected on it Kingston House to show her
contempt of the scandal that was busy with her name.

It was now, so to speak, that Thackeray's *Beatrice*,
turned forty, became transformed into the *Baroness Bernstein*. Age having failed to sober her love of notoriety, or
avarice, that vice of advancing years, to check it, Miss
Chudleigh's actions, which no longer had the *cachet* of
youth to excuse them, startled the world by their astound-
ing eccentricity. On the completion of Kingston House
the constant whirl of excitement in which she lived urged
her to celebrate the occasion by an entertainment. For
this she made a royal birthday serve as a pretext, in order
to prove to the world that her favour in the highest
quarters was as great as ever. The splendour of the *fête*,
in which no expense was spared to make it a success, was,
as she intended, the talk of the town.

"Poor thing!" exclaimed Horace Walpole in a letter to
a friend describing it, "I fear she has thrown away above a
quarter's salary!"

À propos of this *fête*, at which all the Royal Family were
present, though "the Court was in mourning," some idea
of the extraordinary eccentricity that Miss Chudleigh
displayed on this occasion may be gathered from the
following account by Walpole:—

"A scaffold," he says with his characteristic mockery,
"was erected in Hyde Park (opposite Kingston House) for
fireworks. On each side of the courtyard were two large
scaffolds for the virgin's tradespeople. There were also
illuminations of the King and Queen, and one was a

cenotaph of the Princess Elizabeth (who had lately died), a kind of illuminated cradle with the motto : 'All the honours the dead can receive.' This burying-ground was a strange codicil to a festival, and what was more strange, about one in the morning this sarcophagus burst out into crackers and guns."

While as an illustration of the licence of the age, which sufficiently explains why the mistress of the Duke of Kingston was tolerated in the best society, Walpole adds significantly, "to show the illuminations without to more advantage, the company were received in an apartment totally dark, where they remained for two hours, which caused people to say jestingly that it would not be surprising if Miss Chudleigh's *fête* was the cause of more birthdays."

In other words, the standard of morals, which in spite of the moralists changes from age to age, permitted society at this period to recognize a duke's mistress.

It was also on this occasion that the Princess of Wales, forgetting the bond of union between herself and Lord Bute, laughingly rebuked her favourite for the precisely similar relation that existed between the latter and the Duke of Kingston. Whereupon Miss Chudleigh, who was always famous for her power of repartee, cleverly retorted—

" *Votre Altesse sait que chacun a son But(e).*"

V

NOTORIOUS as all Miss Chudleigh's actions still continued to be, they were at least now free from the reproach of gallantry that had rendered them so conspicuous previous to her intimacy with the Duke of Kingston. She was, says Walpole, "chaster as Kingston's mistress than as

AUGUSTA, PRINCESS OF WALES
[*From an old German print*]

Hervey's wife." Her belated respectability was, however, due less to any inclination she had suddenly conceived for virtue than to a sordid desire to render herself indispensable to her rich lover. In this she succeeded so well that she eventually secured both his title and his fortune.

But the complete subjection of the Duke was not effected without a struggle. His Grace did not consider an occasional infidelity on his part as being in the least inconsistent with his devotion to his elderly mistress. Miss Chudleigh, on the contrary, held quite a different opinion, and supported it in a manner that had her lover been less enslaved, must have snapped the chain by which she held him. At last, finding that words had no effect on the Duke, she had recourse to deeds.

Being informed at some Court function that he had taken "a pretty milliner from Cranborn Alley down to Thoresby," her vexation was so great that she decided to take a course of the waters at Carlsbad in order to teach him, by absence, to miss her.

With this object she had a special and very singular travelling coach built, which she equipped with every possible contrivance conducive to comfort, and when it was ready she set out with a troop of servants. Instead of going direct to Carlsbad, her eccentric habits led her first to Berlin. Here the friendliness with which she was welcomed by Frederick the Great so flattered her vanity that she prolonged her visit to his capital, which she electrified by an extravagant and dissipated mode of life. She even went to the length of giving the Prussian Court an illustration of the manner in which she had acquired and maintained her prestige at the Court of England. Frederick, describing in a letter to the Electress of Saxony the wedding festivities of his nephew, wrote that "nothing particular happened to distinguish them from any similar occasion except the appearance of an English lady, a Miss

12

Chudleigh, who, after having emptied a couple of bottles, staggered so in dancing that she almost fell on the floor."

Frederick was, however, too accustomed to such exhibitions among the ladies and gentlemen of his own Court to take offence, and as his extraordinary visitor saw fit to apologize by sending him "an English plough" as a present, he took advantage of the occasion to honour her with a specimen of his doggerel verses, in which he sang the praises both of herself and the plough. It was on the strength of this honour and some letters he wrote her, that Miss Chudleigh in later years was wont to boast of "my great friend the King of Prussia."

She was destined to have the satisfaction of being able to include the Empress Catherine and the Pope in the list of her royal friendships. But perhaps on none of the Crowned Heads of Europe, whose recognition she converted into intimacy to enhance her own importance, did she make so great an impression as on the Electress of Saxony. The name of Miss Chudleigh had long been familiar to this princess from the dispatches of the Saxon envoy in London. For in those days diplomatic dispatches —especially in times of peace—were chiefly composed of all the social tittle-tattle of the Courts to which their writers were accredited, and since the doings of the "virgin Chudleigh" had for years been one of the chief topics of conversation at St. James's, they had likewise formed an important feature of the Saxon minister's correspondence. The Electress, who had found in this correspondence all the enjoyment afforded by a racy society novel, was naturally anxious to meet a woman of whom she had heard so much, and in whom she recognized a kindred spirit. Consequently, when she heard that the original of the heroine of her English envoy's dispatches was in Berlin, she became most anxious "to possess her at Dresden."

As the Saxon Court lay on the road to Carlsbad, Miss

Chudleigh was only too pleased to gratify her own vanity and the Electoral curiosity. The Electress, whom her conduct was incapable of shocking, found her all and more than she had hoped. Indeed, so gracious was the " virgin's " reception, so close the intimacy between her and the Saxon princess, that it is a wonder she ever returned to England at all.

Anxiety, however, as to whether the Duke of Kingston had learnt the lesson she had set him, at length urged her to tear herself away. I do not know if she ever got as far as Carlsbad, or if, as Lord Chesterfield declared, she ever really had the slightest intention of going there, but her Continental tour certainly effected all she desired. In spite of the racketing and tippling in which she had indulged, she returned in blooming health, and found to her delight that the Duke *had* learnt his lesson. He swore never again to have any commerce with bewitching milliners or actresses, and to emphasize his intention to remain faithful to one who was so necessary to his happiness as Miss Chudleigh, he besought her once more to become his duchess.

She had never ceased to regret that second visit to Lainston, when she had, of her own accord, so to speak, remarried the husband she hated. But for that unfortunate indiscretion, she might successfully have defied Hervey to prove she was his wife, and have been the Duchess of Kingston these ten years. The anxiety she had suffered from the numerous infidelities of the Duke had embittered these regrets, and when his Grace offered her marriage on her return from her German tour, Miss Chudleigh's audacity, encouraged by the friendship of her Crowned Heads, led her to take the first step in what was to prove the most audacious act of her whole life.

Shortly after her arrival in London from Dresden, Hervey approached her with a proposal for divorce. Much as she desired her freedom, she was, however, unwilling to obtain it in this way. Utterly careless how she shocked or startled the world, no one was more careful than she to save herself from its laugh. Ridicule was, in fact, the only thing of which she was afraid, and since to inform the world that she had been Hervey's wife all these years, as she would be obliged to do, would but expose her folly as a welcome target to the malice of her enemies, she utterly declined her husband's proposal.

She, however, was ready with a counter-proposal, which was only capable of originating in a head so eccentric as hers. This was to bring an action against Hervey, who should enable her to do so by reviving the old rumours of their marriage with which he had persecuted her in her youth. Whereby, swearing that she had never been legally married to him at all, a perjury in which he would support her by failing to disprove her, she would obtain the nullification of the marriage.

"She could," she said, "easily reconcile this oath to her conscience, particularly as the ceremony was so scrambling and shabby a business that she might as safely swear that she was not married as that she was."

Seeing the position in which he would be placed by such a suit, Hervey naturally refused in his turn, and sent her word that "he would see her damned before he would help to make her a duchess."

Knowing, however, that he was quite as anxious as herself to be free, and aware that he had a pressing need of money, she overcame his resistance by the offer of a heavy bribe Hervey now fell in with her plan with a display of energy that was a little too zealous to be altogether agreeable to her vanity. It goaded her, nevertheless, to the proper pitch of indignation and removed whatever fear she had of the exposure of her perjury, which the absence of any witnesses failed to disclose. Her marriage with Hervey was declared void, and he was restrained from molesting her " to the great danger of his soul's health, no small prejudice to the honourable Elizabeth Chudleigh, and the pernicious example to others." He was also sentenced to pay a fine. Such a case was naturally a nine days' wonder, but its result failed to convince the public. Rumours of Hervey's collusion were rife, and people even went so far as to state the exact sum he had been paid. It was said to be £14,000, which was probably a correct estimate; and since Miss Chudleigh was herself known to be many thousands of pounds in debt at the time, public opinion naturally concluded that the Duke of Kingston had paid the bribe.

" A grosser artifice," declared the Attorney General at the Duchess of Kingston's trial for bigamy some years later, "than this suit was, I believe, never fabricated."

Freed from Hervey, Miss Chudleigh, now forty-nine, was at last enabled to gratify her ambition which she made haste to do. Her marriage to the Duke of Kingston was celebrated by the Archbishop of Canterbury with great pomp. The presence of the King and Queen at the wedding manifested the high favour she enjoyed at Court. But Society, which had previously been willing enough to shut its eyes to the notorious connection between Miss Chudleigh and the Duke of Kingston, saw fit to disapprove of the ceremony which rendered the connection respectable. At Thoresby the " county " refused to call on the new duchess. The marks of royal esteem, however, which she had received, and a marriage settlement of £4000 a year more than compensated her Grace for her vanished popularity.

It was not long before the Duke had occasion to wonder, like Society, how he had come to be inveigled into matrimony. He had looked forward to settling down quietly on one of his numerous estates; unfortunately, the Duchess had a restless disposition, and insisted on carrying him

about with her from place to place in search of amusement, which she loved as strongly at fifty as she had done
at twenty.   Nor when found, would she consent to enjoy it
alone. Pleasure, she declared, was no pleasure to her unless
" her dear lord," as she called the Duke, shared it with her.
Thus having taken a fancy to fishing, which developed into
a passion, she would spend whole days, regardless of
weather, with rod in hand, always accompanied by her
unfortunate husband, " whose boots, like her own, she filled
with rum to keep him from catching cold."

" On these occasions," says the Duke's valet, in a scurril-
ous little book he wrote on the Duchess, who dismissed
him, " I have known her use two quarts in a day, being
obliged to change her clothes twice or thrice during this
time, and standing from morning till evening in the wet,
sometimes too without catching a single fish.   Indeed, I
believe every pound of fish she caught cost the Duke five
guineas."

He had, moreover, not only to endure her vagaries but
her temper as well.   " Quarrel," to quote the valet again,
" they did not, for it takes two to make a quarrel ; and the
Duke was by nature shy, gentle, and courteous.   But she
hectored and domineered over him, dismissed his servants,
directed his actions, and covered him with mortification by
her passionate and violent behaviour, both in public and
private."

After four years of this slavery, his Grace was suddenly
stricken with paralysis.   The Duchess, whose treatment of
her husband had embittered, if not shortened, his life, now
did all in her power to prolong it.   But while she
"journeyed him about with the futile idea of retarding the
irrevocable decree of Omnipotence by means of a change
of air," her anxiety was increased by the most sordid
consideration of her own future welfare.

In anticipation of her widowhood, for which his delicate

health had prepared her, she had shortly after her marriage induced the Duke, whose title would die with him, to make a will in her favour, by which she would inherit his entire fortune. This his Grace had done, but influenced more by a desire to disinherit a nephew whom he disliked than to prove his affection for his wife, he had attached a condition to his bequest by which she would forfeit her fortune if she married again.

The Duchess was aware of this humiliating restriction to her future freedom, and had endeavoured in vain to get it removed. But she was not the woman to accept defeat while there was the least possibility of overcoming it, or to consider the morality of the means she employed. Consequently, when she finally realized that her efforts to save the Duke were useless, she sent "her swiftest footed messenger to her solicitor." When this gentleman, a certain Mr. Field, arrived, the Duchess desired him to execute another will for the Duke to sign, in which the annoying restriction should be removed. But Field, finding the Duke to be in a state of imbecility, utterly refused to oblige her. The Duchess was, of course, highly incensed, but the honesty of the lawyer served her far better than his complicity would have done. For had the Duke's nephews in their furious efforts to upset the validity of his will been able to prove that he had signed it at a time when he was incapable of knowing what he was doing, she would undoubtedly have been stripped of everything. Whereas in the day of adversity, the condition which she had deemed so offensive proved a blessing in disguise.

VI

ON the death of the Duke of Kingston, the Duchess appeared overwhelmed with grief. Between Bath where he died and Thoresby where she buried him, she "had a fit at every place where the body of her dear lord halted." But the grave had no sooner closed over him than she regained her wonted cheerfulness. As soon as she could arrange her affairs, she decided to travel, and never having been to Italy, she chose Rome as her destination.

Her reception here was similar to that which she had experienced at Berlin and Dresden. Ganganelli, under the title of Clement XIV, held the Papal throne. The moderation and tolerance which he displayed on every occasion, had won him the *soubriquet* of the "Protestant Pope." To such a character, the rich and unconventional Duchess was a welcome visitor, and his gallant Holiness carried the toleration for which he was noted to the point of assigning her as a lodging, the palace of one of his cardinals, and according her the privileges of a sovereign prince.

In return for this hospitality, the Duchess, remembering the old Romans' love of spectacles, determined to provide their amiable and degenerate descendants with one. She had, during the Duke's life, had a yacht built, in those days as great a novelty as in these a luxury, and to amuse the Romans as well as to advertise her wealth, which now and not beauty opened to her the doors of Courts, she ordered it to be brought to Italy and conveyed up the Tiber.

The yacht on its arrival proved all she had expected of it. The Romans compared her to Cleopatra. She became the queen of fashion, and spent enormous sums in balls, *fêtes* and equipages—in short, on everything that could afford her an opportunity of exercising her passion for display. She had a theatre, which cost her, in singers and dancers, more than the revenue of many Italian states, and at her own expense she one night illuminated the Colosseum.

Favoured with the friendship of the Pope, enjoying a splendid income and all the prestige of rank and popularity, the Duchess of Kingston seemed to be floating more serenely on the crest of the wave of Fortune than at any time in her life. Nevertheless, while she was revelling in all these extravagant follies, events were shaping themselves in England which were to plunge her from the zenith to the nadir.

Ann Cradock, the maid of her aunt, Mrs. Hanmer, and now the only surviving witness of her marriage with Hervey thirty years before, finding herself reduced in circumstances, applied to Field, the Duchess's solicitor, for relief. He refused her the slightest assistance and also to believe her story of the Duchess's first marriage, which for a family solicitor was injudicious in the first case, and rash in the second. For Cradock, finding him impervious to pity, threatened to blackmail his client. But this threat, which had not the slightest effect on Field, who in spite of his integrity was, it must be confessed, scrupulous to stupidity, had dire results for the Duchess.

Driven from Field's office, Ann Cradock went straight to the house of Evelyn Meadows, the disinherited nephew of the Duke of Kingston, and told him her story. Meadows, who had succeeded neither to the title nor the fortune of his uncle, was only too glad of the opportunity to exploit the bigamy of the Duchess. He at once befriended Cradock, and having consulted with his lawyers, brought a bill of indictment for bigamy against the supposed Duchess. Field had notice of the procedure, and now, thoroughly alarmed, sent to urge her Grace to return in order to prevent outlawry.

Realizing her situation, she resolved to return at once. To procure the money needful for the journey she applied to Jenkins, the English banker in Rome who had, says the *Authentic Detail* contemptuously, "acquired a large property by small means, commencing with the purchase of a little finger of a mutilated statue and ending as banker to all the British travellers who visit the tutelary residence of St. Peter." But the same post which had brought Field's letter to the Duchess, brought one to Jenkins from her adversaries, which induced him to conspire with them to prevent her return by withholding the money she required. This he had no right whatever to do, since he held securities on her account which fully guaranteed him against any sum she was likely to need. To refuse her demand, there-fore, placed him in an awkward position, from which he could think of no more skilful means of extricating himself than to be out when she called.

After calling several times at his office and meeting with the same reply, her Grace naturally imputed his conduct to design. So "she pocketed a brace of pistols with which she always travelled to defend her diamonds," and returned again to the banker's, where, on receiving the same reply as before, "she sat down on the steps of his door and declared she would remain there, were it a week, a month, or a year." Thus out-manœuvred, Jenkins at length appeared, and as the Duchess was blessed with that fiery eloquence with which women of spirit are frequently famous, the banker's conversion was not of the gentlest. He even then attempted to prevaricate, but the pro-duction of the pistols on her part produced the money on his.

Depositing her plate and other valuables in the Papal Bank for greater security and leaving her palace and its

contents to the care of a young English maid, her Grace
now set out hurriedly for England. But the strain of her
ordeal with Jenkins, and her growing anxiety as to what
might await her in England, threw her into a fever before
she reached the Alps. For a few days her attendants
despaired of her life, but though the fever abated her fear
increased as she proceeded. At Calais the knowledge of
her guilt and the vindictiveness of her enemies again brought
her to a halt. In imagination she already saw herself " in
the worst cell of the worst prison of London," so before
running her neck of her own accord into the noose, she
cautiously endeavoured to assure herself of her safety. An
interview with the famous Earl of Mansfield, who chanced
to be passing through Calais to Paris, and who had been
one of her many admirers long years before, in the days of
her beauty, reassured her sufficiently to enable her to cross
the Channel. On her arrival in London she went at once
to Kingston House where every preparation had been made
to receive her.

Misfortune is the test of friendship, and while it carries
away in its flood the glittering favour and flattery of the
world it seldom fails to leave behind some jewel of the lost
treasure sparkling in the mud. In men from whom she
had no right to expect consideration the Duchess found
active and zealous friends. The Duke of Ancaster, among
others, came forward with offers of assistance which were
eagerly welcomed. Bail was found for her, she was told
that the ecclesiastical decree which had freed her from
Hervey was, like Fate, irrevocable. Thus encouraged by
her solicitors and her powerful friends she became quite
reconciled to the dangers of the trial.

The reputation of the Duchess and the revelations that
were expected at the trial excited public interest to a high
pitch. Under such circumstances it was of course impossible, with her love of notoriety, that she should fail to feed

the curiosity of which she was so prominent an object. She rehearsed in public the *rôle* in which she was about to appear as the star in the great legal drama at the House of Lords. To acquire, so to speak, the air of the law, she enveloped herself in the atmosphere of the bar. Gentlemen of the robe were in constant attendance on her. State trials formed the staple subject of her conversation. Her drawing-room was turned into a law library, or rather into a lawyer's office. "Books of cases were purchased in abundance, precedents were blotted with ink, pages doubled down and pins stuck in the several notes of references." While, instead of taking the air in her coach with her "diamonds at her back," as she was wont, she stuffed her carriage with Taylor's *Elements of Civil Law*, Cooke's *Institutes*, and "some history of the Privileges of the Peers to be doubly married."

But in the midst of all this absurd display of indifference while waiting for the trial, her Grace's peace of mind was suddenly disturbed by a blow from quite a different quarter. Samuel Foote, the playwright, who was at this time at the zenith of his fame, having become acquainted with the principal events in the Duchess's life, determined to use them as "copy." He therefore wrote a farce which he called a "Trip to Calais," in which the chief character was a gross caricature of her Grace under the name of Lady Kitty Crocodile.

Foote wrote this piece less with the idea of giving the public the benefit of his wit than with the intention of using it as a means of extorting a sum of money from the Duchess to suppress it. With this end in view he contrived to let her know by a third person that the Haymarket Theatre would produce the play in which she was "hit off to the life." The Duchess hereupon sent for Foote, who took the play with him to prove by reading it to her, he said, that the report she had heard was unfounded.

SAMUEL FOOTE

To face page 188

Obtaining her consent he proceeded to read, selecting scenes in which the allusions were only too evidently meant for herself. Her indignation finally boiled over, and she exclaimed—

"This is scandalous! Why, what a wretch you have made me!"

"You, Madam!" replied Foote in mock astonishment, "this is not designed for your Grace, it is not you!"

Forcing herself to be calm, she begged him to leave the piece for her own perusal. He readily complied. But its perusal thoroughly convinced the Duchess that Kitty Crocodile was a caricature of herself. As she had ever been particularly sensitive to ridicule, and dreaded it more than ever at the present moment, she wrote Foote the next day asking if he would sell her the play and what sum he wanted for suppressing it. Carried away by the success of his plot to extort money from her, and his own greed, the knave had the boldness to ask £2,000, by which in the end he got nothing.

Staggered by such a demand, she offered him fourteen and then sixteen hundred pounds, and actually had a cheque drawn for this amount. But Foote would not abate one guinea of his original price. This species of blackmail, which was perhaps the more immoral in that it was unindictable, might not at any other time have attracted much notice, but on the present occasion it was so clearly a low advantage taken against a woman when least able to resent it that her friends chivalrously came to her rescue. The Lord Chamberlain was apprised of the circumstance, and he forthwith forbade the performance of the play. This led to a remonstrance from Foote, who, discovering that his greed had lost him everything, threatened to publish the play as a book. But here again he over-reached himself, for the Duchess, acting on the advice of her friends, threatened in such an event to prosecute him for extortion. This alarmed Foote and he wrote to apologize to her Grace.

Delighted at her triumph, the Duchess was fired with the desire to "rub it into" her persecutor. To Foote's apology she therefore made the following characteristic reply—

"SIR,

"I was at dinner when I received your ill-judged letter. As there is little consideration required I shall sacrifice a moment to answer it. I know too well what is due to my own dignity to enter into a compromise with an extortionable assassin of private reputation. If I have abhorred you for your slander I now despise you for your concession; it is a proof of the illiberality of your satire when you can publish it or suppress it as best suits the needy convenience of your purse. You first had the cowardly baseness to draw the sword, and, if I sheath it until I make you crouch like the subservient vassal as you are, there is no spirit in an injured woman nor meanness in a slanderous buffoon.

"To a man my sex alone would have screened me from attack, but I am writing to the descendant of a merry-andrew, and I should prostitute the name of manhood by applying it to the name of Mr. Foote.

"Clothed in innocence as in a coat of mail, I am proof against a host of foes; and conscious of never having intentionally injured a single individual, I doubt not but a brave and generous public will protect me from the malevolence of a theatrical assassin. You shall have cause to remember that though I would have given liberally for the relief of your necessities, I scorn to be bullied into a purchase of your silence.

"There is something, however, in your pity at which my nature revolts. I will keep the pity you send until the morning before you are turned off, when I will return it by a Cupid with a box of lip salve, and a choir of choristers shall chaunt a stave to your requiem.

"E. KINGSTON.

"*Kingston House, Sunday,* 13*th August,* 1775."

That the Duchess should have *felt* as she did is excusable, but nothing could have been more ill-advised than to have *written* in such a strain. It was a dangerous letter to address to such a man as Foote, whose wit and satire had gained him the name of the English Aristophanes. His reply was scathing in its mockery. Till his apology the affair had been private, but exasperated by his defeat, Foote now published the correspondence, whereby, to her Grace's mortification, he at least succeeded in getting the laugh of the town on his side.

But the Duchess would not let the matter drop. Giving the rein to her resentment she employed one "Parson" Jackson, an Irish adventurer of the lowest type, to attack Foote with his own weapons in a gutter newspaper of which he was the editor. To Jackson's attacks Foote replied by changing the title of the censored "Trip to Calais" to "The Capuchin," in which he suppressed his caricature of the Duchess and inserted one instead of Jackson, whom he lashed under the name of Dr. Viper. Thus altered, the piece was produced at the Haymarket, and, by reason of the well-known circumstances to which it owed its conception, met with considerable success.

The affair having now become a quarrel between Foote and Jackson, the Duchess had an excellent opportunity of withdrawing from the extremely undignified situation in which she had placed herself. But Jackson, smarting under Foote's lash and anxious for vengeance, easily persuaded her to believe that Dr. Viper of "The Capuchin" was really another Lady Kitty Crocodile of "The Trip to Calais" made more offensive than ever. Thus egged on by Jackson, the Duchess wrote a letter to the *Evening Post*, to which, as Walpole says, "not the lowest of her class who tramp in pattens would have set their mark."

On the strength of the charges contained in this letter Foote was arrested, but acquitted at his trial, in which he had the full sympathy of the public. His spirit, however, had been broken by the malevolence with which he had been persecuted; he gave up his theatre and died the following year. But pity he does not deserve. Popular and successful though his plays were he was less a playwright than a blackmailer, the more dangerous because the blackmail he levied was unindictable. Received, by virtue of his brilliant wit, "in the first circles of fashion," he had thrived for years on his libels till he fell foul of the Duchess of Kingston.

The manner in which she had given him his quietus caused her to lose, at the moment when she had most need of it, the respect and sympathy of the public. In a sketch of this kind it is unnecessary to recapitulate her trial for bigamy in detail. Its fame has made it classic among *causes célèbres* in England. Corruption characterized the whole proceedings both before and during the trial. Witnesses were bribed on both sides; on the Duchess's an attempt was even made to purchase Ann Cradock, though without success. Nor was Justice itself unwilling to be bought. It was intimated to the Duchess before the trial that if she would pay £10,000 the proceedings against her should be stopped! It would have been well for her had she accepted this offer. Her legal advisers, however, who had no desire to be docked of a farthing of their fees, urged her to refuse. One eminent lawyer, to whom she paid £20 for every consultation, which he made so frequent that he almost lived in her house, and who afterwards assisted to convict her, declared that "he would forfeit his right hand and reputation if her Grace had anything to fear."

As may be expected, the interest manifested by the public in this trial was extraordinary. During the five days it lasted five thousand persons were admitted to watch the proceedings, including the Queen and most of the Royal Family. But it was a generation whose favour Elizabeth Chudleigh no longer enjoyed. From the first it was evident that the feeling was against her. Hannah More, who was among the spectators, wrote, "she had small remains of that beauty of which kings and princes were once enamoured." The Duchess, however, appeared courageous, or brazen enough; but if outwardly calm "no tongue," she confessed in her memoirs, "could describe the tortures she endured." To keep up her spirits she resorted to the extraordinary expedient of "being bled every time she left the bar"!

With such a stage it goes without saying that the Duchess should live up to her reputation for eccentricity, which employed in her youth as an advertisement had become second nature from the practice of years. Consequently, besides being bled every day of the trial, her Grace endeavoured to create the impression of innocence by clothing herself in white, a colour adopted as well by some lady friends who supported her at the bar of the House of Lords. Moreover, although she had engaged counsel, she undertook her own defence, and spoke, she says, "with a lucidity and precision that could not be surpassed by the most experienced lawyer."

As a matter of fact, overwhelmed by the unexpected strength of the evidence against her, the Duchess scarcely defended herself at all. Her conviction was a matter of course. She was deprived of her ducal title and condemned to death, which was then the punishment for

13

bigamy. On hearing her sentence she fainted, but " soon recovered, aided by a good conscience " and pleaded the privilege of a peeress for exemption from so terrible a fate. This privilege she was entitled to claim, for in disproving her right to be known as Duchess of Kingston the trial had established the fact that she was Countess of Bristol, Hervey having finally succeeded to the title. For a peeress the punishment for bigamy was to be branded on the palm of the hand, but as the case was without precedent it was uncertain whether the branding was done with a hot or a cold iron. The Attorney-General was for the former torture ; Lord Camden for the latter. Such a divergency of opinion reduced the sentence to an absurdity, and on the advice of her old friend, Lord Chief Justice Mansfield, who declared that she had already been punished severely enough, she was at once liberated.

The trial was one of the biggest legal farces ever played in this country, but by upsetting the decision of the Ecclesiastical Court, on the strength of which Miss Chudleigh had married the Duke of Kingston, it established for the future the inferiority of that Court to the Civil Jurisdiction.

But the vengeance of the Duke's nephews was not satisfied. To deprive the woman he had married of her title was nothing in comparison with depriving her of her fortune. In doing this they had not the ghost of a chance, and only succeeded in ruining themselves in the attempt. They, however, obtained a writ against the Duchess, who though no longer possessing any right to the title, still continued to use it, and to be known by it. But she was too quick for them. Informed that the writ was to be served on her, she sent out invitations to a grand dinner at Kingston House, and causing her carriage, which was well known in London, to be driven about the principal streets to give the impression she had no intention of quitting the

Representation of the Trial of the Dutchess of Kingston

THE TRIAL OF THE DUCHESS OF KINGSTON
[*From an old print*]

country, she slipped off in disguise the same night to Dover and crossed to Calais in an open boat.

She was never seen in England again, never daring to return, from a wholesome fear of the law of which she had shown her contempt, and which prides itself on neither forgiving nor forgetting a slight.

VII

THE love of change and excitement which had ever characterized the Duchess of Kingston did not abate with years. Exiled from England, this restlessness developed in her a spirit of vagrancy, rivalling that which possessed the Wandering Jew. Flitting ostentatiously from place to place, surrounded by sycophants and adventurers who preyed on her vanity and her fortune, tricked, duped, ridiculed and *fêted* wherever she went, her name acquired a European notoriety. In Poland a Prince Radzivill "lived only on her smile," but the Duke of Kingston's restraining condition, on which she enjoyed the use of his great fortune, caused her to refuse his hand. At Munich her "dear Electress" of Saxony, who was on a visit to her brother, the Elector of Bavaria, caused this prince to welcome her with open arms. In her declining years the Duchess had two stock topics of conversation—her friendship with Crowned Heads and her "persecutions." To help her to forget the latter the Elector created her Countess of Warth. Her "dear friend the King of Prussia" gave her the warmest invitation to reside in Berlin, while the King of France, she boasted, "could refuse her nothing." Maria Theresa was apparently the only sovereign who refused to receive her.

There are many piquant and astonishing stories related

of the Duchess of Kingston, from which a better idea of her bizarre character at this period of her life may be formed than from any portrait it is possible to draw of her. Like most of these stories, the following is grossly malicious, nevertheless it is worth repeating for the cleverness of the caricature, in which the resemblance to her Grace is unmistakable. It is so like "Lady Kitty Crocodile" that Foote might have been the author had he been alive when the incident occurred. The story in question is taken from a curious book entitled *An Authentic Detail of Particulars Relative to the Late Duchess of Kingston.*

It should be stated by way of preface that the Duchess, on leaving Rome for England prior to her trial, had left the palace she occupied in charge of a lady companion—a handsome young English girl—and a Spanish friar whom she had employed as a sort of major-domo. This fellow had taken advantage of the Duchess's absence to seduce the girl, after which he had made off with everything of value in the palace that he could conveniently dispose of. The news of this affair reached the Duchess during her residence at Calais, where she resided for some months after her flight from England, in order to watch the progress of the action in which her husband's nephews, having deprived her of his title, were endeavouring to strip her of his fortune. Her Grace hereupon instantly set out for Rome to secure what remained of her property, if not to recover what had been stolen.

"On her arrival," says the author of the *Authentic Detail,* "the question was how the property embezzled by the friar could be re-obtained. The girl sobbed, shed tears in abundance, on her knees entreated forgiveness, but with all this submissive penitence she could scarcely obtain a moment's attention.

"'You must have known the friar broke open the escritoire,' exclaimed her Grace. 'Where are the candlesticks?

What ! is all the linen gone ? By the living God, he has stripped the palace !'

" ' Indeed, your Grace,' pleaded the girl, ' I—he——'

" ' I wish that you were both in the galleys. What is all your nonsense to my property ? Could not you play the fool together without robbing me ? The diamond buckle of my dear lord duke ! The devil confound the villain ! Find him, hussy, or I'll have you punished !'

" Here a message of condolence from his Holiness was notified, and the messenger being ushered in, the Duchess changed her manner to suit the occasion thus—

" ' What I have lost is of considerable value; but to take advantage of a poor innocent young creature is more distressful to me than the trifles he has taken. My dearest lord left me an ample fortune ; I wish to make others happy with it. This unfortunate girl I took from a child, and meant to have provided for her as a mother. I forgive her, poor thing ! My most humble and dutiful respects to his Holiness. *Hélas !* When I think of my troubles they almost overwhelm me. With my dear duke (tears) every happiness was buried. But God is all-sufficient. His Holiness knows how I have been persecuted ; but I forgive my persecutors. Poor Belisarius ! how ungenerously was he treated ! I often thought of him during my persecution. . . .' "

In the following story her Grace is seen in quite another aspect. This episode, which might be called the "Duchess as the victim of Adventurers," has been described by various persons likewise after the manner of Foote, to whose treatment it is admirably adapted. This particular version, however, has the merit of being by her Grace herself. It should be observed that the heroine of the tale speaks of herself as a stranger, and with all the impartiality of an uninterested person.

"During a visit to Italy, when she ruled almost like a sovereign at Rome, she one day received a visit from an Albanian prince named Worta, who was certainly the handsomest man that nature ever produced. He was magnificently dressed, absolutely glittering with jewels, from the waving plume of his hat to the brilliant hilt of his sword. The Duchess of Kingston was no longer young, but she still retained sufficient of that beauty which had once ranked her as the loveliest woman in England to make her believe Prince Worta when he vowed her charms had subdued his heart. She loved him with that excess of passion that is felt by some as they decline in years, when they seem to gather all the energies of their being into one last effort of tenderness. This strange passion conquered all the lesser feelings of her soul. Their marriage was decided on, but deferred until the Prince should return from Holland.

"Meanwhile the Turkish Ambassador at Paris considered it his duty to make some inquiries about this Prince Worta, and he searched and searched until he at length discovered that the fascinating Prince was only a Greek adventurer of the worst character, who had fled from Constantinople to escape the punishment of a theft. The pretended Prince was arrested and put in prison. Next morning when the gaoler visited his cell he found him dead, poisoned by a liquid which he had concealed in a ring, and which he always carried about him for use in case of detection. On his table lay the following letter, addressed to the Duchess of Kingston, which gave a correct idea of this singular man and proved the falsehood of the report that her Grace was aware of his true character.

"'Elizabeth, I do not write to you to justify myself, or to say that I have been the victim of human injustice. No, I am above that; I acknowledge that I am really guilty. But I am not an everyday culprit. I entered the lists against Fate, and was for a time successful; now it is her turn, I am overcome and I yield.

"'I admit that I am but a low adventurer, born in the humblest grade of society. I acknowledge that I merited the punishment which I should have received had I not fled from Constantinople, and I know that I am unworthy of the love you gave me. Well, with the sole resources of my own genius, by the single aid of my own unconquerable will, I have given myself the education which fortune denied. I have acquired the manners and deportment of a prince, though my father was only an ass-driver at Trebizond. Which of your powdered puppets, born to wealth and titles, could have done as much?

"'Farewell, Elizabeth, farewell. In one short hour my career in the world will be at an end. Farewell again, but not for ever—we shall yet meet in the home of souls like ours, where, stripped of earthly prejudices, each shall be judged upon his individual merits. Until this happy day, farewell, farewell, beloved!'

"This unfortunate event," she goes on to say, "nearly overwhelmed the Duchess. Her crushed affections and her wounded pride waged fearful warfare in her breast; but she was obliged to meet Society, to cloak her agony in smiles, and hide from a censorious and ill-judging world the struggle that rent her soul."

It was on this occasion that, being invited to visit some famous tombs, she made the reply: "Ce n'est pas la peine de chercher des tombeaux, on en porte assez dans son cœur."

This Worta was, as he said, "no everyday culprit," but a brilliant adventurer of the picturesque type peculiar to the eighteenth century. His real name was Stefano Zannowich, and he was the son of an Albanian pedlar whose trade, assisted by gambling, had been sufficiently profitable to enable him to educate his son at the University of Padua. It was here, no doubt, that he developed his poetical gifts. A volume of poems by him is extant which prove him to have been endowed with a strong sense of beauty, feeling, and romance. On leaving Padua at eighteen he travelled over Europe, and on returning to Italy conceived the idea of freeing Albania. This led him to declare that he was a descendant of the famous Albanian hero George Kastrioti or Scanderbeg, and to assume the title of Prince of Albania. Failing to gain the credit he anticipated among his compatriots, he then took the name of Worta and went to Poland, where his insinuating appearance and address gained him the esteem of several noble Poles, from whom he obtained considerable money. In Albania he had written a Life of Scanderbeg; in Poland he wrote a book on the future of the Poles; both works, like his poems, breathed the spirit of patriotism. On leaving Poland he travelled through Germany under several aliases. In Berlin he procured an introduction to Prince Henry of Prussia, the brother of Frederick the Great, and made the most of the favourable impression he created on him.

He was next heard of in Holland, where he passed as a priest, and was imprisoned for debt. The deplorable state in which a visiting magistrate found him, coupled with the peculiar charm of his manners, excited such pity in the magistrate that he paid the adventurer's debts and released him. His second arrest was due to the detection of a gigantic swindle which he perpetrated on the Dutch Government. To escape punishment he committed suicide. The strangest trait in his character was sensibility, which is scarcely to be expected of one who lived entirely by duping others. He appears to have become warmly attached to his various dupes, and his letter to the Duchess was probably sincere.

VIII

THERE were times when the spirits of vagrancy and
vanity which possessed the Duchess of Kingston would
combine to entice her to render herself conspicuous.
Perhaps their most successful effort was that which inspired
her to visit the Court of Russia. She had long desired to
add the Empress Catherine to the list of her crowned
friends, and when on returning from Rome to Calais she
learnt that the action to upset the Duke of Kingston's will
had failed, she determined to realize this desire. The distance
and difficulties of such a journey were no obstacle to her,
though she was now past sixty.

"To go from Calais to Petersburg," she said, "is like
going from London to Hampton Court."

As the journey was invariably made by land, her Grace
resolved to reverse this custom and go by sea. For this
purpose she had a vessel specially built which was "as
comfortable as a hotel." Like the coach in which many
years before she had made the "circle of Germany," it was
a curiosity worthy of inspection, and the talk it occasioned
attracted great attention to the Duchess's forthcoming
adventure. This was exactly what she desired, and she
took advantage of the general curiosity her luxurious yacht
excited to form an acquaintance with the Russian Ambassador in Paris, as the person best suited to furnish her with
the letters of introduction she required, and which, owing to
her disgrace, she could not obtain in England.

Since the main object of the journey was to obtain the
friendship of the Empress, her Grace determined to make
her bid for it in advance by adding to Catherine's art
treasures at the Hermitage a Raphael and a Claude
Lorraine from the Duke's collection at Thoresby, which

she believed to be clever copies, but which turned out to be originals of great value. "This," says the *Authentic Detail*, "occasioned as many conferences between the Duchess and the Ambassador as would have been requisite to adjust the differences of Europe."

The manner, indeed, in which this Russian tour of the Duchess of Kingston was stage-managed, so to speak, both by accident and design, was well calculated to excite the curiosity of the Muscovites. England being at war with her American colonies, to avoid being captured by the privateers of the latter, with which the seas swarmed, the Duchess placed her vessel under the French flag. This made it necessary to hire a French crew, the selection of whom almost occasioned a mutiny, for they refused to sail under her English captain, an old and experienced servant. He was, therefore, summarily dismissed, and his place given to "the master of a fishing smack, who undertook to brave the billows of the Baltic."

As for her Grace's suite, its composition was even more sensational than the incidents connected with that of the crew. "Depending on her choice," says one of her biographers, "it was as whimsical an assemblage of characters as were ever blended." From the French priest, whom the crew insisted on having to say Mass for the welfare of their souls, and who enjoyed great favour with her Grace, the "whimsicality" of all may be judged. "Though not of the mendicant order," says the same biographer, "the abbé was in habit as mean as a beggar, and arrived from Paris without any incumbrance of baggage, except his violin, which was the constant companion of his leisure hours."

The voyage in the end was so uneventful as to warrant the Duchess's comparison to a trip from London to Hampton Court. Her reception, however, surpassed even her expectations, and "produced a scene unusual to the

Muscovites." Catherine, who was herself the most ostentatious and splendid of individuals, showered favours upon her singular visitor. In the first flush of success the Duchess, whose vanity was flattered to the utmost, announced her intention of spending the remainder of her life in Russia. To give stability to her words she purchased an estate for twelve thousand pounds, to which she gave the name of Chudleigh, by which it is still known.

Life in Russia, however, in spite of the imperial favour she enjoyed, was not "roses, roses all the way." The British Ambassador and his wife stubbornly refused to receive her or to recognize her claim to be styled the Duchess of Kingston. When her novelty had worn off, the Ambassador's neglect and constant reiteration of the scandals associated with her past were not without their effect on the Empress. Mortification rekindled the old longing for change, and at last, after a two years' residence in Russia, the Duchess made a tiff with Catherine over a decoration she coveted, and which was refused, an excuse for shaking the dust of Muscovy from her shoes. Not being able to sell " Chudleigh " except at a great loss, she established on it a vodka still and left her ship's carpenter in charge of it. Eccentric as her choice seemed, it proved to be a good one. On her death the property under his management had doubled in value.

Paris was her Grace's next and last domicile. She liked Paris extremely, and admiring the Hotel Coq-Heron, in which she resided, she purchased it and made it the rendezvous of every one distinguished either by talent or rank. The salon of the Duchess of Kingston was not so eccentric as might have been expected, and though rank rather than talent—with the exception of Glück, who was a frequent visitor—was to be found in it, she escaped the ridicule to which she was so sensitive. Her suppers were celebrated for their refinement and luxury, and she managed even in Paris to acquire and to keep another royal friendship.

The Duchess of Bourbon took the greatest interest in her. It was, too, on the Duchess of Kingston that the Empress Catherine's son and successor, the Grand Duke Paul, paid one of his first visits when he came to Paris, as the Comte du Nord. Madame d'Oberkirch, who accompanied the Grand Duchess on this occasion, thus describes the impression she received of the Duchess of Kingston.

"Although this lady," she says, "was then sixty-six years of age, she still retained traces of more than ordinary beauty, and her deportment was the most dignified I ever beheld. She moved with all the grace and majesty of a goddess, and our own lovely queen (Marie Antoinette) alone could rival her in the just proportions of her figure. Her great knowledge of society, her wit, and her brilliant imagination, which reflected as a mirror all that passed before it, gave a brilliancy to her conversation that I have seldom seen equalled. But I do not deny that her principles were too harsh and her tone of mind too severe. She was proud and self-willed, opposed to almost all received maxims, and yet varied and inconstant both in her fancies and opinions."

The Hotel Coq-Heron was quite large enough for her needs, but the love of ostentation urged her to purchase the royal residence of Saint-Assise that came into the market on the death of the Duke of Orleans, " Égalité's " father. The possession of this property, however, afforded her little enjoyment, and a law-suit in which it involved her was the immediate cause of her death. For in her rage on learning that the case had been given against her, she burst a blood-vessel from the effects of which she died two days later, in her sixty-ninth year, and one year before the Revolution.

In spite of her apparent reckless expenditure, she was

very shrewd in the management of her affairs. Saint-Assise, for which she was thought to have paid a price far in excess of its value, proved to be a highly profitable investment. Horace Walpole had predicted from her well-known eccentricity that " the Empress Catherine and the Whore of Babylon would be her co-heiresses." Her will was indeed a curious document. Many people who had expected legacies were disappointed, and many others who were in nowise connected with her received valuable presents. To the Countess of Salisbury of the day she left her pearls, for no other reason than that they had once belonged to the Countess of Salisbury of the reign of Henry IV!

Many of the things she disposed of were presents she had received, the value of which was no small proof of the charm she must have possessed at an earlier period of her life. Perhaps the most striking feature of her will was the generosity she displayed to the nephews of her husband who had ruined themselves in the attempt to dispossess her of her fortune. She made them her residuary legatees. Considering the unblushing viciousness of her youth and the cynical selfishness of her later years, even the virtue of this act was called in question. There is reason to believe, however, that the verdict of her contemporaries, whose opinion has been generally accepted by history, was not altogether just to the Duchess of Kingston. The following story, related of her by the Baroness d'Oberkirch, though it is not in any sense an attempt to palliate the evil life of this woman, at least proves that she was not incapable of spontaneous acts of generosity.

" In 1785," says Madame d'Oberkirch, " some person told her that the nephew of the Duke of Kingston, he who had sought to deprive her of her property, was in great distress at Metz, and in momentary danger of being arrested for debt. Contrary to the expectation of her informant, she felt no joy, but asked his address, and immediately wrote to him, telling him that she had forgiven him the injury he had done her and would now be his friend and try to extricate him from his difficulties.

" She went to Versailles, and obtained from the King an order by which the arrest was prevented. She then hired a house for him near Paris and allowed him a pension for life. For this generosity and clemency she was much and justly praised."

Other actions of a similar nature might be related of her. Unfortunately they are conspicuous by reason of their rarity.

One word will suffice to sum up the waste of her life— Idleness! It is one of the seven deadly sins.

THE COMTESSE DE LAMOTTE

1756—1791

THE COMTESSE DE LAMOTTE
[*From an old French print*]

V

THE COMTESSE DE LAMOTTE

1756—1791

I

HENRI II of Valois, King of France, is remembered almost entirely by reason of his relation to three persons whose names are very famous in history—his father, his wife, and his mistress: Francis the First, Catherine de Medici, and Diana of Poitiers. His celebrated devotion to the fair Diana, whose initial he intertwined with his own over the portals of the Louvre, did not, however, prevent him from devoting himself to other and lesser beauties as well. By one of these, Nicole de Savigny, he had a son, to whom he gave the name of Henri de Saint-Remy, Baron de Valois. The King also provided for his offspring by granting him valuable estates in Champagne in the neighbourhood of Bar-sur-Aube, and creating him a gentleman of the bedchamber. Thus protected and supported, the royal bastard in due course married, and proceeded to add to the ranks of the nobility, already swollen by similar additions, another family of illustrious origin.

Fortune, however, did not favour the Saint-Remys of Valois, and two centuries later the descendants of Henri II and Nicole de Savigny had so degenerated that Jacques de Saint-Remy, the last but one of the Barons of Valois, had sunk to the level of a common peasant. Through the extravagance of his ancestors he had succeeded to an estate encumbered with debt and a château so dilapidated as to be uninhabitable. But instead of attempting to retrieve the fortunes of his family, he did his best to ruin them irretrievably. A gambler and a drunkard, he sold acre by acre all that remained of a once splendid estate to provide himself with money for his debauches, in which he had for his boon-companions the peasants of the neighbourhood, with whom he fought as well as drank. His marriage with the daughter of a gamekeeper completed his degradation, for his wife was as ignorant and as vicious as she was low-born. Having parted with his last acre, and found a purchaser even for the roofless château, he and his family moved into a filthy hovel, where the children, Jacques, Jeanne and Marianne, aged three, two, and one respectively, "naked and nourished like savages," lived on the charity of the parish, or on what their father, now turned poacher, could steal.

"My father," relates Comte Beugnot, who as a youth lived at Bar-sur-Aube, "remembers having seen the head of this unhappy family; he was a man of athletic build, who lived by poaching in the forests and even by stealing cultivated fruit from gardens. The inhabitants and authorities suffered him from fear in the one case, and in the other from the renown that still attached to his ancient name."

In those days it was the custom for nobles to keep the title deeds to their estates and their parchments of nobility in the strong-room of their castles. This fact was the principal motive during the Revolution of the terrible Guerre aux Châteaux! the peasants believing that by destroying the châteaux and manors they would destroy the proofs on which the nobles based their claims to their lands, who would thus be powerless to dispossess those who seized them. But though the degraded and depraved Baron de Valois, in parting with every acre he had possessed, had been obliged to part with the title deeds, he still kept his parchments of nobility, and in maudlin moments of drunkenness he was in the habit of drawing them from their hiding-place, under the filthy pallet on which he slept, to forget, if possible, his present misery in the contemplation of the proofs of his former splendour.

From continually seeing her husband blubbering over these documents, his wife had attached an importance to them that was utterly fallacious. She conceived the idea that their possession might be made the instrument of securing the restoration of her husband's ancestral estates, or at all events of relieving herself and her family from the destitution into which they had sunk. With this object in view she finally made up her mind to go to Paris and solicit the influence of some powerful personage connected with the Court. Her husband, who was as ignorant as herself, was readily persuaded to listen to her, and the whole family started one spring night in the year 1760 to walk to Paris, which was one hundred and fifty miles distant. The necessity, however, of having to carry in her arms the youngest child, Marianne, induced the " Baroness " to leave her " on the window-sill of the house of one Durand, a farmer, who, being now the possessor of the greater part of her husband's estates, was deemed the proper person to care for her."

The vagrants were two weeks on the road, and arrived at Paris in a state of extreme destitution. They did not enter the city, but hung around the outskirts, shifting from one suburb to another till they finally settled down at Boulogne opposite St. Cloud. On hearing their tale, the curé to whom they appealed gave them some assistance, but their principal means of support was by begging. This was done for the good-for-nothing parents by their children, Jeanne and Jacques, who were sent daily into the streets and told to implore the passers-by " to take pity on two poor orphans descended in a direct line from Henri II of Valois, King of France." As such an appeal was well calculated to stamp the little beggars as impostors, they generally returned empty-handed to be beaten by their mother, " whose stick often broke in her hand."

The father finally succumbed to drunkenness and want, and through the kindness of the curé was admitted to the Hôtel Dieu in Paris, which owed its existence to the benevolence of Madame de Pompadour, and where in a ward of this charitable institution the scion of the House of Valois breathed his last.

A few days later the " Baroness " gave birth to a daughter to which she gave the name of Marguerite. On her recovery, being in spite of her state of abject poverty still, possessed of some claim to good looks, she endeavoured to employ them in procuring the means of existence. She invested this questionable little capital, however, in a manner which made the payment of the dividends it earned still more questionable. For she replaced her husband by a former soldier from Sardinia, named Raymond, a vagrant like herself.

Begging still continued to be their sole means of support, and while Jeanne and her mother appealed to the passers-by in the suburbs, Raymond, who had the audacity to palm himself off as the Baron de Valois, would take Jacques and

the parchments of nobility and try to excite the pity of
those who frequented the Gardens of the Tuileries. After
having been arrested several times as an incorrigible
impostor and vagrant, the authorities finally expelled him
from Paris altogether. Hereupon the " Baroness" disappeared with him, leaving her wretched children to shift
as best they could.

Four weeks after her departure, Jeanne, now eight,
carrying her little sister Marguerite, aged four, on her back,
happened to be begging on the road between Passy and
Paris, when the Marquis and Marquise de Boulainvilliers
passed in their coach and four. The road was steep, and
the heavy coach was proceeding slowly when suddenly the
Marquise heard a voice exclaim—

" Kind lady, take pity on two poor orphans descended
in a direct line from Henri II of Valois, King of France."

Such an appeal and the sight of the pitiful little waif
who made it, barefooted, ragged, emaciated, and carrying
on her back an equally forlorn creature almost as big as
herself, awoke the curiosity and pity of the Marquise. She
was for relieving their distress on the spot. The Marquis,
on the contrary, declared the children were impostors and
ordered them to be gone. But the naturally quick intelligence of Jeanne, which misery had sharpened exceedingly, had detected the impression she had produced
on the Marquise, and she continued to hobble under her
heavy burden alongside the coach, repeating the stereotyped
formula she had been taught, and which was the only one
she knew to excite compassion.

The Marquise de Boulainvilliers, who was one of the
most sympathetic and charitable of women, to oblige her
husband, refrained with difficulty from tossing Jeanne a
coin. But she inquired of the child where she lived, and
the next day sent a servant to ascertain from the curé if
the little beggars were impostors or not. The curé was, of

course, unable to confirm the royal descent of the children but he told what he knew of them.

This was quite sufficient to excite the liveliest pity in the benevolent Madame de Boulainvilliers. She had the three children brought to her château at Passy—in those days a village on the outskirts of Paris—whither she was going from her house in the capital when Jeanne had first attracted her attention. After the rags, dirt, and vermin with which they were covered had been removed, and they had been properly scoured, clothed and fed, the little waifs were far from being unprepossessing in appearance, and the Marquise resolved to burden herself with the education of the orphans.

Jeanne and her sister Marguerite were placed under the care of a Madame Leclerc, who kept a school for girls at Passy, whose husband likewise took charge of Jacques. Two years later, Marguerite having died of small-pox, Madame de Boulainvilliers, whose interest in her *protégés* increased with time, sent for Marianne, the child who had been abandoned by her parents on the window-sill of a farmer at Bar-sur-Aube, and who had been cared for by him. In thus taking upon herself the up-bringing of this family, the kind-hearted Marquise at first had no further intention than to provide them with the means of later earning their living respectably. Consequently, when Jeanne was fourteen, she was removed from Madame Leclerc's, where her sharp intelligence had made the most of her opportunities, and apprenticed to a dressmaker in Paris.

Unfortunately, this did not at all conform with the girl's own inclination. "Ruled," she writes, "by an indomitable pride which I received from nature, and which the kindness of Madame de Boulainvilliers, by opening to me a glimpse of a more brilliant future, had rendered more acute, I could not but shudder when I reflected on my position. 'Alas!'

I said to myself, 'why am I sprung from the blood of the Valois?'" As a milliner's apprentice life became unendurable to her; she was now obliged to do the most menial work, washing, fetching water, cooking, ironing, sewing, and waiting upon even the servants themselves. Hard work and discontent having impaired her health, which, owing to her early experiences, was far from strong, Madame de Boulainvilliers was induced to release her from this apprenticeship and take her as a maid. With her quick wits and the superior education she had received from Madame Leclerc, the girl insinuated herself so cleverly into her benefactress's good graces that she speedily converted herself from maid into companion.

As she grew the "blood of the Valois" became a monomania with Jeanne de Saint-Remy, it seemed to impregnate her thoughts no less than her veins. Was she, the descendant of the King of France, born to remain in service? Impossible! She had not forgotten Fontette, the village in which she had lived before her parents moved to Paris, young though she was at the time. But it was with pride, not pleasure, that she recalled it. Time and the altered conditions of her life had soothed the bitterness of the memory of the squalid hovel in which she had lived; and the "blood of the Valois" was sufficient to purify the recollection of its shame. No, the Fontette that Madame de Boulainvilliers' *protégée* thought of was the Fontette of which the Barons de Valois had been the lords of the manor. The more she thought of it the more she believed that she and her brother and sister had been wrongfully cheated out of it, till it became the one great object of her life to recover the ancestral estates—to be, in a word, the "Lady of the Manor of Fontette" herself.

From constantly harping on the subject of her pedigree, Madame de Boulainvilliers finally consented to verify officially this alleged descent from Henry II. Hozier, the celebrated genealogist of the French nobility, was employed to make the necessary investigations, in the course of which he satisfied himself as to the truth of the Saint-Remys' boasted connection with the House of Valois. The Marquise, having thus obtained the proofs of the young Saint-Remys' descent, determined to bring their destitute condition to the notice of the King. To accomplish this satisfactorily, she consulted with her relation the Marquis de Chabert, an admiral who, on her recommendation, had given Jacques some small berth in one of the ships of the fleet he commanded. Struck by the zeal and aptitude the young sailor had displayed on his first voyage, from which he returned about this time, Chabert had taken a good deal of interest in his history, and he arranged that Saint-Remy should be presented to Louis XVI as the Baron de Valois.

This presentation took place on the 6th May, 1776, two years after the King's accession, and when the Baron de Valois was twenty-one. Two ministers, Necker and Maurepas, were in attendance on the King, who was pleased to recognize the title which young Saint-Remy, on the advice of Chabert and the Marquis de Boulainvilliers, who accompanied him, had assumed. Louis further consented that his eldest sister Jeanne should henceforth be styled Mademoiselle de Valois, while Marianne should be known as Mademoiselle de Saint-Remy, in accordance with the former custom of the family. As these were but empty honours after all, the King was urged to supplement them with some sort of pecuniary assistance. This he did by granting each member of the family a pension from his privy purse of eight hundred livres, or thirty-two pounds a year. In addition to this the young Baron de Valois received a commission in the navy, and a grant of four thousand livres for his outfit. He shortly afterwards joined his ship at Brest, and died nine years later at the early age of thirty, having greatly distinguished himself in his brief career.

Thus did Fortune, assisted to a large extent by her skill in playing upon the credulity and sympathy of others, transform the wretched little beggar-maid into a lady of title.

II

THOUGH Mademoiselle de Valois was loud in expressing her gratitude for the benefits she had received from the King, in her heart of hearts she really thanked him for nothing, as the saying is. Convinced as she was of her royal descent, the King's recognition of the fact seemed to her a mere act of supererogation. While, as for his generosity in granting her a pension of thirty-two pounds, could royal sympathy with royal distress have manifested itself in a manner more beggarly, more ridiculous, more insulting?

The sovereign, moreover, had suggested the advisability of the sisters of the Baron de Valois leaving Madame de Boulainvilliers and residing in a convent, where, as he had no desire to see the "House of Valois" perpetuated, he perhaps hoped they might be induced to take the veil. Madame de Boulainvilliers had taken the hint, and her *protégées* were sent to board at the Abbey of Yères. This had completed the vexation of Mademoiselle de Valois, but as it was impossible for her to vent her spleen on Louis XVI, whom she had never seen, she vented it on the Marquis de Boulainvilliers, who, having secretly seduced her, she thought ought to have managed the affair better.

Too crafty to betray the truth of her relations with

the Marquis to his wife, whose good-will she was anxious to retain, she gave that good lady to understand that she was far from objecting to the change, as she had been so troubled by the unwelcome attentions of the Marquis that she felt it would have been impossible for her to continue to reside under the same roof with him. She succeeded in conveying this information so cleverly that, while she aroused Madame de Boulainvilliers' resentment against her husband, of whose infidelity she had previous reason to complain, she avoided incurring it herself. During the two years that Mademoiselle de Valois resided at Yères she kept in close touch with her benefactress, who had a country seat near by at Montgeron, and even renewed, in secret, her former relations with the Marquis.

At last, however, according to Réteaux de Villette, she, and her sister as well, were so compromised by the visits of the Marquis, that they deemed it advisable to leave Yères before their conduct reached the ears of Madame de Boulainvilliers and deprived them for ever of her favour. The Marquise, as credulous and as easily duped as she was good, was made to believe that if they remained at Yères they were expected to take the veil —a sacrifice that neither Mademoiselle de Valois nor Mademoiselle de Saint-Remy could bring themselves to make. They therefore prayed their " mother," as they called her, to get them admitted as boarders at the Abbey of Longchamps, which, being near Paris and close to Passy, would enable them to maintain their connection with the family of Boulainvilliers.

This famous nunnery, whose name has been perpetuated by a famous race-course on which it formerly stood, and of which only a picturesque ivy-clad tower and windmill escaped the demolishing rage of the Revolution, was at that period at the height of its renown. It had ever been

in great vogue in the world of fashion, because of the
laxity of the regulations, which had led to such irregu-
larities among those who had taken the veil no less than
among those who were only boarders, as earned it in a
previous age the reputation of being another Rabelaisian
Abbaye de Thélème, whose motto was, "*Fay ce que voul-
dras.*" A reforming Archbishop of Paris, however, had in
the end so severely punished the offenders who had made its
name a by-word, that Longchamps had gone out of fashion
as a fashionable boarding-house, with the result that its
revenues had almost completely disappeared. The advent
of an opera-singer as a boarder, some fifty years prior to
that of Mademoiselle de Valois, had resuscitated the old
favour it had enjoyed. This lady, having taken the veil,
suggested to the Abbess giving sacred concerts in Lent.
The idea appealed to the Abbess, and the concerts became
the rage. All Paris flocked to hear them. "It was found
that the setting in of the spring fashions might be fitly
made to coincide with the eve of Easter;" and it is interesting to note that from the route taken by this fashionable
pilgrimage the present fashionable and world-famous
Avenue des Champs Elysées owes its origin. Eventually,
however, another reforming Archbishop put out a stop to
these concerts, which had gradually developed into operatic
performances in which the voices of the nuns were assisted
by those of stars of the opera, some of whom even disguised themselves as women "for the sake of propriety."
But though Longchamps had a second time "fallen off" as
a fashionable resort, the discipline was still very lax, and
as a "home" for young girls of the type of Mademoiselle
de Valois and her sister offered special attractions.

The expectations, however, that they had built on their
change of abode were not destined to be realized. It is
true the Marquis used to ride over to Longchamps from his
château at Passy, just as he had been in the habit of doing

from Montgeron to Yères, but if the Abbess and her nuns were inclined to shut their eyes, the other boarders were not, and at last the Abbess was obliged to inform the sisters that they could not receive the visits of any gentleman on any pretence whatever. At about the same time they were also deprived of the consolation of imposing on their "dear, kind mother," through whom they hoped they might eventually procure husbands worthy of their inflated opinion of their rank. For the Marquis was detected defrauding the excise by means of a secret distillery in the cellar of his Paris house. The discovery created a great sensation, and both the Marquis and his wife were forbidden to appear at Court. Covered with mortification, they left Paris and its neighbourhood, and retired to another part of the country till the affair blew over.

Deprived thus of the protection of Madame de Boulainvilliers, and finding themselves in bad odour at Longchamps, the sisters decided to return to Bar-sur-Aube. On their arrival they lodged at the poorest inn in the town, gave out that they had come to "claim the manors of Essoyes, Fontette, and Verpilière," which had belonged to their father. The news of the King's recognition and their connection with Madame de Boulainvilliers had reached Bar-sur-Aube, and they counted, upon their return, to make a stir of which they were prepared to take full advantage. In this they were not mistaken, and it was not long before they found a home in the house of a certain Madame de Suremont, the wife of the principal local functionary, where they were "very elegantly entertained at the rate of four hundred livres (sixteen pounds) per annum."

Young Beugnot, to whom reference has already been made, and who was at this time an ardent admirer of Jeanne, has described in his *Memoirs*, written many years later, the impression produced on the staid society of

Bar-sur-Aube by these "fugitive princesses," as he speaks of them.

"As they were almost without clothes," he says, "when they arrived, Madame de Suremont lent them on the day of their arrival two white dresses, but without much hope of their being able to wear them, for the dresses had been made for her figure, which was most voluminous. What, then, was her surprise when she discovered the next morning that the bodices fitted them to perfection. They had passed the night in cutting them out and remaking them. They acted in everything with the same freedom, and Madame de Suremont soon began to find the unceremoniousness of the princesses carried too far."

Indeed, Mademoiselle de Valois soon manifested a desire to practise on M. de Suremont the powers of fascination she had exercised so long and so cleverly on the husband of her benefactress.

"The demoiselles de Saint-Remy," says Beugnot, "who were only to remain one week with Madame de Suremont, stayed in her house one year. The time passed as it passes in a little provincial town—in quarrels, reconciliations, statements, justifications, and frightful intrigues, which never went beyond the walls of the city. Meanwhile the genius of Mademoiselle de Valois developed even in so narrow a circle. She played preludes before attacking the principal piece. She had taken complete possession of M. de Suremont, and covered with the blind attachment felt for her by this worthy man the spiteful things she distributed among all who came in contact with her, including Madame de Suremont herself, who has since often repeated to me that the most unhappy year of her life was the one this demon passed in her house."

"Mademoiselle de Valois was not," continues Beugnot, "exactly handsome, but she was well formed. Her blue eyes were full of expression and arched with black eyebrows;

her face was rather too long and her mouth too wide, but the latter was adorned with fine teeth, and her smile was enchanting. Her hands were pretty, her feet small, and her complexion of dazzling whiteness. She had a naturally quick and penetrating understanding, and entirely lacked the moral sense."

Her deficiency in this latter quality, it should be stated in justice to her, was perhaps due less to a natural tendency to depravity, as in the case of the Empress Catherine, than to the ineradicable impressions of shameless vice, poverty, and indecency that had been stamped upon her nature when a child.

Among Mademoiselle de Valois' numerous admirers at Bar-sur-Aube the most persistent and the most favoured was Nicolas de Lamotte, a subaltern in the Gendarmerie[1] stationed at Lunéville, who was on a visit to his mother at Bar-sur-Aube. He was not good-looking, but he had a good figure and looked well in his scarlet uniform embroidered with silver braid. His manners were agreeable, but his character was weak, and his wits none of the sharpest. In fact the nickname " Momote," which his comrades had given him in contemptuous chaff, and which he did not resent, very aptly describes his insignificance. Being the nephew of M. de Suremont, he had more frequent opportunities of meeting Mademoiselle de Valois than any other of the young men with whom she flirted, and Madame de Suremont, perceiving his attachment, furthered it to the best of her ability.

Lamotte was scarcely the sort of *parti* that Mademoiselle de Valois would have chosen for a husband, since he had

---

[1] The Gendarmerie of the *ancien régime* must not be confused with the force of the same name of the present time. Before the Revolution the Gendarmerie was the smartest of the French cavalry regiments, and consisted of four companies, known as the English, the Scotch, the Flemish, and the Burgundian Guards. It was to the latter that Lamotte belonged.

no fortune beyond a trifling three hundred francs a year
that his uncle allowed him, in order to enable him to
remain in the army.   Nevertheless, she herself had neither
fortune nor the prospect of one, and she was getting on
in years—she was now four-and-twenty ; moreover, fascinating though she was, her conduct had not been such as to
recommend her as a wife to most men.   Consequently,
when Lamotte, who was head over ears in love, proposed
marriage, she accepted him.

To satisfy her vanity she had her banns published in the
parish church of Fontette, and went there to hear them
read.   " All the peasants," she says, " rose from their seats
on our entrance.   We received the holy water and consecrated bread in the seat of honour ; the bells were rung,
and everybody testified their joy.   I gave them money, for
which they expressed their gratitude by drinking to my
health and that of the Baron de Valois.   Then they conducted us around the domains of my ancestors."

The wedding, however, took place at Bar-sur-Aube ;
" and not a moment too soon," says Beugnot, " for exactly
one month afterwards the bride gave birth to twin sons,
who died a few weeks later."   Lamotte acknowledged
them as his, and they were baptized in his name, but local
gossip was inclined to " attribute them to M. de Suremont
or the old Bishop of Langres, who had been very attentive
to Mademoiselle de Valois."

It was impossible that one so proud of her name should
consent to sink it in that of Lamotte, which was quite
devoid of distinction.   So she styled herself de Lamotte-
Valois, and even assumed the title of Comtesse.   For
though her husband had no right to the title of Comte, he
had by some error been thus gazetted on receiving his
commission, and his wife was not the woman to let any
chance slip that increased her importance.

Shortly after his marriage, Lamotte's furlough having

expired, he returned with his bride to his regiment at
Lunéville. From the start the couple had a hard struggle
to maintain themselves. To provide herself with a suitable
trousseau the Comtesse de Lamotte-Valois had raised one
thousand livres on her pension, while the Comte, who had,
as Beugnot says, "at least sufficient brains to acquire
debts," was obliged to sell a cabriolet and horse which
he had bought on credit. The sum he obtained through
this questionable transaction was very soon exhausted.
Then began a life of shifts and expedients: borrowing
from friends and neighbours as long as they could be
induced to lend; raising money from usurers at an ex-
orbitant rate of interest; and even by begging, which
came easy to the Comtesse, who, having solicited alms in
the streets as a child, did not hesitate now when in a tight
corner to appeal by letter to the various rich acquaintances
she had made through her connection with Madame de
Boulainvilliers.

She also had other means of keeping the pot boiling
of which Lamotte knew nothing, or at which he winked.
With her "enchanting smile" she soon had the whole
garrison of Lunéville dangling at her heels. In her little
salon, where none of the pretty furniture was paid for and
it was so pleasant to spend the evenings, a tale of distress
told by a fascinating woman of bailiffs and duns and an
unfeeling husband, and accompanied by sighs and glances,
could not fail to melt the heart and open the purse. At
least the Marquis d'Autichamp, the colonel of Lamotte's
regiment, was not proof against such wiles. In a word, it
was a case of Becky Sharp and Lord Steyne over again.

Suddenly, when the cloud of debt that hung over the
couple was darkest and seemed on the point of bursting
and utterly overwhelming them with its thunder and
lightning, the Comtesse heard that the Marquis and
Marquise de Boulainvilliers were at Strasburg. The idea of

rushing thither and appealing to her "kind and honoured mother," from whom she had been so long separated, no sooner flashed into her brain than she was on the road. Surely, she argued, the protection of which she had had so many proofs in the past will not fail her now ?

On reaching Strasburg, she and her husband, who accompanied her, learned that Madame de Boulainvilliers was staying in the neighbourhood, at the palace of Saverne, as the guest of the Cardinal-Archbishop, Prince Louis de Rohan, Grand Almoner of France. Hereupon they drove out to Saverne and put up at the village inn, from which the Comtesse wrote her benefactress to apprise her of her arrival and to ask to be permitted to call upon her. Madame de Boulainvilliers at once went to her *protégée*, and thinking, perhaps, as the weather was fine, that her carriage was a pleasanter place in which to hear the Comtesse's story than the stuffy parlour of the inn, took her for a drive. On the road they met the Cardinal, whereupon Madame de Boulainvilliers stopped her carriage, and as his Eminence approached it, presented her companion to him.

" The name of Valois," she added, observing the surprise of the Cardinal on hearing it, "really belongs to her, but she has unfortunately no means of supporting it with dignity."

As a friend of Madame de Boulainvilliers he could but offer the hospitality of Saverne to the Comtesse, whose "enchanting smile" no doubt caused his invitation to be more cordial than such formalities usually are. The Comtesse was not the woman to refuse such an invitation, and she and her husband spent two or three days in the splendid palace of the Cardinal at Saverne. Madame was now in her element, and played the cards the Fates had dealt her with wonderful skill. Monsieur, who realized her superiority, regarded her with amazement, and not without

15

a certain fear—much as Rawdon Crawley regarded Becky Sharp. The Marquise de Boulainvilliers was quite overcome with emotion at the tale of her "dear daughter's" sufferings, and to Becky Lamotte's intense satisfaction undertook to pay her debts.

Nor could the Grand Almoner of France, whose generosity was proverbial, especially where a pretty woman was concerned, fail to be touched by the strange life-story of his charming guest. It was impossible to imagine a more interesting story, told by a more attractive woman. So, under the spell of her insinuating voice and caressing manner, he too came to the rescue and promised to exert his influence to obtain promotion for Lamotte.

III

When the Lamottes returned to Lunéville with the whole or the greater part of their debts paid, they might, perhaps, miserable as was their united income, have managed to scrape along somehow. But the Comtesse had very grand ideas of life that were quite out of keeping with her condition. Her short visit at Saverne had completely unsettled her. She could think of nothing, talk of nothing but the Cardinal, his vast influence, and his stately red-sandstone palace, where he lived literally like a king. Obsessed with her descent from the Valois, she felt that she was born to enjoy splendour and power. Destiny surely never intended that she should pass her days in poverty in dead-and-alive Lunéville. As a Valois her place was at Versailles! Once there she might become another Madame de Pompadour; stranger things had happened. At any rate she had had enough of Lunéville, and if she

CARDINAL DE ROHAN
[From an old French print]

To face page 226

was to be poor she would be poor in a place where she could at least console herself with the sight of the rich. Besides, it was not in Lunéville that she would ever obtain the restitution of the manors of Essoyes, Fontette, and Verpilière, which had formerly constituted the estate of the Saint-Remys of Valois.

It was utterly useless to remind her that her father had disposed of the last acre he had possessed, or that even if a claim to the manors had a vestige of right on which to found itself, it was her brother, and not she, to whom the restitution would be made. She was a woman, and had a woman's way of reasoning in such matters. With her it was not a question as to who was to benefit by the restitution—that was a matter which would be very amicably settled—but of the restitution itself, and there did not exist in her mind the slightest doubt that there *was* a way by which it could be effected.

On returning from Saverne she renewed her investigations with greater energy than ever, and eventually discovered through her lawyer at Bar-sur-Aube that the lands at Fontette which her father had sold had passed into the possession of the Crown. Their restitution, then, depended solely on the King. This was an immense feather in the Comtesse's cap. In the face of legal reasoning she had scored a point by sheer persistency. Nothing now could prevent her from going to Paris to plead her case. Her lawyer, Beugnot's father, lent her one thousand livres— presumably on the strength of his belief in her powers of fascination. It is only fair to add that the Comtesse afterwards, in the period of her dishonest prosperity, did not forget this service, and repaid Beugnot in full.

Dividing this money equally with her husband, she sent him to Fontette to ascertain the exact nature of the steps necessary to be taken to recover this and the two other adjacent manors ; while she herself set out for Paris. On reaching the capital the first thing she did was to present herself at the house of Madame de Boulainvilliers, where, to her unfeigned dismay, if not regret, she found her benefactress lying dangerously ill. She found a temporary home, however, in the Boulainvilliers' establishment, which she says might have been a permanent one had she been willing to accept the "downright proposal" of the old reprobate Marquis to remain as his mistress.

No doubt he did make such a proposal, and no doubt she would have accepted it had the *quid pro quo* equalled her demands or her needs. Nor is it at all unlikely that her husband, who, having foolishly resigned his commission and as foolishly dissipated the last livre that she had given him, had joined her in Paris, would have objected to a luxurious *ménage à trois*. But the Marquis appears to have been very niggardly, and his proposal, made, by the way, while his wife was dying, was rejected with scorn by "insulted virtue." On her own stating the Comtesse was always the victim of calumny and malicious persecution !

After the death of Madame de Boulainvilliers she was consequently obliged to seek another place of abode. As she had an idle husband as well as herself to provide for, a situation of which the difficulties were increased by the rejection of her petition to the King, life at Paris did not appear to offer any greater prospect of the luxury she wanted than Lunéville. On the contrary, the misery and humiliation of the existence she was now called upon to face were infinitely greater than any she had experienced in Lunéville. The couple seem to have known all the horrors of poverty but ill-health and imprisonment. Indeed, even the latter Lamotte only escaped by flight into the country, lying hid in some village outside of Paris till his clever wife managed to raise the money to pay the debt that threatened his liberty. Their furniture, purchased on credit, was constantly being pawned or seized ; they

were ever on the move, now being ejected, now slipping
off to avoid paying the rent. Quarrels with landlords
and tradespeople were of constant occurrence. On one
occasion the Comtesse even threatened "to throw the
landlady down the stairs." And a square meal was many
a day a luxury.

Young Beugnot, who had been one of her admirers at
Bar-sur-Aube, and was now studying law in Paris, more
than once appeased the pangs of hunger she suffered.

"I could not ask her to dine at my lodgings," he says,
"because I had no regular establishment, but now and
then she did me the honour to accept an invitation at the
Cadran Bleu, and astonished me by her appetite. She had
a remarkable taste for good beer, and nowhere found it
bad. She would eat from absence of mind two or three
dozen cakes, and this absent-mindedness was so frequent
that I could not but perceive that she had dined very
lightly, if she had dined at all."

The young law student also gave her the benefit of his
legal advice free of charge, and drafted the petitions she
was continually sending to ministers and persons of influence. For the rejection of her petition to the King by no
means prevented her from pressing her claim to Fontette
in other quarters. Having by dint of her name got access
to Calonne, the Controller-General, she besieged him with
demands for assistance, but in vain. On one occasion she
threatened to remain in his office "till he thought fit to
provide her with another home." He at last lost all
patience with her and refused to receive her when she
called. Madame Du Barry "flung her petition into the
fire"; while the Duchesse de Polignac, the well-known
favourite of the Queen, coldly informed her that "she
served no one but her personal friends."

The Comtesse de Lamotte, however, was not the woman
to succumb to discouragement, and one cannot help

admiring the indomitable perseverance she displayed in the face of all reverses. Having failed to accomplish anything by her petitions, she took a room at an inn at Versailles and sought every possible occasion of forming a connection, no matter how humble, within the palace. Somehow, some day, she thought, she might manage to attract the attention of some member of the Royal Family.

In this way she made the acquaintance of a door-keeper, through whom she succeeded, on one occasion, in getting into the palace. Finding herself in an ante-room of the private apartments of Madame, she suddenly dropped in a swoon. Such an event naturally caused commotion. Madame was informed that a poor Comtesse de Valois had fainted from starvation in the attempt to solicit her interest to obtain justice. The name alone was sufficient to command consideration. Madame and Madame Elizabeth were much concerned; they sent her some relief and even appealed to Calonne, the Controller-General, who was playing ducks and drakes with the little money that was left in the Treasury. Thus solicited, he promptly doubled her pension. So much may perseverance accomplish!

But what is sixty-four pounds a year to a woman like the Comtesse de Lamotte-Valois? Regarded as mere cash the sum was less than nothing; nevertheless, skilfully handled, it would go far. On the strength it gave to her vaunted pedigree it provided her with credit. She let it be understood, in her plausible way, that she was connected with the Court; the name of some member of the Royal Family was constantly on her lips, and she was always glibly boasting of the favour she enjoyed with Madame, with the Comte d'Artois, with the Queen. The report of her boasted influence began to spread, and not only was she offered credit by tradespeople, but bribes and presents from place-hunters who wished to employ her to push their interests at Court. In this way she received a thousand francs from a M. de Ganges, who wanted a post that was about to become vacant; while "some silk merchants at Lyons who desired the patronage of the Queen sent her a case of superb stuffs valued at ten thousand livres."

Intoxicated by the ease with which she found she could impose on the credulity of the public, she descended from her attic and launched forth into reckless extravagance. Beugnot, whom the Comtesse's appetite, so suggestive of compulsory fasting, had astonished on the occasions when she had gone with him to the *Cadran Bleu*, was now more astonished than ever at the style in which she lived. He noticed, however, that the company she entertained was scarcely the sort that one so intimate with Royalty as she professed to be would be likely to frequent. The titles of the countesses and marchionesses to whom Beugnot was introduced at the Lamottes' would, he thought, hardly bear investigation, while the men, with the exception of Father Loth, Madame's confessor—she was very regular in attendance at church!—himself, not the most impeccable of his kind, would most certainly never have been received at Versailles.

At her table Beugnot once met a Comte de Valois who, having heard that she had been recognized by the King, had come up from the country to press a similar claim. She called him "cousin" and treated him with the greatest consideration, till one day, having inadvertently let slip that he was a cobbler by trade, she requested him to leave the house. It was afterwards discovered that he coined as well as cobbled in the village he came from!

IV

But the Comtesse de Lamotte knew that though you may deceive people part of the time you cannot deceive them all the time. The credulity that she had imposed upon began to demand fresh proofs of her vaunted influence; failing them, what vengeance might it not wreak? And how was she to produce these proofs? The manor of Fontette, which had previously been necessary to her vanity, became now essential to her safety. Money, realizable property of some kind she must have. Lamotte, who had tried to procure it with the aid of luck in the gambling dens of the Palais Royal without success, had become a card-sharper. He was not only a fool, but his reputation cast doubts on hers. She even declared to Beugnot that she regarded him as "an obstacle."

In such circumstances it is not to be supposed that she would be likely to forget the Cardinal de Rohan and the favourable impression she had created on him at Saverne. His aid, indeed, had been the first she had solicited on arriving in Paris. To call on so great a personage in what she considered the fitting manner, she had begged Beugnot to provide her with a carriage.

"There are only two ways of asking alms," she told him, "at the church door and in a carriage."

As Beugnot was aware of her previous experience in the art of begging, he did not question the truth of this observation, and kindly consented to oblige her.

"She decked herself out," he says, "in her finest feathers, no doubt hired for the occasion, practised on me her most coquettish airs, and made the Rue Vieille du Temple, where she was living, redolent with the odour of her perfumes. She asked me to accompany her, but I declined."

As the result of her " enchanting smile "—or was it the carriage ?—his Eminence received her affably, but since he had been out of favour for many years at Court his influence, on which she had counted to effect the restitution of the Valois estates, could avail her nothing. The Comtesse, however, was not the woman to let so fine an acquaintance drop, and she had greater need of his purse, which was long, than of the influence of which he was so short. So, while besieging Calonne and the others, she did not fail to pay frequent visits to the Hôtel de Rohan, where at least she succeeded in making herself welcome. The Cardinal used to make her small donations from the funds of the Grand Almonry, of which he was custodian. But she afterwards indignantly denied that she had ever received alms from him.

" The daughter of the Valois," she said, " was not the woman to accept five louis in charity."

Nevertheless, being in sore need of money, she was glad enough to receive even smaller sums. And at her trial a letter of hers to a Minister was produced, in which she thanked him for forty-eight francs he had given her out of pity for her distress. Slight, then, as was the assistance she had received from the Cardinal, it was welcome not only for the temporary relief it afforded, but for the connection it established, a connection which the scheming Comtesse was always hoping would " lead to something." It was destined, indeed, to lead both of them far, and began by leading the Comtesse to a complete and useful knowledge of his Eminence's history and character.

From the start Madame de Lamotte had discovered the reason why Prince Louis de Rohan, Cardinal-Archbishop of Strasburg, Grand Almoner of France, the richest of all the princes of the Church, had no influence at Court. Twelve years before, when Ambassador at Vienna, he had incurred, by his notoriously dissolute life and utter contempt for religion, the animosity of the Empress Maria Theresa. She regarded him as the "representative of the devil rather than of the Most Christian King," and to obtain his recall she endeavoured to impart her animosity to her daughter, the Queen of France. In this Maria Theresa succeeded so well that Marie Antoinette not only conceived the greatest dislike and contempt of the prelate, but inspired similar feelings in Louis XVI. Versailles was thus closed to Rohan, and he never went there but once a year, on Assumption Day, in his *rôle* of Grand Almoner, to celebrate mass in the Royal Chapel.

He had tried to compensate himself for his disgrace by the royal splendour of the state he kept in his superb red-sandstone palace at Saverne, or in Paris, where scandal declared that "he emulated in secret the vices of the Roman emperors." He regretted, however, the world where, for a time, he had played a not inconspicuous part. His rapid advancement, his illustrious family—proud as their superb device, *Roi ne puis, prince ne daigne, Rohan je suis*—and his vast wealth awoke his latent ambition. The flatterers who surrounded him compared his ability to that of Richelieu, Mazarin and Fleury, the three Cardinals who had governed France. It was more than his right, it was his duty, they told him, to become First Minister. Intoxicated by their flattery he believed them, and his desire for power developed into a passion, into a fixed idea.

One obstacle alone stood between him and the summit of his ambition—Marie Antoinette; a fascinating and dazzling obstacle to this consecrated voluptuary, so dazzling that it became confused in his mind with the summit from which it kept him. He did not bear the Queen the slightest resentment for her animosity to him. He believed it was due to the influence of his enemies. He felt certain that if he could but meet her, get into communication with her, he could win her esteem.

Nor was he altogether wrong in supposing he could please her. La Belle Eminence, as he was called, was the type of courtier for whose society Marie Antoinette had the greatest inclination. He was sensitive, dreamy, generous, extravagant, witty to a degree, very elegant, and though forty-eight still one of the handsomest men of his time. It is true he was debauched, but then, if the truth be told, so were d'Artois, Besenval, Coigny, Lauzun, and all the others with whom the Queen of Hearts was most intimate.

" He had," says the Baroness d'Oberkirch, " the gallantry and politeness of a grand seigneur such as I have rarely met in any one."

Having learnt all this from her intercourse with the Cardinal, the Comtesse de Lamotte had also discovered that he was extremely credulous. The year before her arrival in Paris, when she and her husband were passing through Strasburg on their way back to Lunéville from Saverne, they had heard mention of a mysterious man who had just arrived there, and whose singular appearance and conduct were exciting the greatest curiosity. He not only professed to be able to cure any malady, but would accept no payment for his services, even giving money to those who were poor. He professed also to have discovered the secret of perpetual youth, and to possess the philosopher's stone. He called himself Count Cagliostro. But the success of his magic and the impressive mystery in which he enveloped himself led the superstitious to believe him to be the Wandering Jew, a belief that he indirectly encouraged.

The Comtesse de Lamotte was the last woman in the world to be gulled by the quackeries of such a man, and, beyond sneering at the gullibility of the Strasburgers, she probably never gave the charlatan another thought till she met him at the Cardinal's when she came to Paris. She had taken the measure of the man at a glance, and the faith that the Cardinal had in him, by exposing to her his gullibility, was the basis on which the success of her famous duping of his Eminence rested.

The Cardinal did not believe that Cagliostro was the Wandering Jew ; but he did believe in his boasted power of divination. Did he not possess " a diamond engraved with the arms of Rohan, worth twenty thousand livres," that Cagliostro " had made out of nothing," when, as his Eminence told the Baroness d'Oberkirch, " I was present during the whole operation, my eyes fixed on the crucible ? " Such evidence of the credulity of the Cardinal filled the Comtesse with the desire to emulate the quack, whose ascendency over the frivolous prelate, who did nothing without consulting him, excited her admiration and envy. This she displayed in a manner so flattering to Cagliostro that he in his turn became the dupe of the Comtesse, and thus unwittingly helped her to exploit his victim for her benefit.

Having already discovered, as she herself admits, " that credulity was a mine which, properly worked, would furnish a far richer yield than charity was ever likely to do," the Comtesse only required a favourable opportunity of testing the mine she discovered in the Cardinal. The sequel to her fainting-fit in Madame's apartments in Versailles, which enabled her to make capital out of her boasted influence at Court, had deceived the Cardinal as well as others. He never dreamt of asking for a tangible proof of the amazing claim of this insinuating beggar to whom he had been in the habit of giving money out of charity. When, therefore, having wound herself into his confidence, she boldly declared she would reconcile the Queen to him, Rohan believed her, because he wanted to believe her.

" I was completely blinded," he admitted at the subsequent trial, " by the intense desire I had to obtain the good graces of the Queen."

His " incredible credulity " having brought him so far,

COUNT CAGLIOSTRO

[*After Bartolozzi*]

To face page 236

there was no reason why it should not carry him any distance from common-sense that the artful Comtesse chose. Accordingly, she quietly disentangled herself from her other dupes, from whose vengeance when the scales fell from their eyes she had everything to fear, and fixed her attention entirely upon the Cardinal. Thus his Eminence was induced to begin a correspondence with the Queen, which was "graduated and shaded in such a way as to make him think that he had succeeded in inspiring her Majesty with the greatest interest and the most complete confidence." In order to remove all suspicion from the mind of the Cardinal as to the genuineness of the letters he received from the Queen, the Comtesse found it necessary to employ an accomplice to imitate the handwriting and signature of Marie Antoinette. For this purpose she required a trusty forger, and, as luck would have it, she had one to hand in Réteaux de Villette, a friend of her husband's, who "had a talent for imitating handwriting and loved her to adoration."

As the object of this forged correspondence was to extract a large sum of money from the infatuated Cardinal, the Comtesse de Lamotte proceeded with the greatest care before she mulcted her dupe. In order to test his willingness to obey the Queen in every particular, as he declared, she sent his Eminence to Saverne, and brought him back to Paris, on the most capricious pretexts. The Cardinal obeyed these strange commands of his royal mistress, not, however, without complaining to the Comtesse of her delay in bringing about his long-desired interview with the Queen. Thinking it wiser to satisfy him before she made the demand on his purse that she contemplated, the Comtesse found it necessary to employ another accomplice, this time to personate the Queen herself!

Here again luck aided her. The Comte de Lamotte passing through the gardens of the Palais Royal on his way to the gambling-hell he frequented, was struck one day by

the remarkable likeness a certain girl he came across bore
to the Queen.   He lost no time in scraping an acquaintance
with her, and, having heard her story—a sad one—promised
to interest a "lady of the Court" in her.   Mademoiselle
Leguay, a gentle, unsuspecting creature, whose extremely
simple and confiding nature had already been the cause of
her betrayal, lent a ready ear to Lamotte's promises.   Not
long afterwards Lamotte brought the "lady of the Court"
to his *protégée's* lodging.   Having taken a seat, the Comtesse, according to the girl's evidence at the trial, "drew
out a pocket-book, and, opening it, showed me several
letters which she declared were written to her by the
Queen.

"But, madame," I answered, "all this is a mystery to
me ; I cannot understand it."

"You will soon understand it, my pet," she returned ; "I
possess the Queen's full confidence.   We are like hand and
glove together.   She has just given me another proof of
this trust by commissioning me to find her a person to do
something which will be explained at the proper time.   I
have made a choice of you, and, if you like to undertake it,
I will make you a present of 15,000 francs.   If, however,
you do not think my word sufficient, and desire to have
security for 15,000 francs, we will go at once to a notary."

"From that moment," added Leguay, "I was no longer
myself."

Having thus obtained the accomplice she needed, the
Comtesse, "whose confidence was never bestowed absolutely on any one," merely instructed the girl in the part
she had to perform.   In the first place, to keep up her own
rôle of patronage, the Comtesse introduced her dupe to the
people who frequented her house as the "Baroness d'Oliva"—
an anagram, by the way, of Valois—and made a great deal
of her.   Finally, when d'Oliva was told that Marie Antoinette wished her to impersonate herself on a certain night in

the Park of Versailles, "which," says the Comtesse in her
Memoirs, " it was not difficult to make her believe, for she
was very stupid," the Cardinal was brought back once more
from Saverne, where he was alternately fuming, and seeking
happy omens from the incantations of Cagliostro.

On this occasion the Comtesse went herself to Saverne,
" disguised as an abbé," in order to announce to him the
Queen's intention to grant him the interview he desired.

" It was a dull night," stated d'Oliva in her evidence,
relative to the famous episode in the Park of Versailles,
when the Comtesse made the Cardinal believe he had had
an interview with Marie Antoinette ; " not a speck of
moonlight, nor could I distinguish anything but those
persons and objects which were familiar to me. It would
be quite impossible for me to describe the state I was in.
I was so agitated, so excited, so disconcerted, and so
tremulous that I cannot conceive how I was able to
accomplish even half of what I had been instructed to do."

This was to offer a rose to " a great nobleman," who was
to believe he received it from the hand of the Queen, and
to say to him, " You know what this means."

The Cardinal, " covered in a long cloak and with the
wide brim of his hat turned down over his face," no sooner
found himself in the presence of the counterfeit queen than
he fell on his knees and kissed her hand, which at the
same time let fall the rose it held. But before he could
utter a word, the artful Comtesse, to avoid the almost
certain risk of detection, rushed up, and murmuring
" Quick, quick! away, away! we are watched!" drew "her
Majesty" away.

The Cardinal, who had not the least doubt he had met
the Queen, especially since he had "the rose as a proof,"
was now so firmly convinced that he was about to be recalled to Court as Minister, that when, in the next of the
forged letters he received from the Queen, he was asked

for "a loan of 50,000 francs for certain charitable purposes," he instantly complied. A month later the Comtesse got another sum of 100,000 francs out of him.

The poor "Baroness d'Oliva," who had been promised 15,000 francs as the reward for her strange service to the Queen, was paid 4,268 francs by bit-and-bit instalments, and then dropped by the "lady of the Court," who no longer needed her.

V

THE first thing the Comtesse de Lamotte did with the money she thus obtained was to return to Bar-sur-Aube. Her object was twofold. She wished to dazzle the people who had known her former poverty, both as a child and at the time of her marriage. And she wished to purchase Fontette since there was no other way of obtaining it. To be the "Lady of the Manor of Fontette" was as much a fixed idea with her as the desire to be Minister was with the Cardinal.

The return of the Lamottes to Bar-sur-Aube, and their doings during the few weeks they spent there, gave the quiet little provincial town plenty to talk of. They first of all paid all their debts, and this created so favourable an impression that most of the best people called on them and accepted the hospitality which the Comtesse paraded more like a *parvenue* than the descendant of the Valois. While the negotiations for the purchase of Fontette were in progress—negotiations never destined to come to anything—Madame de Lamotte bought a house in Bar-sur-Aube, "for which she paid twice as much as it was worth." She wished a place, she said, "where she could spend the summer months till her château was rebuilt."

MADEMOISELLE D'OLISVA.

MADEMOISELLE LEGUAY, "BARONESS D'OLIVA"
[From an old French print]

Her extravagance, however, soon wasted the 150,000 francs she had swindled out of the Cardinal, and it again became necessary to invent fresh means of profiting by his credulity.

It was at this juncture that the ever-fertile imagination of the Comtesse first conceived the idea of spiriting away the famous diamond necklace, which Böhmer and Bassenge, the Court jewellers, had for ten years been trying to sell in vain. One word—vanity—will suffice to explain how it was that those two Saxon Jews, who might have been credited with at least some of the hereditary shrewdness of their race, if with no business ability, having locked up all their capital in a necklace they couldn't sell, should have persistently refused to break it up and dispose of the stones in the ordinary way, whereby after ten years they had come to the verge of ruin.

To break up their "matchless jewel" was the last thought that ever entered their heads, and when it was suggested to Böhmer by Marie Antoinette he felt highly affronted. Worry appears finally to have affected Böhmer's brain, and at the sight of him at Versailles, people used to exchange smiles and tap their foreheads significantly. For, Bassenge having failed to find a purchaser for the necklace in any of the Courts of Europe, Böhmer proceeded to offer it periodically to Marie Antoinette, till he and his diamonds became as great a nuisance to her as the Comtesse de Lamotte and her claim to Fontette had been to Calonne. Nevertheless, Böhmer had persisted in his belief that the Queen's objections to purchase the necklace would eventually be overcome, till in the course of ten years he too, like Rohan, had become obsessed with a fixed idea.

It thus happened that Böhmer, having heard that a certain Comtesse de Lamotte was said to have great influence over the Queen, called on her to implore her to exert it in his behalf. Remembering all she had heard of

16

the jeweller, and coupling it with his belief in her influence, the Comtesse instinctively compared him with the Cardinal. The credulity of each was due to precisely the same cause, and since she had duped one, why should she not dupe the other? The idea acted like a spur to her powers of invention. It required months to fabricate the intrigue by which she obtained the possession of Böhmer's necklace, but the idea—like those which inspire all great masterpieces, of crime as well as of art—was conceived in a moment.

The mind which was capable of *forging* a queen skilfully enough to deceive the Cardinal was too alert and crafty to be caught in the act of raping the jeweller of his diamonds. The Comtesse obliged Böhmer to call on her three times before she finally consented to employ her influence in his behalf. The infatuated jeweller, who believed in her influence, just as the Cardinal did, because he wished to believe in it, offered her a thousand livres for her services. But she grandly declined to be bribed. Intending to have the whole necklace, she would not accept so much as a single gem. Besides, it was wiser that Böhmer should understand from the start that the Comtesse de Lamotte-Valois, as the intimate friend of the Queen of France, was too great a personage to receive payment for the favours she conferred.

"If it be in my power to be of service to you," she said, with gracious dignity, "that in itself will be my recompense. And mind," she added, "you do not say that I have had anything to do with the matter."

That night, for the first time in ten years, Böhmer slept peacefully.

The story of the robbery of the famous necklace, and the

subsequent trial of the Comtesse de Lamotte and her accomplices, is one, to judge from the number of times it has been told, of which the interest seems to be inexhaustible.

Vizetelly's *Story of the Diamond Necklace* is by far the best and most detailed account, while those who are content to dispense with details will find Carlyle's notable essay the most picturesque and dramatic. But though the popularity of the story may be regarded as a legitimate excuse for its repetition, it is impossible here to give more than a brief *résumé* of the affair.

Having resolved to get possession of the necklace, the Comtesse proceeded in the matter with a boldness, confidence, and cunning which lacked only the complete success of her plans to have given them the stamp of genius. To divert all suspicion from herself, she had need of an accomplice, one who could be relied on to obey her instructions implicitly, and who in the end could be made to bear the responsibility, and thus relieve her of the consequences of the fraud. She therefore chose the Cardinal, who seemed to have been sent to her by the devil expressly for her purpose.

He was at Saverne, whither, after swindling him without his knowledge out of 150,000 francs, she had sent him by one of her forged letters to mark time, so to speak, till she could invent fresh means of exploiting his unbounded credulity. He had taken with him his Rose, precious souvenir of that meeting with the Queen, which had come to an end almost before it began, and the name of which he bestowed on one of the walks in his park. He had also taken with him Cagliostro, on whose powers of divination this arch-dupe depended to foretell the probable date when the Queen, as she promised, would send him the letter that should make him the happiest man in France, the letter that summoned him to Versailles, the Ministry, and the arms of Marie Antoinette.

But after six months of exile, the impatience of his Eminence was beginning, in spite of the Rose and Cagliostro, to sap the power even of his credulity. It was, therefore, essential to the Comtesse to recall him to Paris without further delay, though in doing so, after the interview in the Park of Versailles, she ran the risk of ruining her plans. No risk, however, was ever too great to frighten the Comtesse; and she never tried to solve difficulties before she was actually confronted with them. The first thing was to bring the Cardinal to Paris; time enough to find means of soothing his impatience when she got him there.

"I desire," she dictated to her forger, Réteaux de Villette, who wrote the letters the Cardinal believed were written by Marie Antoinette, "to hasten your return, on account of a secret negotiation which I am unwilling to confide to any one but yourself." And the writer went on to explain the immense obstacles that still had to be surmounted before the Cardinal could publicly enjoy the favour he deserved.

His Eminence no sooner received this letter than he started immediately for Paris, though the cold was intense and the roads buried deep in snow. On his arrival the Comtesse informed him on behalf of the Queen that the negotiation entrusted to him was the purchase of Böhmer's necklace.

"The Queen," said the Comtesse, "wishes the purchase to be a secret for the present, so as not to offend the King, who might be annoyed at her extravagance; and being short of money, for the moment she can think of no one but you who personally and from the high consideration you enjoy would be a guarantee in the eyes of the jewellers."

The price of the necklace, she informed the Cardinal, was 1,600,000 livres (£64,000), which the Queen had agreed to pay in four instalments of equal amounts at intervals of six months. The Cardinal, as usual, consulted his "oracle" as to how he should act, whose advice or "divination" was inspired in this instance, as before, by his faith in the Comtesse's boasted influence with the Queen—faith which made Cagliostro unconsciously Madame de Lamotte's accomplice and involved him too in the swindle of which he was both innocent and ignorant.

The Cardinal, accordingly, acting on the advice of the quack, gave Böhmer the necessary guarantee, and having received the necklace handed it over in due course to the Comtesse, who till this moment had apparently nothing to do with the transaction beyond putting Böhmer into communication with his Eminence. Having thus got possession of the necklace, the Comtesse promptly proceeded to pick the diamonds from their setting, whereupon Lamotte crossed the Channel and disposed of the greater part of the stones to "Gray of Bond Street."

The *dénouement* to this bold swindle occurred six months later, when the first instalment of 400,000 livres became due. To avert any suspicion from attaching to herself, the Comtesse had in the meantime continued to delude the Cardinal by means of her forged letters, in which, as the day of reckoning drew near, he was given to understand that as the Queen's financial difficulties continued, it would be necessary for him to procure an extension of time for her from Böhmer. By this action the Comtesse hoped that the Cardinal, remembering he was security for the Queen, would advance the 400,000 livres himself. This in the event of a scandal would convince Böhmer that the Queen really possessed the necklace, while it would involve the Cardinal too seriously to permit him to back out of further payments. For the wily Comtesse knew her victim too well to doubt that he would pay for the necklace sooner than face the scandal of a law-suit which would expose him to ridicule and shame. It would also give her time to invent a plausible means of breaking off the Queen's correspondence with him, whereby he should be made to believe that he was the dupe of Marie Antoinette instead of herself—a deception which the actual hostility of the Queen would prevent him from ever discovering.

To play this pretty little farce in the most convincing manner, the artful impostor actually brought the Cardinal on the day of reckoning 30,000 livres, which she declared " the Queen desired him to offer Böhmer as interest," requesting him at the same time to obtain the extension of time at which she had hinted in her letters. The utterly unsuspicious Cardinal did as he was requested, but Böhmer refused to regard the 30,000 livres as interest, and being hard pressed himself for money, reminded his Eminence that he should expect him, as security for the Queen, to pay the remaining 370,000 livres due.

But Rohan, believing that the guarantee he had given Böhmer was merely a matter of form, had made no provision to meet the engagement ; and rich though he was, he could not in a moment when suddenly called upon find so large a sum. Alarmed, however, by the jeweller's threats, he undertook to pay the instalment in full as agreed in a day or two. With this assurance Böhmer was obliged to be satisfied, but he began to have a suspicion that there was something crooked in the transaction ; a suspicion that nearly drove him completely out of his senses, when on imparting it to Madame Campan, the Queen's lady-in-waiting, she gave him plainly to understand that if he imagined her Majesty had bought his necklace, or had ever had any intention of doing so, he was mad. Böhmer hereupon rushed off in a great state of agitation to Madame de Lamotte, whom he regarded as the Queen's intermediary in the purchase of the necklace, in spite of the fact that beyond soliciting her influence at the commencement he had had no dealings with her at all.

The Comtesse, realizing that Böhmer's interview with Madame Campan upset her original scheme, was unable at a moment's notice to invent another. But, as it was necessary to do something, she thought it best to confirm Madame Campan's statement. So she coolly told the distracted jeweller that he was being victimized.

"But the Cardinal," she added, reassuringly, "is, as you know, very rich ; he will pay. Go to him."

The Comtesse had every reason to believe that Böhmer would take her advice ; but, though she did not doubt Rohan would pay for the sake of his own credit in the matter, knowing that Böhmer's interview with the Cardinal would disclose her imposture to the latter, she sought to render her safety doubly sure. So she proceeded to warn Réteaux de Villette, her forger, and Mademoiselle Leguay d'Oliva, her forged Queen, on whose evidence alone she could be convicted of the fraud, that if they valued their liberty the sooner they got out of the country the better. Terror gave them wings, and they started immediately ; the former taking refuge in Geneva, and the latter in Brussels. The Comtesse herself thought it as well to leave Paris for a while, so she and her husband returned to their house in Bar-sur-Aube, where they proceeded to astound the neighbourhood with their ostentatious style of living.

Had Böhmer taken her advice, she might have continued to enjoy the spoils of her brilliant swindle in safety ; for the Cardinal, sooner than face a scandal which, apart from the ridicule to which it would expose him, meant his ruin, would have paid for the necklace as he tried to do. But instead of going to Rohan the maddened jeweller went to the King !

It was Assumption Day, the one day in the year on which the Cardinal was entitled to appear at Versailles, when as Grand Almoner he celebrated mass, which it was

customary for the Royal Family and the Court to attend
in state.   He and the Court were waiting in the Œil-de-
Bœuf for the King and Queen to appear in order to
accompany them to the Chapel of St. Louis, when a door
was opened, and instead of the King and Queen a chamberlain appeared and summoned the Grand Almoner to the
Sovereign.   Everybody knows what followed.   Böhmer,
having obtained an audience of Louis XVI, had related
to that amazed monarch all the details relative to the
purchase by the Queen of the famous diamond necklace.
This story, repeated in the presence of Marie Antoinette,
whose honesty and virtue alike it impugned, stung her to
fury.   Exasperated by Böhmer's assertion that she had
purchased his necklace, which for ten years she had refused
to do, she might have excused him on the ground of his
insanity.   But when he charged her with having employed
Rohan, whom she hated, to purchase the necklace through
the intervention of a confidante, of whom she had never
heard, she was transported with rage.   Forgetting that she
was a Queen, which she did too often, she remembered
only that she was a woman, and without thinking of the
consequences, insisted that the Cardinal should be arrested
and her reputation publicly vindicated.   Louis XVI, whose
misfortune it was always to be guided by her when he
shouldn't, and never when he should—a misfortune that
cost him in the end crown and life—consequently ordered
the immediate arrest of the Grand Almoner, who, attired
in his pontifical robes, was carried off from Versailles to
the Bastille like a common criminal before the eyes of the
whole Court.

To have arrested him in any case was most unwise,
but to have arrested him like this was the height of folly.
It insulted the whole house of Rohan, which was powerful
enough to resent the insult ; it made a great scandal of a
common swindle by implicating the throne, whose dwind-

ling prestige was thus extinguished; and it gave to the national discontent a new and dangerous hope.

Perhaps nothing illustrates the impression created on the popular mind by the publicity given to this affair than the manner in which the news of the arrest of the first prince of the Church was received by the Parliament of Paris, the old enemy of the Court.

"Grand and joyful business," cried one of the deputies, rubbing his hands. "A Cardinal in a swindle! The Queen implicated in a forgery! Filth on the crook and on the sceptre! What a triumph for ideas of liberty!"

Alas, for the "ideas of liberty" that depend for their realization on such means! Some of the filth in which they originate is sure to cling to them too.

The news of the Cardinal's arrest reached Bar-sur-Aube a few days later, and greatly disturbed the Comtesse de Lamotte. Beugnot, who chanced to be with her when she was informed of it, and was sufficiently acquainted with the intimacy of her relations with the Cardinal to suspect that she might be closely involved in the affair, advised her to flee without delay. But though frightened by the unexpected turn of events, she determined to remain and boldly face the situation. Let them arrest her, if they liked, she would defy them to prove her guilt. Were not the only witnesses whose evidence could incriminate her safe across the frontier? No, she would remain, and if arrested deny everything. She consented, however, to Beugnot's suggestion that she should burn all her letters and papers.

The process was scarcely finished when she was seized. By some extraordinary error the authorities charged with her apprehension failed to secure her husband, who no sooner saw his wife on the road to the Bastille than he quietly slipped across the frontier. Lamotte was a fool as well as a knave, but like many fools he possessed a certain shrewd cunning. If, he thought, the King of France was capable of arresting the Grand Almoner, he was capable of obtaining the arrest of a lesser mortal, even though the soil on which his victim stood was no longer French. He therefore chose England as his place of refuge, in the belief that it would be less willing to oblige the King of France than any other country in Europe.

His fool's cunning, indeed, served him better than the more brilliant craft of his wife's other associates. For Brussels gave up the "Baronne d'Oliva," and Geneva Réteaux de Villette; while Cagliostro and his wife, and a whole host of the Cardinal's and Comtesse's mutual friends were likewise seized. In a fortnight "the Bastille," as Carlyle says, "had opened its iron bosom to them all."

But dangerous as was her situation, Madame de Lamotte's audacity did not desert her. In her effort to save herself she did not hesitate to throw the burden of her guilt on any one she thought capable of bearing it. Thus Marie Antoinette, the Cardinal, and even Cagliostro were all accused by her of being in the plot to rob Böhmer. Her impudence and cleverness, however, did not save her in the end. Her forger and her counterfeit Queen completely vindicated Marie Antoinette, and laid the guilt where it belonged.

After a long and sensational trial, she was "condemned to be flogged, naked, having a halter round her neck, to be branded on the shoulder, and imprisoned for life in the Salpêtrière."

Her accomplices were treated more leniently. Réteaux de Villette was banished for life from the country, and Mademoiselle Leguay d'Oliva was discharged as a victim of the Comtesse, as was Cagliostro, though the trial exposed his quackery and he was, on regaining his liberty, ordered to leave France. The Cardinal, to the inexpressible mortification of Marie Antoinette, was acquitted with honour, but the King afterwards exiled him.

As for Lamotte, he received a similar sentence to that passed on his wife, whose "Valois blood," he said, "had overheated her imagination." But the sentence was never executed, for he would not accept any of the bribes made him to leave England, where in spite of numerous attempts of "the King of France" to arrest or kidnap him he remained in safety till the Revolution.

VI

It was three weeks before the punishment to which the Comtesse de Lamotte was condemned was enforced. During this time she remained in the Conciergerie, whither she had been transferred from the Bastille during her trial, in complete ignorance of her conviction.

"At length," she says, "the 21st of June arrived, that eventful day which will live in my remembrance as long as memory itself shall live—the day the most accursed in the calendar of my misfortunes."

She was under the impression that she was to be banished the country, and it was deemed advisable not to undeceive her, in the hope that her surprise, when informed of the terrible nature of her sentence, would deprive her of the strength to resist, and so enable those charged with the disagreeable duty of inflicting the punishment to effect the object the more easily. Consequently, she was called at five in the morning and "told that her lawyer wished to see her." She rose instantly and, wrapping herself in a cloak, went quickly to a room where, instead of her lawyer, she found eight men and the registrar who had her sentence in his hand.   At the sight of these men she realized that she had been duped.   She was seized with a terrible fright and tried to fly, but the door of the room had been locked behind her.   One caught her roughly by the arm, another by the skirt, and in a second they had bound "her little delicate hands."

Her fright turned to rage.

"Why such precautions?" she asked boldly.   "I cannot escape you.   If you were executioners you could not treat me worse!"

She still believed it was only a question of conveying her to the convent to which she was banished.   But the registrar, as soon as her hands were bound, ordered her to go on her knees to hear her sentence.   This she haughtily refused to do, whereupon one of the men who held her gave her a sudden blow behind the knees, which brought her to the ground; a halter was then slipped round her neck, and the registrar proceeded to read the sentence.

When she heard that she was to be whipped and branded, she fell into a fit.   While unconscious, she was removed to the Court of the Conciergerie, where the punishment was to be inflicted in full view of the public.   Owing to the hour, however, there were very few present.   Here she regained her senses, and at the sight of the whip and the branding-iron "commenced to utter cries not of terror, but of fury."

Addressing the people who were looking on, she exclaimed, "If they treat thus the blood of the Valois, what lot is in store for that of the Bourbons?"   The sight of this shrieking, struggling woman in the hands of eight men "drew groans of indignation from the crowd."   Encouraged by these signs of sympathy, the wretched

Comtesse shrieked and struggled the more, till it was found necessary to tear her clothing from her to mark her with the iron. During this operation she launched forth the foulest calumnies against the Queen. To silence her, they put a gag into her mouth, but not before she bit a piece out of the hand of one of her tormentors. Gagged, bound, and naked, she still continued to struggle, so that the branding-iron which marked her on the shoulder with the letter V[1] glanced off and marked her a second time on the breast.

Fortunately, in the midst of the process, she lost consciousness, and the whipping which followed the branding was "slight and pro forma." As soon as the sentence was executed she was thrown half-naked and half-dead into a cab and driven at full gallop to the Salpêtrière. On the road one of the doors of the cab flew open, and those who accompanied her had barely time to prevent her from throwing herself under the wheels.

At the Salpêtrière fresh horrors awaited her. On her arrival she was taken extremely ill, and remained totally insensible for three quarters of an hour. As soon as she began to recover she was placed by some of the attendants in a bed, which one of her fellow-prisoners was kind enough to give her. "This," observes the Governor of the prison, Madame Robin, in her official report, "was fortunate for Madame de Lamotte, otherwise she would have been under the necessity of lying in a bed full of vermin with six old women."

Of all the brutalities of the *ancien régime*, which was so fair without and so foul within, none justified the awful purge of the Revolution more than the prison system. The Salpêtrière, where women criminals were confined, was a typical French prison, neither the worst nor the best

---

[1] It is a curious coincidence that the V with which she was branded stood for Valois as well as for Voleuse (thief).

of its kind. The Comtesse de Lamotte in her Memoirs has given a very graphic description of it, in which for once she may be relied upon not to exaggerate. Space prevents quoting her in full, but the following extract will perhaps be sufficient to convey the impression of horror she received when on the day after her arrival she was able to take observation of her surroundings.

She was seated in a small court, when a great number of women approached her, "making a most dreadful clattering with their wooden shoes."

"As soon as they saw me," says the Comtesse, "they exclaimed, 'Oh! there she is, that is the lady from the Court.' These poor creatures, whose appearance spoke a variety of wretchedness, approached and invited me to see the place destined for my reception. Some took me by the arm and led me to what they called the dormitory, the place where they slept and worked. I had no sooner entered the door of this infernal mansion than I recoiled with terror, but there were many women behind, who prevented me from running back, or I must have fallen, so great was my horror at the sight of this hall, containing one hundred and twenty-seven women, who, from their appearance and behaviour, might have been reared in the forests, for they were almost as wild and savage as tigers, having always in their hands either stones, bottles, or chairs, ready to throw at the head of any who displeased them.

"At the sight of this hideous spectacle I shrank back, while big tears rolled down my cheeks, and with a stifled voice I said, like a child unconscious of what passed around me, 'Poor Valois! oh, poor Valois!'"

The Comtesse de Lamotte escaped from the Saltpêtrière,

about a year after she entered it, under most mysterious circumstances. Six months prior to her flight she received notice, she says, from without that she would be assisted in any attempt to escape. She believed that this offer of help came from the "Queen or the Cardinal," but she never discovered who her mysterious correspondent was. It was certainly not the Queen, who had every reason to dread the liberty of a woman who had so shamefully calumniated her. Nor was it likely to have been the Cardinal, who had no desire to have the scandal reopened, as it would surely be by the Comtesse's escape. But the considerations that would weigh with the Cardinal were not likely to be regarded by his powerful family, who were at bitter feud with the Queen. In any case it is impossible that Madame de Lamotte should have escaped in the elaborate way she describes without the secret connivance of her gaolers.

Everything was done by her mysterious, unknown correspondent from without, whose instructions she merely followed. She was furnished with clothing for herself and a fellow-prisoner, who was to accompany her as a maid ; and when she left the Saltpêtrière she was provided with money to enable her to leave the country. After having had many curious and dangerous adventures, she finally reached London, where she found her husband.

The Lamottes were now in great distress. Of the sixty odd thousand pounds, at which the famous necklace they had stolen was valued, there remained scarcely anything. To live, the Comte, who had always been an inveterate gambler, had recourse to the gaming-table and the race-course. The Comtesse took to calumniating the Queen as a mine, which, if skilfully worked, might yield gold.

" It was an arrow I still preserved," she confesses frankly,

" as the best in my quiver, resolving to threaten, but not to shoot till reduced to the last extremity."

In pursuance of this resolution, she let it be known that she intended to write " an exact detail of the extraordinary events which had contributed to raise her to the dignity of confidante and favourite of the Queen of France." This report, as intended, reached Versailles, and the Duchesse de Polignac, happening to come to England at this time to take the cure at Bath, was commissioned to buy off the Comtesse. This she did, and Madame Campan asserts that she had seen " in the Queen's hands a manuscript of the infamous Memoirs of the woman Lamotte, and which were corrected by the very hand of M. de Calonne in all those places where a total ignorance of the usages of the Court had made this wretch commit the most palpable errors."

But Madame de Lamotte was a liar and a swindler by instinct ; she had no sooner received payment for her Memoirs than she proceeded to break her word and publish them. This edition obtained a wide sale in England and Holland, whither Lamotte went for the purpose of smuggling another edition across the frontier into France. The fall of the Bastille rid him of all fear of arrest, and he returned to France. The edition he brought with him, of his wife's scandalous libel, in which Calonne, the personal enemy of the Queen, had collaborated, was secretly purchased by Louis XVI, who, dreading its influence on the public, had it burnt in the ovens at Sèvres.

In the meantime, while Lamotte was in France, his wife, who in spite of the Revolution had too wholesome a fear of the Saltpêtrière to return to Paris, was reduced to dire straits in London. For her widely-circulated Memoirs she scarcely received anything ; nor did her husband remit her

the proceeds, or any portion of them, of his sale of the
French edition. On the contrary, he left her to bear the
full brunt of the debts he had incurred in England.
Executions were repeatedly levied on her ; her furniture
was sold or pawned, and even her maid, the same who
accompanied her from the Saltpêtrière, sued her for
wages.

The purchase of her slanderous Memoirs by the Duchesse
de Polignac on behalf of the Queen gave her the idea of
publishing the same slanders again in the form of a
" Justification " of her life, in the hope of extorting more
money from the throne. The Duc d'Orléans, the infamous
Jacobin prince of the blood, was informed by Lamotte of
her intention ; and in his desire to increase the popular
hatred of Marie Antoinette, whose husband he wished to
supplant, he encouraged the Comtesse to carry out her
design by the bestowal of a liberal bribe. It was understood that when the work was completed it would be
purchased by the Orleans party for dissemination in their
campaign of calumny against the throne. But the Comtesse,
whose husband was now doing filthy work for the government of Louis XVI as well as for the Duc d'Orléans, was
induced, in the hope of obtaining a higher price, to enter
into negotiations with the former for the sale of her
work.

It was now her turn to be duped. For the agents of
the King, with whom she was in negotiation, having led
her to believe that on surrendering the manuscript an
annuity would be settled on her for life, suddenly left
her in the lurch when the unexpected and fatal flight of
the Royal Family created a situation which henceforth
rendered calumny valueless as a weapon for extorting
money.

At the same time, the agents of the Duc d'Orléans,

17

finding how she had been playing fast and loose with them, decided on a brutal revenge. Aware of the dread of the Comtesse to return to France—a dread that was causeless now that the Revolution had begun, but which the memory of her punishment still made very real—they proposed to kidnap her and convey her to Paris. To this end they obtained a writ against the wretched woman on the ground that she owed one of them a hundred guineas. Armed with this order for her arrest, they presented themselves at her house and requested her to accompany them. Madame de Lamotte had been warned by her husband to beware of the agents of the Duc d'Orléans. Knowing that she had not incurred the debt she was charged with, she had every reason to be terrified when the men whom she had tricked in the negotiations over the publication of her book appeared with an order for her arrest. But, though frightened, she did not altogether lose her presence of mind. She was sufficiently acquainted with the laws of the country to know that, being a married woman, she was immune from arrest for debt. Nevertheless, as her persecutors assured her, it was necessary for her to *prove* she was married ; and as she could not do this, the proofs of her marriage being in France, they insisted in carrying her off.

The Comtesse, however, seizing a favourable moment, suddenly opened the door and locked her enemies in. She then rushed down the stairs into the street. Had she been less agitated she might have succeeded in making good her escape. " For there were some hackney-coaches," observes Lamotte in recording this event in his Memoirs, "stationed before the house, into one of which she might have got and been driven in a few minutes into another county, where, had her persecutors discovered her retreat, it would have been necessary for them to procure a fresh warrant before arresting her. But instead of adopting this very obvious course, she took refuge in a neighbouring house where she was known, and whither she was pursued by her tormentors, who had watched her movements from the window above as soon as they had succeeded in releasing themselves."

In spite of the efforts of the owner, who was a friend of the Comtesse, to keep them out, they forced their way in, and declaring they would take all the consequences of trespass, proceeded to search the house. The fugitive had taken refuge in a room on the top floor, whither she was traced by her pursuers, who, failing to induce her to open the door, proceeded to batter it down, whereupon the hunted woman, distracted with terror, jumped out of the window.

But luck was against her. For though "her thigh was broken in two places, her left arm fractured, and one of her eyes was knocked out, in addition to which her body was a mass of bruises, she lived for several weeks." While her pursuers immediately seized her almost lifeless body, and with disgraceful indifference to her sufferings refused to surrender it to the friends with whom she had sought refuge till they had got bail for its security.

This shocking incident appears to have attracted as little attention as her death, which followed some weeks later. In spite of the prominence that one would think would have been given to the death of so notorious a public character, the *Gentleman's Magazine*, one of the most popular journals of the day, merely recorded the event as follows—

"August 26, 1791.—Died at her lodgings, near Astley's Riding School, Lambeth, the noted Countess de Lamotte, of 'Necklace' memory, who lately jumped out of a two pair of stairs window to avoid the bailiffs."

Of all the persons connected with Madame de Lamotte, directly or indirectly, by blood, marriage, or implication in her frauds, her husband alone lived to a green old age. He survived till 1831, after a life chequered to the end with adventure.

A quarrel with her sister before the "Necklace" affair saved Mademoiselle de Saint-Remy from being involved in the famous trial. Unlike her brother, who had been foolish enough to commute his pension and entrust the proceeds to the Comtesse to employ in procuring his advancement, she refused to gamble with her little income, which resulted in the severance of all connection between the sisters. Mademoiselle de Saint-Remy went to board at the Abbey of Jarcy, where she was living when arrested as a suspect during the Terror. She, however, escaped the guillotine and died in 1817 in a German convent, whither she had gone on her release.

Cagliostro and Réteaux de Villette both ended their days in the prison of St. Angelo at Rome. The simple "Baroness d'Oliva"—who when put *hors de cour* at her trial thought it was an order prohibiting her from going again to Versailles, and promised the judge to obey it !— died the following year in great poverty.

The Cardinal was eventually permitted to return to Saverne. He allowed himself to be elected a member of the Third Estate in the States General, but when the Revolution, with which he at first sympathized, began to put its hands on Church property he crossed the Rhine. The remaining ten years of his life were spent very discontentedly, but safely, on a small German property he possessed.

As for Böhmer, the Revolution, by confiscating the Cardinal's benefices, the revenue of which had been charged by the Court with the payment of his " matchless jewel," completed his ruin. His troubles affected his reason and shortened his life.

THE DUCHESSE DE POLIGNAC

1749—1793

VI

"Dost thou dream of what was and no more is,
   The old kingdoms of earth and the kings?
Dost thou hunger for these things, Dolores,
   For these in a world of new things?
But thy bosom no fasts could emaciate,
   No hunger compel to complain,
Those lips that no bloodshed could satiate,
   Our Lady of Pain."

SWINBURNE'S *Dolores*.

THE DUCHESSE DE POLIGNAC

1749—1793

I

ADMIRED by many, loved devotedly by a few, and born to be worshipped by all if ever queen was, Marie Antoinette, even in the days when she could still smile, was never popular.

She was too natural in a world too artificial; she was virtuous, and the world in which she lived ridiculed virtue; she was good, sympathetic and generous, and the people by whom she was surrounded were malicious, cynical, and covetous. Above all, she was too triumphantly beautiful; the radiance of her presence inspired resentment.

"The jealousy of the women," says the Prince de Ligne, "whom she crushed by the beauty of her complexion and the carriage of her head, ever seeking to harm her as a woman, harmed her also as a queen. Fredegonde and

Brunehault, Catherine and Marie de Medicis, Anne and Theresa of Austria, never laughed. Marie Antoinette when she was fifteen laughed much; therefore she was declared 'satirical.'

"Because she was friendly to foreigners, from whom she had neither traps nor importunity to fear, they said she was 'inimical to Frenchmen.'

"An unfortunate dispute about a visit between her brother, the Elector of Cologne, and the Princes of the Blood —a dispute of which she was wholly ignorant—offended the etiquette of the Court, which then called her 'proud.'

"She dined with one friend, and sometimes went to see another after supper, and they said she was 'familiar.'

"Because she was sensible of the friendship of certain persons who were devoted to her, she was declared to be 'amorous' of them. Sometimes she required too much for their families, then she was 'unreasonable.'

"She gave little *fêtes* and superintended the management of them herself—that was 'bourgeoise.' She bought St. Cloud for the health of her children, and they pronounced her 'extravagant.'

"Her promenades in the evening on the terrace at Versailles, or on horseback in the Bois de Boulogne, or sometimes on foot round the music in the Orangery, 'seem suspicious.' Her general loving-kindness was termed 'coquettish.' She feared to win at cards, at which she was compelled to play, and they said she 'wasted the money of the nation.'

"She laughed, danced, and sang till she was twenty-five, and they called her 'frivolous.' Because she refused to take sides in quarrels, they termed her 'ungrateful.' And when she foresaw misfortune and ceased to amuse herself, they called her 'intriguing.'"

From criticism to aspersion is but a step. The people caught the trick of disloyalty from the Court. The real

MARIE ANTOINETTE ("LA PANTHÈRE AUTRICHIENNE")
[*From a very rare French print*]

To face page 266

"conquerors of the Bastille" were not the frenzied mob to whom de Launay surrendered the citadel, but the noblesse of France, the *noblesse enversaillée*, as the old Marquis de Mirabeau scornfully termed them. "*L'Autrichienne*" thus became *la panthère Autrichienne.* It was the Court that inspired the epigrams which "tempered despotism." The Revolution had commenced at Versailles long before it broke out in Paris.

But the hostility which finally led Marie Antoinette to the scaffold was made up of many elements beside the spite of women of quality. Everybody, in a word, lent a hand to the construction of that fatal legend; the King's aunts and the King's brothers; Frederick the Great and Joseph II; Madame de Lamotte and Cardinal de Rohan; Calonne, d'Orléans and Lauzun, the heron-plume duke; Court and Capital; princes and valets; Versailles and Europe. "And Marie Antoinette"—admits M. de Nolhac, one of her most enthusiastic admirers—"herself built it up by her innocent frivolity, her diamonds and 'her Polignac.'"

This last element was the match that exploded the mine of hatred which blew the *ancien régime* to pieces. In 1789 the name of Polignac was the French for hate.

Like all the families belonging to the noblesse of the sword, the Polignacs were of very ancient origin. They claimed, indeed, to be descended from Sidonius Apollinaris, the celebrated poet-statesman of the fifth century, who married the daughter of a Roman emperor and, though never a priest, became a bishop and even a saint. Polignac, they said, was a corruption of Apollinaris. The descendants of Saint Sidonius, however, appear to have completely lost themselves in the mists of antiquity, for history cannot find any trace of them till the eleventh century, when a certain Sieur de Polignac, having distinguished himself in the First Crusade, settled down in the Velay and proceeded to plant a genealogical tree which is still flourishing.

Till the Revolution made the Polignacs historic, the family had produced but one member of any note. This was Melchior, Abbé and later Cardinal de Polignac. Destined, as a younger son, for the Church, his father sent him to Paris to be educated. He made the best of his opportunities, and having attracted the attention of Cardinal de Bouillon, went to Rome with him as private secretary. Here the suppleness of his character procured him many powerful friends. It was chiefly, if not entirely, due to his influence that the quarrel between Louis XIV and the Pope was ended.

"I do not know how it is, my dear Abbé," his Holiness said to him, "but though you always appear to be of my opinion, I finish by being of yours."

Such a man could not fail to impress Louis XIV, whose genius for recognizing ability in others was the chief source of his greatness, and he sent the Abbé de Polignac on many important diplomatic missions. It was he who persuaded Louis to sign the Treaty of Utrecht, which was so humiliating to his pride and so necessary to France. The Grand Monarque, who could not endure to be contradicted, declared that the Abbé de Polignac was the only man who had ever done so without vexing him. It was on the recommendation of James II of England that the Pope created him Cardinal.

In spite of his active political life, he found the time to cultivate his taste for literature and art. He spoke and wrote Greek and Latin with perfect purity, and was as distinguished a Latin poet as he was a French writer. Voltaire and Madame de Sévigné held him in high esteem. His principal work was the *Anti-Lucrèce*, a remarkable

MELCHIOR CARDINAL
DE POLIGNAC

After Rigaud

[*From an old French print*]

tour de force that gave him a European reputation. During his embassy at Rome he maintained, in the most conspicuous manner, the traditionary *luxe* of the Court he represented. His palace was not only famed for its lavish hospitality, but for the superb art treasures it contained. Polished, adroit, supple, crafty, and accomplished, Cardinal de Polignac was, in a word, one of the finest specimens of the courtier-priest that the *ancien régime* produced, a type which, like the age that produced it, has ceased to exist.

On his death in 1741, in his eightieth year, his fortune passed to a nephew who had married a Mazarin-Mancini. It is strange to note how the Mazarin blood always rendered notorious the families in whose veins it flowed. The Polignacs, with the exception of Cardinal Melchior, were never heard of till his nephew married a Mazarin.

There were four children of this union, two sons and two daughters. The latter were both named Diane, in accordance with a custom that had obtained in the family since the days of François I, as an acknowledgment of their indebtedness to Diane de Poitiers, whose favour had helped the Polignacs on in the world. One of these Dianes was the family stepping-stone to fame. She obtained—through what influence is unknown, for the Polignacs at the time, in spite of the celebrated Cardinal, were still only of the provincial noblesse, without fortune or influence—the post of lady-in-waiting to the Comtesse d'Artois.

"In Diane de Polignac," says de Goncourt, "the woman was nothing and wit everything. She had only to speak to make one forget her figure, her face, her clothes, the little, in fact, that she had received in the way of beauty or did to obtain it. A malicious manner of seizing on the ridiculous, a certain piquant turn of mind, a talent for epigrammatic conversation, rendered her not only amusing, but almost seductive, in spite of nature."

She was soon "the heart and soul of the Court," and
in spite of the scandal of her *liaison* with the Marquis
d'Autichamp—the same who commanded the Gendarmerie
at Lunéville when the Lamottes were in garrison there
—she succeeded in ingratiating herself into the favour of
the Royal Family, with whom she was always a *persona
grata*. To enable her to retain her post of lady-in-waiting,
of which the salary was totally inadequate to support one,
like herself, without private means at Versailles, the King
affiliated her to one of the religious chapters, so numerous
under the *ancien régime*, which conferred on its members
the title of canoness and a considerable income without
requiring from the beneficiary any return whatever. Later,
as a further mark of the royal esteem, the lay *chanoinesse* was
created a countess in her own right, and promoted from
a mere lady-in-waiting of the Comtesse d'Artois to the
head of the household of Madame Elizabeth.

It was, however, to the favour of her sister-in-law, the
Comtesse Jules, rather than to her own, that Diane de
Polignac owed these latter honours. On the other hand,
it was entirely to Diane that the Comtesse Jules, afterwards Duchesse de Polignac, owed in her turn the royal
patronage she exploited so profitably for herself, her family,
and her friends, and so disastrously to the throne, the Court,
and the nation.

In 1767, when Yolande Gabrielle Martine de Polastron
was married at seventeen to Comte Jules de Polignac, she
little dreamt of the dazzling future in store for her. The
marriage was one of convenience in a more literal sense
than the term usually implies—for in such marriages
there is usually some mutual material advantage. In
the present case, however, the marriage was merely the
formal alliance of two very old, very proud, and very
insignificant provincial families, too poor to make a profitable bargain in the marriage market. The Comtesse

Jules brought her husband scarcely any *dot*. For the first eight years of their marriage, their income never exceeded 8,000 livres, or £350. They lived chiefly at Claye-en-Brie, in a dilapidated country house belonging to Comte Jules. Now and then they came to Paris and took a second-rate apartment in some shabby-genteel quarter. On these occasions they were never seen in society. Only twice during this period of obscurity did they attempt to avail themselves of the privilege of their birth and go to Court: on the marriage of the Dauphin to Marie Antoinette, and again at their Coronation—when they were lost in the crowd of courtiers. They not only could not afford to go to Versailles, but if Madame de Lamotte is to be believed, they were frequently in as low water as herself.

" In my humble station of milliner's assistant," she says, " I often called upon the Duchesse de Polignac from Madame Boussel's to obtain payment, only to receive fair words instead of money. Before the smile of royal favour no tradesman would trust her, and she had not even a dress in which to be presented at Court."

Even when Diane de Polignac obtained her post at Court, it was some time before the Comtesse Jules appeared publicly at Versailles. She went there frequently, however, to see her sister-in-law. On one of these occasions Diane presented her privately to the Comtesse d'Artois, when Marie Antoinette arrived unexpectedly, and thus met for the first time her future favourite.

The appearance of the Comtesse Jules was well calculated to produce a favourable impression on the Queen. She was, to begin with, very beautiful.

" Hers," says M. de Nolhac, " was the beauty of the brunette with blue eyes. No portrait, not even Madame Vigée Lebrun's, adequately conveys the charm on which all her contemporaries dwell, and to which even her enemies submitted while they cursed it."

The Duc de Lévis, one of her contemporaries, declared that "hers was the most heavenly face that eyes could behold. Her glance, her smile, all her features were angelic. She was like a painting by Raphael."

Comte de Tilly, that *blasé* in beauty, who was one of the pages of the Queen when Madame de Polignac first came to Court, becomes almost lyrical when recalling her. According to him, her charm lay not so much in her beauty as in her utter lack of artificiality. She was perfectly natural. When Tilly first beheld her, she was wearing "something *négligé*, with a rose in her hair." At the Court of Versailles, where etiquette had set its stamp even on simplicity itself, the "graceful negligence" of the Comtesse Jules, and her style of dressing, was sufficient to give her a special *cachet*—the *cachet* of originality.

Marie Antoinette, who was herself always at war with the absurd conventions of the Court, felt at once drawn to the beautiful stranger. She expressed her astonishment at not having seen her at Court before, and wanted to know the reason. The Comtesse Jules, having no false pride, frankly acknowledged that neither she nor her husband was in a position to come to Versailles. Such a candid admission touched the Queen, and, resolving to keep up the acquaintance, she desired to be informed the next time that Madame de Polignac came to Versailles to visit her sister-in-law.

With each visit the favourable impression the lovely Comtesse Jules had produced on the Queen deepened. Discovering that she had a charming voice, Marie Antoinette invited her to her concerts, admitted her to her private dances, saw her on every possible occasion. In a very short time the acquaintance ripened into intimacy. But this perpetual coming and going between Paris and

Versailles put the Comte and Comtesse Jules to an expense they could ill afford to incur. It is impossible to go to Court, either formally or informally, on an income of three hundred and fifty pounds. So the Comtesse Jules at last informed the Queen that, flattering as was the "smile of royal favour," she felt compelled by force of poverty to cease coming to Versailles. To Marie Antoinette, however, the intimacy had now become a pleasure she could not do without. In order, therefore, to prevent her friend from leaving her, she realized the necessity of providing her with the means of maintaining herself in a befitting manner. In other words, to fix the Comtesse Jules at Court, it was necessary to find a post for her husband.

The appointment of first equerry of the Queen had just become vacant, and with her characteristic impetuosity Marie Antoinette at once bestowed it on Comte Jules. At the same time she installed her favourite in an apartment close to her own.

It was from the date of the bestowal of these favours that the family of Polignac, insignificant for so many centuries, commenced to count for something in the world.

II

THE situation and character of the Queen were conducive to the formation of the romantic friendship she had conceived for the Comtesse Jules. To Marie Antoinette love was a necessity, and when she met "her Polignac," her heart was starving for sympathy. She wanted so much to be loved, to be understood; but everywhere she met with nothing but indifference, criticism, or insult. She would have loved her husband, but it took him eight years

18

to find out her worth—eight childless years of marriage.
And this childless state had but whetted her hunger for
love the more. Each time that a child was born in the
Royal Family she had suffered bitterly. It needed not
the reproaches of the filthy street-songs, which she had
heard hummed at Versailles itself, to remind her of her
obligation to the nation. She wanted a Dauphin as much
as France did; she longed to be a mother. As de Goncourt
says, "this torture, so unnatural for a young queen, so hard
for one so emotional to bear and to be forced to hide,
explains all her caprices."

Not having a husband or a child on whom to lavish the
pent-up tenderness of her nature, she sought a friend—a
"bosom friend." But in spite of all the triumph of her
youth and beauty; in spite of the admiration she commanded even from those who criticized and aspersed her,
she could not find the pearl of the oyster of love—an affinity.
Scandal, watching her quest without comprehending its
motive, gave her lovers galore. But it was love she sought,
not a lover; and Lauzun, Coigny, Besenval and the others
passed out of her life at the time when, to the world, they
appeared to enter it. Conscious of her own virtuous intentions, she did not perceive the evil of theirs till they had
spattered her with the mud of their declarations.

A great similarity of character and tastes had drawn her
to the Princesse de Lamballe. This "king descended, god
descended," as Carlyle calls her, who was to pay for her
devotion with her life, was, so to speak, a sort of *feminine*
Marie Antoinette. She was the Queen without the
masculine energy of her character, without the vigour of
her impulses, her passions, or her pride. But Madame de
Lamballe, imprisoned like herself in royalty, seemed a
companion in misfortune, rather than a kindred soul; and
"the heart of the queen sought the heart of a friend
who had nothing in common with the *éclat* of the throne."

Such a friend Marie Antoinette believed she had at last found in the Comtesse Jules de Polignac. Charmed by her beauty, her lack of affectation, the simplicity of her manners and style of dressing, the caressing tones of her voice, the grace of her movements—in a word, by her alluring outward appearance, the Queen loved her for a certain air of disinterestedness and honesty that distinguished her from every other woman at Court.

In a sense Marie Antoinette was not mistaken in the opinion she formed of the character of her friend. Personally the Comtesse Jules was not altogether unworthy of the love of the Queen. She was really as amiable, gentle and unaffected as she seemed ; without malice, envy, or even ambition. She did not seek the power she acquired, nor did she greatly desire it. It is true that she did her best to retain it, and abused it ; but in this she was guided by her anxiety to benefit her family and her friends. She cared little or nothing for the benefits she herself derived from her friendship with the Queen. She was, moreover, unaware at the time of the evil she wrought, and probably never realized how much it contributed to the hatred that led Marie Antoinette to the scaffold. Her private life was singularly free from reproach. If the Comte de Vaudreuil, who, with Diane de Polignac, governed her as she governed the Queen, was her lover, the *liaison* was totally devoid of scandal. She was devoted to her children and loyal to her friends. Nevertheless, it is less as a woman that she must be regarded than as an influence. As such no favourite who ever reigned at Versailles was more fell. In this respect the odium in which she was held was fully justified.

Of all the elements of which this fatal " influence " was composed the most mischievous was the air of disinterestedness that captivated Marie Antoinette. It was really the callous indifference of an unemotional woman. The affection with which the Comtesse Jules was honoured left her cold. She could not feign what she did not feel, and she was cunning enough not to try. This unresponsiveness to the heart that impulsively poured its confidences into hers, and sought its sympathy, only served to increase the love of the Queen.

In the midst of the storms of jealousy and envy of the Court which assailed her by reason of the favour she enjoyed, the Comtesse Jules never lost her imperturbable calm. Observing the effect her frank indifference produced, she turned it to account with a craft that was the more consummate from its utter apathy. Learning of a plot to undermine her in the early stage of the friendship, she informed the Queen of it.

"We do not love one another enough yet," she said, "to be unhappy if we separate. I feel that it has come to this already. Be warned, let me leave you before it is too late. Soon I should not be able to bear quitting you."

Her carriage was waiting to take her from the palace, and she would have gone without regret had the Queen taken her at her word. But she had no intention of going; it was to the interest of her family and friends that she should remain. As she expected, Marie Antoinette threw herself on her neck and implored her to stay. The Comtesse Jules kept up the comedy, which she contrived should be witnessed by several persons, till she had the Queen conjuring her on her knees.

This "disinterestedness" was the secret of the vast fortune and the honours Marie Antoinette lavished on "her Polignac." But though the Queen wore out her gratitude she could never intoxicate it. At the height of her favour, when she was rich beyond the dreams of avarice, Madame de Polignac always preserved the air of a woman who regretted the grandeur of the position to which she was condemned.

This "disinterestedness" was also the secret of the incalculable injury the Queen received from the intimacy she formed with Madame de Polignac. For the tantalizing indifference of her favourite caused the Queen to conduct herself in a manner that exposed her to criticism, aspersion and vilification. In the hope of capturing the heart that eluded hers, Marie Antoinette resolved at all costs to get on the same equality with her friend. She abolished without a thought or a care all the awe and sacredness pertaining to the majesty of the throne, which even Louis XV had been careful to preserve. She treated the "salon Jules," as the Court called the favourite's apartments at Versailles, as her own ; and was in the habit of going there at all times without being announced.

"Here," she would say on entering, with her charming smile, " I am no longer queen, but myself."

Dropping the dignity expected of her in private, she refused to conform to the etiquette demanded of her in public. To the scandal of the Court, Marie Antoinette would stroll arm in arm with her friend through the corridors of Versailles ! They forgot, or pretended to forget, that the charming Duchess of Burgundy, whom the Queen resembled in many ways, had shown a similar disregard for etiquette, without giving offence, and that at the Court of Louis XIV, too.

Perhaps the most signal instance of her subversion of etiquette to friendship was her conduct at the birth of Madame de Polignac's youngest son—he who, as if he had inherited the fatal influence of his mother, was destined some fifty years later, in the revolution of 1830, to give the final *coup de grâce* to the Bourbons. In order to be near his mother, who was confined at Passy, Marie Antoinette persuaded the King to move the Court from Versailles to La Muette, where, from its close proximity to Passy, she was able to pass whole days at the bedside of her friend.

But try as she might she could not persuade the Comtesse Jules to give herself up completely to friendship, who, by defying, as it were, the benefactions of the Queen, provoked them the more.

III

THESE "benefactions," which precipitated the fall of the monarchy by their extravagance, were of two kinds—those due to the spontaneous generosity of the Queen, and those due to the solicitations of the favourite, who, though she never solicited anything for herself personally, was far from being indifferent to the wants of her friends and relations.

Marie Antoinette had nothing mean in her nature; when she gave she gave bounteously, but the benefits she conferred on Madame de Polignac passed all bounds. In order that her friend might have the *tabouret* of a duchess, the most coveted distinction a woman could have at the Court of Versailles, the Queen got Comte Jules created a duke and peer of France. Learning that her duke and duchess were in debt to the extent of 400,000 livres, she paid their debts, and obtained for them the estate of Fenestrange, which brought in 70,000 livres a year. Fifteen months later, on her recommendation, the Duc de Polignac was made Director-General of Postes and Haras, an appointment under the old *régime* that corresponded to that of Postmaster-General of the present time. It was worth 80,000 livres a year. When the daughter of her favourite was eleven, Marie Antoinette said to her mother—

"Shortly, I suppose, you will be thinking of marrying your daughter. When you have selected her husband remember the King and I wish to provide her with her *dot*."

The *dot* of a royal princess in the reign of Louis XV had been 6,000 livres. But Marie Antoinette provided the daughter of the Duchesse de Polignac with the monster *dot* of 800,000 livres. The lucky husband of Mademoiselle de Polignac was the Comte de Guiche, the eldest son of the Duc de Gramont. That his wife might not have to wait till he succeeded to the dukedom of which he was the heir before having her *tabouret*, the Queen got him created Duc de Guiche.

All these favours were conferred by the Queen not so much as marks of her esteem for the Duchesse de Polignac as in the hope of conquering her indifference. So assailed, it surrendered; but the heart of the Duchesse manifested its submission to the heart of the Queen by demanding further proofs of the strength of the affection to which it succumbed.

In this way she obtained for her son-in-law, the Duc de Guiche, the post of Captain of the Guards, a much-coveted sinecure, the reversion of which had been previously promised to another. For her sister-in-law, Diane de Polignac, whom the King, in order to enable her to remain at Court, had already made a lay canoness of a convent in Lorraine, she procured the title of Countess, and promotion from lady-in-waiting to the Comtesse d'Artois to Superintendent of the Household of Madame Elizabeth. For her aunt, the widowed Comtesse d'Andlau, who had brought her up, and to whom she was deeply attached, she obtained a pension of 6,000 livres a year, which would have been the pension of her husband had he lived to receive the Marshal's baton he had expected. She sent for her brother, the Comte de Polastron, and his beautiful wife. The former was easily satisfied. He resembled her in that he wanted nothing, being of a contented, indifferent nature, "occupying himself solely with his violin," and the colonelcy of a regiment, which was obtained for him. His wife was more ambitious, she coveted the post of *dame du palais* to the Queen, which the favourite easily procured for her, and which enabled her to "fix" the heart of the fickle Comte d'Artois. Their amour was the last idyl of the Court of Versailles.

In a word, the Duchesse de Polignac neglected none of her numerous kindred. An insignificant uncle, who had no claim on her save that he was an uncle, she made a bishop; while she sent her stupid old father-in-law as Ambassador to Switzerland.

"Within four years," Mercy, the Austrian Ambassador, wrote Maria Theresa, "it is calculated that the Polignac family have procured for themselves, in great posts and other benefits, without deserving anything of the State, and by pure favour, close on 500,000 livres of annual income."

Kaunitz, Maria Theresa's famous minister, was not so polite. He called the favourite and her family "a gang of thieves."

The spectacle of this hitherto unimportant family, whose rise was in proportion to the ruin and misery of the kingdom, exasperated the best people and isolated the throne. The Court became jealous and envious; and from the Court the irritation spread to Paris, and thence throughout France. Soon the name of Polignac was on every tongue; and linked with that of Marie Antoinette in the ribald songs of the people, it did incalculable harm to the Queen.

Maria Theresa and Joseph II, shrewd observers of affairs, and persons for whose opinions she had the greatest respect, warned her of the folly of exciting the public ill-will. But Marie Antoinette was deaf to all arguments or remonstrances. She even went the length of quarrelling with her mother, sooner than desert her friend. The report that the Polignacs would be given Bitche, an

THE DUCHESSE DE POLIGNAC AND THE COMTESSE DE POLASTRON
(From a miniature in the Collection Thiers at the Louvre)
[Reproduced by the courtesy of the " Revue de l'Art Ancien et Moderne," Paris]

To face page 280

estate in the royal domain with a revenue of 100,000 livres a year, excited such a storm of indignation that it was deemed advisable by the family to abandon the idea of obtaining it. The Queen, however, was indignant at the public malignity, and scorned the lampoons that attacked her and her favourite. And in the end the Polignacs got Bitche.

This "pillage," as Mercy called it, finally culminated, as far as the share of the favourite and her immediate kindred were concerned, in the appointment of the former to the post of Governess of the Children of France. This post, of which the importance was second to none at Court, had ever been the special preserve of royalty or the greatest families. The Princesse de Lamballe had held it for a time. When she relinquished it, the Queen had given it almost as a matter of course to the Princesse de Guéménée of the haughty house of Rohan, who considered it as their *right* after royalty. But this arrogant claim, to which custom had given a certain strength, the Queen determined to disregard when the disgraceful failure of the Prince de Guéménée compelled his wife to resign the appointment.

Marie Antoinette, however, aware of her friend's distaste for the pomps of the Court and the exigencies of a grand position, did not at first think of her retiring friend as a candidate for the post vacated by the Princess de Guéménée. When it was suggested to her by the old Baron de Besenval, who was one of the Polignac coterie, the Queen declared in surprise—

"Madame de Polignac! You do not know her, baron. She would not accept the responsibilities and duties of this great post."

Besenval, however, craftily insinuated the contrary.

"What could be more natural and proper," he said, "than that the intimate friend of the Queen should have the care of the Queen's children? Who could be so devoted to such a charge? Besides, the public expect it."

And the wily intriguer showed the Queen a gazette in which it was taken for granted that the Duchesse de Polignac would succeed the Princesse de Guéménée.

Marie Antoinette acted at once on Besenval's suggestion, but it took her several days before she could persuade the Duchesse to accept the post. The perfect trust the Queen displayed in her by this favour moved the favourite more than all the wealth and honours that had been showered on her. For the first time in the history of their friendship she was really touched.

When the Baron de Besenval triumphantly informed her of the success of his ruse, the imperturbable Duchesse turned upon him and cried passionately—

" How absolutely I hate you all! You are sacrificing me to your own ends. It is enough ! "

By conferring this appointment on the Duchesse de Polignac, Marie Antoinette arrayed the whole of the powerful family of Rohan against her—a circumstance which was to cause her dire humiliation at the time of the " Diamond Necklace " affair.

The resentment of the great families of the Court was reflected in the growing dislike of the people for the Queen and her favourite, which manifested itself even in trivialities. For the favours enjoyed by the Polignacs which cost the State nothing were criticized as much as those that emptied the Treasury. The simple *négligé* style of dressing affected by the Duchesse, who never wore diamonds, says Madame Campan, was adopted by the Queen. Simplicity in dress thus became the fashion, and, by levelling the magnificence of the great ladies of the Court to the reach of the women of Paris, helped in its small way to abolish respect and increase discontent. The people who had inveighed against Marie Antoinette for her extravagance were now equally offended by her economy. The exhibition at the Salon of a portrait of the Queen painted "*à la* Polignac" showed the light in which she was viewed by her "charming vile subjects," as the Prince de Ligne called the Parisians. "Some declared that she dressed like a *femme de chambre*, others that she wanted to ruin the Lyons trade."

IV

As the Governess of the Children of France, the Duchesse de Polignac was no longer able to live in the informal manner she liked. She was obliged to move from her small apartments adjoining the Queen's into the official apartments of the Governess—splendid apartments, considered the finest, at Versailles. Here etiquette demanded that she should entertain in a style worthy of her position. Three times a week she received the Court and Paris, when also strangers of distinction would avail themselves of the opportunity of being presented to the favourite. But Marie Antoinette on visiting her, as she did every day, could no longer say, "Ici, je suis chez moi." The *salon* of the Duchesse de Polignac had become the *salon* of the Queen of France.

It was in order that her friend's official duties should not deprive her altogether of the pleasure of the former familiar intimacy that Marie Antoinette obtained Trianon from the King. But she was to discover that friendship such as she desired was impossible for a Queen of France. As her affection for the Duchesse grew in strength, a party formed which looked to it as the means of advancement. The friends and relations of the favourite took care that this party should be comprised only of themselves.   So intrigue crept into Marie Antoinette's little informal court, where she tried to live like a queen on leave, so to speak.   All hoped that Trianon would lead to great things at Versailles. The most foolish had their thirst, their hunger, their objects, their importunities.   They tore off their masks, unleashed their ambitions, revealed their wants.   Not content with procuring money and appointments, they sought power.   To please the friend who ruled her, Marie Antoinette made and unmade ministers without rhyme or reason, or without in the least considering the public good; often, too, against her wish and will.   Calonne, so fatal to France, and the monarchy, so hostile to the Queen, was the creature of the Duchesse de Polignac.

The leader of this insatiable *entourage* was the Comte de Vaudreuil.   He was the son of a Governor of Haiti and a rich creole.   Coming to France when young, his fortune and connections had opened Versailles to him, where he quickly attracted attention.   Till disfigured by small-pox he had been the handsomest man at Court, and even after this affliction "when he spoke, his face turned handsome and shone."   Everybody listened to him, for he was a master of the art of French conversation of which the tradition expired with him.   Cultivated and intellectual, he adored art and literature, "discovered" Fragonard, "and once a week entertained only geniuses at dinner."   He set the fashion, without being a dandy, and knew to perfection the art of pleasing.

"I have known but two men who knew how to address a woman," said the Princesse d'Hénin once to Horace Walpole, "Lekain on the stage, and M. de Vaudreuil in society."

As a patron he was magnificent.   It was he who obtained permission for the censored *Mariage de Figaro* to be performed at the Comédie Française after it had been privately

THE COMTE DE VAUDREUIL
(After Madame Vigée-Lebrun)
[By permission of MM. Plon-Nourrit et Cie.]

To face page 284

acted in his own house. He was very fond of acting, and was always in the principal *rôle* at Trianon. Grimm said that "he was the best amateur actor in Paris."

Connoisseur, patron, courtier, he was also a soldier. On arriving in France, he had entered the army and became the companion in arms and intimate friend of the Comte d'Artois, whom he accompanied on his abortive expedition to capture Gibraltar, and followed later into exile. His immense income derived from sugar plantations in Haiti having been crippled in the American War of Independence, the Comte de Vaudreuil turned intriguer. Cousin of the Duchesse de Polignac, whose beauty and charm captivated him, he cast over her a spell from which she neither could nor would free herself. "She was the slave of this creole planter," as Michelet expressed it in his fierce denunciation of the dying Court. For him she obtained a pension of 30,000 livres and an estate, promotion in the army, post of Grand Falconer, the *cordon bleu*, and the governorship of Lille. But the Comte de Vaudreuil did not halt on this fine road. It was really he who made Calonne minister, and who in return bled the Treasury for his benefit to the extent of 1,800,000 livres !

The Duchesse de Polignac's friendship for him had from the start been a grievance to Marie Antoinette ; and this rivalry, in which she felt that she was always beaten, at last shook her affection. Vaudreuil's intrigues and impertinence helped to accelerate her disillusionment. For having forced the Queen against her will to accept Calonne, he believed her to be so completely "the slave of his slave" that he could force her to appoint him Governor of the Dauphin, a post he greatly coveted. Here, however, Marie Antoinette drew the line, and Vaudreuil's resentment was so great that one day at Trianon "he vented it on the Queen's favourite billiard cue, which he broke in two."

But to withdraw from this friendship, the sacred fire of which, she discovered to her sorrow, had been kept alight by herself alone, was no easy matter for the Queen. It was not only rapacity and intrigue that had made a party of the *entourage* with which the Duchesse hemmed her in, but Marie Antoinette's own necessity. She realized that the Court she had estranged and the people who took advantage of such an estrangement to increase the difficulties of the sovereign, alike regarded her as an enemy to be got rid of, the more dangerous because of the exasperating fidelity of the King. Thus menaced she was obliged to defend herself, and what more natural than that in her isolation she should have found in the friends of her friend the means of defence? Under such circumstances, she naturally dreaded to create fresh enemies by freeing herself from the insatiable crew into whose hands misguided friendship had betrayed her.

Nevertheless, though pride as well as necessity prevented an open rupture, the Queen gradually withdrew from the Duchesse. One day she could not help remarking to Mercy that "Madame de Polignac was so changed she scarcely recognized her." She still, however, continued to visit her; but now it was observed that she had formed the habit of " sending a footman beforehand to ascertain the names of the persons who were at the Duchesse's." If the list did not suit her, as frequently happened, the Queen would stay away.

Madame de Polignac saw the cooling of the friendship with indifference. Sure that she would retain all the advantages it had conferred on her, she made no attempt to hold it. The Duchesse's friends, however, beheld the decline of her favour with dismay. To please them she one day asked Marie Antoinette to explain why she no longer visited her without first learning whom she would meet.

"Because," was the reply, "you receive certain people whom I do not care to meet."

Knowing that it was Vaudreuil whom the Queen especially meant, the Duchesse dared retort—

"I do not think your Majesty's being pleased to come into my *salon* is a reason for claiming the right to exclude my friends from it."

Thus dismissed, as it were, by the favourite, the Queen was no longer seen at Madame de Polignac's.

V

THE isolation of Marie Antoinette, to whom everybody now attributed all the evils which were rapidly increasing, exposed her to the gravest danger. Vilified, calumniated, threatened, her wounded heart sought consolation in another friendship, and she formed an intimacy with one of her ladies-in-waiting, the Comtesse d'Ossun, a sister of the Duc de Guiche.

"Her new friend," says M. de Nolhac, "was a complete contrast to the fascinating Polignac; but she had solid worth of character, and no hidden ambitious designs." By a strange coincidence Madame d'Ossun occupied the apartments adjoining the Queen's, which had formerly been the Duchesse de Polignac's. The people Marie Antoinette met here were almost entirely foreigners, of whom the celebrated Fersen was the most favoured by her notice. The partiality she evinced for these strangers excited the anger of the Polignacs and the Court generally.

"You are right," she said sadly to some one who explained to her the offence caused by her preference for foreigners; "but they at least do not ask me for anything."

The Polignac *salon* pelted the d'Ossun one with epigrams,

in which the most malignant allusions were made to the Queen. The Comte d'Artois was drawn away from her by his devotion for Madame de Polastron, whose hair Marie Antoinette had dressed with her own hands for her first presentation ; while the Comte de Vandreuil openly sympathized with Cardinal de Rohan in the "Diamond Necklace" affair. The Duchesse alone remained the same —amiable, and indifferent.

But Marie Antoinette did not allow herself to sink to the level of the ingratitude she experienced. It is true she had her revenge, but it was at least a noble one. For Madame de Polignac falling ill at this time was ordered by her doctors to take the cure at Bath for two months, whereupon, since no Governess of the Children of France had ever been absent from Court for so long a period, she was obliged to tender her resignation of her post. But Marie Antoinette refused to accept it.

This act, totally misunderstood by the people of Paris, now ripe for revolution, rendered the Queen and her "favourite," as the Duchesse was still called, more hated than ever. Nor did it modify in the least the ill-will of the Court. When the suppression of the Court sinecures commenced, the rage of the Polignac *salon* passed all bounds. The Baron de Besenval was as usual the spokesman of the party. His great popularity had increased his natural impudence, which had been tolerated on account of his grey hairs and his wit. He had once dared to make love to the Queen, who was too kind-hearted to ruin him. He had never forgiven her for the rebuff he had received, and now he deliberately accused her of conniving at, if not being directly responsible for, the ruin of those whose fortunes she had made.

"It is frightful," he told her, "to live in a country where one is not sure of possessing to-morrow what one has to-day. Such a thing is only possible in Turkey!"

When a Queen of France could be thus addressed by a courtier, Marie Antoinette needed not the fall of the Bastille to tell her that the Revolution had begun.

Having reached the abyss, the last act of the Court of Versailles was to plunge into it. *La Cour se suicida.*

On the fall of the Bastille, the Comte d'Artois and the Princes of the Blood, whom the people included in their hatred of the Polignacs, urged the King to leave Versailles for the army, and declare war on Paris. This "Conspiracy of Trianon," as it was called, failed. The King preferred to go to Paris alone, "to restore confidence." As such an act was tantamount to abandoning the Princes and the Polignacs to the popular vengeance if they continued to remain at Versailles, Louis XVI ordered his brother and his cousins to leave the country immediately.

At the same time Marie Antoinette sent for the Duc and Duchesse de Polignac.

"The King is going to Paris to-morrow," said the Queen in a voice broken with emotion, when they appeared "If he should be asked—— I fear the worst. There is yet time to save you from the fury of my enemies. By attacking you they mean to attack me. Do not be victims of your devotion to the monarchy, but go!"

The fall of the Bastille, the popular hatred, the danger of the Queen, the Revolution, in fact, had extinguished the last spark of their resentment. They were aristocrats of the old aristocracy of the sword; at the menace of danger to the throne all their loyalty returned, and they displayed all the courage and chivalry of their caste. They refused to forsake the Queen.

At this moment of agitation the King entered.

"Come," said Marie Antoinette to him, "help me to persuade these devoted officials, these faithful friends, that they must leave us."

It was only by commanding them as their sovereign to

19

depart, that the Duchesse and her husband would consent to abandon the throne. Dismissal under such circumstances touched the heart of the favourite more than all the favours she had received. Her imperturbable indifference, which had so deceived and baffled the Queen, was at last shaken. Too late she realized the value of the heart she had spurned. Overcome with remorse and despair, she passionately proclaimed her love and loyalty, and on her knees implored the forgiveness of the woman whose heart and life, whose name and career she had blighted.

Though Marie Antoinette had long been disillusioned and disenchanted, the ashes of the old friendship were not yet cold. "The friendship of the Queen," says Tilly, "was not always sustained at the supreme pitch. It resembled a beautiful day, which is not without its clouds, but which always finishes with a fine evening." The memory of the past, the thought of the future, and the unmistakable if belated devotion of the woman kneeling at her feet, touched Marie Antoinette to the quick. In the hour of parting she forgot and forgave all.

* * * * * *

Three hours later, at midnight, the Polignacs were ready to depart. Furnished with passports and "disguised as a merchant of Bâle returning home," the Duc de Polignac, accompanied by his daughter the Duchesse de Guiche, his sister the Comtesse Diane, the Comtesse de Polastron, and the Abbé de Balivière, entered the carriage that was waiting. The Duchesse, "disguised as a chambermaid, took her seat beside the coachman." As the carriage started the following note from Marie Antoinette was put into her hands—

"Adieu, la plus tendre des amies! Que ce mot est affreux! mais il est necessaire. Adieu! Je n'ai que la force de vous embrasser."

Thus fled the Duchesse de Polignac from the Court in which for fifteen years she had been supreme. The last of a long line of royal favourites, last and most fatal, fleeing like a criminal in the dead of night before the popular fury which drove her into exile.

VI

THE journey of the exiles across France enabled them to discover how universal and ominous was the popular disaffection. No village through which they passed was so small or so remote but echoed with the fall of the Bastille. Everywhere they learnt how deep was the hatred for the Queen and the name of Polignac. When they reached Sens they found the town in the possession of the mob. Crowds flocked round their carriage and asked if they came from Paris.

"Are the Polignacs still with the Queen?" demanded a man, thrusting his head into the carriage, that proceeded at a snail's pace.

The hate that inspired the question warned the fugitives of their peril. It was the first acquaintance of the *grandes dames* of the old Court with Terror. One can imagine their fate had the mob suspected for a moment that the whole family of Polignac was in their hands.

They were saved by the coolness of the Abbé de Balivière.

"The Polignacs?" he answered quietly; "they are far enough from Versailles now. Those evil persons have been got rid of."[1]

---

[1] The Abbé de Balivière was a typical abbé of the old *régime*. He passed his life in "hunting and gambling, though he never went to

And the carriage, with the beautiful execrated Queen's friend on the box beside the coachman, seen of all Sens, passed on in safety. Her disguise, however, did not altogether conceal her identity. At the next stopping-place a man suddenly whispered to the Duchesse as she alighted—

"Madame, there are still some honest people in the world. I recognized you all at Sens!"

After three days and nights of such experiences the party reached Switzerland worn out with fatigue and anxiety, the latter rendered the greater by reason of their uncertainty as to the fate of the Princes with whom Vaudreuil had fled, and as to what had happened since they left Versailles. On arriving at Bâle they found Necker, whom they informed of his recall to the Ministry, "of which he was ignorant, or pretended to be." Between the Polignacs and Necker there had been a desperate struggle for power. It was their influence that had chiefly brought about his dismissal, which in turn had brought about the events that had occasioned their own fall. At such a moment for the banished favourite to meet him returning in triumph was particularly humiliating, but the thought of the Queen, to whose heart hers had responded too late, forced her to ask him a favour. Marie Antoinette had

---

bed without saying his prayers." He was a great favourite of the Polignacs, and one of the most rapacious of the party that formed around the favourite, who regarded him as her jester. Tilly says of his rapacity and frivolity "that during the American War he remarked one evening to Madame de Polignac—

"'There is frequent mention in the *Gazette* of l'Abbaye (*la baie*) de Chesapeak. It must be a good benefice, and if it ever falls vacant and M. de Rochambeau is victorious, I shall ask the Queen to obtain it for me.

But from this, as his behaviour at Sens proved, it must not be concluded that he was a fool. "If he uttered follies," says the Duc de Lévis of him, "he never committed them."

begged the Duchesse to send her a line as soon as she was safe, and this Madame de Polignac humbled herself to ask Necker to take.

She had her revenge, however, for it was not long before Necker, borne to Versailles on the crest of popularity, had to flee in his turn from the hate of the people.

The Duc de Polignac soon found Switzerland uncomfortably near France, and the exiles went to Italy. At Turin they found the Princes and Vaudreuil; the consolation of meeting with her old friend or lover again was enhanced by the receipt of several letters from the Queen which breathed the purest friendship. But this respite was of short duration. Vaudreuil went off to recruit the Army of the Princes, and the Duc de Polignac, who never got over the shock of his perilous journey across France, found Turin "unsafe." So the Polignacs moved on to Rome. Here the Duchesse was shown the greatest kindness by Society. She would have liked to have settled in Rome till it was possible for her "to return to Versailles as the King had promised." But the news of the progress of the Revolution made the efforts of the Emigrant *noblesse* to stop it the more frantic. They could never stay long in any place. From Rome the Duchesse went to Venice, and here once more she had the society of Vaudreuil to sustain her when the news came of the fatal flight to Varennes and the hopeless situation of the Royal Family.

The death of her aunt the Comtesse d'Andlau occurring at this time intensified the grief of the Duchesse, which turned to despair when she heard of the fall of the Monarchy, and the crushing defeat of the Emigrant army. Naturally tranquil and accustomed to a life of repose, the continued suspense and anguish of her mind, the perpetual moving from one place to another, and all the humiliations to which the *noblesse* in exile were subjected, finally made her ill. But her illness, for which the doctors could find no name, was really the nostalgia of separation from the friend she had learned too late to love.

After the execution of Louis XVI she grew weaker and weaker. "Trembling for the life of the Queen," says the Comtesse Diane, "and having the regicide's axe constantly before her eyes, she ceased to fear death." From her husband and her children, and from all her relations and friends whose fortune she had made at so fearful a cost she received the greatest tenderness. But neither their tears nor prayers nor the devotion of Vaudreuil, who now left her no more, could cure her of the broken heart of which she was dying.

In Vienna, at the Court of the brother of "la panthère Autrichienne," whither the Polignacs had gone on the defeat of the allied kings, it was impossible to keep from her the news of Marie Antoinette's death. But dreading the consequences of informing her of the details of that shameful assassination, they merely gave the Duchesse to understand that her friend had died naturally. Her husband added "that he even regarded the event as a happy one, since it freed the unfortunate Queen from the hands of bloody monsters." She appeared to believe them, but she was not deceived. From that moment all hope of restoring her to health was abandoned, and she expired peacefully seven weeks after the Queen, for whose ruin she, more than any single person, was responsible.

The Polignacs fared better than most of the Emigrant *noblesse*. The Duc, after his wife's death, went to Russia, where he remained for the rest of his life, which, owing to the generosity of the Empress Catherine, who made him colonel of her Preobajenski Guards, was as comfortable as it had been at Versailles.

The Duchesse de Guiche, the "Guichette" of Trianon,

and the Comtesse de Polastron, followed the fortunes of the exiled Court, and never experienced the sordid misery of exile. The former was accidentally burnt to death at Holyrood when Louis XVIII resided there during the Emigration. The latter, the beautiful Egeria of the Comte d'Artois, died in London of consumption, and in the odour of sanctity. For the sake of her beauty and charm, as well as out of pity for her exiled lover, the *amende honorable* was made very light for her by her confessor. He permitted her in dying to bid farewell to her lover, who, the most fickle of men till he had met her, remained faithful to her even after her death.

The men of the family fared better than their lovely womenfolk. They all lived to return with the Bourbons after Waterloo, and not only recovered all they had lost, but gained fresh fortunes and honours.

Vaudreuil was made a duke and peer of France. The sons of the Duchesse de Polignac were created princes.

LOLA MONTEZ

1818—1861

LOLA MONTEZ
[*After Steiler*]

To face page 299

VII

"By the hunger of change and emotion,
  By the thirst of unbearable things,
By despair, the twin-born of devotion,
  By the pleasure that winces and stings,
The delight that consumes the desire,
  The desire that outruns the delight,
By the cruelty deaf as a fire
  And blind as the night."
                                    SWINBURNE'S *Dolores*.

LOLA MONTEZ

1818—1861

I

IN the latter part of the year 1860, a clergyman of the
Protestant Episcopal Church of America received a pressing request to visit a woman who was dying in one of the
charitable institutions of New York, and to minister to her
spiritual wants. He, of course, complied with the summons,
and during the few remaining weeks of the woman's life
he did all in his power to console her spirit, which
was grievously tormented with a deep conviction of sin.
This death-bed repentance was of such an exceptional
character that he afterwards published an account of it
in a little pamphlet entitled *The Story of a Penitent*, "in
order to bear witness to the mighty power of the Holy
Ghost in changing the heart of one who had been a great
sinner."

"In the course of a long experience as a Christian minister," he wrote, " I do not think I ever saw deeper penitence and humility, more real contrition of soul, and more bitter self-reproach than in this poor woman. She was overwhelmed by the thought that Christ's blood could save such a sinner as she felt herself to have been. When I prayed with her nothing could exceed the fervour of her devotion, and never had I a more watchful and attentive hearer than when I read the Scriptures. When she was near her end, and could not speak, I asked her to let me know by a sign whether her soul was at peace and she still felt that Christ would save her. She fixed her eyes on mine and nodded her head affirmatively. If ever a repentant soul loathed past sin I believe hers did."

Thus, in the odour of sanctity, died Lola Montez, the most original and notorious adventuress of the nineteenth century.

Though her name is, perhaps, unfamiliar to most of the present generation, there are many still living who remember when it occupied the attention of the world. Indeed, so notorious was Lola Montez fifty years ago, that she was the cause of more newspaper paragraphs than any woman has ever been. "Ouida" in the heyday of her popularity never excited more extravagant speculation as to her identity and origin than did this brilliant and daring adventuress. It was said that she was born in Spain, in India, in Turkey, at Geneva, at Havana, at Montrose. Some insisted that she was the child of noble parents who had been stolen by gypsies in her infancy; others that she was the daughter of a Scotch washerwoman and Lord Byron. She herself delighted to add to the mystery and increase her notoriety by claiming a parentage and a nationality that inquiry easily disproved—while those who knew the facts preferred to remain silent from fear of exposing themselves to the shame of acknowledging their connection with a woman for the cause of whose degradation they might perhaps not unjustly be deemed responsible.

The truth of her birth, however, when eventually discovered, was found to be much less fantastic than rumour had conceived it. Her father, far from being Lord Byron, proved to be merely an insignificant captain in the British army, though of good enough family, being the son of a Sir Edward Gilbert of Limerick, whose wife had been a beauty in her day; while her mother was an Oliver of Castle Oliver, with a dash of Spanish blood in her veins, a fact on which her daughter afterwards based the romantic fiction of her noble Spanish origin. Her birth, however, was none the less irregular, for her father and mother had made a runaway match, and Lola was born two months afterwards at Limerick. This event occurred in 1818. She was baptized Marie Dolores Eliza Rosanna Gilbert, but she was always called Lola, which is the diminutive of Dolores.

The parents of the young couple refused to have anything to do with them, and Gilbert, who was on leave at the time of his marriage, rejoined his regiment, which was stationed in India, taking his wife and child with him. Seven years later he died of cholera at Dinapore, and his widow shortly afterwards married a Captain Craigie. This second experiment in matrimony of Lola's mother was destined to be much luckier than the first. Craigie was a brave, honourable, kind-hearted, Dobbin-like man, whose devotion to his profession, in which he showed much ability, was rewarded by rapid promotion.

Gilbert had been his friend, and having married his widow he was quite willing to be a father to his child

Mrs. Craigie, however, had little or no affection for her daughter. Constantly found fault with by her mother, whose violent temper she inherited, and spoilt by the Indian servants who had the entire care of her, Lola had become a burden of which the selfish parent was anxious to be relieved. The child, moreover, had arrived at an age when Anglo-Indian children are usually sent to Europe, so Mrs. Craigie took advantage of the new and friendly relations her marriage had given her and sent Lola to her husband's people in Scotland.

The Craigies possessed all the virtues and vices of the Scotch Calvinists; that is to say, they were plain-living, simple-minded, highly respectable people, of very narrow and strict religious views. They, no doubt, meant to be kind to Lola, but they were the last people in the world to whom the neglected, passionate child should have been entrusted. She was as incapable of understanding them as they were of understanding her. The cold restraint to which she was now subjected only served to develop all the rebellious instincts of her violent nature. She stayed but a short time with the Craigies, but it was long enough to have a baneful influence on her impressionable mind. Alas, if Calvinism but had a *heart*, how empty hell might be!

From the Craigies at Montrose, Lola, to her delight and scarcely to her good, was removed to London to the family of Sir Jasper Nichols, commander-in-chief of the forces in Bengal, with whose family Mrs. Craigie was very intimate. As Lady Nichols had decided to educate her daughters in Paris, Lola accompanied them. The six or seven years she was at school here were probably the happiest of her life. When she was fourteen she and the Nichols girls were sent to Bath to a finishing-school preparatory to their *début* in Indian society, and at the expiration of this finishing process, Mrs. Craigie came to England. She had

promised one of her friends, Sir Abraham Lumley, an
Indian judge, to bring him back a wife ; and since her
daughter had developed into an attractive girl of marriageable age, she considered she could hit on no better choice
for Sir Abraham, who was both rich and old, than Lola
herself.

Dreading lest her scheme, if it became known, should
meet with opposition likely to thwart it, Mrs. Craigie wisely
kept silent on the subject. The dresses, however, that she
ordered for her daughter were so much more suited for a
bride than a *débutante* that Lola's suspicions were aroused.
These were confirmed by the answers she got to her
questions, and having ferreted out the scheme, she refused
to be sacrificed on the altar of her mother's avarice. Her
resistance only served to provoke her mother, who
determined to use force, if necessary, to compel her child
to obey her. Hereupon, Lola appealed to a Captain
James, a young officer who had travelled home from India
on the same ship with her mother, to save her from a
detestable fate. This James did most effectually by
eloping with Lola the very next day himself.

The couple crossed over to Ireland, where no clergyman
could be found willing to marry one so young as Lola without her mother's consent. To obtain this James sent his
sister to Bath, but it was not without some difficulty that
Mrs. Craigie, who was highly exasperated at the manner in
which her schemes had been upset, could be persuaded
to give the necessary permission. But as in the case of
her own runaway match, of which she disliked to be
reminded so forcibly, she utterly refused, as her own
parents had done, to have anything more to do with her
daughter.

After eight months in Ireland, the greater part of which
was spent in the country, where existence was so wearisome
that the husband and wife found plenty of time in which

to test the truth of the old maxim of marrying in haste and repenting at leisure, James was ordered to join his regiment in India. And as Gilbert had done before him, James took his wife with him. Here the seal was set to the striking parallel between Lola's marriage and that of her parents. As in the latter instance, it was not long before the bond that united Lola to her husband was severed—not by death, however, but by the temptations with which Indian society surrounds good-looking and attractive Benedicts and their wives.

On the voyage out Mrs. James had amused herself by flirting, innocently enough, with the admirers her vivacity and beauty won her. Among these she had found not the least amusing to be "the captain of the ship, a profound thinker, who defined love as a pipe which is filled at eighteen, and smoked till forty." Up country she continued her flirtations on horseback, while her husband "spent his time drinking porter and sleeping like a boa constrictor." On the arrival, however, of a fascinating Mrs. Lomer, such a creature as Kipling might have created, Captain James woke up and took to flirtations on horseback too, which finally ended in a gallop with Mrs. Lomer to the Neilgherry Hills from which they neither returned.

Deserted by her husband, Lola found herself for the first, but by no means the last, time in her life in a very critical situation. Her mother was the only person in the world on whom she had the slightest claim, or who could be expected to provide for her. She was living in Calcutta, where Craigie filled the important post of Deputy Adjutant-General of the Forces in India. To go to her under ordinary circumstances would have been both natural and easy, but it was only bitter necessity that compelled Lola to appeal to her mother, whom she knew had never forgiven her for eloping with the man who had now deserted her.

Indeed, Mrs. Craigie's first impulse was to refuse to receive her daughter, and it was only the fear of the scandal to which such an action would give rise that prevented her from acting as she felt on Lola's arrival in Calcutta.

Under such conditions, it was impossible that the deserted wife could find a home with her mother. Consequently the kind-hearted Craigie, desiring to pacify one and to provide for the other at the same time, proposed that Lola should find once more a temporary home with his people in Scotland till some arrangement could be made with her husband. To such a proposal Lola could not but consent, and she returned to England, her step-father with Dobbin-like generosity "slipping a cheque for a thousand pounds into her hands when bidding her good-bye."

The thought of going to the Craigies at Montrose, or, as her step-father had suggested, of patching up the breach between herself and her husband, by no means appealed to Lola. An American lady with whom she became intimate on the voyage suggested to her as an alternative that she should go on the stage. Lola at once jumped at the idea, and as the possession of a thousand-pound cheque and jewelry valued at about the same amount served to fire her desire for independence, she resolved to follow her American friend's advice the moment she arrived in London.

This decision was the turning-point in her career, which till then had been characterized by folly rather than by deliberate evil. To hold the Craigies responsible for this step, which was destined to have so base an effect on Lola's character, is, of course, out of the question. But at this juncture of her life, had she been able to recall the home at Montrose with affection, which Calvinistic charity once again offered her, it is highly probable that history had never heard the name of Lola Montez. For passionate,

20

wilful, and headstrong though she was by nature, she was also very impressionable. Sympathy, on perhaps the sole occasion of her life that she received it, instantly and completely melted her heart, which a lifetime of hardship, disgrace, and the contempt of the world had turned into stone; while, her frivolous and selfish attention having once been called to injustice and oppression, reform found her an ardent and faithful partisan. *Tout comprendre, c'est tout pardonner* is the dazzling inscription on the gates of Paradise.

Having, therefore, made up her mind to support herself after a fashion that is particularly calculated to attract and console emotional beauty in distress, Lola no sooner reached London than she sought out Fanny Kelly, who was then the leading trainer for the stage in England. This experienced woman was not long in discovering that her pupil would never make a living as an actress, and very honestly told her so; suggesting, however, at the same time that with application and proper instruction, she might become a *danseuse* of distinction.

To Lola it made not the least difference in what capacity she appeared before the public. So she at once procured a Spanish dancing-master, and when she had learnt all he could teach her she went to Spain for six months to acquire an "atmosphere." Here, possessing a natural aptitude for languages, she picked up enough Spanish to support her claim, to which her looks added weight, to be considered a Spaniard; and, adopting the name of Lola Montez, returned to London to seek an engagement as a Spanish dancer.

This she quickly procured by the impression her singular and striking beauty created upon Benjamin Lumley, the manager of Her Majesty's Theatre, who, though under no illusions as to her accomplishment as a dancer, counted on the attraction of her person to secure the plaudits of an audience which, he knew from experience, set a greater value on the looks than on the talent of his artists.

It was Lumley's habit, when he had a new dancer to introduce to the public, to secure for her beforehand, if possible, the favour of the press by inviting its representatives to witness a private exhibition of her dancing. In an old book, entitled *You have heard of them*, a well-known journalist of the day, who was present at one of these rehearsals at which Lola performed, thus describes the impression she produced upon him.

"Nadaud, the violinist, drew the bow across his instrument, and she began to dance. Her figure was even more attractive than her face, lovely as the latter was. Lithe and graceful as a young fawn, every movement that she made seemed instinct with melody. Her dark eyes were blazing and flashing with excitement, for she felt that I was willing to admire her. In her *pose* grace seemed involuntarily to preside over her limbs and dispose their attitude. Her foot and ankle were almost faultless. No one who has seen her will quarrel with me for saying that she was not and is not a finished *danseuse*, but all who have will as certainly agree with me that she possesses every element which could be required, with careful study, to make her eminent in her vocation."

I do not know if Lola Montez was superstitious, though the influence of the Hindustani servants who had the sole charge of her in childhood was well calculated to make her so. But if she was, the fact that her *début*, on the success of which her future depended, was to be made under Lumley, whose name was the same as that of the old Indian judge who had been the cause of her unfortunate marriage, might very well have seemed to her an ill-omen. She did not, however, appear at all nervous when the curtain rose and she pirouetted out into the middle of the stage.

It was the height of the London season, and the theatre was filled with one of those audiences which spell triumph or failure for a new star. Everything was seemingly in her favour. *The Tarantula*, the piece of the evening, was a popular success. Of the beauty of the *danseuse* there could be no two opinions. " The dance she was to perform was as well adapted as any dance could be," to quote the above-mentioned journalist again, " not to expose her deficiencies." Lumley, as usual, had "squared" the Press. And the omnibus boxes on each side of the stage were filled with the "bloods," who now-a-days at similar entertainments are wont to occupy the front rows of the stalls, and are more intent on watching a pretty leg or an ankle than on criticizing a *pas*.

But no sooner had the Spanish dancer appeared than an ominous hiss came from one of the boxes, and Lord Ranelagh, the *arbiter elegantiarum* of the day, drawled out in a voice loud enough to be heard all over the house—

" Why, it's Betty James ! "

The hiss which had come from the box in which he sat was at once taken up by the box opposite, and gradually spread through the house. Lola, however, went on with her pirouetting as if the hisses were applause, till Lumley, whose experience told him too well that her failure, in the face of so hostile a reception, was irretrievable, angrily ordered the curtain to be rung down. It fell on her dancing and her career as a *danseuse* in England at the same time.

Nevertheless, there were many who had admired the unfortunate *débutante*, and the *Illustrated London News* was loud in its regret that she did not appear again.

When the news that Mrs. James intended to go on the stage reached India, where she had been well known, Mrs. Craigie put on mourning as if her daughter had died, and sent out to all her friends the customary funeral letters.

James, in the meantime, had behaved still more unfeelingly. For, desiring to retrieve the position he had lost by his desertion of his wife, he took advantage of the gossip that the officers of the ship on which she had gone to England brought back to India, and applied for a divorce on the ground of her misconduct on the voyage home with a Mr. Lennox. Lola, however, took no steps to defend herself, and the court consequently passed judgment in favour of James. Whether the charge was true or not, it proves James, in the light of his own previous conduct, to be so contemptible that his wife might consider herself fortunate to obtain her freedom, even at the cost of such a stain on her reputation.

II

LOLA'S failure placed her in an extremely critical position. Her capital had almost entirely oozed away in that sort of insensible perspiration common to women who have never been taught the value of money. The divorce court and the stage had completely cut her off from all her former connections, while the door to the stage itself—as far as London was concerned—was ignominiously closed to her by the hissing of a couple of boxes filled with dandies. But she always had at her disposal an immense fund of pluck and determination. Refusing to abandon the profession she had adopted, she managed somehow to procure an engagement to dance in the ballet of the Opera at Dresden. Here she obtained a favourable reception ; and likewise in Berlin, where the attention she attracted caused her to be engaged to dance at a *fête* given by the King of Prussia. Her success, however, was inconsiderable, and it was not till two years later that Europe first became aware of the existence of such a person as Lola Montez.

Many extravagant stories were afterwards current of this period of obscurity, in which fact was so cleverly blended with fiction that it was as difficult to disprove as it was to verify them. Lola was ever wide awake to the value of advertisement, and she never hesitated to lie where her own antecedents were concerned. As a liar she was always picturesque. She may or may not have been "reduced to sing in the streets of Brussels to keep herself from starving." And it may or may not be true that the connections she formed in Saxony and Prussia opened the way for the most flattering reception in Russia, "where the Emperor Nicholas, attracted by her beauty and ability, employed her as a political spy." As a second-rate dancer she was no doubt often without an engagement and in want; while it is equally probable that she was ready to fill an engagement wherever one offered, and consequently became acquainted with most of the capitals of Europe, and even had the pleasure of pirouetting on occasions before Royalty itself. It is more than likely, however, that when "out of a job," Lola Montez, with her beauty and charm, had other and more congenial means of maintaining existence than singing in the streets. Nor can there be the least doubt that had she really been a "secret political agent," her vanity would have compelled her to prove the fact beyond dispute.

It is perhaps just as well that no authentic record of her life during this time exists. At all events it was a period of apprenticeship, and when it ended Lola only wanted, as she said, "a nice round lump sum of money to carry out her original plan, that is, trying to hook a prince." To this end she had learnt the Almanac de Gotha pretty well by heart.

According to her version, the events which caused her to come to Paris, to which city belongs the credit of having discovered this celebrated adventuress, were of the most sensational description. For the sake of the admirable portrait it contains of her, I will give her story in detail, or, rather, the story as it was published by a clergyman to whom she related it.

"It was in Warsaw that her name first became involved in politics. The Paskevitch, Viceroy of Poland, an old man, fell most furiously and disgracefully in love with her. Old men are never very wise when in love, but the vice-king was especially foolish. Now the director of the theatre was also Colonel of the Gens d'Armes—a disgraceful position of itself, and rendered peculiarly so by him, from his having been a spy for the Russian Government. Of course the Poles hated him.

"While Lola Montez was on a visit to Madame Stein-killer, the wife of the principal banker of Poland, the old viceroy sent to ask her presence at the palace one morning at eleven o'clock. She was assured by several ladies that it would be neither politic nor safe to refuse to go ; so she went in Madame Steinkiller's carriage, and heard from the viceroy a most extraordinary proposition. He offered her the gift of a splendid country estate, and would load her with diamonds besides. The poor old man was a comic sight to look upon—unusually short in stature, and every time he spoke he threw his head back and opened his mouth so wide as to expose the artificial gold roof of his palate. A death's-head making love to a lady could not have been a more horrible or disgusting sight. *These generous gifts were most respectfully and very decidedly declined.* But her refusal to make a bigger fool of one who was already fool enough was not well received.

"The next day the Colonel-director of the theatre called at her hotel to urge the suit of his master. He

began by being persuasive and argumentative; and when
that availed nothing, he insinuated threats, when a grand
row broke out, and the madcap ordered him out of her
room.

"Now when Lola Montez appeared that night at the
theatre, she was hissed by two or three parties who had
evidently been instructed to do so by the director himself.
The same thing occurred the next night, and when it came
again on the third night, Lola Montez, in a rage, rushed
down to the footlights and declared that those hisses had
been set at her by the director, because she had refused
certain gifts from the old prince his master. Then came a
tremendous shower of applause from the audience; and
the old princess, who was present, both nodded her head
and clapped her hands to the enraged and fiery little Lola.

"Here, then, was a pretty muss. An immense crowd of
Poles, who hated both the prince and the director, escorted
her to her lodgings. She found herself a heroine without
expecting it, and, indeed, without intending it. In a moment
of rage she had told the whole truth, without stopping to
count the cost, and she had unintentionally set the whole of
Warsaw by the ears.

"The hatred which the Poles intensely felt towards the
Government and its agents found a convenient opportunity
of demonstrating itself, and in less than twenty-four hours
Warsaw was bubbling and raging with the signs of an
incipient revolution. When Lola Montez was apprised of
the fact that her arrest was ordered, she barricaded her
door; and when the police arrived, she sat behind it with
a pistol in her hand, declaring that she would certainly
shoot the first man dead who should break in. The police
were frightened, or at least they could not agree among
themselves who should be the martyr, and they went
off to inform their masters what a tigress they had to
confront.

GENERAL PASKEVITCH, VICEROY OF POLAND

To face page 312

"In the meantime the French consul came forward and gallantly claimed Lola Montez as a French subject, which saved her from immediate arrest. But the order was peremptory that she must quit Warsaw."

This highly picturesque account in which the adventuress characteristically sought to turn the hissing she received in Warsaw into a compliment, lacks but a single detail to give it the seal of absolute truth. Paskevitch, so famous in those days as the " Pacificator of Poland," was all that Lola described ; she herself was quite capable of all the violence which she attributes to herself; she did dance at Warsaw and was hissed ; and, whether on the same night or on another, but certainly while she was in Warsaw, there was an attempt at insurrection on the part of the Poles when there were several hundred arrests. But of one thing we may be quite sure : had the vice-king of Poland really made the offer to Lola Montez that she said he did, she would gladly and instantly have accepted it.

She confided to Vandam, the author of *An Englishman in Paris*, that she had been brought to Paris by a Pole whose mistress she was at the time. At all events, whether she left Warsaw of her own accord, or whether she was expelled, she realized that the opportunity of associating herself with the events that occurred there at the time of her departure offered her a unique advertisement of which she was quick to take advantage. It helped her to obtain an engagement at the Porte Saint-Martin ; and knowing the critical nature of the Parisians, she also counted upon it to attract their attention to her personality in the hope of diverting it from her dancing, with regard to which she had long ceased to foster any illusions.

Nevertheless, her hopes of success were again doomed to be dashed. In spite of her beauty and the *réclame* of an expulsion from Poland in the sacred cause of liberty, she was again ignominiously hissed. Exasperated by this rebuff, she gave vent to her disappointment in one of those violent exhibitions of temper for which she was afterwards so notorious. For de Mirecourt says that " she made faces at the audience, and taking off her garters flung them into the pit."

Of course, after this her name was withdrawn from the bills. But she gained the notoriety she desired in another and more profitable way. For the rumours associated with her name had attracted Dujarrier, the editor of *La Presse*, to the Porte Saint-Martin on the night of her appearance, and he was so struck with her beauty that he made her acquaintance. The result was that Lola Montez became his mistress, and was introduced to all his associates, men who were either acquiring fame or who had already acquired it, like Balzac and Dumas.

Becoming intimate with these people, she quickly became a noted figure in Paris. Unknown before, she did her best to heighten the mystery of her past. It was now that the extravagant and contradictory stories concerning her origin and antecedents first arose. Her fame penetrated into the most exclusive quarters ; and her wit, her dazzling beauty, and her costumes formed as many topics of conversation in the *salons* of the noble Faubourg as on the boulevards.

Vandam, who did not like her, declared that " her gait and carriage were those of a duchess, for she was naturally graceful, but the moment she opened her lips the illusion vanished, at least for me ; for I am bound to admit that men of far higher intellectual attainments than mine, and familiar with very good society, raved and kept raving about her."

Gustave Claudin was greatly impressed with her intelligence, and remarked in his Memoirs that " in the eighteenth century, the adventuress, as one called her, *eût joué un rôle.*" In the nineteenth century, however, in spite of its attempts to restrict irresponsible personal ambition, there were still many opportunities for men and women to express their individuality in the old, audacious and dramatic fashion. All over Europe at this time personality was busily engaged in exploiting the new democratic order of things for its own profit. And Lola's star was in the ascendant.

Dujarrier was not the least brilliant member of the intellectual set in which the adventuress now found herself. Young, rich and talented, he was an enthusiastic Republican, and his opinions were well calculated to appeal to one so emotional as Lola Montez, who for the last two years had been embittered by the hardships and degradations of an unsuccessful career, which at the best seldom wins the respect of the world. Infected with Dujarrier's Republican ardour, she took a keen interest in political questions, and became so ardent a Republican herself that " in her heart she sickened that she had not been born a man." The spontaneity and passion with which she adopted the ideals so dear to Dujarrier deepened his attachment for so sympathetic a mistress, and he desired to marry her.

To Lola the prospect of becoming the wife of such a man promised the fulfilment of the utmost she could ask of life. It restored her self-respect and awoke all that was good in her. Fate seemed suddenly to have showered on her wealth, luxury, love and position. As the wife of Dujarrier, whose genius had struck some exquisite hitherto unknown chord in her nature, what noble deeds might she not accomplish? to what heights of fame might she not rise?

It was, however, but a fleeting glimpse of Paradise that this emotional adventuress had obtained. The zeal with which Dujarrier's clever pen championed the rights of the people and denounced tyranny, created for him numerous enemies in the class whose political principles were the opposite of his. Among these the most dangerous was Beauvallon, whose paper, the widely circulated Royalist *Globe*, was at daggers drawn with *La Presse*. It was inevitable that the rivalry of the editors of these papers should lead to a duel, and an article by Dujarrier finally provoked a challenge. The meeting took place in the Bois de Boulogne, and Dujarrier fell shot through the brain.

Lola, having been informed by a letter from her lover of his approaching encounter with Beauvallon, immediately on its receipt rushed off to the spot to stop the duel and met his dead body being brought back. Beside herself with grief, she flung herself on the corpse and covered it with kisses. The affair did not end here. Dujarrier's friends, exasperated by his untimely end, accused Beauvallon and his seconds of foul play. They were arrested, and the trial, which took place at Rouen, attracted the greatest attention from the number of celebrities who were called as witnesses. Lola, though she had not been summoned, insisted on appearing as the person most interested in avenging Dujarrier. He had left her in his will eighteen shares in the Palais Royal Theatre, worth about 20,000 francs.

Vandam was among those whom the public curiosity attracted to Rouen. "I was there," he says, "and though the court was crowded with men occupying the foremost ranks in literature and art and Paris society, no one attracted the attention she did. She was dressed in mourning—not the deepest, but soft masses of silk and lace —and when she lifted her veil and took off her glove to take the prescribed oath a murmur of admiration ran through the court."

Her evidence was not of the least importance, but she wanted to create a sensation and she succeeded—from inherent love and need of advertisement, which was more than ever necessary to her now that Dujarrier's death reduced her to her former means of existence.

" I was," she declared passionately, " a better shot than Dujarrier, and if Beauvallon wanted satisfaction I would have fought him myself."

Such an attitude under the circumstances was well suited to win her popular sympathy, and she easily became a heroine for a few days in Paris. But her day was over, and shortly afterwards she left Paris. No one knew or cared what had become of her.

" In six months," says Vandam, " her name was almost forgotten. Dumas, though far from superstitious, was glad she had disappeared. ' She has the evil eye,' he said, ' and will bring bad luck to whoever links his destiny with hers.' "

About eighteen months later, however, the name of Lola Montez came once more very prominently before the public, and this time under circumstances so amazing as to give her a world-wide reputation. For, having returned to her former vocation, she secured an engagement in Munich, where she danced to please the King, if not the people, and so cleverly that her performance has become one of the most romantic historical episodes in the nineteenth century.

III

AT this time Ludwig I was the King of Bavaria, and a more singular personality has seldom occupied a throne. Born in 1786, his youth had been passed in the tumult of the Napoleonic invasion of Germany. His father, Max Joseph, was a clever and able man, by whose opportunist statesmanship Bavaria managed to maintain not only her existence, but her independence. The lessons of the French Revolution had not been thrown away on Max Joseph. The knowledge they imparted to him had been acquired by hard and bitter experience. He had lost all his ancestral possessions on the Rhine, he had been surrounded by the Jacobins, seen his standard torn down, and been obliged to flee for his life. The sovereignty of Bavaria to which he had succeeded was all that was left him, and that, too, was menaced. The Holy Roman Empire was breaking up, the spirit of revolution was rampant everywhere. It was no time to think of patriotism, to join Austria or Prussia in a last stand against the French. He found it to his interest to join the latter; and to prove the sincerity of his pledges, Wittelsbach though he was, he did not hesitate to give his daughter in marriage to Eugène Beauharnais, the step-son of the magnificent Corsican *parvenu* who had dominated Europe. In return Napoleon made him king—he had before been only an elector—and increased the territory of Bavaria with important acquisitions.

In pursuing this course Max Joseph had been enthusiastically supported by his subjects of all classes. But though the Bavarians, more than any other state in Germany, had welcomed with joy the gospel of the French Revolution, they objected to an alliance which, however great were its material advantages, had made Bavaria the vassal of Napoleon. The instinct of race which the crushing humiliations of Jena, Austerlitz and Wagram had aroused in Germany was as keen in Bavaria as elsewhere, and the Bavarians became as anxious to break the bonds which tied them to France as they had previously been to form them. This spirit of patriotism was felt and expressed by no one more vehemently than the young Crown Prince Ludwig.

It was no ordinary love of country with which he was

inflamed. On a visit to Rome when he was eighteen he had formed a close friendship with a certain Martin Wagner, a young German painter whose name and influence on him were by a strange coincidence similar to those of another and better known Wagner, whose fame was afterwards so closely linked with that of the Crown Prince's better known grandson, the immortal "Mad King" of Bavaria. For Wagner, the painter, awoke in Ludwig I that passionate and all-absorbing love of art and beauty that was the chief trait of his character, just as Wagner, the musician, awoke in Ludwig II a similar and equally characteristic passion.

To cut short this first fascinating visit to Rome, as he was obliged, in order to return to Germany and serve with the Bavarian army under Napoleon, was intolerable to the high-strung and romantic young prince. German to the core, this military service forced upon him at such a time above all others, under a foreign conqueror and against his fatherland, branded him deep with hate of Napoleon. Burning with the "Greek spirit," if ever prince or youth burned, like a true Greek, love of art and love of country blended in Ludwig.

"It would be the happiest and proudest day of my life," he once said, "if Strasburg, the town where I was born, should once more become a German town."

His patriotism was intensely personal. German freedom meant to him the awakening of Germany to the love of the Beautiful. Both together formed his creed. He proclaimed his faith in it openly, passionately, regardless of danger, seeking converts everywhere. Napoleon, who inspired such terror and respect in all whom he dominated, failed to terrify Ludwig. He bitterly resented the idea that his sister should be given in marriage to Eugène Beauharnais, and when Napoleon came to Munich for the match he turned his back on him in public.

To Napoleon, who was very desirous that Beauharnais should succeed Max Joseph on the throne of Bavaria, such a slight was well calculated to urge him to extremes to accomplish his purpose. It was said that he contemplated removing Ludwig from his path as he had done the Duc d'Enghien. But if he really said, " *Qui m'empêche de fusiller ce prince?* " as was rumoured, he contented himself with the utterance of his wish, and trusted to Destiny to perform more regularly an act which, though he had the courage, he had not the folly to take upon himself.

Great, however, as were the influences that were brought to bear upon Max Joseph to abandon Napoleon, he stubbornly refused to do so, until faith in his power, which from the astonishing evidences he had had of it he was justified in deeming irresistible, was shattered by the Conqueror's mad excursion to Russia. His delay was inspired by the soundest statesmanship, as the Bavarians themselves afterwards recognized. For it gave to Bavaria, whose territory had been so extended by Napoleon, an immense importance in Germany, which saved her from absorption when the map of Europe came to be made afresh after Waterloo.

Ludwig, as soon as possible, took advantage of the peace this event brought to his distracted fatherland to rush back to Rome to worship the Beautiful. There was nothing now to interfere with his devotion, and he lived the life of his dreams, a free and unconventional life among painters, sculptors and architects, to whom he was a veritable Prince of Bohemia. He refused to enter any other society, to form any other acquaintances. His house was a temple to the Beautiful, crammed with marbles, bronzes and pictures, open only to enthusiasts and "true Greeks." Here he dispensed lavish hospitality on his "comrades," among whom Thorwaldsen and Canova were the most famous; and at all these *al fresco* lunches or suppers of the gods,

LUDWIG I., KING OF BAVARIA
[*From a German print*]

To face page 320

where the conversation was confined to artistic subjects, it was ever the Prince who was the most inspired and inspiring.

There are many, especially those whose ambition has grown luxurious with ease and plenty, who, in an atmosphere so favourable to dilettanteism would have exhausted the creative faculty in beautiful emotions. But Ludwig belonged to the caste of genius, and his dreams were to him, like Samson's hair, the source of a marvellous vigour. He returned to Germany the greatest connoisseur of the nineteenth century, to preach the gospel of art to his countrymen and to "make of Munich such an honour to the fatherland that no one who had not visited it could pretend to know Germany."

That he succeeded, all who know Munich will agree. This city as it exists to-day is the outward and visible form of his dreams. As such it is the most remarkable masterpiece of the modern world, for Ludwig not only imagined it, but when finished signed his work with his own personality. The spirit of the Beautiful which pervades both the treasures and the very life itself of Munich, and has made it the chief art centre in Germany, is the soul of Ludwig I. To the creation of this German Athens he consecrated his whole life and all that he possessed, even his throne itself. It is estimated that he spent out of his private purse over 30,000,000 marks on art, and over 20,000,000 on scientific and other institutions. To the eminent archæologists who excavated for him in Greece, and the famous painters who purchased pictures for him all over Europe, he said, "Only the very best is good enough for me." The efforts of the former are to be found in the superb Glyptothek, while those of the latter may be seen in the Pinakothek. They are the most wonderful collection of sculpture and paintings that one man has ever made either in ancient or modern times.

21

When he succeeded his father Max Joseph in 1825 no sovereign in Europe was so popular. The part, insignificant though it was, that he had played in the troublous times of Napoleon, had served as his introduction, so to speak, to his future subjects, and the acquaintance formed under such favourable circumstances had ripened into a close intimacy. His independence of thought, his utter unconventionality in moving among the people, his friendships and love of art, excited the keenest interest and sympathy.

The "artistic temperament" in a prince has always a great attraction for the people. In countries where their power is dominated by that of the throne an artistic prince is supposed to be either soft and malleable, or democratic in his ideas. The fact that, with certain remarkable exceptions, the contrary generally proves to be the case by no means tends to dispel this popular impression. Though they have been deceived over and over again, the people, who are children that never grow up, are always fascinated by the sight of an artist or a philosopher on the steps of the throne. Nor are they to be blamed. For if such an unusual spectacle eventually proves disappointing it never fails to be picturesque.

Ludwig was naturally humane and simple; but democratic though he was in his manner of life, he had a very strong sense of the divine right of kings. He manifested at first, however, every intention of maintaining the liberal *régime* which Bavaria had enjoyed under Max Joseph, whose French Revolution experiences had taught him the wisdom of adopting it. But with Waterloo reaction had set in all over Europe, and after the Revolution of 1830 in France, Ludwig began to fall more and more into line with the rest of the German princes whom Metternich had charmed into full reaction. The Roman Catholic Church had ever been a great power in Bavaria, and its splendid

ritual, if not its creed, was eminently calculated to impress
the artistic mind of Ludwig. Led by the Jesuits, the party
of reaction, the party of Austria and Metternich, gradually
got the upper hand. And in 1846, when Lola Montez
arrived in Bavaria, the King and the country had for over
ten years been in the hands of an Ultramontane Ministry
which was absolutely out of sympathy with the ideas and
desires of the people.

The latter during the twenty years since their artistic
king had come to the throne had gradually changed their
opinion of him. They had early made the discovery that
the "artistic temperament" is quite as unconventional and
free in regard to morals as to manners, and Ludwig was
too catholic in his passion for beauty to despise it when
endowed with life. In such a man everything connected
with him was of interest, and his love of a beautiful woman
having become even more widely known than his love of
art, every opportunity had been given him to become
as great a connoisseur of the fair sex as of a statue or a
picture. And none of these opportunities had he neglected.
Any and every beauty who came to Munich was sure of an
enthusiastic welcome from him. Heaven only knows how
many had come to him from all over the globe in the
course of his reign. Their portraits were instantly painted,
and may still be seen in the royal palace at Munich—
the finest collection of fair women in existence. A
Lovelace, there was also a touch of the minnesinger in
Ludwig. In moments of exhilaration he wrote poetry,
passionate doggerel set to a Greek metre, and for inspir-
ation was in the habit of spending a couple of hours
a day in silent and solitary communion with these
portraits.

At first, as his plain and good Queen chose to shut
her eyes to his frequent infidelities, his people decided to
shut theirs too. But when infidelity and reaction joined

forces in the character of the King, the people no longer talked of the "irresponsibility of genius," but of its "incapacity."

Such were Ludwig I and his people when suddenly Lola Montez sprang into their midst, alert and radiant, like a live spark blown by the wind upon combustible matter.

IV

MUCH has been written in German upon this period of Bavarian history, but the truth has been so entangled by prejudice that it has been impossible to unravel it. Those who could have spoken with authority either wilfully lied or remained silent. Nor did Lola Montez herself ever deign to throw the least light on the events of her life in Bavaria, confining herself on every occasion when she conversed on the subject to such matters as were known to everybody.

The Jesuits, her inveterate enemies, maintained that she was the agent of a secret revolutionary society sent to disturb the public peace and overthrow the Government. But this was a calumny devoid of all truth, for Lola Montez, though imbued with republican ideas and keenly interested in political questions, was never connected with any secret society whatever. When circumstances raised her to power in Bavaria she had to depend solely on her own ability, and the party on which she relied for support was formed and financed by herself.

As far as one can surmise with any degree of probability she had no political object whatsoever in view when she arrived in Munich, but came thither just as any dancer

would have come in the pursuit of her professional career.
The object of her life before she met Dujarrier, she had
told Vandam, was to "hook a prince"; and when Dujarrier's death obliged her to return to the stage, she had
returned likewise to her original purpose. Consequently,
knowing, as all the world knew, Ludwig's notorious weakness for female beauty, it is highly probable that she
hoped to exploit it when she selected Munich as the scene
of her reappearance.

There are various stories describing how Lola first met
the King, but here again the darkness of Cimmeria veils
the truth. It is certain that she danced in the ballet of
the opera. On her first appearance some hissing was
mingled with the applause which her beauty, if not her
dancing, elicited. On the second she took the house by
storm. The King was present on both these occasions,
as well as at her third appearance, which was equally
triumphant, and with which her career as a dancer came
to an end. Five days later she was presented at Court,
when Ludwig astonished his ministers by introducing her
to them as his "best friend."

At first not a word of protest was raised against her.
The heads of the army, the ministers, the students, and
even the people appeared to have fallen as completely
under her spell as the King himself. She seemed set upon
pleasing and fascinating everybody. During this period
of universal popularity, at Fürstenried, where she resided
with Ludwig, pending the furnishing of a little palace in
the Barerstrasse which he had given her, Lola held recep-
tions at which the most prominent and brilliant people in
Bavaria were to be seen.

Had she been content with her social triumphs it is
possible she might have long continued to enjoy them, and
have ended her days in a peaceful, prosperous, and aristocratic oblivion; for she was a very lovely woman with a

magnetic personality. But the position she had secured so magically dazzled her, and being naturally restless and ambitious, she was tempted to grasp the power that flattery dangled before her. Through her favour with the King she became the channel through which he was approached. Being very intelligent, surrounded as she was by persons who held reactionary, moderate, or very advanced opinions, she quickly acquired an intimate knowledge of the political situation in Bavaria. Being keenly interested in political questions, she naturally formed her own opinions on the situation. From the experience she had picked up in her wanderings over Europe she understood the extent of the popular discontent that was everywhere apparent, and fully realized the danger to which the policy of reaction exposed Ludwig.

Being strongly republican at heart, she would, under other circumstances, have welcomed the revolution she knew to be impending in Europe. But her own interest was now too closely associated with Ludwig's for her to desire the overthrow of his throne, and she resolved to save it for him, if possible, while there was yet time. The first step in this direction was to get rid of the Ultramontane Ministry of reaction and embark the King on a liberal policy of reform. She was too strongly imbued with the spirit of democracy to be appalled by the difficulties or dangers of such a task, and politics were her passion.

Her machinations, subtle though they were, brought her into open conflict with the Church of Rome, whose power in Bavaria was very great. The power of Ludwig, however, weakened though it was by unpopularity, was sufficient for Lola's purpose. Infatuated with the infatuation of a man of sixty, he was merely a tool in her hands, and all who criticized or worked against her only earned his enmity.

Realizing the strength of her influence over the King, the Ministry at first used every art to win her to their side. "A nobleman was easily found who was willing for a consideration to immolate his pride by marrying her." Austrian gold was tried, Metternich offered her a million florins if she would leave Bavaria—all to no purpose. Then came threats and plots. Gold was sowed in the streets of Munich, and when at last revolution broke out, it was not the superior tact or sagacity or virtue of her enemies, but brute force, that drove Lola Montez from Bavaria.

In the meantime, Europe looked on in amazement at the remarkable persistency, fearlessness, and ability with which the adventuress held her own. She had received a palace and splendid gifts from Ludwig, but with the cupidity and vanity common to women in her position she demanded a title. Ludwig was only too willing to please her, but, according to the Bavarian law, before she could be ennobled it was necessary that she should be naturalized. Such a proposal, had Lola been willing to act with instead of against the Ministry, would have met with no opposition. But now they determined to make a final effort to crush their enemy by refusing the King's request.

Ludwig, hereupon, highly incensed, immediately overruled the law and officially created Lola Montez, Baroness of Rosenthal and Countess of Landsfeld. To enable her to maintain these dignities he gave her an income equivalent to about £5,000 a year, with which he burdened the Treasury. And as if this was not sufficient to proclaim the power she had acquired, he forced his Queen, a plain and good woman, who was universally esteemed, to receive the new Countess, and decorate her with the Order of St. Theresa, which she had herself created and which bore her name.

After this there was nothing left for the Ministry to do but to resign, which they did. Ludwig accepted their resignation with every mark of contempt, and acting under the influence of his mistress, who now became the virtual ruler of the State, he formed a new Ministry composed entirely of advanced liberals, famous in Bavarian history as the "Lola Ministry."

In retiring, the reactionary Cabinet shot a Parthian shaft at the King in the form of a "Remonstrance" on the scandal of his private life. Never was moral indignation more vindictive and insincere than that which this remarkable document breathed. But the sympathy that might have been felt for a Ministry which contained a man of such integrity and weight as Dr. Döllinger,[1] driven from power by a strolling dancer of ill-fame, was turned to ridicule by the tone of maudlin sentiment in which the ministerial indignation at the royal depravity, so long tolerated with equanimity, was expressed.

The *Times*, in a leader on the situation in Munich, lashed the fallen Ministry with contempt for the malice and mawkishness of their complaint. Commenting on their statement that "individuals like the Bishop of Augsburg" (the head of the Roman Catholic Church in Bavaria) "every day shed bitter tears in consequence of what is passing before their eyes," the *Times*, without finding any excuse for Ludwig's shortcomings, declared—

"It is seldom that we find any connection between politics and pathos, nor is there any bias whatever in favour of sentimental statesmanship. If it had been customary in England for ministers to moan and weep over the private immoralities of their royal master, what constant showers of tears would have been falling in the days of certain

---

[1] Dr. Döllinger was a famous Catholic divine, and friend of Gladstone. He acquired great celebrity many years later by his refusal to accept the doctrine of Papal Infallibility.

monarchs we might enumerate ! We could name statesmen who would never have had their pocket-handkerchiefs away from their eyes. We need not go very far back to picture a premier crying his eyes out at an actress having gained some ascendency over the heart or mind of his royal master.

" Poor Canning would have had a hard time of it during his brief ministry, and as to Lord Eldon, his well-known tendency to

> ' Drop tears as fast as the Arabian trees
> Their medicinal gum.'

might have originated in his having a touch of the Bishop of Augsburg's leakiness, whose head appears to be a reservoir with a couple of mains continually turned on."

In those days the opinion of the *Times* was regarded with profound respect all over Europe, but its lash on this occasion failed to have any effect on the fallen Ministry and the party they represented. To regain the power they had lost, the reactionary element in the country, which was very strong, backed by the Church of Rome, which was still stronger, waged a relentless war against the " Spanish dancer." She was declared to be, among other things, the Beast mentioned in the Apocalypse.

But the Countess of Landsfeld was proof against vilification and calumny. To the abuse of the Jesuits she replied in a letter which was published in the *Times*, and very plainly and concisely put the situation in a nutshell. At the same time she publicly denied in the *Times*, and in the press of Munich, that she was not what she purported to be —a Spanish dancer. And she added, if not to the confusion regarding her origin, at least to the humour of the stories, by stating that she was " the daughter of Torero, the most popular *toreador* in Spain," to the amazement of

that individual, who as publicly hastened to deny the
impeachment.

But her war with the forces of reaction commanded by
the Jesuits was not confined to battles of words.   The key
to the situation was held by the students who were members
of the various clubs of which the University, according to
the German custom, was composed.   At Munich there were
five of these clubs, named after the five provinces of Bavaria
—Franconia, Istria, Palatinate, Bavaria, and Suabia.   With
the side they joined would in the end lie the victory.   Their
sympathies were decidedly liberal, but " the king's mistress "
offended them in one of the tempests of passion to which
she was subject by obliging the Head of the University,
who had insulted her, to resign.   This made the students,
who were as violent and impulsive as Lola, her enemies.
Hoping to rectify her error by sowing dissension among
them, she created a sixth club known as the Allemania.
They wore caps of bright red trimmed with parti-coloured
gauze.   Their motto was " Lola and Liberty."   England is
the only other country in which the mistress of a king has
thus been identified with the cause of the people.   In the
reign of Charles II both Nell Gwyn and the Duchesse de
Mazarin were for a time regarded by the people and the
Protestants (!) as their chief champions.

The other clubs utterly refused to recognize the Allemania,
which they called " Lola's creatures."   Fights were of everyday occurrence.   On one occasion Lola herself joined in the
fray.   One day as the Allemania were being pursued through
the streets they were taunted by a saying of the Countess
of Landsfeld to which wide circulation had been given : " A
bad horse may buck, but not a whole stable."   This drove
the Allemania to fury, and, as they sought refuge in a café,
one of them drew a dagger and precipitated himself on his
tormentors.   It was taken from him, but the police dared
not arrest one of the powerful Countess of Landsfeld's

A CARICATURE OF LOLA MONTEZ IN BAVARIA

[*From a German print*]

protégés, who sent and implored her protection. She came at once, on foot and alone, convinced that she could quell any tumult by her mere presence. But in this she was mistaken. As soon as she was recognized she was hissed, hustled, mobbed. Realizing her danger, the intrepid creature appealed at several doors for shelter, but, in the face of such a disturbance, none dared open. As she passed the Austrian Legation its doors were pointedly shut in her face.

Ludwig, informed of the desperate plight of his " Lolotte," as he called her in the doggerel sonnets he dedicated to her, instantly went to her rescue. Elbowing his way through the threatening, yelling mob that surrounded her, he offered her his arm and led her to the Church of the Theatines near by. Here she was no sooner safe than she snatched a pistol from one of the officers who had accompanied the King and threatened to discharge it into the mob. To ensure her return to her palace alive it was necessary to send for a detachment of soldiers.

The following week she persuaded the King to close the University for a year. This was her greatest blunder. Until then the people on whom the " Lola Ministry " had conferred many benefits had neither been touched by the tears of the Bishop of Augsburg, nor scandalized that "Venus," as their priests told them, " should have driven the Virgin from Munich." When groaning under oppression, the " divine " people, like drowning men, never question the moral character of their deliverer—till afterwards. Then a great deal of insincerity is uttered about a spotless reputation being the first qualification in a leader of the people. So it was in this case. Having got the Code Napoleon, and many much-needed reforms out of the democratic sympathy of Lola Montez, the people were ready enough to join the students on the slightest provocation and clamour for the banishment of the King's foreign mistress.

But Ludwig, who had not trembled before Napoleon, was not the man to tremble before the people, the insincerity of whose belated moral indignation was as apparent to him as that of the reactionary party. He replied that "he would rather lose his crown than part with the Countess of Landsfeld." His refusal was no sooner made known than barricades were erected in the streets; and with the cries of "Down with the Concubine!" that were raised under the windows of his palace, were mingled cries of "Long live the Republic!"

The riot was quelled, but the whole country was now in a ferment. Alarmed at the popular exasperation, the members of the Upper House, who represented the moderate and rational elements in the kingdom, went in a body to the Palace to convince Ludwig of the necessity of conforming to the universal demand. After some hours of argument and persuasion they finally succeeded in wringing from him an order for the expulsion of his favourite.

The news spread rapidly, and an immense multitude of all classes of the community assembled round the palace of the Countess to help in the execution of the order. According to all accounts, she displayed the greatest courage and coolness. Undaunted by the sight of the mob yelling under her windows, she declared her intention of going to the King and receiving her banishment from his own lips. She was told it was impossible, and that if she wished to escape being torn to pieces there was no time to lose. It was only when her palace was on fire that she would admit the game was up. Then, "disguising herself as a boy," she accepted the protection of the troop of horse which had been ordered to escort her to the frontier.

Thus fell Lola Montez after a reign of two years. No woman in her position had wielded such power since Louis XV made his *amende honorable* to God and dismissed the

Du Barry. She had, moreover, used her power entirely for the benefit of the people and displayed, unskilled though it was, ability of a high order. Her chief blunders had been due to her violent and ungovernable temper, which in the end estranged even those dependent on her.

But the passions she had unchained in Bavaria in her struggle to maintain her position, were not calmed by her expulsion. Revolution was in the air. To save the monarchy it became necessary for the King to abdicate. This event following only a fortnight after the Countess oɪ Landsfeld's exile, completed in a striking manner the drama of her connection with Bavaria.

Ludwig accepted his destiny with great dignity and without a trace of bitterness. It was said that he even welcomed abdication, which was made easier for him by the accession of his son than it usually is to a fallen prince. There was no suggestion of banishing him, and he remained in Munich, which he continued to beautify at his own expense. Off the throne his incapacity as a king was forgotten; he became what Nature had intended him to be—a teacher of the Beautiful. In this *rôle* his supremacy was unquestioned, and he recovered a popularity far greater than that which he had lost. Fourteen years later, the equestrian statue of him which rides in the Odeon Platz was erected by public subscription and unveiled on his birthday. On the pedestal was inscribed—

" A tribute of gratitude from the town of Munich."

Ludwig I lived for twenty years after he lost his throne, dying at Nice in 1868 at the age of eighty-two. His last words were, " Give my thanks to every one in Munich." Bavaria at once claimed his body, and buried him as the pupils of a great artist might bury a Master they loved. The occasion created a deep impression on the minds of all who recalled the circumstances under which he had been forced to abdicate twenty years before.

V

FOR a fortnight after her expulsion, Lola Montez hovered about the frontier expecting to be recalled. It was said that she even returned to Munich in the male disguise in which she had fled and had an interview with Ludwig. The rumour has never been confirmed. If true, whatever hopes she might have built on a personal appeal to the infatuated old man were doomed to disappointment. On learning the news of his abdication, she finally abandoned all idea of returning either to him or to Bavaria, and went to Switzerland.

She was now once more reduced to the necessity of earning her living by her wits. She had saved nothing. All the money she had received had been spent on her political supporters. Her palace had been burnt to the ground with all it contained. Of the splendid gifts that Ludwig had showered on her she only retained a few diamonds and her title of Countess. In fact she was poorer than when she had entered Bavaria.

"I came to Munich," she said, "with one hundred thousand francs, *Louis les a mangé!*"

So she resolved to return to the stage, not as a dancer, but as an actress, relying for financial success on the celebrity her name had acquired. Early in 1849 she left Switzerland for England, where she was advertised to appear at Covent Garden Theatre in a drama entitled *Lola Montez, or a Countess for an hour*. The Censor, however, refused to license the piece for political reasons. She attracted considerable attention, nevertheless, and the small lodging-house in Half-Moon Street in which she lived during her stay in London, became the nightly rendezvous of young men of fashion, who found, according to the Hon.

Frederick Leveson-Gower, "her animated conversation entertaining, though she had lost much of her good looks."

Among these gilded dandies who thought to obtain notoriety by associating themselves with so famous an adventuress, Stafford Heald, of the 2nd Life Guards, fell desperately in love with her. He had just come of age and into a fortune of four or five thousand a year. Lola Montez was quite aware that her waning beauty made her future means of existence more and more problematical. She was weary of the strain of excitement and struggle; after the turmoil and scandal of the life she had led, she longed for rest and even respectability. So though Heald was ten years her junior, and a fool into the bargain, she fascinated him into marrying her.

She soon realized her mistake. Heald's aunt, who had brought him up, was so exasperated at his marriage that she became obsessed with this "Countess of Landsfeld," to the extent of ferreting out her past. Discovering that she had been previously married, the outraged Miss Heald naturally decided to "look into the divorce proceedings" of Captain James and his wife. In the course of her investigations, having ascertained that some legal formality was wanting to make the divorce complete, she gave the rein to her passion and, regardless of scandal, brought an action for bigamy against the Countess.

A summons to attend the Marlborough Street Police Court and answer the charge was levied on Lola as she was getting into her carriage to take her daily drive in the Park. She affected the greatest unconcern and smilingly obeyed the summons, attended by her husband, who during the inquiry "held her hand, which he repeatedly raised to his lips." To the triumph of his vindictive aunt, who was present, the inquiry ended ominously for his fascinating wife. She was remanded on bail of one thousand pounds, which was instantly furnished by the devoted Heald. But London was cheated of the highly sensational trial to which it was looking forward by the sudden flight of the couple.

Marriage under such circumstances, and between two persons so ill-suited to one another, was bound to be a failure. Embittered by disappointment, Lola's temper, which had ever been violent, became more and more passionate. The slightest thing was sufficient to excite her to fury. It is probable that these outbursts were occasioned by a disordered nervous system ; while they lasted they had all the appearance of fits of insanity.

Lola and her Guardsman, however, continued to live together for two or three years, chiefly in Spain, whither they had fled on leaving England. Their quarrels were of daily occurrence, and in one of them Heald was stabbed. He ran away from her more than once, but her fascination over him was so strong that he invariably returned to her. At last this life became intolerable to Lola, and she left him and the two children she had borne him. What became of them is unknown. Heald, who had been obliged to sell out of the army, and whose fortune and life were ruined by his irreparable infatuation, was shortly after his desertion found drowned at Lisbon.

Lola Montez was next heard of in Paris, but she failed to find the reception she expected among the people she had known there several years before. An American theatrical manager, whose acquaintance she made, persuaded her to go to America with him as a theatrical star. She crossed the ocean in the same vessel with Kossuth, and made her first appearance as an actress in New York in a drama which had been specially written for her, called *Lola Montez in Bavaria*, and in which she represented herself as the dancer, the politician, the Countess, the revolutionist, and the fugitive. The piece ran for five nights. She then toured in the same drama through the States. In New Orleans she met with a very hostile reception, and was obliged to leave the town. In San Francisco she married, for the third time, one of the leading citizens of the place, an Irishman by the name of Hull, from whom she was divorced a few weeks later. Wherever she went the fame of her exploits in Bavaria drew large audiences to see her, but the money she made was as quickly spent.

Having exhausted the curiosity of the Americans, she next proceeded to Australia and appeared in her stock *rôle* as " Lola Montez in Bavaria " at the Theatre Royal, Sydney. She announced that the proceeds of the performance would be given to the " wounded at Sebastopol." Her reception was very favourable, and her Australian tour was very profitable. In Melbourne she won great popularity by horse-whipping Seekamp, the editor of *Ballarat Times*, in his office, on account of an article he had written reflecting on her character. The same night she received an ovation at the theatre on explaining to the audience that she had offered to fight him with pistols.

She did not always score, however, in her horse-whipping adventures, which were of rather too frequent occurrence. Her castigation of Crosby, the lessee of a theatre in which she was acting, whom she accused of cheating her, led to an encounter with his wife, an athletic woman, who broke Lola's wrist in the fight and left her unconscious.

On leaving Australia she returned to England, where, attracted out of curiosity to Spurgeon's Tabernacle, she was so impressed by the sermon she heard that she resolved to leave the stage. She now became a public lecturer. In this new *rôle* she went a second time to America. Her lectures, though well received by the press, did not prove remunerative, and she was fast sinking into the extreme of poverty, when by chance she met a Mrs.

22

Buchanan who had formerly been at school with her at Bath. This woman played the part of the Good Samaritan to the unhappy adventuress, whose proud spirit was now humbled and broken by hardship, degradation, contempt, loss of self-respect, and despair.

The Christianity that Mrs. Buchanan professed and practised was of a type with which Lola Montez had never before come into contact. On a nature so emotional as hers, its message of love and pity could not fail to produce the deepest impression, and Mrs. Buchanan's loving-kindness had its reward in the passionate repentance of the miserable creature who experienced it.

The change that was now wrought in the character of Lola Montez was the most remarkable of all the incidents in her sensational career. She declared her intention to consecrate the remainder of her life to the rescue of the wretched of her own sex. There was no doubt of her sincerity. She threw herself with all her old fire into the work, but her zeal soon exhausted her health, shattered by the dissipations of the past. Warned, by a stroke of paralysis, of her approaching end, she faced it in the manner stated at the beginning of this memoir. She had just completed her forty-third year.

An obituary notice of the dead woman, whose name had been so long and ignominiously before the public, contained the following significant statement :—

" The news of her illness reaching her mother, Mrs. Craigie, who was still living, came from England to America, in the hope of inheriting her daughter's money ; but on finding she had nothing to leave, she took the next ship back."

After this of what use is a moral ?

Lola Montez was beautiful, gifted, and neglected. In the early Christian centuries she would have been an Empress like Theodora, or a holy prostitute like Pelagia.

SOURCES

DUCHESSE DE CHÂTEAUROUX

La Duchesse de Châteauroux et ses Sœurs	Goncourt
Les Maitresses de Louis XV	Goncourt
Les Mesdemoiselles de Nesle	Capefigue
La Seigneurie de Courbépine	Lambert
Mémoires	Marquis d'Argenson
Mémoires	Comte de Maurepas
Mémoires	Duc de Luynes
Mémoires	Duchesse de Brancas
Mémoires	Madame du Hausset
Mémoires	Duc de Richelieu
Nouveaux Mémoires du Maréchal de Richelieu	Lescure
Histoire de la Décadence	Abbé Soulavie
Journal	Barbier
Mélanges	Boisjourdain
Histoire de France, Vol. xviii	Michelet
The Real Louis XV	Haggard
Vie Privée de Louis XV	
Correspondance de la Duchesse de Châteauroux	

DUCHESS OF KENDAL

The Four Georges	Thackeray
The Four Georges	Justin McCarthy
Memoirs	Electress Sophia
The Princess Sophia's Journal	
Reminiscences	Horace Walpole
Letters of Lady Mary Wortley-Montagu	
Official Baronage	Doyle
History of England	Lord Stanhope
Diary	Countess Cowper
Sir Robert Walpole	Coxe
Memoirs	Lord John Hervey
The Love of an Uncrowned Queen	Wilkins
Caricature History of the Four Georges	Wright
Briefe des Herzogs Ernst August zu Braunschweig-Lüneburg an Johann Franz Diedrich von Wendt	Herausgegeben von Erich Graf Kielmansegg

EMPRESS CATHERINE II

Memoirs	Princess Dashkof
Memoirs	Empress Catherine
The Story of a Throne	Waliszewski
The Romance of an Empress	Waliszewski
The Courtships of Catherine the Great	Walizsewski
La Messaline du Nord	
Cathérine II de Russie et ses favoris	
Vie de Cathérine II	Castéra

22 *

ELIZABETH CHUDLEIGH

Life and Memoirs of Elizabeth Chudleigh .
Histoire de la vie de la Duchesse de Kingston
Les Aventures trop amoureuses
An Authentic Detail of particulars relative to the Duchess of Kingston .
Mémoires . . . . Baronne d'Oberkirch
Original Anecdotes . . . . Whitehead
Memoirs of the Court of England . . . . . . Jesse
Twelve Bad Women . . . . Vincent
Historic Oddities . . . . Baring-Gould

COMTESSE DE LAMOTTE

The Story of the Diamond Necklace . . . . . Vizetelly
The Diamond Necklace . . . . Carlyle
L'Affaire du Collier . . . . Funck-Brentano
Mémoires . . . . Comtesse de Lamotte
Mémoires . . . . Comte de Lamotte
Mémoires . . . . Comte Beugnot
Mémoires . . . . Rétaux de Villette
Mémoires . . . . Baronne d'Oberkirch
Histoire de France, Vol. xix . . . . . . Michelet

DUCHESSE DE POLIGNAC

Marie Antoinette . . . . Goncourt
Marie Antoinette . . . . Nolhac
La Vraie Marie Antoinette . . . . Lescure
La Duchesse de Polignac et son temps . . . . Schlesinger
Les Derniers Jours de Trianon . . . . . . Capefigue
Le Duc de Lauzun et la Cour de Marie Antoinette . . . Maugras
Mémoires . . . . . . Comtesse Diane de Polignac
Mémoires . . . . Prince de Ligne
Mémoires . . . . Duchesse de Gontaut
Souvenirs . . . . Comte Tilly
Le Salon de la Duchesse de Polignac (in *Revue des Deux Mondes*, 15 Sept., 1890) . . . . Du Bled
Les Reines de l'Emigration (La Comtesse de Polastron) . . Vicomte de Reiset
The "Introduction" by Léonce Pingaud to "La Correspondance intime du Comte de Vaudreuil."

LOLA MONTEZ

Autobiography and Lectures of Lola Montez . . . .
Some Fair Hibernians . . . . Frances Gerard
An Englishman in Paris . . . . Vandam
Bygone Years . . . . Leveson-Gower
You Have Heard of Them . . . . "Q"
Mes Souvenirs . . . . Claudin
Lola Montez . . . . Mirecourt
Story of a Penitent . . . .
Players of a Century . . . . Phelps
Lola Montez in die Karikatur . . . . . . Fuchs
The *Times*, 16 Dec., 1842; 2, 8, 9, 12, 18 March, and 9 April, 1847; 24 March, 1848; 9 Aug., 1849; *New York Herald*, 20 Jan., 1861.

INDEX

RICHARD CLAY & SONS, LIMITED,
BREAD STREET HILL, E.C., AND
BUNGAY, SUFFOLK.